FURY OF THE STORM

Lightning struck only a few yards away, and as though waiting for just such a signal, the horses and longhorns took the cue. As one, they struck out in a gallop, back toward the east. Lonnie and Dallas were in the lead, trying to get ahead of the stampede. Mindy leaped into the saddle of Becky's horse, kicking the animal into a run. Lonnie and Dallas were directly in the path of the herd, waving their hats and firing their Colts.

The fury of the storm, with its rolling thunder, drowned out the sound of the shooting. There was no stopping the stampede, and Lonnie galloped out of its path. But Dallas continued firing. Frightened by the shooting and the oncoming herd, his horse nickered, rearing. Dallas was flung from the saddle, while the frightened horse tried to get out of the path of the stampede. Dallas stood there as though stunned. The leaders of the stampede had already galloped past Lonnie, and while he kicked his horse into a gallop, there was no way he could reach Dallas in time. Then from the other side of the charging herd——just seconds ahead of the leaders——came Mindy on Becky's bay horse. It seemed for a moment that Dallas and his rescuer were lost, but Mindy extended her hand, Dallas took it, and swung up to the saddle behind her . . .

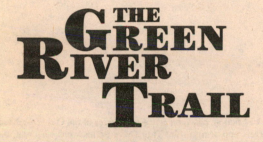

THE GREEN RIVER TRAIL

Ralph Compton

St. Martin's Paperbacks

This is a work of fiction, based on actual trail drives of the Old West. Many of the characters appearing in the Trail Drive Series were very real, and some of the trail drives actually took place. But the reader should be aware that, in the developing of characters and events, some fictional literary license has been employed. While some of the characters and events herein are purely the creation of the author, every effort has been made to portray them with accuracy. However, the inherent dangers of the trail are real, sufficient unto themselves, and seldom has it been necessary to enhance their reality.

THE GREEN RIVER TRAIL

Copyright © 1999 by Ralph Compton.

Trail map design by L. A. Hensley.

All rights reserved.

For information address St. Martin's Press, 175 Fifth Avenue, New York, NY 10010.

EAN: 978-0-312-97092-5

Printed in the United States of America

St. Martin's Paperbacks edition / January 1998

10 9 8 7

AUTHOR'S FOREWORD

Jim Bridger, just eighteen, had been working in St. Louis as a blacksmith when he joined William H. Ashley's Missouri River Expedition. It was his introduction to the West, and he spent the next twenty years as a trader and fur trapper in Idaho, Colorado, and Utah.

The fur trade began to die in the 1840s, leaving many of the mountain men such as Bridger at loose ends. But Oregon Territory had been opened in 1841, and Fort Laramie was the only major outpost between Independence and the end of two thousand miles of treacherous trail. Having long traded with the friendly Shoshones, Jim Bridger—aided by another mountain man, Louis Vasquez—built a trading post on Black's Fork, where it fed into the Green. Bridger believed it would be a godsend to the Oregon-bound emigrants on the trail west, while drawing regular trade from Wyoming's friendly tribe, the Wind River Shoshones. Bridger's trading post prospered for four years.

It was time for Mormons to find a home, and Brigham Young chose a remote spot in the valley of the Great Salt Lake in Utah. Preparations were made for the Saints to migrate by wagon and on foot with handcarts to carry their goods across a little-known wilderness.

But trouble lay ahead. In July 1847, the first settlers arrived at what is now Salt Lake City. They built shelters, planted crops, and through irrigation the desert began to thrive and blossom. But Gentiles—the name for non-Mormons—began arriving, and when gold was discovered in California, things went from bad to worse. Gold seekers, attempting to avoid the crossing of the treacherous South Pass, passed through territory Mormons saw as their own.

After numerous clashes with Mormons, Bridger realized he must give up his trading post. There were good reasons for Bridger's decision. First, there was the ever-present danger from militant Mormons, who were now within just a few miles of the trading post. Second, the army was planning to build more forts in the western territories. Third, the railroad would be coming, eliminating most of the need for frontier outposts, private or government-owned. The Union Pacific Railroad would open up the nation to commerce with the High Plains.

In the spring of 1853, what Jim Bridger had foreseen came to pass. He and Louis Vasquez fled the trading post just ahead of a horde of Mormons who overran the trading post and captured it. Eventually, the trading post—or fort—would be sold to the United States government, and it would take soldiers to dislodge the Mormons. But as Bridger and Vasquez rode out for the last time, Bridger was content. He had become weary of being a storekeeper, and in the back of his mind was the lush graze along Green River in northeastern Utah. There a man could build a cattle or horse ranch that would be the envy of the frontier, if he chose to do so.

The territory was rich in minerals. Coal, lead, gold, and silver were to be produced in great amounts, but the area developed slowly because of conflict that ensued between Mormons and the federal government. But copper was the chief metal. Bingham Canyon had the largest open-pit copper mine in the country. But both mining and smelting were controlled by big eastern-owned companies, resulting in a Mormon distrust of industrialization. In 1848, at the end of the Mexican War, the region passed to the United States, and a large area, of which the present state is a part, became Utah Territory. Congressional acts forbidding polygamy were passed in 1862, 1882, and 1887. Not until the religious group discontinued the practice did the territory become the state of Utah. The year was 1896.

THE
GREEN RIVER TRAIL

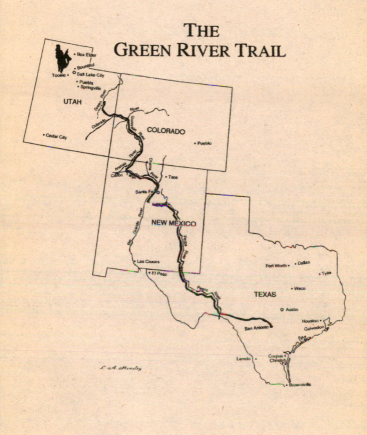

PROLOGUE

San Francisco, California. June 1, 1853.

Four men rode across the Sierra Nevada, bound for south-western Wyoming. Their pack mule followed on a lead rope. At twenty-three, Lonnie Kilgore was the oldest of the four. Dallas Weaver was a year younger, while Dirk McNelly and Kirby Lowe were both several months shy of twenty-one. They reined up on a ridge to rest the horses and the pack mule.

"I'm glad I got to see California once," Dirk McNelly said, "but I've never been so glad to be leavin' a place in my life. It ain't natural, everything always bein' green. I like to see the falling leaves."

"I reckon you'll be seeing plenty of them in Texas," said Kirby Lowe. "Remember, in just four years each of us has come out of the California goldfields with more than ten thousand dollars. Raising cows in Texas, starving through the dry years, and fighting the Comanches, you wouldn't see half that much coin if you lived to be a hundred."

"That's the gospel truth if I ever heard it," Dallas Weaver said. "Trouble is, what are we goin' to do with what we've earned? A couple of bad years in Texas could break us.''

''Then maybe we'd better not settle in Texas,'' said Lonnie Kilgore. ''Remember, on our way west, when we spent a couple of days at Jim Bridger's trading post in Wyoming?''

''Yeah,'' Dallas Weaver said. ''Bridger's an old mountain man, and what he don't know about this high country likely ain't worth knowing.''

''I'm thinking of something he said while we was there,'' said Lonnie. ''He talked about that range along the Green River in northeastern Utah, where the grass reaches up to a horse's belly. He thought it would be grand for horses, cattle, or both. In the summer, herds of cattle could be driven into Washington, Oregon, Nevada, and California.''

''That ain't all,'' Kirby Lowe said. ''It'll be a while in coming, but the San Francisco newspapers was plumb full of stories about the building of the Union Pacific, a transcontinental railroad. It'll run across southern Wyoming near where Bridger's trading post is now. I doubt any of us will live long enough to see a railroad reach Texas.''

''A railroad can be as much a curse as a blessing,'' said Dirk McNelly. ''It'll bring in droves of sodbusters, and it'll mean the end of free range.''

''Forget about free range,'' Lonnie Kilgore said. ''We have money to buy land, and if the price is right, we can buy a lot of it. Once you got a title to it, nobody can root you out. That's my thinking.''

''The farther we are from civilization, the less the land will cost,'' said Dallas Weaver, ''but I'm not sure about this Green River range. Bridger was already having trouble with the Mormons when we was there four years ago, and he ain't even *in* Utah.''

''Once we've filed on land and have a title to it, it's ours,'' Lonnie Kilgore said. ''I'm not one to fight with my neighbors, but I won't be pushed around. I think we should talk to Bridger about this range, and unless somebody's already claiming it, we should consider buying four sections—or maybe eight—depending on the price.''

''Eight sections!'' said Kirby Lowe. ''My God, that's more than five thousand acres.''

''With the Green River running through it,'' Dirk McNelly said. ''I like that.''

''So do I,'' Kirby Lowe said, ''but before we settle out here, I'd like to ride to Texas and see my folks. I ain't seen 'em since I was sixteen.''

''I ain't so sure my folks will want to see me,'' said Dirk McNelly. ''My old man called me a fool for wantin' to go gallavantin' off to California. I had to sneak off in the middle of the night.''

''After we talk to Bridger, if all this still seems like a good idea, we'll be going back to Texas,'' Lonnie Kilgore said. ''We'll need cattle. We may have to rope the varmints out of the brush, but we can do that, if we must.''

''What about horses?'' Kirby Lowe asked. ''Even when it's hard times in Texas, a good horse can set you back two hundred dollars.''

''There are some fine horses in California,'' said Lonnie Kilgore. ''Once we've brought a herd of longhorns from Texas, we can bring in some brood mares from California.''

''One thing we have to consider is the Indians,'' Dallas Weaver said. ''From what Jim Bridger said, the Utes and Paiutes don't take kindly to whites coming into the territory.''

''By now,'' said Kirby Lowe, ''there ought to be enough Mormons there to keep them busy. At least the Wind River Shoshones are friendly.''

''Yeah,'' Dirk McNelly said, ''but they're too far north, in the Wind River Mountains.''

''I think this is another case where we'll have to depend on Jim Bridger's advice,'' said Lonnie Kilgore.

The four of them rode on, still dressed as Texas cowboys, even after four long years in California. In each saddle boot there was a treasured Hawken rifle, and each of them had a tied-down Colt revolver on his right hip. Not until late afternoon did they discover they were being followed. Again, they had stopped to rest the horses, and it was Kirby Lowe who spoke.

"Maybe my eyes are playin' tricks on me, but I'd swear I saw some dust back yonder a ways, along our back trail."

"Whether you did or didn't, this is no time to gamble," said Lonnie Kilgore. "There's always a horde of *hombres* around a gold camp who'd rather steal their gold than work for it. Remember last year, when three miners were bushwhacked when they rode out bound for home?"

"Yeah," Dallas Weaver said, "and the bushwhackers were never caught. I think we'd do well to ride on a ways and then double back. This ain't the kind of country where a man rides unless he has to. We can set up a little welcomin' party of our own."

"We'll ride to the foot of this ridge," said Lonnie Kilgore. "There we'll leave the mule and our horses, doubling back on foot."

They rode on, leaving a clear trail for their pursuers. Reining up in a thicket, they tied the mule and their horses.

"Dallas," said Lonnie, "you and Dirk double back to the south and then west, keeping within range of the trail. Kirby, you and me will head north a ways, and then west. I'll challenge these riders, and since we'll be shooting from cover, we'll let them make the first move. They *could* be other miners on their way home."

"Well, hell," Dirk McNelly said, "if they are, we still may have a fight on our hands. They're likely to think we're bushwhackers aimin' to take their gold."

"Maybe not," said Lonnie Kilgore. "Bushwhackers don't shout a warning."

The four men separated in twos, taking the north and south sides of the back trail. A vengeful sun bore down on them, and the armpits of their shirts were soon soaked with sweat. They waited for more than an hour, their patience growing thin, before hearing the distinctive sound of trotting horses. There were four riders, and they looked like anything but miners. They rode on, and when they were within gun range, Lonnie Kilgore shouted a challenge.

"Rein up. Identify yourselves and tell us why you're trailing us."

There was a moment of shocked silence. Then, as one, the four went for their guns. It left the four friends from Texas little choice. Lonnie shot the lead man out of the saddle, while Dallas, Dirk, and Kirby accounted for the other three. Spooked by the shooting, their horses galloped down the ridge. There was dead silence, and none of the four who had been gunned down seemed alive.

"We might as well search them," said Lonnie, "and see what we can find. Then we'll go after their horses and search their saddlebags."

"Lord, I hope they wasn't miners on their way home," Dirk McNelly said.

"I doubt they were," said Lonnie Kilgore. "Bushwhackers wouldn't have challenged them, and if they didn't have mischief on their minds, they wouldn't have gone for their guns. They made the first move, and it was the wrong one. When a man pulls iron, it's evidence aplenty that he's up to no good."

Each of them searched one of the dead men, and it was Dallas Weaver who recognized one of them.

"This is Jake Doolin," said Dallas. "He's been hanging around for months, and as for mining, he ain't hit a lick. There's been some strong suspicions that he's one of a pack of coyotes who kill miners for their pokes."

"I've heard that," Lonnie said, "but nobody said it too loud. There was no proof."

"There is now," said Kirby. "Sure as hell, the four of 'em aimed to kill and rob us."

"Question is," Dirk said, "what do we do with them? I can't see ridin' all the way back to San Francisco to tell the law what we done."

"We'll leave them where they lay," said Lonnie, "and anything we find that we can use, we'll take with us."

Searching the bodies of the four men, they came up with more than a thousand dollars in gold coin.

"Unless somebody's hit pay dirt in Texas, that'll buy three hundred cows," Dirk said.

"Now," said Dallas, "let's round up their horses. We can take them with us, and it'll be the start of a remuda for the trail drive from Texas."

They soon found the four horses grazing and caught them without difficulty. There was a rifle in each saddle boot. But the saddlebags were a disappointment, for there was only a change of clothing, clean socks, and jerked beef.

"They didn't aim to travel far from town," Lonnie said. "They'd ride just far enough to do their killing and robbing, and be back at the gold camp before dark."

"It'd be a shame, leaving these four good horses and saddles," said Dirk, "but there's a little matter of us having no bills of sale on any of 'em. They're all branded, too."

"Mex brands," Lonnie said. "They likely were stolen somewhere below the border, and as long as these four dead coyotes have been hanging around San Francisco, I doubt anybody's asked for a bill of sale. We'll take those four horses with us on lead ropes."

The four friends rode out. Three of the men had the newly acquired horses on leads, while Lonnie Kilgore led the fourth horse and the pack mule. They made camp for the night near a water hole in Nevada. They poured water on their small fire well before dark.

"I have some serious doubts about the direction we're headed," Lonnie said. "I think we ought to ride due north and take the Oregon Trail to Bridger's trading post. Remember, when we was there before, Bridger told us the Mormons was settling around the Great Salt Lake? If we ride a straight line from here to Bridger's, we'll be passing right through the Mormon settlements.''

''It'll take us maybe a day longer,'' said Dallas, ''and we'd come out somewhere in Idaho, I reckon.''*

''Them Mormons has had four years to settle out here since we talked to Bridger,'' Dirk said. ''There must be thousands of 'em by now. I kinda like that idea of ridin' north from here, and then taking the Oregon Trail to Bridger's.''

''One thing wrong with that,'' Kirby said. ''We'll have to cross South Pass.''

''That won't be a problem,'' said Lonnie, ''since we have no wagons. Horses and mules can make it, even if we have to dismount and lead them. If we settle along the Green, I'll gamble that we'll be in trouble with the Mormons soon enough. I think we'd do well to go north from here until we reach the Oregon Trail. Even with crossing South Pass, we can still make it in about six days.''

''I like that,'' Dallas said. ''Nothing but a fool fights, if he can avoid it.''

''I'll go along,'' said Dirk. ''We'll likely have all the Mormon trouble we can handle after we bring that trail drive from Texas.''

''Count me in,'' Kirby said. ''We got to claim the land, get us a herd of cows and some prime horses. Then will be soon enough to fight with anybody that don't like us.''

They had reached an agreement, and there seemed little else to do except roll in their blankets and get some sleep.

*Near the present-day town of Twin Falls, Idaho.

Southeastern Idaho Territory. June 6, 1853.

It had been ten years since Oregon Territory had been settled, and deep wagon ruts marked the trail. There was also a litter of horse and mule bones, attesting to the devilish terrain.

"I've always heard it said that nothin' breakable ever got across South Pass without bein' broke," said Kirby Lowe. "Look at all the glass."

"I think we ought to dismount and lead all the horses across," Lonnie said. "We'll get there sometime tomorrow."

"How far you reckon it is from here to Bridger's trading post?" Dirk asked.

"Maybe two hundred and fifty miles," said Lonnie. "It'll take us a mite longer than the six days we was countin' on, but I think there'll be less risk. I want to talk to Bridger before we get too involved in the troubles of the territory."

Southwestern Wyoming. June 10, 1853.

The sun was two hours high when the four Texans approached the log building that was Jim Bridger's trading post. Suddenly there was the sound of a shot, and lead thunked into a pine just ahead of the four horsemen.

"Rein up and identify yourselves," a voice commanded.

"We're Texans, on our way home from California," Lonnie shouted.

"Dismount and come on," said the voice, "and don't make no funny moves."

The four dismounted and, leading their horses and the pack mule, reached the front of the trading post. The door opened, and Louis Vasquez stepped out, a Hawken rifle under his arm. Lonnie spoke.

"You're Louis Vasquez, and four years ago, on our way to California, we spent two days and nights here. I'm Lonnie Kilgore, and my *amigos* are Dallas Weaver, Dirk McNelly, and Kirby Lowe."

"I remember them, Louis," said Bridger from the gloom of the trading post. "Put your horses in the corral and come in."

Bridger had lighted a coal oil lamp to dispel the gloom within the building. There were surprisingly few goods remaining in the trading post.

"You must have been doing a landslide business," Lonnie Kilgore said, looking at the small stock that remained.

"No," said Bridger. "I'm abandoning the post. It's just a matter of days before it'll be overrun with Mormons. I have an Indian friend keeping me posted as to their progress. Wovoka?"

The Indian seemed to materialize out of the shadows, a Hawken rifle under his arm.

Bridger spoke. "This is Wovoka Shatiki, a Shoshone. Wovoka, this is Dallas Weaver, Lonnie Kilgore, Dirk McNelly, and Kirby Lowe. They're returning from California on their way to Texas."

Without hesitation, Dallas extended his hand and the Indian took it. The procedure continued, with Lonnie, Dirk, and Kirby taking the Shoshone's hand.

"I reckon the Mormon situation has worsened since we were last here," Lonnie Kilgore said.

"It has," said Bridger. "Wovoka's been watching them, and time's running out."

"They come," Wovoka said. "Ten suns, mebbe."

"If it's any of my business," said Lonnie, "where do you aim to go from here?"

"I reckon Vasquez and me will ride north and spend some time with Wovoka's people, the Wind River Shoshones. When this territory opens up—and it will—the government will need scouts. Me and Louis aim to be ready.''

"That's mainly the reason we came back this way," Lonnie Kilgore said. "We wanted to discuss with you the possibility of buying title to maybe eight sections of land along Green River, to the east of here. We would return to Texas and bring a herd of longhorns. But we're a mite skittish about buyin' into a range war.''

"I doubt it'll come to that," Bridger said. "Utah's been declared a territory of the United States, and it'll be just a matter of time until the Federals in Washington have to put a stop to all the hell-raising.''*

"In Texas," said Dallas Weaver, "we ain't above some hell-raising ourselves, if there's no other way. This Green River range is soundin' better to me all the time.''

"If you can buy title to the land and hire enough riders to defend it, I don't believe you'll be sorry," Bridger said. "I reckon a man's religious beliefs is his business, but it ain't wrote down nowhere that a bunch like these Mormons can take over a whole territory and drive everybody else out.''

"That's about the way we feel," said Lonnie Kilgore. "That is, if nobody's claimed the Green River range.''

"Nobody has," Bridger said. "The Mormons are mostly settled east of there, around the Great Salt Lake, but that ain't stopped them from laying claim to the whole territory.''

"Well, I'll challenge any man who tries to run me off land after I've bought and paid for it," said Dallas Weaver. "How do the rest of you feel?''

"I'm with you until hell freezes," Lonnie Kilgore said.

"Count me in," said Dirk McNelly and Kirby Lowe in a single voice.

"Ugh," said Wovoka Shatiki, obviously pleased.

"Wovoka wants to stay and fight," Louis Vasquez said.

*The government sent soldiers in 1857. The confrontation ended peacefully.

"Kill," said Wovoka.

"Wovoka," Bridger said, "maybe you ought to join these *hombres*, if they settle along the Green. I think there'll be some fighting before this thing is over."

"No drive cow," said Wovoka. "Not be squaw."

The men resisted the urge to laugh. Lonnie Kilgore spoke to the Indian.

"You won't be driving cows, *amigo*. We're goin' to need a scout while we're trailing a herd from Texas. Our next drive will be from California. We'll be bringing in a herd of horses. How do you feel about them?"

"*Bueno*," Wovoka said. "Horse good."

"Wovoka can gentle any horse alive," said Bridger. "If he does nothing else, you'll do well to include him in your outfit. He don't like the idea of going with Louis and me to the Shoshone village until the government decides to hire us as scouts."

"I think I can speak for us all," Lonnie Kilgore said, "as long as Wovoka joining our outfit won't leave you at a disadvantage."

"It won't," said Bridger. "Louis and me have many friends among the Wind River Shoshones."

"If we aim to buy Green River land, where do we start?" Kirby Lowe asked.

"The nearest government outpost is Fort Laramie," said Bridger. "Captain Stoddard is the post commander there, and I know him well. Tell him what you want and that you're there on my recommendation."

"We're obliged," Lonnie said. "Since you're giving up the post, why don't you and Louis take up a couple of sections alongside ours?"

Bridger laughed. "Louis and me are wanderers. We been here thirty years, and since we started this trading post, it's the longest we've been in one place. Once we leave here, we aim to ride to Fort Laramie and have Captain Stoddard pass along the word that the United States government has got itself a pair of scouts.''

"He's right," said Louis Vasquez. "I'll never stay this long in one place again, unless I'm buried there.''

Come the dawn, the four Texans decided not to delay their departure. They would ride on to Fort Laramie.

"A good idea," said Bridger. "Get your titles to that Green River graze as soon as you can. When you get dug in, Louis and me will ride down there for some of that good Texas beef. On the trail to Texas and on the way back with the herd, let Wovoka scout ahead. He can track a lizard across solid rock, and he's a dead shot with a Hawken or Colt.''

In a silent farewell, Bridger and Vasquez extended their hands, and Wovoka Shatiki took them. He then followed the four Texans out to the corral, waiting for them to saddle their horses.

"Wovoka," Lonnie said, "you're welcome to ride any of these four horses on lead ropes, if you choose to. They belonged to some gents that tried to bushwhack us, and they won't be needin' them no more.''

The grin never reached the Indian's lips, but it was in his eyes. It was a kind of justice he appreciated, and he nodded. The five men mounted and rode eastward. Fort Laramie was two hundred miles distant.

Fort Laramie, Wyoming. June 13, 1853.

"Bridger's right about that," Captain Stoddard said, when the Texans met with him. "The army's ready to hire scouts, and they prefer mountain men.''

"Bueno," said Lonnie. "Bridger said him and Louis Vasquez will be ridin' over to see you within the next few days.

Now let's get down to our reason for being here.''

"Go ahead," Captain Stoddard said.

"We aim to settle along the Green River in northeastern Utah," Lonnie said. "We're on our way to Texas for a herd of cattle and reckoned we'd better secure the land first."

"I suppose Bridger made you aware of the . . . ah . . . unrest in Utah Territory," Stoddard said.

"He did," said Lonnie, "and that's why we want title to our spread. If it's ours legally, we'll be within our rights shootin' any varmints trying to take it from us."

"That's exactly right," Captain Stoddard said, "and the government will welcome your settling there. I can mark off your holdings on a land map, give you a receipt for your money, and lock it in my office safe until it can be taken to the nearest U.S. land office. I believe the range you have in mind can be had for a dollar an acre. Generally, whites are reluctant to settle *anywhere* in Utah Territory because of the constant trouble there."

"We want a total of eight sections," said Lonnie, "with four on each side of the Green, adjoining. That's twelve hundred and eighty dollars each, and we're prepared to pay right now."

The four Texans had brought in their saddlebags, and each proceeded to count out the correct amount on Captain Stoddard's desk. Stoddard then wrote each of them a receipt.

"By the time you return from Texas," Captain Stoddard said, "I should have the deeds for you. One of you can ride up here and get them. Good luck."

"We're obliged," said Dallas Weaver. "Now we need to visit your sutler's store."

"Go ahead, and welcome," Captain Stoddard said.

Wovoka Shatiki had waited for them, remaining with the horses, outside the sutler's. As the Texans approached, there were half a dozen whites gathered there, and Wovoka had his back to the wall and a Colt in his hand.

"That's enough," said Lonnie quietly. "You men back off."

"You bastard," said one of the threatening whites, "is this your damn Indian?"

"He's *nobody's* Indian," Lonnie said coldly. "He's a man in his own right, and he's part of my outfit. Move in on him, and the four of us are right behind you."

In the silence that followed, there were distinctive snicks as the four Texans drew and cocked their Colts. Without a word, keeping their hands away from their weapons, all the whites backed away. Wovoka holstered his Colt. His dark eyes met those of the four men he had chosen to ride with. They had sided with him, claimed him as one of their outfit, and Wovoka Shatiki would not forget.

1

The four Texans and their Indian companion rode out of Fort Laramie, heading south.

"One thing we ain't settled," Dallas Weaver said. "Where are we going to start buying cows once we reach Texas?"

"I'm figuring San Antonio," said Lonnie. "Most of us have kin around there. They've had four years of natural increase since we've been gone. They may have cows for sale."

"Somethin' else we ain't considered," Dirk McNelly said. "We'll be a while just buying the herd, and we're gonna be needing some riders. Snow will be flying in the high country by the time we're ready to start the drive."

"It may be," said Lonnie. "If it is, we may not be able to begin our drive until spring of next year."

"I wouldn't mind that," Dallas said. "There's a little gal in Uvalde that cried when I left four years ago. If I play my cards right, she might be going to Utah with me."

Kirby Lowe laughed. "She's got a ring through some *hombre*'s nose, and maybe three younguns by now. Where do you fit in?"

"Hell," said Dallas, "she wasn't but thirteen when I rode west. Won't cost me nothin' to find out where I stand. She'll be seventeen now, and at twenty she'll be past her prime. How many cows are we aimin' to buy, anyhow?''

"I'm thinking of a thousand head for each of us," Lonnie said, "depending on the cost. I doubt we'll get any decent stock for less than three dollars a head, and it might be more than that. If we pay as much as three-fifty, that's thirty-five hundred dollars for each of us. That, plus what we've paid for the land, will have taken almost half the gold we brought out of California. There'll be wages for our riders we hope to hire in Texas, and God knows how much we'll have to pay for a decent horse herd."

"Catch wild horse," said Wovoka, who had been listening. "There be many wild horse in *bastardo* Crow country." He pointed north.

"Thanks, Wovoka," Lonnie said. "That's something we'll have to consider. Have you hunted these wild ones to the north?"

"*Sí,*" said Wovoka. "Hunt Crow. Take horse."

Dallas Weaver laughed. "If we go horse-hunting, I think we'd better catch the wild ones running loose and gentle them ourselves. We may be facing a showdown with the Mormons. We don't want the Crows coming after us from the other direction."

"I think Wovoka is referring to Montana Territory, along the Yellowstone," Lonnie said. "I've heard there are many wild horses there, and we have as much right to them as anybody else."

Wovoka nodded, pleased.

"We won't be gettin' any of them high-stepping, Spanish-trained horses from California, then," said Kirby Lowe.

"No," Lonnie said, "but we won't be paying two or three hundred dollars apiece for them, either. As the frontier becomes settled, there'll be a real need for a tough little horse that can turn on a nickel and give you some change. He'll need the strength to hold a twelve-hundred-pound steer at the end of a rope. The army will be needing more and more horses as they build more forts and send more soldiers.''*

"This all sounds like a dream to me," said Dirk McNelly. "I reckon we'd better get the four thousand cows from Texas and put 'em to grazing along the Green River before we start horse-hunting. How many riders are we aimin' to hire in Texas?"

"At least five, maybe more, if we can find them," Lonnie Kilgore said. "Wovoka will be scouting ahead, and with a point, two flank, and two swing riders, we'll need three of the others riding drag."

"That's eight," said Kirby Lowe.

"We must have more horses," Lonnie said, "and with a decent remuda, that means at least two horse wranglers. We'll need at least two more pack mules, and the wranglers will be responsible for them, too."

North Texas. June 19, 1853.

The outfit had ridden across eastern Colorado and Indian Territory's Panhandle.

"I can tell we're in Texas," Kirby Lowe said. "It ain't rained here since we left."

"It may have rained farther south, where we're going," said Dallas. "It's closer to the Gulf of Mexico."

"I'm not wishing anybody bad luck," Dirk McNelly said, "but if Texas has had two or three dry years, we won't be payin' near as much for cows. What good's a cow when the sun's burnt all the grass to a crisp and there ain't no rain in sight?"

"You'd better hope that hasn't been the case here," Lonnie

---

*These were the first "quarter horses," but the breed was unnamed until 1941, when the American Quarter Horse Association came into existence.

said. "We'll be here awhile buying our herd, and they'll have to eat."

They crossed the Canadian River and rode south, which would take them directly to San Antonio. It had indeed been a dry year in Texas, and there was little greenery to be seen.

San Antonio, Texas. June 26, 1853.

It was nearly dark when the five weary riders reached San Antonio.

"Let's stay at a hotel tonight and meet with our kin tomorrow," Lonnie suggested.

"Good idea," said Dallas. "I got to wash off the trail dust and get me some new duds."

Wovoka got only as far as the stable where they left the horses.

"No like hotel," Wovoka said. "No like town."

Lonnie talked the hostler into allowing the Indian to spend the night in the hayloft.

"If he's that skittish, he'll get awful damn hungry before we get out of Texas," said Kirby Lowe.

"I reckon when we split up, he can go with me," Lonnie said. "My folks have a barn with a hayloft. He can stay there."

The following morning, the four Texans approached the livery with caution, wondering how they could feed Wovoka. They found him sitting cross-legged in the early morning sun, his back against the stable wall.

"Wovoka," said Lonnie, "it's time for breakfast. We eat."

"Eat," Wovoka said. "Much hungry."

It was still early, and there was nobody but the cook in the cafe they chose. Wovoka sat down calmly enough, waiting.

The cook wasted no time getting to their table, and with his eyes on Wovoka, he spoke.

"Gents, it ain't my personal feelings, but most folks that comes in here takes a dim view of settin' down with an Indian."

"He's part of our outfit," said Lonnie, "and he stays. The sooner you can get us some grub out here, the sooner we'll be on our way. Bring us plenty of coffee. Scramble us two dozen eggs, and bring a couple of platters of ham. You got biscuits?"

"Yeah," the cook growled.

"Bring us all of them," Lonnie said.

When the order came, Wovoka's reluctance vanished like the morning dew. He ate like it might be the last meal he'd ever see. The four Texans served themselves, and Wovoka ate everything else.

"My God," said Kirby Lowe, "he never ate nothin' but jerked beef all the way here. Didn't Bridger ever feed him?"

Wovoka kept eating, and Lonnie spoke to the cook.

"Bring us another round."

"There ain't no more biscuits," the cook said. "You got 'em all."

"Then bring more ham, eggs, and coffee," Lonnie said.

It was with considerable relief that the distraught cook watched the five of them leave the cafe.

"Well," Lonnie said, "it's time to meet with our kin and break the news. Since we'll be here awhile, let's each take a few days and start asking around for some cows for sale and some riders. We'll meet at my pa's place on July Fourth."

"When we find cows for sale," said Kirby Lowe, "you want us to go ahead and buy?"

"Up to a thousand head," Lonnie said, "and get two or three bulls. See if the owner will allow us to leave the herd on his range until we're ready to move 'em out."

"That may be the hard part," said Dallas Weaver. "If

Texas has had some dry years, it might be reason enough for an outfit selling stock. I think after we've bought 'em it'll be up us to feed 'em."

"If that's how it is," Lonnie said, "don't be quick to buy. Range may be scare."

"Why don't we just find cows for sale, and see what we've learned when we come back together on July Fourth?" said Dirk McNelly.

"I like that better," Dallas Weaver said.

"That might be best," said Lonnie. "Kirby?"

"I agree," Kirby said. "If graze is a problem, we don't want four thousand cows until we're ready to head them north."

"It's agreed, then," said Lonnie. "Scout around. See what's for sale and for how much. And be sure you ask about some riders. Each man will need at least three horses."

There the friends parted company. Each had kin less than an hour's ride from San Antonio. Wovoka Shatiki rode with Lonnie, and when they approached the ranch house where Lonnie had grown up, Wovoka held back.

"Come on, Wovoka," Lonnie urged. "These are my kin. You'll be welcome."

Seemingly against his better judgment, Wovoka rode on. Suddenly the door opened and Willard Kilgore stepped out on the porch. Mary, his wife, was right behind him.

In seconds, Mary was down the steps, meeting Lonnie as he dismounted. Wovoka had reined up uncertainly.

"Ma, Pa," Lonnie said, "this is a friend of mine, Wovoka Shatiki. He's Shoshone."

"Long as he ain't Comanche," said Willard. "Step down, Wovoka, and welcome."

Wovoka dismounted, seeming surprised when Willard Kilgore offered his hand. Wovoka took it, nodding to Mary. A warrior never shook the hand of a squaw.

"Unsaddle your horses in the barn," said Willard, "and come on to the house."

"Wovoka take horses," the Indian said.

Lonnie nodded, knowing what the Indian had in mind. He waited until Wovoka had led their horses toward the barn before he spoke.

"Wovoka prefers the barn to a house. Let's go on in."

Lonnie spoke for more than an hour about what he and his friends planned to do.

"But you've been gone four years," Mary protested. "If you move all the way to Utah Territory, we may never see you again."

"Mary," said Willard, "it's the last frontier for a rancher. A man must be careful. Such an opportunity may not come again."

"I know," Mary said sadly, "and there's the talk of secession. Even war."

"War?" Lonnie asked. "What war?"

"Just talk, so far," said Willard. "The South don't like the Federals denying them what they see as states' rights. Southern states—especially those in the Deep South—already have threatened to secede from the Union. Texans—except for Sam Houston—is ready to take up arms and fight."

"My God," Lonnie said, "it ain't even ten years since Texas became a state, and it was all Houston's doing. He fought like a dog for statehood."

"Sam says he'll quit public office if Texas secedes," said Willard.*

"I can understand his feelings," Lonnie said, "but I think there's a limit to how much pushing around a man can take."

"I told Willard you'd say that," said Mary sadly. "I hate to say it, but I'd rather have you ranching in the wilds of Utah than risk you being killed in a foolish war between the states."

*Sam Houston resigned as governor of Texas in 1861.

"It's still just talk," Willard said. "I doubt there'll be a war, but even if there is, you can't be faulted for taking up ranching on a new range."

"We'll need cattle and we'll need riders," said Lonnie, "and we're prepared to pay."

"Then you should find plenty of both in Texas," Willard said. "We'll always be cattle-poor until there's a way to get the critters to eastern markets."

"There's talk of a transcontinental railroad," said Lonnie.

"I've heard that talk," Willard said, "but *when*? I doubt I'll live to see it."

"If there's a war, I doubt any of us will," said Lonnie.

Dallas Weaver received much the same reception from his kin.

"We hate to see you take up ranching so far away," Otis Weaver said, "but a man has to have room to grow. When do you aim to start the drive?"

"We're not sure," said Dallas. "We'll need to hire maybe six riders, and of course we must find the cattle and some decent bulls. We'll also need a couple more pack mules, and probably some horses."

"You won't have any trouble finding riders," Otis said. "Texas is full of eighteen- and nineteen-year-olds just chompin' at the bit to make their mark in the world. But horses and mules may be a problem. With so much dry weather, most of the range has gone to hell, and few ranchers are keepin' more animals than they need for their own work."

"We've considered that," said Dallas. "We might have to wait until spring to begin the drive."

"Oh, I hope you do," Elvie Weaver said. "There's something you need to attend to before you start the drive. Do you remember Mindy Odens?"

Dallas laughed. "I sure do. She was just a little shirttail girl when I left here, just barely thirteen. I half-expected her to sneak off and follow me."

"She might have been better off if she had," said Elvie. "A year after you left, her Ma died, and since then, old Jess has become a drunkard and a scoundrel. When Mindy was sixteen, she ran away. She came here, and we let her stay until old Jess sent the sheriff to take her home. I think you should talk to her."

Dallas laughed uneasily. "Ma, when I left here, Mindy was a freckle-faced little girl with a chest as flat as a billiard table. She—"

Otis Weaver laughed, and Elvie's face went red with embarrassment. When she trusted herself to speak, she did.

"Dallas, you've been away four years. The little girl you remember is a woman now, and if it wasn't for her sot of a father, she could have any man she wants."

"That may be true," said Dallas, "but she's still not of age. You want me to ride over there, shoot her old daddy, and carry her away?"

"I want you to ride over there and see her," Elvie said. "What you do after that is up to you. Jess spends most of his time in town hanging around the saloons."

"I'll talk to her," said Dallas. "Tomorrow will be soon enough to begin the search for horses, mules, cattle, and riders."

When Dallas reached the Odens ranch, he was amazed at how run-down and unkempt the place looked. There was a single horse in a corral adjoining the barn. Behind the house someone was chopping wood. Dallas reined up, dismounted, and started around the house, and his first look at Mindy Odens took his breath away. She had gathered up an armload of stove wood and was about to head for the house when she saw Dallas. With a glad cry, she flung down the wood and ran to meet him. She flung herself at him, and he was so speechless, he said the first foolish thing that popped into his head.

"You used to have freckles."

She laughed. "Now just a few on my nose. I used to be flat-chested, too. Am I still as ugly as I was when you went away?"

He held her at arm's length and looked at her. Her light hair was like newly grown corn silk, while her eyes matched the bluebonnets on the Texas plains. He swallowed hard a time or two before he was able to speak. When he did, it was straight from the heart.

"Mindy Odens, you're the most beautiful girl I've ever seen."

"Thank you," she said, pleased. "Come on in the house where it's a little cooler. Pa's gone to town."

There was coffee left over from breakfast, and Mindy stirred up the fire in the stove. She then sat down on the other side of the table facing Dallas.

"I was sorry to hear of your ma's passing," said Dallas.

"She was all that kept Pa straight," Mindy said, "and she was just worn out. When she was gone, Pa just went straight to hell. He spends his days in town, begging drinks in the saloons or running up a bar tab where he can get credit. Now tell me about you. Are you back for good?"

"No," said Dallas.

He dreaded telling her of the proposed drive to the Green River range and his intention of remaining there, but she would find out soon enough. So he told her, and long before he was finished, tears crept out the corners of her eyes and rolled down her cheeks. Finally there was nothing more to be told, and there was a long, uncomfortable silence. Mindy finally spoke, and her voice trembled.

"Dallas, when you go, take me with you. I won't ask anything of you except a roof over my head and something to eat. I'm a good cook, and I can chop my own wood."

"I wish I could take you with me," Dallas said, "but if my memory serves me right, you're still only seventeen. Your pa would just send the law after you."

"Let him," said Mindy defiantly. "I'll show the sheriff what I should have shown him already."

She got up from the table and peeled the long dress over her head, leaving her wearing only her boots. Struck dumb, Dallas sat there as she turned first one way and then the other. From her shoulders to her knees, her body was a mass of welts and scars. Some of them were crusted with dried blood.

"Great God Almighty," Dallas said, his voice trembling with anger. "Your Pa did that?"

"Yes," said Mindy. "Every morning before he leaves for town. I'm leaving here, if I have to go to San Antonio or Austin and become a whore."

"Hush that kind of talk," Dallas said. "You're going back to my pa's place with me, and when we're ready to begin the drive, you'll go to Utah."

"But what can you do if Pa sends the law after me?"

"If all else fails," said Dallas, "you can show—or threaten to show—the sheriff those scars all over you. Has he . . . hurt you in any other way?"

"No," Mindy said, "but he's tried. He comes in drunk, tells me I have to take Ma's place, and tries to get in bed with me. I've had to leave the house and sleep in the barn."

"That settles it," said Dallas. "You're not coming back here, if I have to shoot the old varmint. Gather up what clothes you have."

"I don't have much," Mindy said. "I haven't had a new dress since Ma died."

"You'll need cowboy clothes for the trail drive," said Dallas, "and we can get them in town. Is that your horse in the corral?"

"Yes," Mindy said, "but he's wind-broke, thanks to Pa. My saddle's in the barn."

"Wind-broke or not, we'll take our time, taking him with us. Before we begin the trail drive, we'll have to get you a better horse," said Dallas.

Overcome with emotion, Mindy flung herself at Dallas, still wearing only her boots.

"Whoa," Dallas said. "Let me get used to you before you lay too much temptation on me. Take one of your pa's shirts and a pair of Levi's, so you can ride astraddle."

Placing her hands on his shoulders, she leaned back and looked into his eyes.

"I'm not ugly, then?"

"Ugly, hell," said Dallas. "You're beautiful. Now get some riding clothes on. You're making it more and more difficult for me to be a gentleman."

She laughed, and went about rounding up something to wear.

Leaving the cafe Dirk McNelly set out for the Chad Tilden place. There he would inquire about mules, horses, and cattle for sale. He secretly hoped he might have a chance to see Tilden's daughter, April. The girl was within a year of Dirk's own age, and when he had tried to see her before leaving for California, Chad Tilden had asked him to leave. Now, he thought with some satisfaction, April would be of age. When he was within sight of the house, he could see Chad Tilden was on the front porch waiting. Dirk reined up, and Tilden spoke.

"What business do you have here, McNelly?"

"I'm interested in buyin' some mules, some horses, and maybe a thousand cows, if you got any to sell," said Dirk. "Lonnie Kilgore, Dallas Weaver, Kirby Lowe, and me have more than five thousand acres in Utah, and we're taking up ranching there."

"Glad to hear it," Tilden said ungraciously. "None of you ever amounted to anything in these parts. I might have three hundred cows to sell, but no mules or horses. That is, if the money is there."

"The money will be there, if the price is right," said Dirk.

"We aim to compare prices, and we'll let you know. Do you mind if I say hello to April while I'm here?"

"She's gone riding," Tilden said stiffly, "and I don't know when she'll be back."

Dirk wheeled his horse and rode back the way he had come. He wasn't more than a mile from the house when a horse nickered somewhere ahead of him. His mount answered, and Dirk reined up.

"Dirk?" a female voice inquired.

"Yeah," said Dirk. "Is that you, April?"

To answer his question, the girl rode out into a clearing ahead. She had been sixteen when Dirk had left for California four years ago. She had since matured beyond his wildest dreams, and Dirk rode forward to meet her.

"I'd just started out for a ride when I saw you coming," April said, "so I waited. As you probably learned, Pa still doesn't think too highly of you."

"I can understand why he might have felt that way before," said Dirk. "I was sixteen, with nothing ahead of me but Pa's ten-cow rawhide outfit. But I'm back from California, with money to buy horses, mules, and cattle. Lonnie, Dallas, Kirby, and me own eight full sections of land alongside the Green River in Utah."

"You told Pa that?" April asked.

"Yes," said Dirk. "Beyond agreeing to maybe sell some cows, I can't see that it makes any difference to him. He still ain't wantin' me to see you."

"Do *you* want to see me?"

"It's all I've thought about for four years," Dirk said. "I was hoping that me changing from a thirty-and-found rider to the owner of a ranch might make a difference, but I got an idea that your Pa just don't like me."

"I liked you when you were a thirty-and-found rider," said April. "You were always a gentlemen, and I felt safe with you. I can't say the same about some of the other men my Pa allows to hang around. I'm of age, and I can ride where I want. Name a place, and I'll meet you there.''

"I'm staying with my ma and pa until we can buy the horses, mules, and cows we'll be needing for the trail drive to Utah,'' Dirk said.

"If I ride over there after dark, will your family consider me a brazen, wayward girl?''

"No,'' said Dirk. "I've told 'em your pa doesn't like me, but my folks like you, and I can promise you that you'll be welcome anytime.''

"Then I'll ride over there and meet you after dark,'' April said.

They parted, and Dirk had forgotten all about mules, horses, cows, and the proposed drive to the Green River range. His heart felt strangely light, and he didn't care if it did take them all winter to ready the trail drive. He promised himself he wouldn't leave Texas until April Tilden rode beside him.

Riding into Neal and Elene Upton's ranch, Kirby Lowe received an enthusiastic welcome, for the Uptons were friends with Kirby's kin, Burke and Tilda. The Uptons had a young son, as well as a daughter—Laura—who was near Kirby's own age. They had in no way discouraged his seeing Laura, and he believed she liked him. He had dismounted and was climbing the steps to the front porch when the front door burst open and Laura shouted a greeting. She grabbed him, kissing him hard, to the amusement of her parents.

"You left when I was just sixteen,'' Laura said, "and I never expected to see you again. Have you come back to stay?''

"No,'' said Kirby. "I own twelve hundred and eighty acres of good graze, and I'm back to buy some mules, horses, and cattle. Let's set a while, and I'll tell you all about it.''

"There's fresh cake and coffee in the kitchen,'' Elene Upton said. "Let's go there.''

They all listened attentively as Kirby described the lush graze along the Green and the intention of the four friends to establish the largest horse and cattle ranch in the territory.

"How long until you aim to start the drive?" Neal Upton asked.

"We're not sure," said Kirby. "We'll need time to buy some extra horses for a remuda and four thousand cows. We'll need a couple of pack mules, and some bulls, too. Do you have anything for sale? We're paying cash."

"I can spare you maybe three hundred cows and a couple of bulls," Neal Upton said. "I've held off as long as I could. The going price is two dollars and seventy-five cents a head, and that's for prime stock."

"We'll pay three dollars and fifty cents a head for prime stock," said Kirby.

"That's generous of you," Neal said. "Why don't you bring your ma and pa over for Sunday dinner? We haven't seen Burke and Tilda for months."

Laura Upton winked at Kirby across the table, and he had to swallow hard before he could speak.

"I . . . they . . . we'd all like that," said Kirby.

"I'll ride part of the way home with you," Laura said. "We have some catching up to do."

Again she winked at Kirby, while Neal and Elene Upton grinned at the embarrassed cowboy.

"Lonnie," said Mary Kilgore, "I don't know why I didn't think of this sooner. Becky Holt's ma and pa died when their house burned two years ago. Becky's tried her best to hold the outfit together, but one by one her riders have quit for lack of pay. She might be willing to sell all her cattle. There's not much else she *can* do, but none of the ranchers around here have the money to buy."

"I purely hate to take advantage of somebody's hard luck,"

said Lonnie, "but I reckon I can talk to her. How old is she now?"

Willard Kilgore laughed. "Maybe a year older than you. You might sweet-talk her and get all her cows for two dollars a head."

"Willard Kilgore," said Mary, "I'm ashamed of you. Lonnie, if Becky's willing to sell to you, then you treat her fair."

"I aim to, Ma," Lonnie said.

2

San Antonio, Texas. June 28, 1853.

*I*mmediately after breakfast, Lonnie Kilgore rode to the Holt ranch, some ten miles to the east. As he approached, two men came out of the barn. Gus Wilder and Waco Talley had been with the Holts for as long as Lonnie could remember. The two were at the house when Lonnie reined up.

"Get down, cowboy," said Gus.

Lonnie dismounted, shaking their hands. Both men were in their thirties, and their old hats, run-over boots, and faded Levi's and shirts attested to some hard times.

"It's good to see you, gents," Lonnie said, "but I must talk to Becky. Dallas Weaver, Dirk McNelly, Kirby Lowe, and me have bought eight sections of land along Green River in northeastern Utah. We're looking to buy cattle, horses, and mules."

"Then I reckon Miss Becky will be glad to see you," said Waco Talley. "She's played out her hand. Gus and me is stayin' until she decides what to do with this place."

Becky Holt stepped out on the porch, closing the door behind her. The dark shadows under her eyes and the worry lines in her face made her seem older than she was. Finally she spoke.

"Come in, Lonnie, and I'd like Gus and Waco to join us. They've stayed with me to the end, even when I could no longer pay them. I think they deserve to know what I must do."

Lonnie nodded, and the three cowboys followed Becky Holt into the parlor. Most of the upholstered furniture was worn threadbare. The trio sat down on a sagging couch, while Becky took a chair facing them. What she had to say was painful, and she swallowed hard before she began.

"Three years ago, we started losing more than our share of cattle to rustlers. Pa, Gus, and Waco surprised them one night, killing three of them. A few days later—during the day—the house burned. Nobody was here except Ma and Pa, and there was evidence that gunmen had trapped them in the house while it burned. There were shell casings aplenty."

"No tracks?" Lonnie asked.

"Plenty, for a while," Gus said, "but it was comin' on dark, and there was some rain during the night."

"Where we once had three thousand head of cattle, there may not even be a thousand," said Becky. "They're wild as Texas jacks, and it's all but impossible for the three of us to gather them. I can't honestly sell you cows, because I don't know how many there are, or where they are."

"There's Dallas, Dirk, Kirby, and me," Lonnie said. "With Gus and Waco helping, we could round them up in a few days."

"It's slow, hard, dangerous work," said Becky. "I won't have Gus and Waco taking part in this, when their wages are three months behind."

Reaching in his pocket, Lonnie handed each of the men five double eagles. Becky Holt caught her breath, and the harsh lines in her face softened. Lonnie spoke.

"Gus, if you and Waco have nothing keeping you here,

we're needing riders to trail the herd to northeastern Utah. Riders who will stay with us.''

"Let us think on it some," said Gus. "Before we're done gathering the herd, we'll have made up our minds."

"I'll miss you," Becky said, "but go, with my blessing."

Feeling their part in the discussion was over, the two cowboys got up and left the house. Lonnie spoke.

"I reckon it's none of my business, but do you still owe money on this place?"

"Seven hundred and fifty dollars," said Becky, "and I think the only reason the bank hasn't called in the loan is because my pa was a longtime friend of the banker."

"I hate to say this," Lonnie said, "but if the bank has to foreclose, they'll be expecting some cows in the deal. Your pa had cattle when he took out the loan, didn't he?"

"Yes," said Becky.

"Suppose we bought enough cows for you to pay off the bank?" Lonnie asked.

Becky buried her face in her hands, and it was a while before she could look at him. There were tears in the corners of her eyes, and her voice trembled.

"That's awfully generous of you, Lonnie, but the rustlers have beaten me. I just don't have the riders, and I can't afford enough. I'm just hoping I can realize enough out of this place for stage fare back to Missouri."

"You have kin there?"

"Pa does," said Becky, "but I've never seen them. They didn't like Ma, and disowned Pa after he married her."

"So you don't know if they'll welcome you or not," Lonnie said.

"No," said Becky, "but I have nowhere else to go. I'm almost twenty-five, and I expect them to treat me like an old maid."

"You're anything but that," Lonnie said. "Take that worry

off your shoulders and out of your eyes, and you'd be pretty
as any girl in Texas.''

"It's kind of you to say that," said Becky. "You're about
to make me cry, and it's a luxury I couldn't afford since Ma
and Pa died."

It seemed Lonnie had said all there was to say. He stood
up, pausing when he reached the door. To his total surprise,
Becky Holt threw her arms around him, holding him tight. He
put his arms around her, and when she lifted her head, their
eyes met. As though by consent, without a word being spoken,
they kissed long and hard.

"In case you're wondering," Becky said, "that wasn't in
gratitude. I admire the kind of man you've become, Lonnie
Kilgore, and I just hate the thought of me being in Missouri,
while you're somewhere in Utah."

"It'll be a while before we start the drive to Utah," said
Lonnie. "Things could change before then. When can I see
you again?"

"I'm here all the time," Becky said, "but after dark, you'd
better sing out, so Gus and Waco will know who you are.
They've had a bellyful of rustlers."

"I'll be back tonight after supper," said Lonnie. "There
must be some way I can help you dig out of this."

On his way back to the Kilgore ranch, his mind was a
turmoil of possibilities, for he was unable to rid himself of
Becky Holt's troubled face. She was near his own age, yet he
had never thought of her, except for she and her parents being
friends to his family. His only ambition had been to reach the
rich diggings in California. Arriving at the Kilgore barn, he
unsaddled his horse, rubbed the animal down, and went on to
the house. Mary, his mother, was in the kitchen baking pies.
It was hot in the kitchen, and she came into the dining room,
wiping her sweating face with a towel. Lonnie had sat down
at the table, and Mary sat down on a chair across from him.

"It's too hot, being in the kitchen," Lonnie said. "It must be a hundred degrees in the shade."

"I'm baking you some pies while I can," said Mary. "You likely won't have anything like that in the wilds of Utah. Besides, I may never see you again."

"Oh, Ma," Lonnie said, fanning himself with his hat, "I came home this time, didn't I?"

"Yes," said Mary, "but to buy stock. You won't have to do that again. What did you learn at Becky Holt's place?"

"That she's in over her head," Lonnie said. "If the bank calls in the loan, they'll take everything, including the cattle. She won't have anything left to sell."

"That's what your pa says," said Mary. "He's tried to raise enough money among the other ranchers to pay off her mortgage, but nobody has any money to spare. Many of them are behind on their own loans at the bank."

"Ma," Lonnie said, "I have the money to pay off Becky's place free and clear, without it affecting our drive to Green River."

"That's generous of you, Lonnie, but without riders and money to pay them, she'd be in trouble again within a few months. She can ride, rope, and shoot like a man, but it's taking its toll on her. It's one thing for a woman to have a strong man beside her, and yet another when she's alone, with everything falling on her shoulders. Did she tell you what she aims to do when the bank takes her place?"

"She's talking of going to Missouri to stay with some of her pa's family," said Lonnie, "but I think she's just desperate. When Walt Holt married Fannie, he was disowned by his family. At least that's what Becky told me."

"You've learned more from her than any of the rest of us," Mary Kilgore said. "When will you see her again?"

"Tonight," said Lonnie, not meeting his mother's eyes.

"Then we'll have supper early," Mary said, "and you can take Becky one of these pies."

Eventually Willard Kilgore rode in, and Lonnie joined him on the front porch. Talk turned almost immediately to Becky Holt and her seemingly impossible situation.

"Son," said Willard, "there's only one way Becky Holt can come out of this short of bein' stone broke. She's got to pay off what she owes the bank, so she can legally sell the cattle she has left. Otherwise, they'll belong to the bank, too."

"I know," Lonnie said. "With her two riders, Dallas, Dirk, Kirby, and me, we could round up the cattle she has left and find out where she stands."

"She might have far more cattle than she thinks," said Willard Kilgore. "Rustlers won't drag the wild ones out of the brush, and that's likely where the most of them are."

After supper, Lonnie rode back to the Holt ranch, one of Mary's pies wrapped in a clean flour sack. Gus and Waco came out of the barn, recognized Lonnie, and returned to whatever they had been doing. Becky sat on the front porch, and it was obvious to Lonnie that she had taken some time preparing for his visit. He dismounted and climbed the steps to the porch.

"Ma sent you a pie," he said by way of greeting. "I like that dress you're wearing."

"It's the best I have," she said. "I last wore it to Ma and Pa's funeral."

"Becky," said Lonnie, wasting no time, "I'm going to pay off what you owe the bank."

"I can't let you do it," Becky said. "I'd have no way of repaying you."

"All you need is two hundred and fifty cows at three dollars a head," said Lonnie. "Surely you have that many. With Gus and Waco helping, Dallas, Dirk, Kirby, and me can round them up. All of us will be meeting at Pa's ranch on July Fourth. I want you, Gus, and Waco there."

"Lonnie, I appreciate what you're doing," she said, but the sad expression in her dark eyes cast a shadow on her words.

"None of this is going to make you happy, is it?" Lonnie asked.

"No," said Becky. "I was born here, and however hard the times were, it was home. I have this feeling, deep down, that I won't ever be happy with Pa's relations, even if they take me in. I don't mind the hard life on a ranch, and if I could do it all by myself, then I would. But with the rustling, and cattle prices down, and money owed to the bank, I'm whipped."

"Becky Holt," Lonnie said, "when I left here four years ago, I had a mean case of the wanderlust, but this morning, when I saw you, something happened to me. That's why I'm here tonight, to ask you the most important question I've ever asked anybody."

She didn't dare look at him. He took her face in both his hands, and her eyes were closed. Silent tears ran down her cheeks, which had been tanned by sun and wind. For just a moment, Lonnie feared she wasn't going to respond, and then she did. She clung to him until her tears dried, and when her eyes finally met his, something deep inside—not unlike the awareness of salvation—told him he was doing the right thing for them both.

"Becky," said Lonnie, "I want you to marry me."

"But I might not have even enough cows to pay off the mortgage at the bank," she said.

"Damn the mortgage at the bank," Lonnie said. "I want you, and I don't care if there's not a single cow left on this range. I'll pay what's owed the bank so you don't lose the place your pa homesteaded. My pa can look after it, making use of the graze and water, and we'll round up all the cattle we can find. Now, will you marry me?"

"Yes," she said simply. "When?"

"July Fourth," said Lonnie. "Dallas, Dirk, and Kirby will be at my pa's place. Be sure that Gus and Waco come with you, and you can tell them about us, if you want to."

"I wish you would stay the night," Becky said. "I'd just like to show you how happy I am."

Lonnie laughed. "I don't dare. After I've made you an honest woman, you can have your way with me."

When Dallas and Mindy Odens rode in to the Weaver ranch, Elvie Weaver stood on the porch. Dallas dismounted and helped Mindy down. His mother's eyes were full of questions, but Dallas didn't wait for them.

"Ma, I'm taking Mindy back to Utah with me, whatever her pa says or does. Mindy, I want you to go in the house and show Ma how badly you've been beaten. If the sheriff shows up, we may need her to speak up for you. I'll unsaddle the horses."

Mindy followed the older woman into the house and wordlessly removed her clothes.

With a gasp, Elvie Weaver wept as she beheld the welts and scars inflicted by the brutal beatings Mindy had suffered.

"Ma'am, I don't want to be any trouble," Mindy said.

"Hush," said Elvie Weaver. "If he shows up trying to take you back, I'll get a gun and shoot him myself. Come on in here and lie down across the bed so I can doctor you."

Having unsaddled the horses, Dallas went on to the house. He sat down on the porch, waiting. He had no doubt his mother was doctoring Mindy as best she could. While he did not for a moment regret taking Mindy away from her abusive father, he would have to see that she was always with him until they were ready for the drive to the Green River range. He had little doubt that Jess Odens would come looking for the girl and that the situation might well involve the law, but he was equally certain that he wasn't giving Mindy up.

It was late when Lonnie Kilgore returned to the Kilgore ranch, and he was surprised to find a lamp burning in the parlor. Mary Kilgore sat beside the lamp, sewing.

"You're up kind of late, Ma," Lonnie said.

"I had some sewing I'd been putting off," said Mary. "Besides, I wanted to know what you've decided to do where Becky Holt's concerned."

Lonnie laughed. "I've decided to marry her and take her to Utah with me. Does that meet with your approval?"

"You know it does," Mary said. "I stopped just short of suggesting it, because Willard told me to keep my mouth shut. When will you marry?"

"Right here, on July Fourth," said Lonnie, "Dallas, Dirk, and Kirby will be meeting me here. We'll be taking Becky's last two riders with us to Utah, and with Dallas, Dirk, Kirby, and me helping, we should be able to round up what's left of Becky's cattle. With some of the money I would have needed to buy stock, I'm paying off Becky's mortgage at the bank. We want Pa to keep an eye on the place, using the land for graze as he needs it."

"I don't think you should count too much on Becky's cattle," said Mary. "The rustlers have taken advantage of her, and she may not have a cow left."

"Ma, just calm down," Lonnie said. "I'm marrying Becky, not her cattle or the ranch. If she's been rustled dry, then we'll manage. If Pa's agreeable, I'd like for us to have some real festivities on the Fourth. You know, some cakes, pies, and two or three haunches of roast beef."

Mary laughed. "When Willard learns you're marrying Becky Holt, nothing will be too much to ask. He's been worried about what was to become of her, and lamenting all of us being too up against it to help her. We hate to lose you to Utah Territory, but we'll feel better knowing Becky's with you."

San Antonio, Texas. July 4, 1835

Early in the morning—just after breakfast—Becky Holt and her riders Gus Wilder and Waco Talley arrived. Gus and Waco headed toward the barn, for there, beneath a huge oak, Willard Kilgore was roasting haunches of beef over open pits.

Becky barely made it to the porch before she was met by Mary Kilgore. The two of them wept for a moment, while Lonnie stood there feeling useless.

Dallas Weaver and Mindy Odens were next to arrive. Mindy held back, allowing Dallas to explain why she was with him.

"Why, you sneaking coyote," said Dallas, "How did this little old thing happen?"

"Her ma and pa are dead, and I went to see her about buying cattle," said Lonnie, "and I went back to see her that same night. We're keeping two of her riders, and with you, me, Dirk, and Kirby helping, we need to round up the cattle she has left. Rustlers have taken advantage of her, stealing her blind."

"I hope you don't mind me bringing Mindy Odens with me," Dallas said. "Her Pa—old Jess—has become a drunk and has been beating Mindy. She's still a year underage, but I'm taking her to Utah with me if I have to shoot old Jess. I don't want him taking out his rage on my folks, so I'm keeping Mindy with me."

"Mindy's welcome," said Lonnie. "Why don't you go ahead and tie the knot, and let old Jess do his worst?"

"I'm tempted to," Dallas said. "I'll talk to Mindy. She's scared to death the law will take her back to old Jess. I have to handle this in such a way that I can protect her."

"One thing I'd forgotten," said Lonnie. "I don't have a ring for Becky."

"I don't have one for Mindy, either," Dallas said. "Do you have a preacher coming?"

"Not yet," said Lonnie, "but we have all day. I aim to ride into San Antonio and look up old Reverend Henderson. Him and Pa have been friends for years."

"July Fourth or not, there'll be some of the shops open," Dallas said. "Suppose we take Becky and Mindy with us and buy them some rings?"

"That's probably the best idea you've had in your life," said Lonnie. "I only have one regret. Dirk and Kirby will likely ride in while we're gone, and I wanted to see their faces when they learn what we're about to do."

Lonnie and Dallas went into the house, told the girls their intentions, and then went to saddle horses for the four of them.

"Don't take too long," Mary Kilgore said. "Willard's roasting enough beef to feed just about everybody in the county, and I don't want a lot of it left. Hurry back and let's eat."

"We'll have to find Preacher Henderson," said Lonnie, "and bring him with us. Do us a favor, Ma. Don't you, Pa, Gus, or Waco tell Dirk and Kirby what we're up to. I want to see their faces when we show up with the girls and the preacher."

Kirby Lowe arrived at the Kilgore ranch, and he wasn't alone. Laura Upton rode beside him. Kirby helped her dismount. Willard Kilgore, Gus, and Waco had come to the house to greet the new arrivals. Mary Kilgore greeted them warmly, and Willard Kilgore introduced Gus and Waco. Kirby didn't waste any time.

"Laura and me are gettin' married a week from today at my pa's place. Ever'body that wants to come is welcome. Where's Lonnie, Dallas, and Dirk?"

"Dirk hasn't ridden in yet," said Willard. "Lonnie and

Dallas rode into town to fetch something. We're waiting for them to get back so we can eat.''

"Laura," Kirby said, "why don't you go in the house with Mrs. Kilgore? I reckon it'll be great fun surprising these *hombres* when they ride in."

Waco Talley laughed. "I reckon there will be some surprise."

When Lonnie, Becky, Dallas, and Mindy returned, they were accompanied by an elderly man with gray hair and wearing a gray frock coat. Kirby Lowe waited on the porch, anticipating the surprise he had in store for Lonnie and Dallas, but he looked at the women and the old minister uncertainly. The five of them dismounted, and Lonnie was the first to speak.

"Kirby, you know the Reverend Henderson. This young lady is Becky Holt. Before the day's out, she'll be Mrs. Lonnie Kilgore."

Kirby was speechless, and before he could think of a response, Dallas cut in.

"Kirby, this is Mindy Odens. We'll be married the same time as Lonnie and Becky."

There was laughter from within the hall. Kirby still hadn't thought of anything to say, when Mary Kilgore and Laura stepped out on the porch. Her eyes sparkling, Laura went down the steps to stand beside Kirby, and it was she who spoke.

"We have a surprise, too. A week from today, at Kirby's place, him and me will be married. Everybody that knows either of us is welcome to come."

The joke was on all three of the cowboys, and there was considerable merriment at their expense. Finally Kirby spoke.

"It's gonna be hard on old Dirk, the three of us with pretty girls. He'll be ridin' alone, I reckon."

"Before we left for California," said Lonnie, "he was sweet on April Tilden."

"Yeah," Dallas said, "but he told me old man Tilden run him off."

"He shouldn't let that stop him," said Mary Kilgore. "April's at least twenty, and old enough to choose a life of her own."

"She's not married, then," Lonnie said.

"Heavens, no," said Mary. "Chad Tilden thinks no man is good enough for her. She'll die right there under his roof, if he has his way."

"Poor old Dirk," Dallas said. "He wasn't blessed with good looks, but he's as true a friend as a man ever had."

Dirk McNelly, the object of their conversation, rode in and dismounted. He didn't seem unduly surprised at the gathering. Dallas and Kirby looked slantways at Lonnie, hoping he would break the news to Dirk. Lonnie did so, and shaking their hands, Dirk grinned at them.

"The rest of you can take as long as you like," Willard Kilgore said, "but Gus, Waco, the preacher, that Shoshone in the barn, and me is goin' to eat."

Having lived in the county all their lives, the three young women were not strangers, and they settled down to eat together. Lonnie, Dallas, Dirk, and Kirby ate together, for they had much to talk about.

"Startin' tomorrow," said Lonnie, "we got to do a fast roundup."

They looked at him expectantly, awaiting an explanation. Quickly, Lonnie told them of Becky Holt's cattle, of his decision to pay off Becky's loan at the bank, and that he had hired Gus Wilder and Waco Talley to accompany them to Green River range.

"You do things almighty sudden, *amigo*," Dallas said. "All I got was the promise of six hundred cows. No bulls, no horses, no mules."

"Laura's Pa promised us three hundred cows and two bulls," said Kirby.

"I didn't get a damn thing but some hard looks," Dirk McNelly said. "Old man Tilden said he might sell us three hundred cows, if the money's there. People around here still treat me like I'm a thirty-and-found line rider."

"We all know better, don't we?" said Lonnie. "We'll beat the bushes and round up as many cows as we can on Becky's place. Let Tilden keep his damn cows."

"We need to round up enough of Becky's cows, so we can afford to buy some horses with the money we can save," Dallas said. "Then I think when we've rounded them up, we need to stand watch over them until we're ready to begin the trail drive."

"I agree," said Lonnie, "but there's something we've forgotten. We haven't introduced the ladies to Wovoka Shatiki. With all that's happened, I'd forgotten him. He's been in the barn since we got here, sleeping in the hayloft. I've had to take his food to him."

"It looks like you'll have to take it to him this time, too," Willard Kilgore said. "I tried to get him out here, and he wouldn't come."

"No," said Lonnie. "If he's going to be part of our outfit, I won't have him slinking around under cover because he's uncomfortable with us. I'll get him."

To the surprise of them all, Lonnie returned with the Shoshone.

"Kirby," Lonnie said, "move over there and sit beside Laura. Dallas, you'll sit beside Mindy, and I'll sit beside Becky."

Wovoka, stood there uncertainly, seemingly overwhelmed by the array of food.

"Wovoka," said Lonnie, "this is Becky with me, Mindy with Dallas, and Laura with Kirby. Squaws, Wovoka."

Wovoka nodded to them, saying nothing, but there was a light of understanding in his dark eyes. Mary Kilgore quickly got his attention by presenting him with an entire pie.

"Yours, Wovoka," she said.

It was a gesture the Shoshone fully understood, and he relaxed. These people meant him no harm. Willard Kilgore heaped a platter with roast beef, boiled potatoes, and some sourdough biscuits. Wovoka sat down, his back to an oak, and ate all the food. He was invited to take more, which he did.

"I think I'm going to like him," Laura said. "Thank God he's not Comanche."

"He's a Wind River Shoshone, from Wyoming," said Lonnie. "They're friendly. Wovoka has long been a friend of Jim Bridger, and Bridger thought we'd need Wovoka with us."

"Everybody's finished eating except Wovoka," Kirby said, "and he's likely to be at it for a while. Lonnie, when do you and Dallas aim to get hitched into double harness? I'd like to get Laura home before dark."

"I'm not going until I see this," said Laura.

"Then let's get on with it," Lonnie said. "Preacher Henderson, are you ready?"

The old preacher laughed. "Probably more so than either you or Dallas."

The ceremony was short and simple. Wovoka watched it from beneath the oak, where he was still eating.

"Come on, Dirk" said Kirby. "Let's kiss the brides."

They proceeded to do exactly that. Several times.

"Just once, damn it," Lonnie said.

The merriment came to an abrupt halt as a horseman approached.

"Oh, dear God," said Mindy.

Jess Odens reined up, making no move to dismount. He seemed to ignore Mindy, his hard old eyes on Dallas. Finally he spoke.

"I'm here to tell you to keep away from my gal."

"It's you that's going to be kept away from her," said Dallas. "Preacher Henderson just read from the book, and I've put a ring on her finger."

"That's true," Henderson said. "In the eyes of God, she's his wife."

"Leave the Bible-thumpin' out of this, Preacher," said Odens. "It's just him and me."

"Whatever you aim to do," Dallas said, "do it. Mindy stays with me."

"I'll fetch the sheriff, then," said Odens. "She ain't but seventeen."

"*Bueno,*" Dallas said. "Bring the sheriff, and we'll show him Mindy's back and legs. I suspect there are some laws against what you've done to her."

Odens shifted his hard eyes to Mindy, condemning her for revealing his cowardly acts. But the girl's eyes met his with no hesitation. Without another word, he rode away.

3

He's headed toward town,'' Mary Kilgore said. ''Perhaps he is going for the sheriff.''

''Or back to the saloons,'' said Willard.

''Oh, I wish he hadn't come,'' Mindy said. ''He'll find some way of getting back at me.''

''He can try,'' said Dallas, ''but he'll have to step over my dead body.''

''It's a scruffy old coyote like him that'd shoot you in the back,'' Waco Talley said. ''I'd say the sooner we can take the trail to Utah, the better off you'll be.''

''We don't start the drive until we're ready,'' said Dallas. ''My pa's always told me not to start any fights, but to never be afraid to finish one.''

''We may be all of next week rounding up Becky's cattle,'' Lonnie said. ''For every cow or maverick we gather, it'll mean that much more of our money we can spend on some good horses.''

''Waco and me has got two horses each,'' said Gus Wilder. ''The two extras are back at the ranch. With nobody at the house, I think we'd better ride over there and bring them here. A varmint that'll steal cows will steal horses.''

"I think you're right," Lonnie said. "Why don't you and Waco ride over there and get them? Things may get a mite cramped, but I think we'll continue to gather here for whatever time we remain in Texas."

"We have plenty of room," said Mary Kilgore. "This is a large house, and there are rooms upstairs that we never use."

Gus and Waco had saddled their horses. Bound for Becky Holt's place, they rode out.

"It's time I was getting back to town," Reverend Henderson said. "I've enjoyed the hospitality. To you young folks bound for Utah, good luck, and may God go with you."

Lonnie and Dallas each handed the old preacher a double eagle. He nodded his thanks and, mounting his horse, rode back toward town.

"I'd better take Laura home," said Kirby. "I aim to tell her ma and pa that Laura will have some female friends on this trail drive and after we reach Green River range."

"Both of you are welcome to stay the night," Mary Kilgore said. "We have room."

"We appreciate the offer," said Kirby, "but Laura's folks want her to stay there with them until we're ready for the drive to move out. We want all of you at Kilgore's ranch for the ceremony a week from today. Preacher Henderson's already promised to be there."

"We understand," Dallas said. "My ma and pa wanted Mindy and me to stay there with them as long as we could, but I didn't want old Jess Odens causing them trouble, trying to get even with me."

Kirby saddled the horses, helped Laura mount, and the two of them rode out.

"The Indian's gone," said Mary Kilgore.

"He finally got enough to eat and went back in the barn," Lonnie said.

"Come on to the house," said Mary. "I have rooms ready for you and Becky, and for Dallas and Mindy."

"Show the girls the rooms," Lonnie said. "Dallas and me and Dirk had better settle down here in the shade and wait for Kirby. We still have some more plans to make."

"Kirby won't be worth a damn durin' the gather if he spends his nights at Laura's. He won't get any sleep," said Dirk.

"Dirk," Lonnie said, "I doubt Laura's ma and pa will have the two of them sharing a room until Preacher Henderson reads from the book. Kirby knows we're starting the gather tomorrow. If he doesn't make it back tonight, he'll be here at first light in the morning."

Gus Wilder and Waco Talley rode in, leading their extra horses. Dismounting, they led the animals into the barn.

"Gus, before you and Waco unsaddle your horses, come out here for a minute," said Lonnie. "I've just thought of a way the two of you may be able to help us."

The two cowboys came out of the barn, leading their saddled horses.

"Becky had more riders than just the two of you," Lonnie said. "How many were there before some of them pulled out?"

"At one time there was six of us," said Waco Talley. "Sandy Orr, Benjamin Raines, Elliot Graves, and Justin Irwin moved on."

"Do either of you know where they are, or if they're hired on with somebody?" Lonnie asked.

"We ain't seen 'em since they left," said Gus, "but nobody around here's able to hire any riders. You want we should track 'em down?"

"If you know where to find them," Lonnie said. "We'll pay forty-and-found to men who will help us trail the herd to Utah and stay on as part of our outfit."

"These is all good *hombres*," said Waco. "No drunks or hell-raisers. They all have kin in these parts. We might have time to find 'em before dark."

"See if you can," Lonnie said, "and tell them to be here at first light tomorrow. The more riders we have, the less time it'll take to make the gather."

"I hate to mention this," said Gus, "but when they left, they was owed three months' wages. I reckon that would be their only objection to hirin' on again."

"I don't fault them for that," Lonnie said. "Tell them if they'll hire on with us, we'll pay them their back wages. We'll also pay each of you a month's wages in advance before we leave Texas."

"You're *hombres* to ride the river with," said Waco. "We'll do our best to bring them back with us."

The two cowboys mounted and rode out.

"Tarnation," Dallas said, "that's some hell of a payroll we'll have, and so far we ain't bought a horse or a cow."

"There hasn't been a gather on Becky's spread in near three years," Willard Kilgore said. "You may be surprised at the number of cows you'll find there."

"I hope you're right," said Lonnie, "because we must come out of this with money to buy horses, and enough to keep us going for a while."

"If Gus and Waco can find Becky's other four riders," Dallas said, "they should have at least two horses each. That'll help some. We have the four extra horses we brought with us from California, but I'll need one of them for Mindy. The poor old horse her Pa left her is wind-broke."

"There's plenty of daylight left," said Dirk. "I think I'll ride into town for a while."

"As long as you're back by first light," Lonnie said.

Dirk mounted and rode out toward town, but once he was out of sight, he rode south. He rode along a stream, now almost dry, half a dozen miles from Chad Tilden's ranch. He didn't dare hope April would be there, and his heart leaped with anticipation when a horse nickered ahead of him.

"It's me," said April, aware of his caution.

Dirk rode ahead, dismounted, and she came to him.

"Let's find us some shade," Dirk said. "We got lots to talk about."

"Not all that much," said April. "All I have to do is ride out and never go back."

"I know," Dirk said. "and I've set a time. A week from today, at the Kilgore ranch."

"Why there?"

"Because one of my *amigos*—Kirby Lowe—is tyin' the knot with Laura Upton. Just a while ago, Lonnie Kilgore, Becky Holt, Dallas Weaver, and Mindy Odens took the jump. I ain't told them a thing about you. You just be here early in the day, and I'll come and get you. We're going to surprise a lot of folks."

"Yes," said Laura. "Mine especially."

"I know," Dirk said, "and I'll be especially regretful, them not bein' there. But there's no other way we can do it. You're of age, and by the time they hear about us, you'll be wearing your ring and you'll belong to me. Really, I ought to take you to town and buy you a ring so we can be sure it'll fit, but your pa's likely to hear of it, and he'll know we have something in mind."

"I've thought of that," April said. "Take this piece of string, wrap it about my finger where the ring should go, and then tie a knot in it. The loop in the string can be used to get a ring that will fit. But please, nothing fancy."

"After we're hitched," said Dirk, "I aim for us to stay at the Kilgore ranch until we're ready to start the trail drive."

"Why there?" April asked.

"Because your pa may decide to track you down and take you home," said Dirk, "and I can't keep you with me all the time. We have cows and horses to buy. You'll be safe at the Kilgores', and legally your Pa can't force you to leave with him. When we meet here next Monday, bring everything with you that you'll expect to need, because you won't be able to go back for a long time. Maybe never. Are you still sure you want to go through with this?''

''I'm sure,'' April said. ''Just get here early, so we can take our vows before anything goes wrong. I'll be waiting, with both my horses.''

Hating to leave her, Dirk McNelly rode away, headed for town. He *really* hadn't lied to his companions about going to town. He just hadn't told them of the stop he planned to make along the way. Reaching into his shirt pocket, he felt the bit of string that he would need to buy April's ring.

The sun had long since gone down, and the first stars were twinkling in purple heavens, when everybody at the Kilgore ranch retired to the parlor. Suddenly there came the sound of approaching horses. Lonnie and Dallas, keeping within the shadows of the hall, went to the front door.

''Rein up and identify yourselves,'' Lonnie said.

''Gus and Waco, with friends,'' Gus said.

''Come on,'' said Lonnie.

Six riders reined up, dismounted, and left their horses at the hitch rail.

''We got some gents you and the rest of the outfit need to meet,'' Waco said.

''Then come on in the house where there's some light,'' said Lonnie.

Lonnie and Dallas led the six men back to the parlor. Willard Kilgore was bringing in chairs from the kitchen.

''Folks,'' said Waco, ''these *hombres* is Sandy Orr, Benjamin Raines, Elliot Graves, and Justin Irwin. You folks that don't know 'em, I'll let you do your own introducin'.''

With a glad cry and tears in her eyes, Becky Holt got to her feet, and one at a time, took their hands.

''I'm Lonnie Kilgore,'' Lonnie said. ''Becky and me tied the knot today.''

"I'm Dallas Weaver," said Dallas. "Mindy and me just took the same jump."

The two of them shook the hands of the four new arrivals.

"I reckon you all know Mary and me," Willard Kilgore said.

"Well," said Mary, "we know all of you well enough to know you're probably hungry. There's plenty of supper left."

The cowboys grinned in appreciation.

"We are a mite hungry, ma'am," Waco Talley said.

"Give us a few minutes, then," said Mary. "Becky, you and Mindy can help me."

"We'll unsaddle our horses, then," Sandy Orr said. "There's eight. Is there room in the barn for them all?"

"Yes," said Willard Kilgore, "but you'd better take Lonnie with you. There's an Indian in the hayloft."

"My God, not a Comanche, I hope," Benjamin Raines said.

"No," said Willard, "he's Shoshone, but it'll take some time for him to get used to you bein' around."

"His name is Wovoka Shatiki," Lonnie said "He's a long-time friend of Jim Bridger, and Bridger wanted him with us on this trail drive. Come on. I'll go with you to stable your horses."

"Wovoka," said Lonnie, before entering the barn, "these are *amigos*, come to stable their horses."

There was no sound from within the barn. Either the Shoshone understood or didn't want to reveal his position. The men entered the barn, leading their horses. Wovoka still said nothing and made no sound. When the horses were unsaddled and led into the stalls, the men followed Lonnie back to the house.

"Supper's ready," Mary Kilgore announced.

Gus, Waco, and the four riders they had brought with them washed and dried their hands. The table was large enough to seat them all, with chairs remaining.

"Dallas and me will join you at the table," said Lonnie. "We'll tell you what we aim to do. When you're done eating, if you have questions, we'll try to answer them."

Before Lonnie said anything else, he and Dallas removed handfuls of double eagles from their pockets. Two of the coins were placed before Gus Wilder and Waco Talley.

"You already have your back wages," Lonnie said. "This is a month in advance."

Then before each of the four newly arrived riders, Lonnie and Dallas placed eight of the gold coins.

The four new arrivals looked as though they couldn't believe it.

"That's your back wages, and a month in advance," said Lonnie.

"*Amigo,*" Sandy Orr said, "you've just hired yourself some *hombres* that'll stay with you until hell freezes, and then skate on the ice."

There was immediate agreement from Orr's three companions, and one by one they leaned across to shake the hands of Lonnie and Dallas.

"A rider's coming," Willard Kilgore said. "I'll see who it is."

Kirby Lowe dismounted, came in, and Lonnie introduced him to the four new riders.

"I'm glad you fellers joined us," said Kirby. "All of us bein' from around here, it'll be like workin' with kinfolks."

"Dirk McNelly rode to town," Lonnie said, "and he ought to be back pretty soon. He's owner of one of our four spreads."

"Four?" said Benjamin Raines.

"Eight sections," Lonnie said. "Four on each side of the Green River, adjoining one another. Four of us have bought in, and we'll run it as one ranch."

"I'm proud of bein' part of such an outfit," said Justin Irwin.

"We've come up against one big problem," Dallas said. "We'll need at least two more pack mules and one horse. That's the least we can get by with."

"That's an almighty skimpy remuda for such a drive," said Benjamin Raines.

"I know," Dallas said. "Each of you gents has two horses, and with the four that we brought back from California, Lonnie, Dirk, Kirby, and me will have extra mounts. But I'll have to find a horse for Mindy. The old horse she's been riding is wind-broke."

"My God," said Sandy Orr, "that means none of the ladies nor the Indian will have an extra mount. If one of their horses goes lame, we're in trouble."

"Every man working cattle—especially on a trail drive— needs at least three mounts in his string," Elliot Graves said, "but I don't know where in tarnation we'd get the extras. But I do know where we can get a couple of mules. My pa's giving up farming, and he's asking a hundred dollars apiece for them."

"Tell him we'll take them," said Lonnie. "After we're finished rounding up Becky's cows, you can take him the money. We'll need a couple of pack saddles, too."

"You'll likely have to get them in town at the wagon yard," Sandy Orr said. "Most of the folks owning mules only use 'em to draw a wagon or for plowing."

Another rider approached, and Willard Kilgore let Dirk McNelly in.

"Am I too late for supper?" he asked.

"No," said Mary, "there's plenty. Pull up a chair."

"You're too late for one thing," Lonnie said. "While you were gone, we managed to hire the rest of Becky's old outfit. This is Sandy Orr, Benjamin Raines, Elliot Graves, and Justin Irwin."

"I know them," said Dirk, extending his hand. "Good to have you with us, gents."

"We've been talking our situation over, Dirk," Lonnie said. "Elliot can get us a couple of mules from his pa, but we haven't come up with any horses. Each of these six riders has one extra mount, and the horses we brought back from California can be used as extra mounts for you, Kirby, Dallas, and me. We'll still need a horse for Mindy."

"We're pushing our luck, having only two horses for each rider," said Kirby.

"Give me some time the next Monday morning," said Dirk, thinking of April Tilden's second horse. "I think I can come up with that extra horse, and we won't have to pay."

"You ain't aimin' to steal one, are you?" Kirby Lowe asked.

"Hell, no," said Dirk. "I got some important business to take care of after we're done with this gather, and if it all works out like I think it will, we'll have that extra horse."

"Don't spend too much time," Kirby said. "Remember, Laura and me's gettin' hitched."

"I know," said Dirk, "and I wouldn't miss it for the world. I'll be back here pronto."

"I reckon all of you will want to get an early start in the morning," Mary Kilgore said, "and I have your rooms ready. Sandy, you and Benjamin will share a room, and so will Elliot and Justin. I hope that's all right. We now have a full house."

"That brings back painful memories," said Gus Wilder. "Last time I had a full house, with a month's wages ridin' on it, the varmint across the table from me had a straight diamond flush."

The six cowboys followed Mary Kilgore upstairs to be shown their rooms.

"I'm starting to feel better about this trail drive all the time," Dallas Weaver said. "We done the right thing, hiring those six riders."

"Dallas," said Mary when she returned to the dining room, "you and Mindy take the first room to the left at the head of the stairs. Lonnie, you and Becky will take the first room on the right, across the hall. Dirk, you and Kirby will be in the room right next to Lonnie and Becky.''

Dirk laughed. ''Will you be sleepin' tonight, Lonnie? Do we stuff our ears with some cotton?''

''You'd better stuff some cotton in your ears,'' said Lonnie, ''and while you're about it, stuff a handful in your big mouth.''

Becky and Mindy had remained in the parlor with Willard Kilgore while the cowboys had been discussing business. Both women had heard the exchange between Lonnie and Dirk, and were still blushing when they entered the dining room.

''Lonnie,'' said Willard, ''before you rush off to bed, what do you aim for Wovoka to do while the rest of you are gathering a herd?''

''He can stay in the barn,'' Lonnie said. ''He won't be of any use in the gather. Driving cows is squaw work, according to him.''

''Then see that you talk to him in the morning when you take him his breakfast,'' said Willard. ''I still don't think he trusts me.''

Dirk and Kirby climbed the stairs to the room that had been assigned to them.

''Enjoy this while you can,'' Kirby jibed. ''After this week, you'll never get to sleep with me again.''

''I ain't expecting to,'' said Dirk. ''Not even if you was good-lookin', which you ain't.''

Lonnie and Becky entered their room. Dallas and Mindy entered theirs across the hall.

''Mindy,'' Dallas said after closing the door, ''if you're a mite nervous, we . . . can wait until you get used to havin' me around.''

''We'll wait only if it bothers you,'' said Mindy. ''I've been waiting since I wasn't even thirteen. All I ask is that you at least take off your hat, gunbelt, and boots.''

"Hell, I can do better than that," Dallas said. And he did.

Across the hall, Becky sat on the bed while Lonnie struggled to remove his boots.

"When I was much younger," said Becky, "I used to wonder what this would be like."

"Oh?" Lonnie said. "You don't wonder anymore?"

"I never thought the day would come," said Becky, "so I quit torturing myself and put it out of my mind. Now I'm an old woman. I'll be twenty-five, my next birthday."

"I'll be twenty-four," Lonnie said, "and I ain't even close to bein' an old man. Give me half an hour, and I'll prove it to you, unless you aim to set there the rest of the night in your boots, hat, and cowboy duds."

Becky laughed. "I'm waiting for you to take them off. If that doesn't shock you into sleeping in the barn with Wovoka, we'll go from there."

On the Range. July 5, 1853.

"Wovoka will stay here in the barn," Lonnie said, after taking the Indian his breakfast. "Becky and Mindy will be here, and Wovoka will be watching the house from the hayloft. He's been told to fire only warning shots. Pa, if you hear shooting, get out there and see who's coming. We still may not be rid of old Jess Odens."

The ten men mounted and rode out for Becky Holt's range.

"Unless the rustlers have cleaned her out, there should be a decent herd," Gus Wilder said. "There should be three years of natural increase."

"No gather for that long?" Lonnie asked.

"Not since Becky's ma and pa died," said Gus. "She had to bury her folks, rebuild the house, and worry about how she could get the money to pay us. We was willing, wages or no wages, to gather some cows and drive them to market somewhere. Anywhere. But the girl's got her pa's pride, and without the money for such a drive, she wouldn't do it.''

"There was the mortgage, too," Waco said. "She just seemed to lose all hope."

"Trouble was," said Sandy Orr, "there was no place to drive a herd with any hope of gettin' decent money. Folks in New Mexico, Kansas, Louisiana, Missouri, Arkansas, and Mississippi raise cattle, too. It'd be hell, drivin' a herd of three-dollar cows hundreds of miles, only to find the local stock going for two dollars a head."

"That's not going to change until a railroad's in reach," Lonnie said, "and we don't know when it will come. Maybe never, if war breaks out between North and South."

"That's another good reason for settling in Utah Territory," said Elliot Graves. "I'm not of a mind to fight a war started by a bunch of damn politicians. Hell, we ain't even ten years away from the war with Mexico, and we'd have had to fight it ourselves if it hadn't been for old Sam Houston forcing the Congress to admit Texas to the Union."

The ten riders came within sight of the ranch house and the barn, and there wasn't any sign of activity. A light breeze blew out of the west, and from somewhere in the distance came the lonesome cawing of a crow.

"You gents know this range," Lonnie told Becky's former cowboys. "If there are any cows, you should have some idea where they'll be."

"Low-lying areas, where there's some shade and maybe a little water," said Gus, "and there's plenty such places on this six hundred and forty acres. Come on."

Less than a mile from the house, they came up on a stream where there was no more than a trickle of water. Willows grew along the banks, forming a tunnel of greenery. With Gus Wilder and Waco Talley leading, the ten cowboys entered the dim coolness of the overhanging willows.

"Yeeeeaaaaha," Gus shouted. "Yeeeeaaaaha!"

There was a bawling frenzy as the cattle sought to escape the invaders. Down the stream they ran, breaking through the willows and into the sunlight. Quickly the riders headed them and started them milling. There were twelve of the animals, and none of them were branded.

"Two-year-olds," said Justin Irwin. "They're part of the natural increase."

"What are we gonna do with 'em?" Elliot Graves asked. "Soon as we ride on, they'll be right back among them willows."

"That's no problem," said Lonnie. "We know they're in there. When we're finished for the day, we'll drive what we've gathered back to here, and then chase this bunch out to join them. We'll be watching for some good graze, with water, and that's where we'll start bunching them for the night. By the time we're ready to start the drive, we want all these critters to feel like they're part of a herd."

"All bunched up that way, they'll be mighty convenient for rustlers," Gus Wilder said.

"No," said Lonnie. "We're gonna be standing watch, five of us at a time. The first watch until midnight, and the second until dawn."

"We should have thought of that sooner and brought some grub," said Dallas. "The first watch will have a long day and half the night, with no supper."

"I have thought of it," Lonnie said, "and I'm way ahead of you. Ma will have supper ready for the first watch in time for them to ride in, eat, and get back to the herd before dark. Then the second watch rides in, has supper, gets some sleep, and is back here to relieve the first watch at midnight. Next morning, the first watch will have their breakfast and ride back here, so the second watch can ride in and eat."

"We're gonna spend more time ridin' to and from your pa's place than rounding up the cows," said Benjamin Raines. "Why don't we just get a sackful of jerked beef, some coffee, and a coffeepot, and all of us stay out here until the gather's done?''

''It's just a way for us to have some decent meals before we begin the drive,'' Lonnie said. ''Save the jerked beef for the long ride to Utah Territory.''

The ten of them rode on, seeking more cows. Before the day was over, many of the cattle they had rounded up bore Becky's Circle H brand. They rode well beyond the barn and the deserted ranch house, driving before them the cattle they had gathered during the day. The cowboys bedded them down alongside a creek. It was running low, but there was ample water.

''Not the best graze in the world, but it'll get them through tonight,'' Lonnie said.

''Seventy-five of the varmints,'' said Kirby Lowe. ''and at least two-thirds of them are wearin' Becky's brand. If the natural increase continues to be that good, we may come out of here with a right smart of a herd.''

''It's lookin' better than I expected,'' Lonnie said. ''Now we need to decide who's on the first watch. The first watch will have to ride in, eat, and then return here, so the second watch can ride in, eat, get a little sleep, and take over at midnight. Any volunteers for the first watch?''

''I'll take it,'' said Kirby Lowe.

''So will I,'' Dirk McNelly said.

''Count me in,'' said Gus Wilder.

''I'll stay,'' Waco Talley said.

''I'm stayin' too,'' said Sandy Orr.

''All of you ride in for supper,'' Lonnie said. ''Then you'll ride back, allowing the rest of us to ride in, eat, and get a little sleep. When we relieve you at midnight, you'll ride in, catch some sleep, have your breakfast, and then relieve the second watch, so we can go eat. Since there have been rustlers working this range, don't take any chances. Nobody except us has any business out here. If some varmint comes sneaking around and won't identify himself, then don't be afraid to shoot.''

4

On the Range. July 7, 1853.

*T*he third day on Becky's range, the riders gathered more than three hundred cows, many of them unbranded, a result of natural increase.

"With rustlers at work," Dallas said, "I can't understand why there's so many without brands. Thieves ought to take them first."

"Maybe they're bein' driven across the border," said Waco. "*Mejicanos* don't care how many Texas brands a critter's wearing, just like Texans don't care a damn about brands on Mex cows and horses."

"Rustling can get you the rope in Texas," Sandy Orr said. "It just don't seem natural for a gent to risk gettin' his neck stretched over a cow worth three dollars."

"There may be just one man involved," said Lonnie. "He couldn't drive more than a few cows at a time. That might explain why there are so many still here."

"Most folks in these parts won't know we're here gathering

cows,'' Benjamin Raines said. ''The varmint that's taking the cows might show up some night.''

''I hope he does,'' said Dallas.

On the Range. July 9, 1853.

By Saturday, the outfit had gathered 2,025 longhorns, almost half of which bore no brands. Some of the animals were bulls.

''We've hit the jackpot,'' Lonnie said. ''We need only two thousand more cows to complete our herd. I think we'd better leave these where they are for next few days. Pa will need all his graze.''

''Don't forget,'' said Kirby. ''Laura and me's gettin' hitched come Monday. If all of you are there, who's gonna be watching the herd?''

''It'll be in the daytime,'' Lonnie said, ''and I think this varmint does his rustling in the dark. I think we can all leave the herd long enough to watch you get fitted for a double harness. We'll go with the usual watches tonight and tomorrow night. Monday, we'll have to move the herd anyway. They'll need new graze.''

Saturday night—well after midnight—the five riders on the second watch hunkered down under the shadow of an oak. There was Lonnie Kilgore, Dallas Weaver, Benjamin Raines, Elliot Graves, and Justin Irwin. Suddenly one of their horses nickered, and all five men were on their feet, Colts in their hands. Afoot, they started around the herd toward some distant brush. The horse nickered again, and in the pale starlight, Lonnie raised his hand and issued a command.

''Whoever you are, come out of there with your hands in the air. Otherwise, we'll salt down that thicket with lead.''

''Don't shoot,'' a nervous voice said. ''I'm coming.''

The man who emerged had his hands in the air, and even

in the starlight, the riders could see the frightened face of Jess Odens.

"You're a good ways off your range, Jess," Lonnie said. "Why?"

"No law agin a man ridin' across somebody else's range," said Odens.

"There is, if he aims to take another man's cows home with him," Lonnie said.

"I ain't never took a cow that was branded," said Odens. "A maverick's as much mine as anybody's."

"Not if it's part of a natural increase on another man's range," Lonnie said.

"You ain't got nothin' on me," shouted Odens.

"Dallas," said Lonnie, "find his horse, and if he has saddlebags, check them out."

"Damn you," Odens snarled, "you got no right."

"We have every right," said Lonnie.

"There was some interesting stuff in his saddlebags," Dallas said when he returned. "A pair of running irons."

"Hell," said Odens, "them ain't nothin' but cinch rings. You can't prove they ever been used for anything else."

"The hell we can't," Dallas said. "They're blackened. They've been in a branding fire."

"I think we all know what this old coyote's been up to and why he's here tonight," said Lonnie. "Gus, tie his hands behind him. Waco, get your lariat and fashion us a good, strong noose."

"No," Odens bawled. "I ain't done nothing."

"Dallas, fetch his horse," said Lonnie.

Dallas brought the horse. With the help of Gus Wilder, Lonnie hoisted the frightened Odens into the saddle. Waco had the noose ready, and standing up in his stirrups, he let it fall over Odens's head.

"Let me go," Odens begged, "and you'll never see me again. I . . . I'll ride away."

"Lonnie," said Dallas, "come here."

Lonnie joined his comrade, and Dallas spoke softly so nobody else could hear.

"Lonnie, I know he's a thieving, no-account old coyote, but he's still Mindy's pa. For her sake, I'm askin' you not to do this."

Lonnie said nothing, and from the grim set of his jaw, Dallas didn't think he was going to speak. When he finally did, it was to Odens.

"Odens, you're going to get more of a break than you deserve, because you're Mindy's pa, but that won't work the next time. I aim to see to it that everybody within a hundred miles of San Antone knows you're a damn thief. Waco, take off the noose. Dallas, free his hands."

Odens was openly weeping, and some of the cowboys turned away, refusing to witness such cowardice. Lonnie slapped Odens's horse on the flank, and it galloped away into the darkness.

Benjamin Raines laughed. "We really didn't have enough evidence to string him up."

"No," Lonnie said, "but I think we put the fear of God into him, which was exactly what I aimed to do."

"I'm obliged," said Dallas. "I reckon he'll come to a bad end, but for Mindy's sake, I don't want to be involved in it."

"We really ought to spread the word among the other ranchers," Elliot Graves said. "After we're gone, if Odens falls back on his thieving ways, everybody he steals from will have a chance to track down the old varmint."

"I aim for the county sheriff to know what we suspect," said Lonnie. "I feel guilty, us lettin' the old devil loose, because I think once a thief, always a thief. He may straighten up until we head out for Utah Territory and then revert to his old ways."

"Then somebody else can shoot or hang him," Dallas said. "I reckon Mindy knows what he is, but I'd be obliged if none of you gents say anything about us findin' him out here tonight. He's hurt her enough.''

"I won't talk about it until I have to," said Lonnie.

"Neither will I," Benjamin Raines said.

"I'll be quiet," said Elliot Graves.

"So will I," Justin Irwin said.

On the Range. July 10, 1853.

Sunday was quiet, and except for watching the gathered herd, the outfit took the day off. With Gus Wilder, Waco Talley, Sandy Orr, Benjamin Raines, Elliot Graves, and Justin Irwin knowing the Holt range, the gather had been done swiftly and well.

"I wouldn't have dreamed there were that many cows," said Becky during supper.

"Well, I'm glad we didn't find them all before you and me tied the knot," Lonnie said. "I don't reckon I'd like to have you think I was marrying you for your cows."

"If you did, you got a better deal than Dallas did," said Mindy. "I don't have a horse, and unless I can come up with some clothes, I'll be stark naked before we get to Utah."

The men laughed, but it quickly faded, for the women all looked dead serious.

"I reckon we'll have to do some buying," Lonnie said, "but not too much. With just three pack mules, we won't have much room for anything but grub. Then when we arrive, we'll likely have to survive the whole winter on what we take with us."

"I don't think you can take that much grub on three mules," said Willard Kilgore. "Not if you plan to eat during the drive. Am I free to suggest something?"

"I wish you would," Lonnie said. "You've just given us something else to worry about during the drive."

"Sorry," said Willard, "but you must face facts. You have three mules. Why don't you find one more and take a wagon? Fit one with a new canvas top, and fill it with food."*

"That's an almighty good idea," Dallas said, "except that we aimed to travel to Laramie and from there along the Oregon Trail a ways. That'll take us across South Pass, and it's pure hell on wagons."

"Maybe it's a better idea than we think," said Lonnie. "Instead of going to Laramie and following the Oregon Trail, suppose we blaze our own trail? We could travel across New Mexico Territory and southern Colorado Territory, entering Green River range from the east, instead of the north."

"It'll be a lot easier, cooking from a wagon than from pack mules," Gus Wilder said.

"You shouldn't have any trouble finding a wagon for sale," said Mary Kilgore.

"Whoa," Lonnie said. "Before we make too many plans for a wagon, let's see if we're all in agreement. Remember, we'll need a fourth mule. Anybody against the idea of using a wagon instead of pack mules?"

Nobody disagreed.

"That's settled, then," said Lonnie. "Now, who can drive a four-mule hitch?"

"We all can, and you know it," Dirk McNelly said. "I reckon what you're asking is who *wants* to drive one."

"I reckon I am," said Lonnie.

"I can handle a four-mule hitch," Becky Holt said.

"So can I," said Mindy. "Why don't we take turns in the wagon, leaving the riders free to trail the herd?"

"That would end the need for an extra horse," Becky said. "When I'm with the wagon, she can ride my horse."

"Then we'd better get busy tracking down a fourth mule," said Dallas.

*This will not be a chuck wagon, which was invented by Charles Goodnight in 1866.

"I hate to pour cold water on anybody's cook fire," Benjamin Raines said, "but there's something we ain't talked about, and it's bothering me."

"Then let's talk about it," said Lonnie.

"I was up to Fort Laramie once," Raines said, "and it was early October. I was ready to ride south when it started snowing. The damnedest snowstorm I ever saw, and the wind was so cold, it burned your face. The temperature dropped fifty degrees, just in a matter of hours. I was holed up at Laramie a week before my horse could travel. Now we aim to go into this High Plains country, and by the time we leave here, I don't look for us to have more than two months before snow flies. I figure we'll be well into October just getting there, and as much as I favor taking a wagonload of grub, the wagon will slow us down. You can drive a cow just about anywhere, but not a wagon. That means we'll have to drive the herd along a trail that will allow the wagon and mules to follow."

"You should have thought of that before we decided to take a wagon," said Lonnie.

"It's no more his fault than the fault of any of the rest of us," Dallas said. "We've all been so caught up in the drive, we've overlooked the obvious. What Ben's said is entirely possible, and I reckon we'd better begin thinking about what we aim to do."

"We could wait until spring," said Dirk McNelly.

"I thought the same thing," Lonnie replied. "But remember what Bridger told us about those Mormons about to move in on his trading post? Suppose we wait until spring and then discover that they have settled on our range along Green River?"

"Why, they can't do that," said Kirby Lowe. "We'll have title to it."

"The hell they can't," Lonnie said. "Possession has always been nine-tenths of the law, and there may be hundreds of them, compared to the few of us. We can't wait for spring.

Whatever it takes, we must get to Green River and get dug in before too many know we're coming.''

"Dear Lord," said Mary Kilgore, "I can't believe you'll have to fight for range after you've bought and paid for it. Is there no law?''

"No nearer than Oregon or California to the west, and Fort Laramie to the east," Lonnie said. "The Mormons went to Utah to escape the government's bothering them, and I think the government considers it good riddance. Utah may never become a state. We'll be strictly on our own, I think.''

It was a sobering thought, and for a while, nobody spoke.

"We can take some extra canvas with us," suggested Waco. "Then if we're caught out in the open, we can set up some windbreaks. Besides, if we're blazing our own trail, we might find some arroyos deep enough for shelter.''

"Good thinking, Waco," Lonnie said. "We're going to have to begin thinking of ways we *can* make it, instead of dwelling on reasons why we *can't*.''

"That's exactly right," said Willard Kilgore, "and the sooner you get started, the better will be your chance that you'll reach your range before the snow comes. I think tomorrow you should split up, some of you buying more cows, one or two buying a wagon with some extra canvas, and some of you looking for that fourth mule.''

"Damn," Kirby Lowe said, "what about Laura and me? We're gettin' married.''

"Preacher Henderson's supposed to be here in the morning," said Lonnie. "It won't take five minutes for him to read from the book. You can nuzzle up to Laura after we've got this drive ready for the trail. Tomorrow, right after the vows, all of us will get busy, like Pa suggested.''

"Remember," Dirk said, "I have somewhere to go in the morning, before the preacher reads from the book.''

"Then get an early start," said Lonnie. "Time is short.''

The Kilgore Ranch. July 11, 1853.

Preacher Henderson did indeed arrive early. Dirk had not returned, having been gone a little more than an hour. Laura Upton was already there, with her parents, Neal and Elene.

"We're waiting for Dirk," Lonnie said. "I don't know what he had to do that was so all-fired important, but he insisted on being here for the marrying."

"He'd better come on," said Dallas. "On top of everything else, we have to move those cows to better graze."

Meanwhile, Dirk had arrived at the stream where he and April had always met, and found her waiting there. Her second horse bore a neatly tied canvas-wrapped pack.

"I reckon this is it," Dirk said. "Do you still aim to go through with it?"

"Yes," said April.

Dirk nodded, and when he led out, April followed.

At the Kilgore ranch, everybody was on edge, especially Kirby Lowe. He was roundly cursing Dirk McNelly when Lonnie spoke.

"Dust over yonder. Somebody's coming."

"Two riders," Dallas observed. "One of 'em's Dirk, but who's the other?"

"A woman," said Mindy.

"She's right," Kirby Lowe said. "Has old Dirk been pulling the wool over our eyes?"

"We'll soon know," said Lonnie.

The two riders reined up. Dirk dismounted first and helped April down. Only then did he speak, and he was brief and to the point.

"Folks, this is April Tilden. We aim to get hitched along with Kirby and Laura. I'll let them of you that don't know her introduce yourselves."

"We know April very well," said Mary Kilgore, "but this comes as a total surprise. This is a time for a family to be together, April. Where's Chad and Edith, your folks?"

"At home, I suppose," April replied, her eyes on the toes of her dusty boots.

"April's of age, and she's doing this on her own," said Dirk. "Before we rode west to California, her Pa called me a thirty-dollar-a-month line rider, and told me to make myself scarce. I don't think he'd settle for anything less than seeing me strung up or gut-shot."

"We did the only thing we *could* do," April said defiantly.

"Things have changed considerably," said Willard Kilgore. "Dirk's no longer a bacon-and-beans, thirty-dollar cowboy. He'll own a ranch, and the cattle to stock it. I predict that Chad and Edith Tilden will change their minds about a lot of things."

"Maybe," Dirk said, "but April and me don't aim to gamble on it."

April nodded. Her eyes were dry, and there was a grim set to her jaw.

"Then let us get on with the ceremony," said Preacher Henderson.

The ceremony was short, and at its conclusion, Lonnie Kilgore spoke.

"We have many things to attend to. April, you and Laura are to remain here. We'll all be staying here until we begin the trail drive."

"Come on, April, and let's all sit on the porch," Mindy said. "We likely won't see them until after dark."

Lonnie and his outfit mounted and rode out, leaving Willard and Mary Kilgore alone.

"I know April's of age," said Mary, "but I'm worried."

"About what?" Willard asked.

"That Chad Tilden may come looking for April. With a gun," said Mary.

"Legally, he can't do anything," Willard said. "If he shows up, I'll talk some sense into him. Don't mention Chad around April."

"I won't," said Mary. "The poor girl's frightened enough."

Lonnie and the outfit moved their gather to yet another stream on Becky's spread, and there was enough graze for maybe two days.

"Elliot," said Lonnie, "here's the two hundred dollars we owe your pa for those mules. See if he knows of anybody who might sell us another one. We'll pay more, if we must."

Elliot Graves nodded, mounted his horse, and rode out.

"Now," Lonnie said, "it's time for some of us to lay down some money for cows. We need to increase our herd by two thousand. I think Dallas and me can handle that, unless some of the rest of you would like to be in on it. Some of us will have to remain here with our gather."

"I'll stay with the herd," said Dirk McNelly. "The only offer to sell cows that I got, it came from old man Tilden, April's pa, and I'd as soon not have any dealings with him, if we can buy our cattle elsewhere."

"I'll stay with the herd, too," Kirby Lowe said.

"Bueno," said Lonnie. He then turned to Sandy Orr, Benjamin Raines, and Justin Irwin.

The trio shook their heads, and Sandy Orr, spoke for them all.

"We'll stay with the herd. You gents are entitled to get as good a deal as you can, and you don't need any of us for that. Besides, we've been down and out for so long, I'm not sure anybody around here would take us serious, if we showed up wantin' to buy stock."

"Dallas and me will take care of it," said Lonnie, "but you *hombres* are part of this outfit. Don't ever sell yourselves short. Your opinions are welcome."

"We're obliged," Justin Irwin said.

"Yeah," said Benjamin Raines. "You got yourself some cowboys. At least until we're so old and stove-up we can't ride."

"Come on, Dallas," Lonnie said. "Maybe we can make deals for some of those cows today. I'll shoot for a thousand head, and you do the same. We'll meet back here with our gather before the start of the first watch."

"One thing I'd like to suggest," said Gus Wilder. "All of us have kin around here, and I reckon they'll appreciate it if you call on them first. They'll all have cows to sell, and I know they need the money."

"Good thinking," Lonnie said. "Chances are, we may get the rest of our herd without going any farther."

Lonnie and Dallas mounted and rode out. Two hours later, Elliot Graves returned with two mules on lead ropes.

"*Bueno,*" said Kirby Lowe. "Is there a chance he can find us one more?"

"He's goin' to try," Graves said.

"There ain't much need for a wagon until we get that fourth mule," said Sandy Orr.

"Pa says we'll likely have to pay more money for another mule," Graves said. "There's not many outfits that have extra stock, because of dry weather and poor graze."

"Thanks to Lonnie gettin' hitched to Becky Holt, we got half our herd and it ain't cost us a thing. We can afford a couple of hundred dollars for a mule," said Dirk.

"It's just as well Lonnie ain't hearin' you say that," Waco Talley said. "You're makin' it sound like he took the woman just to get her cattle."

"Well, that ain't what I meant," said Dirk. "When they tied the knot, Lonnie didn't know if she had ten cows or a thousand. I figure all of us came out ahead. Especially Lonnie. Becky's one fine-looking woman, and I'd be jealous as hell if I didn't have April."

* * *

Lonnie returned to the herd only minutes behind Dallas. After they had dismounted, Lonnie spoke.

"Gus, that was a good idea, calling on your kin. We made a deal for twenty-one hundred cows, with three hundred and fifty of them coming from each of your kin. They've agreed to let us leave them there until we're ready for the trail. Elliot, is there any chance your Pa can find us one more mule?"

"Maybe," said Graves, "but he reckons it'll cost us more."

"Tomorrow," Lonnie said, "I'll let you have two hundred dollars. Instead of just riding from one spread to another, see if your pa knows who has mules. Now it's time for those of you on the first watch to ride in and eat. Hustle on back, so those of us on the second watch can eat and get a few hours' sleep."

Dirk McNelly, Kirby Lowe, Gus Wilder, Waco Talley, and Sandy Orr mounted and rode out, bound for the Kilgore ranch. They returned just as the sun dipped below the western horizon.

"Dirk," said Lonnie, "you're kind of white around the gills. Anything wrong?"

"Not yet," Dirk said, "but with night comin' on, April reckons her kin will be lookin' for her by morning. Her daddy hates the very ground I walk on, and April's afraid he'll show up raising hell."

"She may be right," said Lonnie. "Being on the first watch, you'll be riding back to the ranch at midnight, and you'll be there in the morning. I think you should stay there long enough to see if Chad Tilden going to show up. You don't think she's having a change of mind about you and her gettin' hitched, do you?"

"No," Dirk said. "She's always known her Pa would explode when she left. She's just a mite on the down side because she's dreading a big fight with her pa. Legally, he can't take her away, but that won't stop him from making April miserable. She's already figuring, with us going so far away, that she'll never see her ma and pa again.''

The Kilgore Ranch. July 12, 1853.

The night was quiet. Come the dawn, the five men on the second watch were relieved by four riders from the first. Arriving at the ranch for breakfast, Lonnie spoke to Dirk McNelly, who had remained at the ranch, and then to Elliot Graves.

''Remember, Dirk, you're to spend some time with April until we know whether or not her pa's coming looking for her. Elliot, do the best you can toward finding us that fourth mule. Dallas and me will ride to town and see about buying a wagon. The rest of you stay with the herd.''

Except for Dirk McNelly, the men rode out toward their various destinations. Everyone had left Dirk and April at the kitchen table, for it was obvious the girl was afraid. As she lifted her coffee cup, her hand shook. Dirk wasn't all that settled himself. He hadn't the faintest idea what he could do if Chad Tilden showed up making demands. All the edge he had—if he had one—was the fact that he and April had spent most of the night together, and everything had been strictly legal.

''A buckboard's comin','' Willard Kilgore shouted.

The sun was noon-high when Chad Tilden reined his team to a halt in the Kilgore front yard. Beside him sat his wife, Edith. Willard Kilgore was there to greet them.

''Step down and come in,'' Willard invited.

''I ain't comin' in,'' said Tilden. ''Not now, not ever. My little girl run away, and you give her a place to hide. I owe you for that.''

''Your little girl is a grown woman, with the right to do whatever pleases her,'' said Willard. ''As of yesterday, she's also a married woman, bound for Utah Territory. The only decent thing for you to do is make peace with her. She and Dirk's in the parlor.''

"That damn no-account Dirk McNelly," Tilden snarled. "He's never had nothing in his worthless life but a horse and saddle. Now you've been a party to the varmint taking my little girl. I want them to hear what I have to say."

The front door opened. Dirk and April stepped out on the front porch.

"Have your say, then," said Dirk.

"As long as I'm alive, neither of you are ever to darken my door again," Tilden said.

"Pa," April said pleadingly, "Dirk's ranch in Utah would make four of yours. Can't you let us go with your blessing?"

"I've had my say," Tilden snarled.

Edith Tilden had sat there white-faced, saying nothing. When it became obvious that Chad intended to drive away, Edith snatched the reins from his hand. Before he was aware of what she had in mind, Edith was out of the buckboard, running toward April, who had started down the steps.

"Woman," Tilden shouted, "I forbid you going to her. It's your damn duty to stand behind me, whatever I say or do."

April paused just short of Edith, for Edith no longer faced her. She had turned back to face her irate husband. In a calm voice, she spoke.

"Forbid and be damned, Chad. I've stood behind you too long. Now I aim to stand beside April, to send her away with my blessing, with the hope that she'll find the happiness that's never been mine."

"You get back in this wagon, woman," Tilden said, "or I'll drive away and leave you."

"Do that," said Edith, "and you'll never see me again. I have kin who will welcome me, because they never liked you. Now I think they saw the cruelty in you that I couldn't see until it was too late."

Edith went to April, and the two clung together.

"Come on to the porch, out of the sun," Mary Kilgore said.

As though by prior agreement, Becky, Mindy, and Laura followed Willard and Mary Kilgore into the house, leaving Dirk McNelly, April, and her mother on the front porch.

"I'm sorry I had to slip away, Ma," said April.

"Don't be," Edith said. "You done what you had to."

Their eventual parting was a tearful one, the visit lasting more than an hour. Through it all, Chad sat in the buckboard. When Edith again mounted the box beside him, he flicked the team with the reins and drove away.

5

A hundred and fifty dollars seems a mite expensive for a wagon," Dallas said.

"It's a Studebaker," said Lonnie. "There's none better, and it comes with everything we'll need to add a canvas top."*

"Take it," said Stapleton, owner of the wagon yard, "and I'll include the canvas at no extra charge."

"You got a deal," Lonnie said, "but we'll need to leave it here for a while. We're short one mule. Do you know of anybody with a mule to sell?"

"No," said Stapleton. "The livery has some horses, but they're a pretty scrubby lot."

"Now what?" Dallas said, after they had left the wagon yard.

"I don't want to disappoint Jess Odens by not doing what I promised," said Lonnie. "I think we have to call on the sheriff and tell him we caught Odens sneaking around our herd. He ain't likely to bother us again, but after we're gone, he may backslide to his old rustling ways, stealing from our kin."

*The Studebaker brothers began building wagons in 1839.

They found Sheriff Jackman in his office, and he listened while Lonnie and Dallas told him of their suspicions.

"I'm obliged," Jackman said, "and I'll keep that in mind. For the last several years, ranchers have complained about losing a few cows at a time, and from what you've told me, I'm more and more inclined to believe it's a one-man operation."

When Lonnie and Dallas rode back to the herd, Dirk was there. But there was no sign of Elliot Graves. Nobody said anything until Lonnie and Dallas had dismounted, and it was Dirk who spoke.

"Lonnie, I'm obliged to you for lettin' me stay with April. Her pa showed up, and he was just as nasty and mean as I was expecting. April's ma was with Chad, and in spite of his threats and hell-raising, she wished April well. That helped some."

"I'm glad," said Lonnie. "Dallas and me just bought a new Studebaker wagon in town."

"*Bueno,*" Kirby Lowe said. "Now all we need is that fourth mule. Elliot's been gone for quite a spell."

"He may have had to ride from one ranch to another," said Lonnie, "and that takes a while. Fact is, the drive may be held up, waiting on that one mule."

"I hope not," said Waco. "Every day we lose looking for a mule may be one more day we'll spend in neck-deep snow on the High Plains."

"If Elliot fails to find one today," Lonnie said, "tomorrow, four of us will begin looking. There has to be one more damn mule that can be had, somewhere in Texas."

Elliot Graves returned empty-handed. After dismounting, he spoke.

"I rode to six ranches, all south of here. Nobody with any mules is of a mind to sell one. I offered as much as two hundred dollars, with no takers. It's not my money, so I'd not risk going any higher without you agreein' to it."

"We've got to have one more mule," Lonnie said, "if we have to pay as much as four hundred dollars."

"That's a hell of a lot of money for one critter," said Kirby Lowe. "Was we to go over the border, we could likely get one for a hundred or less."

"We could also get ourselves shot full of holes," Lonnie said. "That war that we fought with Mexico is still fresh in the minds of *Mejicanos*. There's nothing they'd like better than gettin' some foolish *Americanos* across the river and in their gunsights."

"I reckon you're right," said Kirby. "It was just an idea."

"A bad idea," Dallas said. "Maybe we ought to ride north, to Austin or Waco. None of the spreads south of here is likely to have any extra animals, because of their nearness to the border."

The men on the first watch rode to the Kilgore ranch, had their supper, and rode back to the herd, allowing the second watch to ride in. Willard Kilgore sat on the shaded porch, and Lonnie paused to talk to him.

"Dirk said Chad Tilden was here," said Lonnie.

"He was," Willard said, "and he was even worse than I expected. But April's ma made up for his devilment. April's goin' to be all right."

On Texas Range. July 13, 1853.

"Dallas," said Lonnie, "you, me, Dirk, and Kirby are going mule-hunting. The rest of you stay with the herd. Waco, you're in charge."

The four men mounted and rode out. Lonnie spoke.

"I reckon we'd better not split up. With some of us not knowing what the others are doing, we could end up with two expensive mules. We'll first try the liveries in Austin and

Waco. If we come up dry there, we'll have to split up and ride to individual ranches.''

"It's near two hundred miles to Waco," said Kirby. "There's no way we can ride all that far, beat the bushes for a mule, and be back with our herd before dark.''

"I reckon you're right," Lonnie said. "I'm just anxious to find that blasted mule. If we don't come up with one in Austin, Waco will have to wait.''

Austin, Texas. July 13, 1853.

Lonnie and his companions reined up before the livery. Just above the two wide double doors was a hand-lettered sign that read TARKINGTON AND SONS. LIVESTOCK BOUGHT AND SOLD. The four men dismounted and entered the cool interior of the livery barn.

"What can I do for you gents?" a thin little man asked. His hair—what there was of it—was gray, and he looked at them over the tops of his spectacles.

"You can sell us a mule, if you have one," said Lonnie. "If you don't, then maybe you can direct us to somebody who has one for sale. I'm Lonnie Kilgore. My pards are Dallas Weaver, Dirk McNelly, and Kirby Lowe. We're all from San Antone.''

"I'm Wade Tarkington," the livery man said, "and I do happen to have a mule, but I'll not sell him without a bill of sale, and I don't have one. Night before last, some varmint took one of my best horses, leavin' a lame mule behind. Dang mule, if he wasn't lame, is worth maybe a hundred dollars. The horse that I lost was worth twice that.''

"We're badly in need of a fourth mule to pull a wagon," said Lonnie, "and we're about to take a cattle drive to Utah Territory, so we're not all that concerned about a bill of sale.

If the mule's just lame, we'll pay you two hundred dollars for him.''

''He's just lame,'' Tarkington said, ''and in another two or three days, he'll be good as ever. I'll write you a bill of sale, for whatever it's worth, and you got yourself a mule.''

Lonnie and his companions rode south toward San Antonio. Kirby Lowe led the mule on a lead rope.

''He ain't limping,'' said Dallas, ''and that's a good sign.''

''When we get him to the ranch,'' Lonnie said, ''I'll douse that sore leg with plenty of horse liniment. Otherwise, he looks healthy enough.''

When they reached the Kilgore ranch, Kirby led the mule into the barn, while Lonnie looked for the horse liniment. Willard Kilgore had seen them ride in, and he came on to the barn.

''So you found one,'' said Willard.

''A lame one,'' Lonnie said. ''We'll have to wait on him to heal, but I've doctored him with horse liniment. As soon as he's able, we'll be ready to go. We just bought a brand-new Studebaker wagon in town, and it's just waiting for that fourth mule.''

Lonnie, Dallas, Dirk, and Kirby rode back to the herd and announced the finding and the purchasing of the mule, although he was lame.

''It'll take a while for him to heal,'' said Elliot Graves, ''but that won't take near as long as some of us gallavantin' around Texas lookin' for another one.''

''Tomorrow,'' Lonnie said, ''five of us will begin driving the cattle we've bought, mixing them with this gather. I figure that'll take maybe two days. By then, the mule should be in condition to work. Then we'll be ready to pick up the wagon and load it with provisions for the drive to Green River.''

''Then maybe four days from now, we'll be able to move 'em out,'' Dirk said. ''April's still afraid her old daddy might do something foolish. Like shootin' me.''

"Not unless he aims to shoot some of the rest of us along with you," said Lonnie. "We're an outfit, and we have to side one another. Where we're going, there'll be nobody else we can count on."

On the Range. July 16, 1853.

At the end of two days, another 2,100 head of cattle had been added to the gather.

"They can't stay here more than another day," Waco observed the next morning. "The graze is already gettin' thin."

"They shouldn't be here any longer than that," said Lonnie. "When I ride in to supper, I aim to have another look at that mule. If he's healed, we'll go to town tomorrow, get the wagon, and load it with supplies."

"I need to take Mindy along," Dallas said. "She desperately needs clothes. All she has is worn out Levi's and shirts discarded by her pa."

"I reckon we ought to take Becky, Laura, and April, as well," said Lonnie. "Where we are going, it may be years before any of them will see another store. Whatever any of us are needin', now's the time to get it."

San Antonio, Texas. July 17, 1853.

"Gents," Lonnie said, "today, Dallas, Dirk, Kirby, and me will be riding into town for the wagon. While we're there, we'll load up with supplies. The day after tomorrow, we'll watch the herd while the rest of you ride into town for whatever you may need. The day after that—July twentieth—we'll move 'em out for Green River."

Lonnie and Becky, Dallas and Mindy, Dirk and April, and Kirby and Laura rode into town. Each of the four men led one of the mules. The women headed for the mercantile while the men rode on the wagon yard. The Studebaker wagon they had bought already had the canvas stretched tight across the bows.

"We'll have to buy some harness from Stapleton," Lonnie said.

"I knew we was forgettin' something," said Kirby.

"I didn't forget," Lonnie replied. "Since nobody's had any mules to sell, it's unlikely they'll have any spare harness. We'll have to buy it new."

"Harness for four mules," said Stapleton. "They won't come cheap, because that's all I got. A hundred dollars for the four."

"Tarnation," Dallas said, "that's twenty-five dollars apiece. All four of 'em ain't worth forty dollars, total."

"I reckon it all depends on how bad you need 'em," Stapleton said. "Now, if you was to ride to Fort Worth or New Orleans, the price would likely come down some. But that's my price. Take it or leave it."

"We'll take it," said Lonnie, casting a warning look at his companions.

Quickly they harnessed the mules, and with Kirby at the reins, they started back to the mercantile.

"Sorry," Dallas said. "I didn't mean to speak out of turn. It's just that I don't cotton to bein' robbed by a varmint, even if he does it without a mask or a gun."

"I feel the same way," said Lonnie, "but we had to have the harness. Day after tomorrow, we'll let the rest of the outfit ride in to do their buying. The day after that, we should be ready to take the trail north."

It took most of the afternoon for the sweating storekeeper and his clerks to load all the supplies into the wagon. The women took the time to carefully choose what they would take with them. Lonnie and his companions were pleased to learn that none of the women had chosen any finery. They had limited themselves to clothing suited to the range, such as flannel or denim shirts and Levi's.

"There's some things you're forgetting," Lonnie told Becky. "You'll need a heavy coat, a wool scarf, wool-lined gloves, wool socks, and maybe three pairs of woolen underwear. See that Mindy, April, and Laura include these things in what they're buying."

"All this is going to cost a lot," said Becky, "and none of the four of us have money."

"I don't reckon it'll cost more than six thousand dollars," Lonnie said. "That's what we saved by gathering two thousand of your cows. And though the mortgage was expensive, it's paid off. When we reach the Green River range, I have no idea when you'll see another store."

"I understand," said Becky. She then sought Mindy, April, and Laura to see that each of them bought the items Lonnie had suggested.

About an hour before sundown, the outfit reached the Kilgore ranch with the wagon.

"I got just one complaint," Kirby said. "This damn mule we bought in Austin is purely unsociable. It's unlikely he's ever been hitched to a wagon before, and it gets on the bad side if him, havin' other mules too close."

"Too bad," said Lonnie, "and he's just gonna have to get used to it. We can always put blinders on him so he can only see straight ahead."

"Then we'd better do it," Kirby said. "It's no job for a woman, trying to keep this varmint headed the same direction as the other three."

"Another thing," Dallas said. "He's got to be one of the lead mules, so he can't see another mule in front of him."

"We'll get some blinders for him," said Lonnie. "For now, let's unhitch the teams, get our supper, and relieve the rest of our outfit with the herd so they can eat."

The Kilgore Ranch. July 19, 1853.

"Don't spend your money on ammunition," Lonnie told his six riders as they prepared to ride into town. "We have plenty in the wagon, and two kegs of black powder. Just be sure you get some clothes for snow country."

Lonnie, Dallas, Dirk, and Kirby remained with the herd. It was late afternoon when the riders returned from town.

"Dirk," said Waco, "Chad Tilden's in town, badmouthing you."

"He's got nothing against me," Dirk said, "except that he hates my guts."

"He claims he's missing some cows," said Waco, "and he's telling everybody who will listen that you're responsible. He's makin' it sound like we're adding his cows to our own gather."

"That's a damn lie, and he knows it," Lonnie said. "We can prove when and where we got every one of these cows. He's trying to get back at Dirk, but he's hurting us all. We won't be leaving this range with an unproven charge of rustling hanging over our heads. I'll ride into town and talk to the sheriff. Then I'll face Chad Tilden."

"I'm going with you," said Dirk. "It's me he's after."

"Saddle up and come on, then," Lonnie said, "but let me handle him. Don't let him get to you, forcing you to do something foolish. The rest of you take turns riding in to eat, and don't breathe a word about what Tilden's doing. April feels bad enough already."

"When we last saw Tilden, he was in the Alamo Saloon," said Waco.

"We'll find him," Lonnie said.

When Lonnie and Dirk reached town, the first stars had appeared, and a cooling wind blew out of the west.

"We'll talk to the sheriff first," said Lonnie. "I think he needs to know the real reason Chad Tilden's got a mad on. There must be some kind of law against a man accusing his neighbors of rustling when he doesn't have a shred of proof."

The sheriff's office was closed for the day, and not far from the office they found the lawman eating supper.

"Sheriff Jackman," Lonnie said, "we need to talk to you."

"Pull out some chairs and set," said Jackman.

He said no more, and Lonnie quickly told him of Chad Tilden accusations, and of the probable cause behind them.

"He gets his courage from a bottle," the lawman said. "If you want, after I eat, I'll go after him. A night in jail should sober him up enough that I can talk sense to him."

"*Bueno,*" Lonnie said. "We're leaving on a trail drive to Utah Territory tomorrow, and I don't want anybody spreading lies when we won't be here to stand up for ourselves. If you're going to call his hand, Dirk and me will go with you."

"That might be wise," said Jackman. "Maybe we can bring this to a head while you're still here."

When Sheriff Jackman finished his supper, Lonnie and Dirk followed him to the Alamo Saloon. It was still early, and there were few patrons in the saloon. Chad Tilden sat alone at a table, nursing a bottle. Even as they approached him, he up-ended the bottle, taking a long drink. Nearing the table, the three men paused, while Tilden glared at them through bloodshot eyes.

"Chad," said Sheriff Jackman, "you've been doing some talking, and it appears to be gettin' out of hand. You don't call a man a rustler unless you can prove it. Dirk McNelly's been away for four years, and he ain't been back more than a few days. Him and his outfit's been buying cows, and they can account for every damn cow in their herd. This gent with Dirk is one of his pardners, Lonnie Kilgore. I've known the Kilgores for more than twenty years. Now, if you're hell-bent on stirring up trouble. I'll lock you up for as long as it takes to set your mind straight.''

''I said McNelly's a thief, and he is,'' Tilden growled. ''He come sneakin' around and stole away my little girl.''

''So that's *really* what's biting you,'' said Jackman. ''Chad, April's a grown woman, able to make up her own mind, which she's done. You've lost her only if you're so muleheaded you won't make your peace with Dirk McNelly. He's family, whether you like it or not.''

''That young coyote ain't family to me, and he won't never be,'' said Tilden.

''In that case,'' Sheriff Jackman said, ''you have two choices. You can shut up and go home, or I'll lock you up until I think you're sensible enough for me to turn you loose. What's it goin' to be?''

''I'm leavin','' said Tilden, struggling to his feet.

''Mr. Tilden,'' Dirk said, ''I'm sorry you can't see things different, if only for April's sake. We'll be leavin' tomorrow.''

''Then go, and I don't never want to see either of you again,'' said Tilden. Unsteadily he got to his feet and stumbled through the batwing doors out of the saloon.

''A shame, for the sake of his wife and daughter,'' Sheriff Jackman said, ''but there's no help for it. Tomorrow your outfit—along with Dirk and April—will be gone, and all the hell-raising he can do won't change that.''

''Thanks for your help, Sheriff,'' said Dirk.

The confrontation with Chad Tilden had been a sobering, unpleasant experience. Lonnie and Dirk mounted their horses and rode back to the ranch without speaking.

The Trail North. July 20, 1853.

Only Laura's kin—Neal and Elene Upton—were there to see the drive head out. It was a sad occasion for Becky, Mindy, and April, for they had no blood kin there to wish them well, and they didn't know if they would ever see Texas again. Mary Kilgore tried her best to comfort them. The cattle had been gathered, and among them were the extra horses. With Becky at the reins, the wagon pulled in behind the herd. Lonnie had ridden to the point position, and from there shouted the command they had all been waiting for.

"Head 'em up and move 'em out." Wovoka Shatiki rode beside him.

Dallas Weaver and Dirk McNelly were the flank riders. Kirby Lowe and Gus Wilder were at swing, while Waco Talley, Sandy Orr, Benjamin Raines, Elliot Graves, and Justin Irwin rode drag. Mindy, April, and Laura rode with the drag riders, while Becky followed close behind with the wagon. Until the herd became trailwise—which sometimes took as long as a week—the outfit would have to contend with bunch-quitters from daylight until dark. The herd became unruly almost immediately, with those nearest the tag end breaking away to gallop along the back trail. It required the efforts of all five men as well as the three women to keep the herd moving. It was still early, and the sun had just begun to rise, but already the heat was sufficient to have all the riders and their horses sweating. A cloud of dust—without a breath of wind—followed the herd, covering the riders and the horses with what looked like a thin coat of mud. After chasing some bunch-quitters back to the herd, Mindy rode alongside the wagon for a moment.

"Are you ready to take over the wagon?" Becky jibed.

"No," said Mindy. "With the wagon trailing the herd, you're getting as much dust as I am. I've never got so dirty so fast in my life. I've got sand in places I can't even talk about."

Becky laughed. "I know the feeling. When we stop for the night, I hope there's water enough that I can sit in it neck-deep."

"I have a feeling we won't have much privacy," said Mindy.

"Who needs it?" Becky said. "I'm just takin' off my boots and hat."

Suddenly, from the tag end of the herd, a dozen bunch-quitters fought their way past the drag riders and ran directly toward the oncoming wagon. Their fourth mule was one of the lead team. Skittish, he had been fitted with blinders so he couldn't see to right or left. But he had no trouble seeing a dozen longhorns lumbering toward him, a big, ugly black bull in the lead. The frightened mule reared, braying. His three companions wasted no time in making his panic their own. The four of them, almost turning the wagon over, swung it around and headed back the way they had come. Waco Talley, leaving the other riders to head the bunch-quitters, galloped after the runaway wagon.

"Whoa, you jugheaded bastards," Becky shouted. She was on her feet, leaning on the reins, and slowly but surely, the wagon slowed. She was sitting on the wagon seat wiping sweat from her eyes with her shirtsleeve when Waco caught up. She still had a few choice words to say to the sweating mules. She cussed them and their ancestors back four or five generations.

"Are you all right, ma'am?" Waco asked.

"I reckon," said Becky, "except for being a little put out with these mules. You didn't hear . . . anything I said, did you, Waco?"

Waco grinned. "Not a word, ma'am. It takes considerable talent, gettin' it through a mule's head what you want or don't want him to do. You'll do, ma'am."

"Call me Becky," said the girl.

The trail drive had gone on, and it took a while for the wagon to catch up to the drag riders. Mindy, April, and Laura dropped back, riding alongside the wagon.

"Becky," Mindy said, "the whole front of your Levi's is wet."

"That's sweat, damn it," said Becky.

The drive moved on. Becky increased the distance between the wagon and the drag, to make allowances for other bunch-quitters. Near sundown, they reached a creek. Lonnie waved his hat, a signal that was passed on by the flank and swing riders. It was time to bunch the herd for the night. Near the creek, Becky reined up the teams and climbed down from the wagon box. She had cramps in both legs and felt the need to walk.

"Gus and me will unharness your teams," said Waco.

"Thank you," Becky said. "It's best I don't go near them for a while. I'd be tempted to shoot one of them stone dead."

It had been decided by the four women that they would cook for the outfit, a decision all the men had applauded. Dallas Weaver soon had a fire going.

"Ladies," said Lonnie, "the things you'll need the most often are packed in the rear of the wagon. If you need something that's in too deep, let one of us get it for you. We've got it packed so the load's unlikely to shift, unless we move things around too much."

While supper was being prepared, Becky saw Waco talking to Lonnie. It wasn't until after supper that Lonnie had anything to say to Becky.

"Waco says you're a top hand. I'm not goin' to have to pay you more wages, am I?"

"Probably not," Becky said with a straight face. "I still owe you a fortune for all that finery you bought for me in San Antonio."

"Finery, hell," said Lonnie. "All you bought was men's clothes. I may never get to see you in any female finery."

"How about stark naked?" Becky asked.

"That," said Lonnie, "when it's just you and me. But maybe I'll want to show you off to others. We can't show you off with you not wearing a stitch."

"We can't?" Becky replied, feigning disappointment.

"Lonnie," said Dallas, interrupting, "some of us would like to see that map you have before we get too far along the trail. That's one thing we haven't discussed."

"Here," Lonnie said. "I've drawn a line along the way I think we should take the herd. Just remember, this is a government map, maybe ten years old. Before the first watch rides out, we'll talk some. If there's a better way than I've marked, then let's find it."

Dallas spread the huge map out on the ground. Except for Lonnie, the rest of the outfit joined him in studying it. When Dallas had carefully refolded the map, he spoke.

"I like it. The route you've drawn may be a mite farther, but you've made allowances for water all the way to southern Colorado Territory."

"Yes," said Lonnie. "By driving northwest, we'll reach the Pecos River just beyond Del Rio. From there, we'll follow the Pecos until we're near Santa Fe. There we'll take the Rio Grande on into southern Colorado. The last couple of hundred miles, this map isn't showing any rivers, but southern Colorado is mountainous country. I can't imagine there not being springs and runoffs from rivers farther north."

"Looks like a good gamble to me," said Gus Wilder. "Once we reach the Pecos, we'll be following a river about two-thirds of the way. We got to have water, and there's some better chance of finding decent graze along a riverbank."

"That's what I'm hoping," Lonnie said. "If any of you have ideas as to a better way to go, I'm willing to listen."

Nobody said anything, and Lonnie could tell by the expressions on their faces that they were in agreement with him.

"It's about time for the first watch," said Dallas. "Any change in the way the watches are set up?"

"Not as far as I'm concerned," Lonnie said. "It'll be Dirk McNelly, Kirby Lowe, Gus Wilder, Waco Talley, and Sandy Orr on the first. The rest of us, including Wovoka, will take the second."

"What about Becky, Mindy, Laura, and me?" April asked.

"You're doing all the cooking," said Lonnie. "We don't expect more than that."

"Laura and me are going with Dirk and Kirby," April said.

Lonnie said nothing, expecting to hear from Becky and Mindy on the subject.

"Well, I reckon that puts Mindy and me on the second watch," Becky said.

"We'll try it that way," said Lonnie. "Just so we don't let a handsome woman draw our attention away from the herd."

"That's how it is with Texas men," Becky said. "The horses and cows come first, and the women are stumbling along somewhere in third place."

"This conversation's gone far enough," said Lonnie. "First watch, mount up."

6

On the Trail. July 21, 1853.

*T*heir first night on the trail was peaceful. The herd, for all its activity during the day, was tired. So were the riders. Well before sunup, the outfit was again ready to move out.

"Head 'em up, move 'em out," Lonnie shouted.

Again Wovoka rode beside Lonnie at point. It was Mindy's turn on the wagon box, and Dallas looked back occasionally to see that she was all right. The dust was so thick, the oncoming wagon was just a dim shape in the distance. But Mindy was purposely staying far enough behind the drag riders to allow them time to head any bunch-quitters before the longhorns came face-to-face with the mules, as they had done the day before. By late afternoon, a bank of dirty gray clouds had spread across the western horizon. Occasionally jagged fingers of lightning galloped across the sky. The riders were aware of it, but there was nothing they could do except push on. Foremost in their minds was the fact that, on the plains, a man on a horse was almost always a target for lightning.*

*Lightning was feared, having killed more riders than stampedes.

"Looks like we're all going to get a bath," Becky said.

Becky, April, and Laura, seeking to escape some of the dust that enveloped the drag riders, had dropped back to ride alongside the wagon.

The gathering storm didn't seem any closer, and though sundown was an hour away, Lonnie gave the signal to mill the herd. There was water and some graze, which they just might not be fortunate enough to find before dark if they pushed on. The day had been typically hot. All the animals and riders were drenched with sweat. Mindy reined up the teams near the creek. Dallas Weaver and Kirby Lowe unharnessed the teams. Once the riders had unsaddled their horses, Justin Irwin gathered wood and started the supper fire.

"After supper, before dark," Lonnie said, "some of us ought to gather some dry wood and fill the possum belly beneath the wagon.* Then if it rains all night, we'll still have the dry wood for our breakfast fire."

"Amen to that," said Benjamin Raines. "A man can stand anything as long as there's a pot of hot coffee to chase the chill out of his bones."

But it seemed more and more likely that the storm would blow itself out before reaching them. While the daggers of golden lightning had become more intense, the cloud bank didn't seem to have advanced.

"Feel the air," Gus Wilder said. "It may be a hundred miles away, but she's raining mighty hard over yonder to the west."

The wind, out of the west, had become a cooling breeze.

"As long as there's a chance of a storm," Lonnie said, "nobody takes off anything but his hat. Keep your horses picketed close by."

But the lightning remained distant, and only a few drops

---

*The possum belly: a cowhide slung under a wagon, for storing dry kindling and wood.

of rain fell. Finally there was no more lightning, and the threat of a storm was past. The second watch had just mounted their horses, and Becky was riding beside Lonnie.

"I was kind of hoping we'd have some rain," said Becky. "After a week of this. I'll be smelling so bad, you won't come near me."

Lonnie laughed. "No problem. I'll be smelling just as bad, or worse. We'll cancel one another out."

"How far do you think we've come, today and yesterday?" Becky asked.

"Not more than twenty miles, if that far," said Lonnie. "We'll be lucky to average ten a day, until these critters get the idea they're a herd, and stop galloping down the back trail."

On the other side of the herd, Mindy rode alongside Dallas, neither of them speaking.

"You've been mighty quiet," Dallas said. "Are you already homesick?"

"Maybe a little," said Mindy, "when I remember back to the days when Ma was alive. I have no good memories after she was gone."

"Not even me?" Dallas teased.

"Not yet," said Mindy. "I sort of . . . put the trail drive out of my mind. All I thought of was how different it was going to be with you beside me all the time. By that I mean I wasn't expecting you to be on your horse and me on mine, and our only other time with the rest of the outfit at mealtime."

Dallas laughed. "Oh? You mean man and wife time."

"Yes." She was glad it was dark so he couldn't see her blush.

"I thought we got off to a good start back at the Kilgore ranch," said Dallas.

"We did," Mindy agreed, "but there seems to be no time or place during this trail drive."

"I reckon you're right about that," said Dallas. "We can't get too far from the herd, in case the critters get spooked and decide to run. Another good reason why we must all stay close by is that Comanches might sneak up and slit our throats. When we're out of Texas, that won't change anything. We'll still have the Paiutes to contend with. While we're on the subject, do Becky, April, and Laura feel as neglected as you?"

"I don't know," Mindy said. "We don't talk about . . . such things."

"Maybe you should," said Dallas. "You're all in the same boat until we reach the Green River range."

On the Trail. July 22, 1853.

Their third day on the trail, the herd began to settle down. There were fewer bunch-quitters, and the drag riders were able to keep the ranks closed with little effort. By the end of the day, the outfit was optimistic.

"A good day," said Elliot Graves. "Another good one tomorrow should take us at least halfway to the Pecos."

"Since we're going almost through Santa Fe," Becky said, "can we afford to stop at a store?"

"Maybe," said Lonnie, "but I can't see that we've overlooked anything. What do you have in mind?"

"Some dried apples for making pies," Becky said.

"Damn right," shouted Kirby Lowe. "Sell a few cows if we have to."

There were enthusiastic shouts from the rest of the outfit. Dried apple pies was one of the few sweets that men on the trail could enjoy. Range cooks willing and able to prepare them were treasured.

Lonnie laughed. "You'll get no argument out of me, but you'd better get all the dried apples you can get into the wagon. Once you feed a cow nurse dried apple pie, he'll want it every day. I reckon Wovoka could eat a dozen.''

"I wish we had some right now," said Dallas. "We're still a hell of a long way south of Santa Fe."

"Gents," Lonnie said, "we'll be nearing Del Rio pretty soon. I know it's nothing but a wide place in the trail, but I think we ought to be sure there's no trouble awaiting us between here and there. Do any of you know the country?"

"I do," said Justin Irwin. "I was there just after the war, and already the *Mejicanos* had started violating their treaty, crossing into Texas for horses and cows. I'd be willing to bet my saddle they ain't changed their ways. Wasn't more than fifteen or twenty people in all of Del Rio."*

"You've been there, Justin," Lonnie said. "Why don't you take Wovoka with you and scout ahead, all the way to the Pecos? Watch carefully for the tracks of shod and unshod horses, paying particular notice to where they're coming from and where they're going."

"I'll start out in the morning," Justin said. "I can also judge how far it is to the next water, as we travel toward the Pecos."

"Bueno," said Lonnie.

On the Trail. July 23, 1853.

The next afternoon, Justin Irwin and Wovoka reached the Pecos River. There was a shallows that they immediately recognized as a crossing, for there were many tracks of shod horses, all of them leading south. Justin followed until they were certain the riders were headed straight for the border. Del Rio had one saloon and a general store. Struck by inspiration, Justin pointed to the store. Wovoka chose to remain with the

*Del Rio had a population of fifty in 1855.

horses while Justin went into the store. The storekeeper stared at him in what amounted to surprise.

"You got any dried apples?" Justin asked.

"Maybe twenty pounds," said the storekeeper. "How much do you want?"

"All of them," Justin said, "and wrap them well."

As Justin was leaving the store, a *Mejicano* rode up and dismounted. Tying his reins to the hitch rail, he ignored Wovoka and went on into the store. The man had gone to great lengths to ignore Justin as well, and that aroused immediate suspicion in Justin's mind. He and Wovoka started back the way they had come, and as soon as they were well away from Del Rio and the border, they reined up their horses under cover of some brush. The Indian's keen eyes were first to detect a thin tendril of dust to the south, well after their own dust had settled.

"One *hombre* follow," Wovoka said.

"So that's how it is," said Justin softly. "Let the varmints come on. We'll be ready."

Justin and Wovoka were almost thirty miles from the crossing at Del Rio when they were able to see the trail drive coming. They wheeled their horses and rode beside Lonnie when they reached the point position. Justin quickly related what they had learned.

"So they may jump us within the next two or three days," Lonnie said.

"I think so," said Irwin. "From the shod tracks crossing the border, I'd say this bunch does a pretty good business stealing horses and cows in Texas."

"That's good thinking," Lonnie said. "You and Wovoka may have just saved our bacon. What do you have in the flour sack?"

Irwin laughed. "Twenty pounds of dried apples. If I can sneak them into the wagon, the ladies can surprise us all at supper tonight."

"*Bueno*," said Lonnie. "How much did you pay for them?"

"Ten dollars," Irwin said. "Consider it my contribution to the trail drive."

Justin Irwin rode wide of the herd and the rest of the riders, for he would be returning to the drag position. But instead of stopping there, he rode on to meet the wagon. Becky was again at the reins, and she looked at him, a question in her eyes. Justin rode close, dropping the sack of dried apples at her feet.

"Dried apples," said Justin. "I reckon you'll know what to do with 'em."

"I know," Becky said, "and there'll be an extra pie for you."

Lonnie waited until the herd had been bedded down for the night and preparations for supper were under way before calling the outfit together to hear what Justin Irwin had to say. Quickly, he told them, Wovoka nodding occasionally in agreement.

"What about water between here and the Pecos?" Dallas asked.

"Two more creeks," said Irwin. "Graze ain't nothin' to get excited about, but it'll get us through a night or two."

"I reckon we'd better plan on fightin' a bunch of Mexican outlaws," Kirby Lowe said.

"We're going to, as soon as we know where they are," said Lonnie. "Justin, I'd like for you and Wovoka to scout ahead for the next several days. Just be sure that you don't get too close. These are the kind of varmints that will ambush us."

"They must know we're aiming to trail the herd north along the Pecos," Irwin said, "so they'll be holed up somewhere this side of the river. Wovoka and me will find them."

Preparations for supper seemed to be taking an unusually long time. Instead of one fire there were two. Becky, April, and Laura worked at the larger one, while Mindy hung one of the coffeepots over the lesser fire. Dallas spoke.

"What's holdin' up supper? I'm hungry enough to eat a longhorn cow raw."

"I reckon it's something that'll be worth waiting for," said Mindy. "Just wait and see."

Despite the threat of a fight with Mexican outlaws hanging over their heads, the outfit thoroughly enjoyed the unexpected treat. Wovoka ate four pies, beaming his approval.

"Thank Justin," Becky said, when she was complimented. "He brought the apples."

"Justin, you can scout for us anytime," said Dirk McNelly.

Supper was a jovial affair, but the outfit was somber as the first watch saddled up.

"I doubt they'll hit us so far from the border," Lonnie said, "but we can't afford not to be ready. When you're sleeping, keep your horses picketed and your guns handy."

The first watch began circling the herd, while those on the second watch rolled in their blankets to get as much sleep as they could.

"Lonnie," said Becky, "are you asleep?"

"No," he said, turning over to face her in the darkness.

"Do you *really* think they'll attack us during the night?" she asked.

"No," said Lonnie, "but a wrong guess could hurt us, so we must be ready. I'm expecting them to lay an ambush somewhere between here and the Pecos. If Justin and Wovoka can find it, we'll go after them before they come after us."

"I'm sorry we have to travel so near the border," Becky said.

"So am I," said Lonnie, "but by following the Pecos, we'll have sure water all the way to Santa Fe. We have a good outfit."

"I'm just finding that out," Becky said. "Despite all the years I've been around those men who used to ride for me, I feel like I'm getting to know them for the first time. Justin really surprised me, and not just with the dried apples.''

"I'm truly glad the six of them are with us," said Lonnie. "Honest-to-God Texans have always ridden, lived, and died for their outfit. These men are no different.''

"I'm glad Wovoka's with us, too," Becky said, "although we may go broke feeding him. He had four pies, double everything else, and still looked hungry.''

Lonnie laughed. "I don't remember ever seeing a fat Indian.''

"You just may see one before we reach Utah," said Becky.

Lonnie saw to it that the supper fires had been put out well before dark. He spoke to the first watch as they mounted their horses.

"If there's a bunch of thieves waiting for us, I expect them to lay a daylight ambush. But we can't be too careful. If you see or hear anything unusual, don't hesitate to call for help. But don't fire unless you have to. A muzzle flash makes an almighty fine target.''

April and Laura were saddling their horses to ride with Dirk and Kirby.

"No talking," Lonnie said. "There's no wind, and the smallest sound might be heard a mile away.''

When the second watch took over at midnight, all seemed calm. Suddenly, just ahead of Lonnie, Wovoka reined up, listening. Lonnie reined up, too, but heard nothing. In an instant, the Indian was off his horse and running toward a thicket. From within it came the roar of a gun, the lead tugging at the sleeve of Wovoka's deer-hide shirt. But there was no time for the unseen adversary to fire a second time. Wovoka drew his Colt, and like the rolling of thunder, fired three times. There was the distinctive sound of a body crashing into surrounding brush. Then there was only silence.

"By God, Wovoka got him," Elliot Graves said. "That'll show 'em.''

"It'll show 'em we're wise to what they have in mind," said Dallas. "They likely sent this one coyote to take our measure."

"I reckon you're right," Lonnie said, "but there's no help for it now. Even if they're too far away to have heard the shooting, they'll know we've dealt them a bad hand when this varmint in the thicket doesn't come back. Come first light, we'll go in after him."

The rest of the night was peaceful. At first light, Justin Irwin and Dallas Weaver went into the thicket to see just how effective Wovoka's shooting had been. They soon returned carrying the dead man. He had been hit twice.

"This looks an almighty lot like the *Mejicano* Wovoka and me saw in Del Rio," Justin said. "What do you think, Wovoka? Is he the same *hombre*?"

"*Sí,*" said the Indian, pointing toward an ugly scar that ran along the dead man's left jawbone.

"Wovoka would make a good Pinkerton man," Dallas said.

"I reckon he would," said Justin. "We only saw the Mex for a few seconds in Del Rio, and I don't recall seeing the scar."

"There's one possibility we haven't considered," Lonnie said. "If this coyote followed Justin and Wovoka on his own, the gang he rides with—assuming there is one—won't be aware of us. We still might get by without fighting."

"I bleed just like the gent Wovoka shot last night," said Kirby Lowe, "so I just ain't anxious for a gunfight, and the best way to avoid one is to be ready. I say we go on, still expecting that ambush. If it don't come, so much the better, but if it does, we won't be caught with our britches down."

"That's exactly right," Lonnie said. "While we're not absolutely sure this varmint had time to alert the rest of his outfit to us, we can't afford to gamble that he didn't. We'll go on expecting an ambush until we're well past Del Rio and are on our way north. Justin, after breakfast, I want you and Wovoka to scout at least fifteen miles ahead, with an eye toward a position where a bunch of killers might hole up with long guns and cut down on us.''

''I think they'll wait until we're closer to the border,'' Dallas said, ''which would be the day after tomorrow, but we can't risk that. After riding fifteen miles, suppose Wovoka and Justin split up and didn't allow themselves to be seen in Del Rio? They might then ride along the river, looking for fresh tracks.''

''I'd say it's worth doing,'' Lonnie said, ''unless Wovoka and Justin come up with something within the next fifteen miles. If there's no ambush tomorrow, the bunch will need some time to get into position. It might be possible to find out whether they've already crossed the river. I think the herd's trailwise enough for us to step up the gait. If we can make fifteen miles today and fifteen tomorrow, that'll take us away from Del Rio and the border.''

''*Bueno,*'' said Justin. ''We're not more than thirty miles from the river now. I think if Wovoka and me ride on to the Pecos, we ought to stay there for a while after dark. Mex bandits know they're not welcome on the Texas side of the river, and they might not risk crossing in daylight.''

''*Sí,*'' Wovoka agreed.

''That makes sense,'' said Lonnie. ''Do it, but don't stay later than midnight. We need a deadline, because we're not sure the two of you won't run into unexpected trouble.''

''We don't aim to get ourselves captured, if that's what you mean,'' Justin said.

''That's exactly what I mean,'' said Lonnie. ''If the *hombre* Wovoka shot didn't return to his outfit before following you and Wovoka, the rest of his bunch may come looking for him. They'll not only find the tracks of yours and Wovoka's horses, they'll also find the tracks of this dead varmint's horse from when he followed you. Don't take any big chances. We may have to take it a day at a time. If you don't find them dug in for an ambush today, we'll prepare for one tomorrow."

"Don't hold supper for us, ladies," Justin said. "We may be gettin' in late. Our supper may be river water and jerked beef."

"I feel a lot safer with them scouting ahead," said Becky. "I just wish we could have done this without going near the border."

"We could have," Lonnie replied, irritated. "Hell, we could have taken a more northerly direction and reached the Pecos somewhere north of Fort Stockton. But that would have taken us two hundred miles across Texas plains that haven't seen more than a little rain in the past two years. It's worth fighting a bunch of *Mejicano* outlaws, just to have water all the way to Santa Fe."

"I realize that," said Becky, "but what's wrong with me wishing we didn't have to go near the border and fight outlaws? Stop talking to me like you're my daddy."

"If I was your daddy," Lonnie said, "I'd take a belt to your backside every morning before breakfast, just to keep you in line for the day."

She turned her head just enough to see his eyes, wondering if he was serious. Deciding that he was, she responded, the rough edge of her voice matching his.

"Ah reckon we been too close to one another too long," said Becky, in her best Texas drawl. "From here on to Utah, my blankets won't be spread nowhere close to yours."

"It's just as well," Lonnie growled. "It never gets dark enough for you to do anything except talk. Damn it, you promised to love, honor, and obey."

"I never promised to lay my bare bottom on the ground in a cow camp while you're having your way with me," said Becky.

The affair had erupted into a full-blown argument, with Lonnie and Becky standing toe-to-toe, glaring at one another.

Lonnie went red as a sunset, and while he was trying to think of a suitable scathing response, Mindy laughed. Within seconds, the rest of the outfit had joined in. Even Wovoka understood.

"Damn it," Lonnie said, still half-angry, "every man needs a woman to help him make a fool of himself."

"Most men don't need any help," said Becky, and she wasn't smiling.

"Come on," Justin Irwin said. "Wovoka and me likely won't have any supper, and we ain't goin' nowhere until we've had breakfast."

"*Sí,*" said Wovoka. "Squaw fight, we not eat."

That brought on a new round of laughter. Becky joined in, and Lonnie was forced to do likewise. The Indian had summed it up neatly, and suddenly Lonnie grinned at him. The foolish sparring had ended. At least for a while.

After breakfast, Justin and Wovoka saddled their horses and rode out well ahead of the trail drive. Neither spoke, but Justin noted that his companion still had a spark in his dark eyes. He now seemed more than ever a part of their outfit. When they had ridden what Justin estimated was fifteen miles, he reined up, Wovoka beside him.

"No sign of them," said Justin, "but that don't mean they won't come after us sometime tomorrow. There'll be a moon tonight. We'll ride on to Del Rio, where we can watch the saloon and the crossing."

Wovoka nodded, and they rode out. Long before reaching Del Rio, Justin pointed west. He rode that direction, Wovoka following. They would reach the river somewhere to the west of the crossing, working their way in so that they might observe the crossing and the saloon. The riverbank was overgrown with brush and willows. Justin and Wovoka rode downstream until they found a suitable place to conceal their horses. From there, they continued on foot, halting when they could see the isolated store building and the saloon in the distance. The riverbanks had been cleared for a distance, allowing for the crossing. It could easily be seen, even in the moonlight. Coming up with the very objection that was in Justin's mind, Wovoka spoke softly.

"Per'ap they no cross here."

"It's a chance we'll have to take," Justin said. "They could cross the border anywhere within fifty miles, and there's no way we can watch that much territory. If they don't get here until after dark, they'll likely spend some time in the saloon, and that'll mean what they have planned for us won't happen until tomorrow."

Justin and Wovoka found shade under a willow tree, which was welcome because not a breath of air stirred. The river was at low ebb, flowing sluggishly. Something—probably a frog—plopped into the water.

"One of us can watch as good as two," said Justin. "We can take turns gettin' us some sleep."

Wovoka nodded, pointing to Justin, who sat with his back against the tree's trunk, tilting his hat over his eyes. Doing battle with an enemy was something the Indian well understood, and not once did he take his eyes off the saloon, the store, or the crossing beyond. The sun was low in the west when Justin took off his hat and fanned his sweating face.

"No come," said Wovoka.

"If they're comin' at all, it'll be after dark," said Justin. "I'll watch for a while."

"We both watch," Wovoka said. "Eat."

They sat there in silence, eating the jerked beef they had brought with them, since it seemed there was no way they could return to the trail drive for supper. Justin felt a little guilty, having napped most of the afternoon while Wovoka watched the crossing. But there was a restless excitement in the Indian, for the coming of an enemy was something he well understood. The sun sank below the western horizon, fanning the sky with lurid fingers of crimson marking the way of its

going. Justin wiped the sweat from his eyes on the sleeve of
his shirt. By the time the first stars twinkled in a sea of purple
sky, just a whisper of cooling wind came out of the northwest.

"Another three hours until moonrise," said Justin. While
fully understanding the necessity of it, he was weary of the
inactivity and the waiting.

Wovoka said nothing, and Justin Irwin admired the Indian's
patience. The sky was a mass of stars when the moon finally
lifted its golden head above the horizon. Wovoka got to his
feet and walking downstream a ways, stood there listening. He
then returned to his companion and spoke softly.

"*Hombres* come. Many horses."

Justin listened and could hear the soft thud of horses'
hooves well before he could see the riders. There was a splashing as they rode across the river. Reining up before the saloon,
they dismounted and tied their horses to the hitch rail. In the
lamplight fanning out the door, Justin counted fourteen men
entering the saloon.

"Whatever they have planned for us will come tomorrow,"
said Justin. "Now it's time to ride back to the outfit."

"Per'ap the plan no work, if they no got horses," Wovoka
said.

Justin laughed. "I swear, you're thinking like a hell-for-
leather Texan. What you got on your mind, Wovoka?"

"You watch," said Wovoka.

Wovoka's Bowie knife in his hand, Justin watched the
shadowy form of the Indian as he approached the horses tied
to the saloon's hitch rail. Without a sound, he returned with
two of the horses. In a matter of minutes, he had them all.
Using lariats from the saddles of the horses, Wovoka and Justin quickly fashioned lead ropes. Finally, with each of them
leading seven horses, they rode eastward to join the trail drive.

"Wovoka," said Justin, "that was slick. I never seen nothing like it."

The Indian grunted his appreciation, and they rode on.

7

Leading so many horses, it was past midnight when Justin and Wovoka approached the camp. Lonnie Kilgore issued the challenge.

"Halt and identify yourselves."

"Justin and Wovoka," said Justin.

"Who's ridin' the other horses?" Lonnie asked suspiciously.

"Nobody," said Justin. "They kind of took up with Wovoka in Del Rio and followed us back."

Justin and Wovoka led the fourteen horses into the clearing near the wagon. When they had dismounted, Lonnie spoke.

"Now, what's this all about?"

Quickly Justin explained, giving Wovoka full credit for having taken the horses. When he had finished, Dallas laughed. Benjamin Raines and Elliot Graves joined in. The arrival of so many horses, combined with the laughter, awakened the rest of the camp, and Justin had to repeat the story. There was much more laughter, and only when it had died down did Lonnie speak.

"I never expected anything like this. Suppose those *hombres* were just on their way to the saloon, with no intention of bushwhacking us? That makes us horse thieves.''

"That's not very likely," Justin said. "Why would fourteen men, armed to the teeth, ride desolate country like this unless they stand to gain something by it? If it makes you feel better, once we're beyond Del Rio, you can turn their horses loose."

"Ugh," said Wovoka, not liking the turn things had taken.

"I don't think we owe them the return of these horses," Dallas said, "if they're who we think they are. Notice in every saddle boot there's a long gun?"

"He's right," said Benjamin Raines. "If that bunch comes after us, they'll have to bushwhack us with pistols."

"We can't rule out the possibility they'll do exactly that," Dallas said. "These days, you can shoot some *hombre* and maybe get away with it. But take his horse, and you're likely to be strung up. Since this is something that can't be undone, I reckon we'd better follow our plan, expecting an ambush, until we're well north of Del Rio."

"That's all we can do," said Lonnie. "Justin, I want you and Wovoka out there ahead of us for the next two or three days. If this bunch is coming after us and they're afoot, it won't be easy finding them. Now all of you roll in your blankets and get what sleep you can."

Lonnie mounted his horse and again began circling the herd, aware that Becky rode beside him. Lonnie suspected she had something to say, and she did.

"That may or may not have been such a good idea, Wovoka taking those horses, but I wish you hadn't questioned it where he could hear. He's loyal to us, and I feel better, him being with us."

"So do I," said Lonnie, "and as for taking the horses of an enemy, that's the Indian way. I'm just not sure it's the *right* way at this particular time."

"I am," Becky said. "What can this bunch of thieves do? They certainly can't complain to the law that, while they were on the Texas side of the border, somebody took all their horses.''

''No,'' said Lonnie, ''but let's look at those horses in daylight. I'd bet my saddle that every last one has a Texas brand.''

''Perhaps,'' Becky said, ''but we're on a trail drive, needing to reach your Green River range ahead of winter snow. We can't take the time to ride around south Texas looking for the rightful owners of these horses. Turn them loose, and if they've been across the border for as long as two weeks, they'll return there.''*

''I realize that,'' said Lonnie. ''That's why we're taking them with us. Since we're unable to return them to their rightful owners, we're more entitled to them than that bunch of *Mejicano* outlaws.''

Wovoka was afoot, near enough to hear their words. He sighed with satisfaction, for he had not done wrong.

Southwestern Texas. July 24, 1853.

''Unless that bunch got their hands on some horses almighty quick,'' Lonnie said, ''we won't be hearing from them before tomorrow. But we can't afford to gamble. Justin, you and Wovoka ride at least as far as the next water, and a little beyond, if you can. Boot prints won't be as easy to follow as horse tracks, but that can't be helped.''

After breakfast, Lonnie and Wovoka again rode west. Wovoka rode slightly behind, and occasionally Justin turned his head enough to see the Indian. Wovoka looked grim, as though he'd been unjustly reprimanded. Lonnie made up his mind to talk to the Indian the first time they stopped to rest their horses.

---

*After two weeks or more in the same place, a horse generally considered it ''home.''

South of the Border. July 24, 1853.

The saloon near Del Rio was about to close when the fourteen men stumbled out of the bar to discover they no longer had horses.

"*Por Dios,*" slurred one of the riders. "What are we to do?"

"*Mama mía,*" said Chavez, the leader of the bunch, "what do you think? We walk."

"By the horns of El Diablo," one of the outlaws groaned, "which way? We cannot ambush these *hombres* afoot. They will ride us down."

"We do not be afoot, *estupido*," Chavez replied. "We will again cross the river, and we will find horses. They will be turned loose after the ambush, when we have taken our own, that were taken from us."

So the outlaws started south on foot, with the nearest horses many miles away. They kept a steady pace, but that changed when the sun lifted its golden face above the eastern horizon. Men staggered along until they found some shade, and there they collapsed, heaving for breath.

"*Madre de Dios,*" Chavez shouted, "we do not have much time until the *Americanos* are gone, taking our horses. On your feet."

Their narrow Mexican boots had blistered their feet, and every step was torture. Still they limped on, hating Chavez almost as much as the son of a donkey who had taken their horses.

Fifteen miles east of Del Rio and the border, Justin and Wovoka reined up. Nothing interrupted the stillness, and the Indian looked questioningly at Justin.

"If they aim to try and bushwhack us afoot," said Justin,

"it'll take them longer to get here. We'd better ride on a ways and, if we can, find some sign of their coming."

They rode on, reining up a mile or two from the border.

"They no walk," Wovoka said.

"Not in this direction, anyway," said Justin. "That leaves just one possibility. They're hoofin' it back across the border for some horses. Depending on how far they have to walk, it's unlikely they'll be in a position to come after us before sometime tomorrow. We might as well ride back and meet the outfit."

Seeing the herd coming, Justin and Wovoka reined up, waiting until Lonnie reached them. They then rode alongside him long enough for Justin to relay what he and Wovoka had learned.

Lonnie laughed. "They must really have a mad on, to hike God knows how far into old Mexico. But I think you're right. They're after horses. They know about how much time they have before we reach Del Rio. If they get mounted sometime today or tonight, we'll still have a fight on our hands tomorrow."

Leaving Wovoka with Lonnie at the point position, Justin joined the drag riders. One of them was Kirby Lowe, and he trotted his horse alongside Justin's.

"Where are they?" Kirby asked.

"Looks like they've gone back across the border, probably to get some horses," said Justin. "I reckon we'll know tomorrow."

Not until the day was done and the herd bedded down for the night did Lonnie repeat what Justin had told him. For a moment there was silence as the outfit digested the information.

"So we've just slowed them down some," Dallas said.

"Yes," said Lonnie, "but if they've gone after more horses, that tells us something we need to know. They aim to attack us, and they won't be on foot when they do. The best time for them to attack is when we're nearest the border, and that should come tomorrow. But if it doesn't come tomorrow, they can still come after us. After we reach the Pecos, we can't possibly cover more than fifteen miles with the herd before nightfall. They can still catch up to us and give us hell.''

"If they don't jump us tomorrow," Justin said. "Wovoka and me will still have to scout on ahead. The varmints will know we're expecting them, and they'll ride far enough east or west to circle around and get ahead of us.''

"I'd not be surprised if they wait until we reach the Pecos," said Lonnie. "There may be some prime places for an ambush along the river, and if they don't attack tomorrow, they could figure that as a means of confusing us and catching us off guard. We'll be ready for them tomorrow and several days after that. I can't believe they'd pass up a herd the size of ours so near the border.''

"We got their horses, too," Waco said. "That had to be humiliating.''

Supper was ready, and by the time the outfit had eaten, it was time for the first watch to begin circling the herd. They mounted their horses and rode out. April followed Dirk, while Laura followed Kirby.

"I never thought those ladies would be out there every night," Dallas said, "but there they are. They're like a couple of shadows.''

"We got a couple of shadows, too," said Lonnie. "Mindy rides with you, while Becky's riding with me. It hasn't caused any trouble so far, and it makes them feel better.''

By midnight, big gray clouds had gathered. Two hours before dawn, the rain started. When it was light enough to see, Lonnie, Dallas, Justin, and Elliot used one of the sheets of extra canvas to rig a shelter behind the wagon, where breakfast could be prepared. The dry wood in the wagon's possum belly served its purpose well.

"I hate to mention this," Dallas said, "but if this rain don't soon slack off, there'll be so much mud, this wagon won't be going nowhere."

"There's almost no graze here," Gus Wilder said. "We got to move on."

"Mud don't slow pack mules down," said Sandy Orr needlessly.

"Enough of that," Elliot Graves said. "We all agreed on the wagon. If we'd stuck with pack mules, we'd already be eatin' jerked beef and drinking branch water."

"It's my day on the wagon," said Mindy. "Unless it rains all day, I can try."

"That's about all we can do," Lonnie said. "The wagon's well loaded, and if the ground gets enough water, the wagon will bog down."

The outfit had breakfast as best they could, some of them hunkering down under the canvas stretched behind the wagon, while others got under the wagon.

"She's clearin' up over yonder to the west," said Benjamin Raines.

"We'll give it a little time," Lonnie said. "If the rain slacks pretty soon, we still might be able to go on. But there's no use harnessing the mules, saddling our horses, and taking the trail with the herd until we're sure the wagon can make it."

The skies continued to clear, until the sun came forth and began sucking up the excess water. Wet clothing dried quickly, and the heat was such that the rain might never have fallen. Lonnie and Dallas began harnessing the mules to the wagon.

"Mindy," said Dallas, when the teams had been harnessed, "take them a ways and then bring 'em back. If you don't bog down, then we can probably make it."

Mindy flicked the reins. While the wagon wheels mired a little, the mules had no real trouble drawing the wagon. Several hundred yards away, Mindy turned the team, brining the wagon back.

"Let's try it," Lonnie said. "I don't believe there was enough rain to hurt us."

Quickly the riders saddled their horses. Justin Irwin spoke to Lonnie.

"Wovoka and me will ride on ahead, almost to Del Rio. If we don't see any signs of those *Mejicanos*, I think we'll just hole up somewhere ahead and wait for the rest of you to catch up to us. Otherwise, it's possible they'll arrive and set up an ambush after we've turned back to meet the herd. What do you think?"

"I think that's wise," said Lonnie. "Just be careful as you ride west, and don't leave any obvious tracks. The rain will have wiped the trails clean, and if that bunch is headed this way, we don't want them knowing you and Wovoka are riding ahead looking for them."

"They won't know," Justin said. "Wovoka and me will split up, one of us to the north and the other to the south of the trail."

"*Bueno,*" said Lonnie. "If you reach the river without seeing any of them, both of you move as near that crossing as you can. When they reach the crossing and it appears they are riding toward us, follow as close as you can. Then you might learn where they aim to lay their ambush, and riding wide, you can come back and warn us. Just be damn sure they don't discover you, and don't do anything foolish, such as attacking them."

"Kill," Wovoka said.

"No, Wovoka," said Lonnie. "You'll get your chance at them once we know for sure they're after us. Don't let him forget that, Justin."

"Don't worry," Justin said. "Fourteen of them against two of us is terrible odds. We'll lay low until we see them coming, and once they hole up somewhere, we'll be riding back to tell you.''

''*Bueno,*'' said Lonnie. ''Get going.''

Justin and Wovoka rode out. They had gone not more than a mile when Justin reined up. He pointed to Wovoka and then to the south. The Indian had heard and understood Justin's conversation with Lonnie. He nodded and rode south. Justin rode almost two miles north. Justin would reach the river several miles north of the Del Rio crossing, while Wovoka would emerge an equal distance to the south. Unless the outlaws did some careful scouting, they wouldn't know the trail drive had expected and prepared for their arrival.

Old Mexico. July 25, 1853.

The fourteen weary outlaws had walked twenty long miles into old Mexico before they reached the blind canyon where they had taken stolen horses and cattle. Mostly, during the long journey afoot, they suffered in silence. Now their ordeal was over, and again they had horses. Except for Chavez, all of them collapsed in the welcome shade the canyon rim afforded.

''On your feet,'' bawled Chavez. ''It will be dark before we reach the crossing.''

''*Madre mía,*'' one of the outlaws complained, ''we have no saddles or rifles.''

''We will when we take them back from the *Americanos*,'' said Chavez.

''Let us eat before we go,'' one of the outlaws begged. ''We have eaten nothing since yesterday morning, and then only jerked beef.''

''You will have jerked beef again this day,'' said Chavez, ''if any remains.''

Chavez mounted his horse bareback, and with a sigh of

resignation, his followers all mounted and rode with him. North, toward the crossing at Del Rio.

Del Rio, Texas. July 25, 1853.

"The crossing can't be too far ahead," said Lonnie. "Here I think we'd better take the trail west, until we reach the Pecos. Sometime soon—maybe tonight—we should be hearing from Justin and Wovoka."

Darkness had fallen when the fourteen outlaws again reached the crossing. Less than a mile south of the crossing, Wovoka had heard the horses coming. So had Justin, to the north, and when the *Mejicanos* rode on past the saloon, Justin and Wovoka came together behind them.

"We'll follow them a ways," Justin said. "Our outfit may have already gone west and reached the Pecos."

Less than two miles from the crossing, the outlaws rode west. Wovoka leaned over and by starlight, studied the ground. Finally, he spoke.

"Cow go that way." He pointed toward the west. "*Mejicanos* follow."

"That means we'll have to circle wide enough to get back to the herd, without those no-account varmints knowin' we're coming," said Justin. "If they're armed only with six-guns, they may try to sneak up on us tonight after moonset."

That was exactly the tactic Chavez was considering when he and his companions reined up to rest the horses. He was waiting for just the right moment, and one of the outlaws gave him cause.

"I do not believe we can ambush so many *Americanos* with only the *pistola*," said one of the outlaws.

"Nor do I," Chavez replied. "I think we wait for some of them to sleep. Then we creep close and kill all of those who are on watch, withdrawing before the living can retaliate. If we rid ourselves of half of them tonight, can we not eliminate the others tomorrow night?''

There was mumbled assent from the rest of the outlaws. It seemed far more practical than attempting an ambush with only handguns.

''Come, then,'' said Chavez. ''We shall ride as near them as we dare, attacking during the small hours of the morning, when they least expect it.''

But Justin and Wovoka, aware that the trail drive had gone west toward the Pecos, rode wide to the north, going around the outlaws. Reaching the Pecos somewhere north of the herd, they rode south along the east bank.

''Rein up,'' said Waco Talley, ''and identify yourselves.''

''Justin and Wovoka,'' Justin replied.

The two of them rode in and dismounted. Justin noted with approval that there was no fire. Quickly he related what he and Wovoka had learned.

''Tarnation,'' said Dallas, ''that means they don't have long guns. They aim to attack us sometime tonight.''

''It looks that way,'' Lonnie said. ''Taking us by surprise, they could gun down half of us tonight and the rest tomorrow night. I think, for tonight and tomorrow night, there'll be no first and second watch. We'll all be on watch from dusk to dawn, until this bunch has made their move. Those of you normally on the second watch, mount up. We'll take a position just south of the herd. The rest of you be prepared to join us on either flank if we're attacked. See that every shot counts. Your muzzle flashes will be excellent targets.''

Dallas, Benjamin Raines, Elliot Graves, Justin Irwin, and Wovoka followed Lonnie to the south. A hundred yards beyond the camp, they fanned out in a half-circle, waiting. A pale moon rose, and when it eventually set, the world seemed all the darker for its going. Lonnie looked at the stars and found it was nearly midnight. If there was to be an attack, he didn't expect it until the small hours of the morning. The sound, when he heard it, was slight, and it didn't come again. Lonnie drew and cocked his Colt, its action sounding loud in the stillness.

"It's me," Becky whispered.

"Go back," said Lonnie, irritated. "I don't want you here during the attack."

"But I am here," Becky whispered back, "and Mindy's with Dallas. Both of us have our guns. We have as much right to risk our necks as you have to risk yours."

Lonnie sighed and kept his silence. It was neither the time nor the place for an argument. If the outlaws were close, even a breath of resignation might sound loud in the stillness of the night.

"*Madre de Dios,*" came a whispered exclamation, "they do not watch the herd."

It was evidence enough that the outlaws had intended to gun down the riders on watch. They could then come after the others on another night, having an edge after the outfit had been reduced by half. It was time to issue a challenge, and Lonnie did.

"You men are covered. Drop your guns and come out, your hands over your heads."

Nobody expected the outlaws to surrender, and they didn't. There was a muzzle flash, as one of them fired in the direction of Lonnie's voice. Lonnie returned the fire, and there was a groan of pain. The rest of the outlaws opened fire, their muzzle flashes providing excellent targets. The men from the first watch had circled the outlaws and were firing from a flank position. The outlaws had nowhere to go, except into the river or back the way they had come.

"*Retiro,*" Chavez shouted. "*Retiro.*"

But his command to retreat had come too late. The Texans sent a storm of lead into the thicket where the outlaws were hidden. One of them nearest Chavez got to his feet to run and was quickly cut down. Chavez heard his body fall in the brush.

Not daring to get to his feet, Chavez crawled on his belly until the scattered gunfire was well behind him. He reached the horses and discover they all were there. Under his breath, he cursed all *gringos* in general, and these in particular. Quickly he caught one of the horses, mounted, and kicked the animal into a run, headed south. But he was in a clearing now, under a cloudless sky, and was jolted forward as a slug slammed into his shoulder. On he rode, his only hope being to cross the border before the *Americano* devils caught up to him.

"Hold your fire," Lonnie shouted. "Any of you men who are still alive, it's time to get your hands in the air and give it up. If you don't, we'll salt that thicket with enough lead to finish you. Now what's it goin' to be?"

"Lonnie," said Dallas, "one of them rode away, but we wounded him. I don't think the others are alive."

"We'll keep watch until dawn, just in case," Lonnie said. "If there's no more activity, we'll take a body count."

Chavez crossed the Rio Grande into Mexico, where he reined up, waiting to see if any of the others had escaped. But there was no sound except the whisper of the wind among the trees. Chavez cursed bitterly. The numbness had begun to wear off, and his shoulder hurt. Looking back once more, he kicked his horse into a lope and was soon lost within the shadows.

The Pecos River. July 26, 1853.

"Lonnie," said Dallas, "while we're waiting for breakfast, let's have a look at the bunch that jumped us last night."

"I'll join you," Justin Irwin said. "I can't believe we took them all on and none of us even got a scratch."

"We have you and Wovoka to thank for that," said Lonnie. "We knew they were after us, and they had to come in close enough to use their six-guns."

"We owe Wovoka for taking their horses," Dallas said.

"Otherwise they would have had their rifles. It was a fatal mistake, them coming after us with pistols."

Entering the thicket, they froze, for they were confronted by a grisly sight. Some of the outlaws had been hit more than once. In all, there were thirteen dead men.

"That means one of them escaped," said Lonnie, "and I think he was hit."

"Then there must be some horses along the Pecos south of here," Justin said. "We're goin' to have a decent remuda yet."

"Like those horses Wovoka took, they'll likely all have Texas brands," said Lonnie.

"Maybe," Dallas said. "If I thought they'd wander back to their Texas owners, I'd say turn them loose. But more than likely they'd drift back across the river. We're as entitled to them as anybody."

"Let's get breakfast, if we still have the stomach for it," said Lonnie. "Then we'll look for those horses."

Returning to camp, Lonnie told them of the gruesome results of the gunfight the night before. All were in a somber mood, except Wovoka.

"Maybe we ought to search them," Dirk McNelly said. "It's the same thing as with the horses. If they have money, they can't use it."

"Dirk," said April, "that's a terrible thing, searching dead men."

"No more than they'd have done, if it was us layin' there dead," Dirk replied.

"I know it sounds cruel," said Lonnie, "but it's the truth. While we're about it, we'll take a look at their weapons. Any of them with a Colt, take it, along with any ammunition that's left."

"Why only Colts?" Mindy asked.

"Because there's lots of foreign makes on the frontier," said Lonnie, "and it's difficult finding ammunition for them."

"I go," Wovoka said, pointing toward the fateful thicket.

"Go," said Lonnie, "but breakfast is almost ready. Why don't you eat first?"

Wovoka might not have heard. When one killed another in battle, the dead man's gun, knife, and horse belonged to the victor. The Indian disappeared into the thicket.

"My God," Kirby Lowe said, "I hope he won't scalp them."

"Lonnie," said Becky, "Can't you . . . ?"

"No," Lonnie said. "I can't tell him to ignore his tribal traditions. He's Shoshone, and I don't know how they feel about scalping."

"Maybe he was with Bridger long enough to put some of his tribal traditions behind him," said Dallas.

"Breakfast is ready," Becky said. "We'll save some for Wovoka."

When Wovoka finally emerged from the thicket, he looked like a walking arsenal. He had ten shell belts, each with a holstered Colt. Proudly he placed them on the ground near the cook fire.

"All Colt," said Wovoka.

"*Bueno*, Wovoka," Lonnie said. "What about their pockets?"

The Indian had a blank look on his face, as though he didn't fully understand what had been expected of him. Lonnie reached into his Levi's pocket, took a handful of double eagles, and held them out to Wovoka.

"Take gun, take horse," said Wovoka. He then went to the wagon's tailgate, where Becky had left his breakfast. He sat down on the wagon tongue and began to eat.

Dallas looked as though he were about to laugh, but Lonnie shook his head. Nothing was more devastating to an Indian than having someone laugh at him.

"Gus and me will take a quick look," Waco Talley said.

"Go ahead," said Lonnie.

"Oh, I hate this," Becky said. "It's so uncivilized."

"Sorry," said Lonnie. "We're doing nothing to them that they wouldn't have done to us. At least Wovoka didn't scalp them."

Gus and Waco weren't gone very long. When they returned, Gus carried his hat. When he dumped its contents on a blanket, there was the dull shine of many gold eagles, as well as double eagles.

"Looks to be maybe a thousand dollars or more," Waco said.

"Becky," said Lonnie, "find a place for it near the front of the wagon. Later on, we'll divide it among the outfit. Now let's saddle our horses and find those the *Mejicanos* left behind. Then it's on to the Green River range."

8

Lonnie, Dallas, Elliot Graves, and Justin Irwin started down-river in search of the horses the outlaws had ridden. The animals had been picketed where there was virtually no graze, and it was impossible for them to get to the river.

"No telling how long it's been since they were watered," Lonnie said. "We'll lead them all to water first."

While the horses drank their fill, the riders looked for familiar brands on them.

"They're all branded, and except for that bay, they look like Texas brands," said Gus Wilder.

"There may be some risk, but we'll take them with us," Lonnie said. "I can't see turning them loose, only to have them cross the river back into old Mexico."

"With the fourteen Wovoka took, we've picked up twenty-seven horses," said Dallas. "I think we should begin saddling them and see if they have the makings of some good cow horses."

"Good idea," Lonnie said. "Being from Texas, I'd gamble that all of them have plenty of cow savvy."

When the horses had drunk their fill, the riders led them back to camp, loosing them among their own remuda.

"Not a horse for sale anywhere in Texas," said Dirk McNelly, "and now we got all this bunch without layin' down a peso."

"Don't crow too long and loud," Lonnie said. "If we meet up with a ranger or a U.S. marshal, we'll have some explaining to do. If my memory serves me right, the law can and might hold us responsible for taking horses we know are stolen."

"Well, hell," said Dallas, "we disposed of a gang of horse thieves. That ought to be worth something to Texas lawmen."

"We'll concern ourselves with that if and when the time comes." Lonnie said. "Saddle your horses, hitch the teams to the wagon, and let's get the herd moving."

To allow their own animals a rest, the outfit saddled some of the horses taken from the dead outlaws. The rest of the horses were driven to the tag end of the herd, forming a remuda. Behind them, the drag riders would keep them bunched, as near the cattle as they could. Once the remuda was in position and the herd was moving, Mindy brought the wagon to within a few yards of the drag. The cattle had become trail-wise, and the horses in the remuda followed the herd willingly. By noon, there was a rumble of thunder far to the west, and a dirty gray band of clouds strung out along the horizon. Lightning's jagged golden fingers shot through the clouds.

"Storm come," said Wovoka, who rode beside Lonnie.

"I reckon you're right," Lonnie said, "and the nearer we are to those mountains, the worse it's likely to be."

The dark clouds were driven eastward on a rising west wind, swallowing the sun. The day seemed at an end, with only twilight between them and total darkness. The storm was coming from the west, all the excuse the cattle needed for turning their backs to it and drifting back the way they had come. Lonnie raised his hat and lowered it three times, his signal to mill the herd. The flank and swing riders quickly got ahead of the lead steers, and got them moving in a circle. Some of the cattle, sensing the coming storm, were bawling and snorting in fear. The remuda horses picked up on the fear of the cattle and began nickering, forcing the drag riders to bunch the remuda horses and drag steers at considerable risk. The wagon had caught up to the drag, and some of the steers, breaking free of the advancing drag riders, decided to direct their fury at the oncoming mules and wagon.

"Mindy," Dallas shouted, "turn away from them. Turn away."

The skittish mule who had caused trouble once, chose that moment to repeat what he had done before. But Mindy proved herself equal. Seizing a whip, she popped the ragged end of it on his behind. The mule squealed and tried to run, but was held back by his three companions. Still the drag steers and some of the horse remuda galloped on, coming closer and closer to the careening wagon. But all the Colts taken from the dead outlaws had been piled under the wagon seat. Quickly, Mindy looped the reins about the pole that was the wagon's brake handle, and seized one of the Colts. Once, twice, three times she fired, kicking up dust in the faces of the oncoming steers and horses. Dimly she thought she heard Dallas shouting at her, but it was too late to turn the wagon away from the oncoming stampede. She fired three more times, and it had some effect on the frightened horses and cattle bearing down on her. Quickly she seized another Colt from beneath the wagon seat and began firing into the ground right at the feet of the running horses and steers. Slowly, the running herd eased down to a trot, allowing the drag riders to come between them and the wagon. Slowly, the herd was again bunched together. Mindy climbed down from the wagon, so wrung out she had to cling to a wagon wheel to stand. Dallas left the other riders to bunch the herd, and in a moment was at Mindy's side. His face was white, and his reaction anything but what Mindy had expected.

"You damn fool, why didn't you turn the wagon aside and

get out of the path of the running herd while you had time? You could have been killed.''

"I could have," said Mindy, "but I wasn't."

Dallas continued his tirade until tears rolled down Mindy's cheeks. It was Lonnie who came to her aid. He dismounted, took Dallas's shoulder, and whirled his comrade around so they were facing one another.

"Dallas," Lonnie said, "one more word out of you and I'll beat your ears down to the tops of your boots. There's not a man in the outfit—including you and me—who could have done any better. Maybe not even as well. With a storm coming, we're going to stop here for the night. Mindy, find you a place to sit down and rest for a while."

Dallas said nothing. Mounting his horse, he rode back to join the rest of the riders who were bunching the herd. Becky, April, and Laura had witnessed Mindy's heroics and immediately rode to join her.

"There are times when a man's an unfeeling brute," Becky said. "Give him some time to think about it, and he'll be praising you."

"I didn't expect or want any praise," said Mindy, "but I didn't expect him to chew my tail feathers off at the roots. I thought I was doing what a man would do. Why is it that when a man does something dangerous, he's a hero, yet when a woman does the same thing, she's a damn fool?"

"Men don't like to think of women as being their equals," Laura said. "He's not really angry with you. What's bothering him is that you saw what needed doing, and did it as well or better than any man. Remind him of that, if he starts in on you again."

April and Becky quickly agreed.

"If he jumps on me again," Mindy said, "I have some choice words I learned from him. He may try to force me off the wagon."

"He can't do that," said Becky. "Every man in the outfit

will stand up for you. I can promise you that April, Laura, and me will.''

''Thank you,'' Mindy said.

The herd had been bunched and the outfit was circling it, attempting to quiet horses and cows as the storm approached.

''Don't worry about Dallas, Mindy,'' said Lonnie. ''By tonight he'll be ready to admit he's sorry for what he said. Now some of us had better get busy with that canvas shelter, or there'll be no dry place for cooking and eating.''

While the rest of the outfit circled the herd, Lonnie, Dirk, Kirby, and Gus managed to erect the canvas shelter behind the wagon. They finished just minutes before the storm hit them with all its fury. Gray sheets of rain swept down on them, while the lightning and thunder came steadily closer. All the cattle and remuda horses were on their feet, stamping and milling uneasily. A cow bawled. Then another and another, until there was a bellowing frenzy among the herd. Every man in the outfit was mounted except Wovoka. Under the wagon he sat, awaiting supper.

''Get ready to ride,'' Lonnie shouted. ''They're gonna run!''

Lightning struck only a few yards away, and as though waiting for just such a signal, the horses and longhorns took the cue. As one, they struck out in a gallop, back toward the east. Lonnie and Dallas were in the lead, trying to get ahead of the stampede. Mindy, without any warning, leaped to the saddle of Becky's horse, kicking the animal into a run. She didn't know what had prompted her to do such a thing until she was riding alongside the lead steers. Lonnie and Dallas were directly in the path of the herd, waving their hats and firing their Colts. But the fury of the storm, with its rolling thunder, drowned out the sound of the shooting. There was no stopping the stampede, and Lonnie galloped out of its path. But Dallas continued firing. Frightened by the shooting and the oncoming herd, his horse nickered, rearing. Dallas was flung from the saddle, while the frightened horse tried to get out of the path of the stampede. Dallas stood there as though stunned. The leaders of the stampede had already galloped past Lonnie, and while he kicked his horse into a gallop, there was no way he could reach Dallas in time. Then from the other side of the charging herd—just seconds ahead of the leaders— came Mindy on Becky's bay horse. It seemed for a moment that Dallas and his rescuer were lost, but Mindy extended her hand, Dallas took it, and swung up to the saddle behind her. The stampede was almost upon them when Mindy wheeled the tired horse, kicking him into a run toward the nearest avenue of escape. They escaped with only seconds to spare. A steer in the front rank raked the flank of the horse with a horn, and the animal screamed. Mindy reined up and dismounted, falling to her knees. In an instant, Dallas was off the horse and by her side.

"I reckon I'll always be a damn fool," said Mindy.

"Hush," Dallas said. "When this stampede is over, I have some important things to say to you, and I promise it won't be anything like the last time."

The stampede seemed a lost cause. The riders stood holding the reins of their horses, while sheets of rain were wind-whipped into their faces. The thunder and lightning ceased, but there was no evidence that the rain intended to anytime soon.

"I don't think it'll stop in time for us to begin the gather today," Justin Irwin said.

"Then we'll begin at first light in the morning," said Lonnie.

Even in the rain, Becky took a tin of sulfur salve and began doctoring the bloody trail where the horn had raked the flank of her horse.

"Sorry I had to take your horse," Mindy said, "but he was the closest one."

"Don't be sorry," said Becky. "You did what had to be

done, and you did it well. I'd say there's not a man in this outfit who won't be talking about you around campfires in all the years to come.''

The rain eventually dropped off to a drizzle, and then ceased entirely. The clouds had begun to break up, and there were patches of blue sky. The dying rays of the sun reached above the remaining gray clouds on the western horizon. Darkness was no more than an hour away.

''Too late to begin the gather today,'' Lonnie said. ''All of your picket your horses, and we'll have supper.''

While the riders unsaddled their mounts, Becky, Mindy, April, and Laurel prepared the supper. The meal was a somber affair, each of them aware that gathering the herd would cost them some time they could ill afford to lose.

''Tonight, with the herd gone,'' said Lonnie, ''we might as well get some sleep. Don't take off anything but your hats, and sleep with your horse's reins in your hand.''

Most of the riders gathered a mass of dead leaves, which they placed between one of their blankets and the ground. Mindy made it a point to spread her blankets far from the place where Dallas had unrolled his. To her surprise, he gathered his blankets and brought them next to hers.

''You don't mind, do you?'' he asked. ''I have some talking to do.''

''I hope it's better than what you've said so far today,'' said Mindy.

''Forget what I said,'' Dallas pleaded. ''What can I do? I'm a damned fool.''

''You don't have to do anything,'' said Mindy. ''I just don't want you to jump all over me.''

''You just scared me to death sometimes. I don't want to lose you,'' Dallas said.

''So your fear becomes anger, and you turn on me,'' said Mindy.

''I reckon I do,'' Dallas admitted. ''Can you forgive me?''

"When I know that you're sincere," said Mindy.

"How long is that goin' to take?" Dallas asked.

"I don't know," said Mindy. "When you get a mad on, direct it where it belongs, not at me. You're old enough that you don't need a dog to kick, but if you do, it's not going to be me. The way I feel right now, if I had anything in Texas besides my drunken old daddy, I'd turn around and go back."

"I don't want you going back," Dallas said. "I want you with me."

"In the weeks to come, I'm going to be looking for some proof of that," said Mindy.

Dallas said no more, knowing that nothing less than keeping his promises would satisfy Mindy. Finally he got up and walked along the river.

"You were pretty hard on him," Becky said.

"You were listening to us, then," said Mindy. "Why didn't you bring April and Laura over here?"

Becky laughed. "I didn't have to. They came on their own."

"We wanted to see how you handled him," Laura said.

"Yes," said April, "we're learning from you. Do you aim for him to sleep by himself all the way to Green River?"

"I don't know yet," Mindy said. "If I decide that, I'll tell Lonnie, so he can announce it to everybody."

Along the Pecos. July 27, 1853.

The outfit was ready to begin the gather at first light. Becky, Mindy, April, and Laura remained with the wagon. So did Wovoka.

"There's plenty of guns under the wagon seat," Lonnie said. "Might be a good idea if each of you belted one on until we return."

The ten riders rode out, and Wovoka watched with some

amusement as each one of the four women belted a gun rig about her waist.

"Look at him," said April. "He's laughing at us."

"I think we'll have to excuse him," Laura said. "He's probably not used to a woman carrying a weapon."

"I've enjoyed about all of a man's ego I can stand," said Mindy. "If he keeps grinning at us, I'll see that he never gets another dried apple pie."

The riders began finding grazing horses before they saw any of the cattle.

"Let's ride on," Lonnie said. "Where we find the most cows and horses, that's where we begin the gather. All those between here and there, we can gather on the way back."

They had ridden almost five miles before they judged they had reached the end of the stampede. There, many horses and cattle grazed.

"Mighty unusual for a stampede to run this far," said Kirby Lowe. "Generally, when the thunder and lightning's done, they'll slow down."

"That's something to think about," Lonnie said. "We're still in Texas. Comanches won't care a damn for the cows, but they'd murder us all for so many horses."

"The varmints have been known to take advantage of a stampede, keeping it going," said Waco Talley. "We'd better keep our eyes open."

The riders had no trouble rounding up the scattered horses and cattle. They moved the herd back in the direction the stampede had come, adding more horses and cattle as they found them. Finally they saw no more grazing stock, and driving their gather ahead of them, they started back toward the Pecos.

"Hell, it ain't even noon," Dirk McNelly said. "I can't believe we got them all."

"We'll run some tallies when we get them back to the river," said Lonnie.

The women were surprised to see them returning so soon. The riders separated horses from cows and then ran half a dozen tallies. Lonnie compared the results.

"Damn it," said Lonnie, "we're missing three hundred cows and six horses."

"I reckon we can spare the horses, since we got nothing invested in them," Dallas said, "but that's a lot of cows to lose."

"Then we'll just have to beat the bushes," said Gus Wilder. "Some of them fell out of the stampede and likely wandered north or south. Except for some of that rain that fell last night, I'd gamble the only water is the Pecos. They've had time to get thirsty, and I'd bet my saddle they've headed back toward the river, to north and maybe south of where we are."

"You could be right," said Lonnie. "Before we ride again in the direction the stampede took, I think we ought to ride upstream and downstream three or four miles. Justin, I want you, Sandy, Benjamin, Elliot, and Waco to ride south along the Pecos. Give it a good five miles. The rest of us will ride north, the same distance."

Lonnie and his companions hadn't ridden more than three miles when they began to see grazing cattle. There were also four of the six missing horses. They continued riding upriver until there were no more horses or cattle. They then rode south, gathering horses and cows as they went.

Meanwhile, to the south, Justin and his riders were equally fortunate. There were two of the missing horses, as well as many grazing cattle.

"I think we've gone far enough," Justin said, when they could no longer see any horses or cows. "Let's gather what we've found. With what the others may have found, there just might be enough."

The outfit came together near the wagon within minutes of each other.

"Now we'll tally these new arrivals and see where we

stand,'' said Lonnie. ''I can see we've recovered all the horses.''

Quickly they tallied the new gather of cows, adding the gathers together.

''Forty-one hundred,'' Lonnie said. ''We're short twenty-five.''

''Let's take one more ride along the way that stampede went,'' said Dallas. ''There may be more stampedes before we reach the Green River range, and we flat can't afford to lose so many each time.''

Lonnie sighed. ''All right, we'll have another look. Dallas, Dirk, Kirby, and Gus, you'll ride with me. They rest of you stay here and keep this gather bunched.''

Lonnie and his companions again rode along the muddy route of the stampede. There didn't seem to be any more cattle, and they were about to turn back.

''Wait a minute,'' Dallas said. ''There's a willow thicket down yonder at the foot of this ridge. There may be a water hole there. Shade and water. What more could a cow expect?''

''Graze,'' said Dirk McNelly.

''Dallas has a point,'' Lonnie said. ''It'll take only a few minutes to look into that willow thicket.''

Sure enough, when the riders drew near the thicket, there were cow tracks leading in from the north.

''Some of those dropping out of the stampede to the north only made it back to here,'' said Lonnie. ''Let's run them out of there.''

''Yeeeeahaaa,'' Dallas shouted. Drawing his Colt, he fired twice.

It had the desired effect, driving twenty cows into the open. It was enough.

''Let's hitch up the mules and move out,'' said Lonnie when they returned. ''We've lost some time, but we still have enough daylight left to gain a few more miles.''

"You want Wovoka and me to scout ahead?" Justin Irwin asked.

"Yes," said Lonnie. "We'll soon be out of Comanche country, and we have no way of knowing when we'll encounter Paiutes."

"Kill," Wovoka said.

"That's the one thing I don't like about Wovoka," Becky said, when Wovoka and Justin had ridden out. "He's ready to kill before he knows for sure that we're facing an enemy."

"He may be justified in feeling that way," said Lonnie. "From what Jim Bridger told us, the Paiutes are not only unfriendly to whites, but to other tribes as well. I think we'll be fortunate if we don't have to fight our way across northern New Mexico Territory."

Justin and Wovoka rode what Justin estimated was twenty miles, hunting Indian sign. But there were no tracks except those of wild animals come to water. Justin nodded, and with Wovoka following, rode back to meet the oncoming herd. Reaching the point position, they rode alongside Lonnie, while Justin reported to him.

"Maybe we're not into Paiute country yet," Lonnie said, "but we'll continue scouting. I don't want any unpleasant surprises."

Wovoka remained with Lonnie, while Justin rode back to join the drag riders. It was Becky's day on the wagon. Mindy, April, and Laura trotted their horses until they caught up to the drag riders.

"No Indians?" Mindy inquired.

"None," said Justin, "and no tracks."

Even with having gotten a late start, the drive went approximately ten miles. The sun was already down when they bedded down the horses and cattle alongside the Pecos.

"Keep the fires small," Lonnie cautioned. "No sign of Paiutes yet, but smoke carries a long way at night. Put the fires out as soon as possible."

When the watch changed at midnight, there had been no disturbance. There was graze enough along the Pecos to satisfy the horses and longhorns for at least a night. The next morning, of course, they would again be on the trail. Those just off the first watch rolled in their blankets. They were all asleep, but some little sound had awakened Laura. She sat up, and there was a skunk with its head in her saddlebags.

"Kirby!" she hissed.

"What is it?" Kirby asked sleepily.

"There's a damn skunk in my saddlebag," said Laura in a quavering voice.

"Keep your mouth shut and don't move," Kirby hissed back.

The rest of the camp—including those on the second watch—had apparently heard the exchange, for Laura thought she heard somebody laugh. The skunk had backed away from the saddlebags and stood there looking at her as though considering leaving her something to remember him by. Finally he ambled away into the darkness.

"He's gone," said Laura with a sigh of relief.

With a grunt, Kirby Lowe got up and made his way to where Laura sat.

"How many times have I told you never to leave your saddlebags on the ground?" said Kirby. "Hang them over the side of the wagon box or over a tree limb, but *never* on the ground. Do you have jerked beef in there?"

"Yes," Laura said in a quivering voice.

Kirby took the saddlebags, hanging them over a head-high pine limb. He then returned to his blankets.

"You're not leaving me alone, are you?" Laura asked. "Suppose he comes back?"

"He ain't likely to," said Kirby, "but if he does, keep your mouth shut and don't move a muscle. Get yourself a dose of skunk smell, and it'll be until this time next year wearin' off. Now get some sleep."

"No," Laura said angrily. "I'm going to sit here the rest of the night and watch."

"Go ahead," said Kirby, "but be quiet about it. Strange sounds in the dark are likely to stampede the herd."

Seething with anger, Laura folded her blankets and sat down, her back against a pine tree. Try as she might to stay awake, she felt herself nodding. But suddenly she sat up, not entirely sure what had awakened her. Blaming it on her imagination, she had just managed to calm herself when she heard what sounded like the far-off scream of a woman. It had not been lost on the horses and mules, for she could hear them as the second watch tried to calm them. But there was no movement among those from the first watch who slept. As quietly as she could, taking her blankets, Laura lay down as near Kirby as she could get.

"You don't look like you slept much last night, Laura," said Becky, as the women were preparing breakfast later.

"You know I didn't," Laura said sourly, "and don't pretend you don't know why."

"When you got up this morning," said Mindy, "you looked like you might just cloud up and rain all over Kirby. That wasn't his fault, you know."

"I'm not saying it was his fault," Laura said angrily. "I hate him because all he wanted was to sleep. He didn't care a damn about me."

"You left that skunk an invitation, and he took it," said April.

"If all of you are so damned concerned about Kirby," Laura said, "then you can take turns sleeping with him."

It was a shocking thing to have said. Becky, Mindy, and April turned away, all their faces crimson. Laura immediately regretted her words, for Kirby Lowe had heard her. His face pale, he turned away. Breakfast was a silent meal. The entire outfit knew there was a strain between Kirby and Laura. It was the kind of thing that could be resolved only by the stubborn parties involved, and neither seemed willing to bend in the slightest.

"Justin," said Lonnie when breakfast was over, "you and Wovoka scout ahead twenty miles. Since we've lost some time, I think we ought to step up the gait some. These cows and horses have enough trail savvy, and there's plenty of water, so there shouldn't be any problem."

Justin and Wovoka rode out, as the rest of the outfit saddled their horses and hitched the mules to the wagon. While Lonnie had no wish to involve himself in a foolish fight between Kirby and Laura, he moved Kirby from drag to a swing position. The increased gait resulted in the longest day's drive since the outfit had been on the trail. Everybody was elated except Kirby and Laura. After supper, when the first watch had mounted up to ride, Laura made it a point not to ride near Kirby.

"I never seen so much foolishness between two people," said Dallas.

"I seem to recall you and Mindy had some hard words," Lonnie said.

"Yeah," said Dallas sheepishly, "but we compromised. When she called me a fool, I just admitted it."

The second watch took over at midnight, while those on the first watch settled down to get what sleep they could. Suddenly there was a scream of terror, and everybody was on his feet, reaching for a gun. Dirk McNelly was the first to discover the cause of the disturbance. April was lying belly-down, her Levi's around her ankles.

"What the hell's wrong with you?" Dirk demanded. "Are you tryin' to stampede the herd?"

"Is that all you care about, the damn herd?" April demanded. "I went to the bushes, and something cold and wet touched my behind."

Dirk made the mistake of laughing. "Likely a mule or a horse. It ain't like a cougar was nuzzled up to you. Now get up and fasten your britches. The others will be coming to see what's happened to you.''

But Lonnie and the others had heard enough. It was shaping up like another of those foolish arguments, like the one in which Kirby and Laura had been involved the night before. Those on the second watch resumed their duties, while the first watch tried to sleep.

9

$\mathcal{A}$fter April had calmed down and Dirk had gone back to sleep, Lonnie spoke to his companions on the second watch.

"I think Dirk may have been right," Lonnie said. "That may have been a horse, a mule, or even a cow that scared April. If it was one of the mules, and he's lit out, we may be in trouble. Let's have a look."

"I don't know how any one of 'em could have got past us," said Elliot Graves. "We've been watching pretty close."

But try as they might, they could find only three mules.

"It's that troublesome varmint we bought that was lame," said Dallas, "and we'll never find him in the dark."

"We'll have to wait for first light," Lonnie said. "Another delay."

Then on the wind came a faraway, chilling scream.

"Cougar," said Justin Irwin. "First light may be too late, and the delay may be longer than we expect."

"I heard him a while ago," Lonnie said, "and he's no closer. He's somewhere in those mountains to the west of us, and the wind's from that direction."

"I once talked to a gent that rode the Old Spanish Trail

from Santa Fe to California," Benjamin Raines said. "He claims there's cougars and grizzlies in northern New Mexico and southern Colorado."

"I don't doubt that," said Lonnie. "I'm hoping we can avoid them. It's bad enough that we may have to fight the Paiutes and the Mormons."

Lonnie made the announcement to the outfit before breakfast.

"We're missing a mule, and we can't move on until we find him. After breakfast, Gus, Dallas, Waco, and me will go looking for him."

April made it a point not to notice Dirk McNelly glaring at her. The rest of the outfit didn't look at either of them. Breakfast was a silent affair. Afterward, Lonnie, Dallas, Gus, and Waco saddled their horses and rode out.

"We'll try this side of the river first," Lonnie said. "Half-circles."

They rode almost a mile downriver. From there, they spaced themselves a few yards apart along the river. They would each ride a half-circle around their camp and the herd, ending at the river a mile or so above the herd. When they had accomplished that, there was no sign of the mule, and no tracks.

"He had to cross the river, then," Dallas said. "I reckon April must have scared hell out of him."

"It didn't take much to scare him," said Gus. "That cougar's squall may have got under his hide."

"We'll cross the river and ride half-circles again," Lonnie said. "It's possible, after he scared April, that he went directly across the river. That would account for there being no tracks over here."

They found a shallows and rode across the Pecos. Riding back downriver, they almost immediately found mule tracks.

"Well, we know the little varmint's somewhere on this side of the river," said Dallas.

Following the mule's tracks, they were headed west up a rock-strewn slope. Reaching the crest of that slope, they immediately found themselves facing another. The ground was flint-hard. They were on solid rock, without a sign of any mule tracks.

"I have an idea we're going to reach a higher and higher elevation," Lonnie said, "and not a sign of any mule tracks."

"Along with his other faults," said Dallas, "that mule's part mountain goat."

"Let's stop and listen," Gus suggested. "On solid rock, surely he'll make some noise."

The wind was from the west, and suddenly they heard the desperate, distinct braying of a mule.

"Wherever he is, the little varmint's in trouble," Lonnie said. "Come on."

When they eventually found the mule, his left hind foot was wedged in a rock crevice. The troublesome animal regarded them with sad eyes, while Lonnie tried to free its hoof from the crevice.

"Damn it," said Lonnie, "he's caught for good."

"Won't it come out the way it went in?" Dallas asked.

"Take a look," said Lonnie. "He's been trapped here so long, his leg is badly swollen. It's already been cut, and trying to force it out will only cut it deeper. He won't be of any use to us if we cut a tendon to free him. Dallas, you and Waco ride back to camp. In the wagon is a sledgehammer and an iron wedge. Bring them."

"We may be a while," Dallas said, "if we have to unload some of the wagon."

"In that case," said Lonnie, "get some of the rest of the outfit to help you."

The rest of the outfit was waiting anxiously for the return of the riders who had gone in search of the mule. Quickly they gathered around as Dallas and Waco dismounted.

"Not much time for talk," Dallas said. "The mule's caught

his foot between two ledges or rock, and he's hurt some. Lonnie and Waco's stayed with him, so's he don't struggle around and hurt himself more. There's a sledgehammer and an iron wedge somewhere in the wagon. Lonnie wants it.''

There was a search for the sledgehammer and the wedge, and after unloading part of the wagon's goods, their search was rewarded. Dallas and Waco took the tools, mounted their horses, and rode back across the river.

''Where's April?'' Dirk asked. ''She was here just a minute ago.''

''After last night, I reckon she's upset with you,'' said Becky. ''Now she likely thinks the mule being gone is her fault.''

''Maybe it is,'' Dirk said.

''The mule had already wandered away from the other mules and the horses,'' snapped Becky, ''and even if he hadn't frightened April, he might still be where he is right now. If you're just half as much a man as you should be, you'll find her and tell her none of this is her fault.''

Dirk looked at her, his fists doubled and his face flaming red. For a moment, Becky was afraid of him. Finally, with a sigh, he turned away and went looking for April. Well beyond the herd, he found her sitting cross-legged beside the river, staring into the muddy water. Without a word, he sat down beside her, and it was she who finally spoke.

''I know what the others must think of me. Aren't you afraid some of it may rub off on you?''

''Nobody's blamed you for anything, except me,'' said Dirk, ''and I reckon I shot off my mouth without thinking. That blasted mule was already wandering away when he got to you. If he hadn't gone anywhere near you, he'd still have been gone. Nobody's blaming you for anything. Come on back and join the rest of the outfit. Lonnie, Dallas, Gus, and Waco have found the mule. He's caught a hind leg between two rocks, and they're freeing him.''

"I'll go with you," April said, "but you'll have to forgive me for being a little afraid. I've never been away from home before, and I've never slept in the wilds. I'll do better, if I can."

"Whether you do or don't," said Dirk, his hands on her shoulders, "you're my woman, and I couldn't go on without you. From now on, spread your blankets next to mine, and I'll see that nothing bothers you."

That earned him a smile, and she took his hand.

"We only had to unload about half the wagon," Dallas said, when he and Waco had dismounted. "When we're done with this hammer and wedge, I'd like to suggest we stash them under the wagon seat. The rest of the outfit's trying to pack the wagon back the way it was."

"You can stuff them in your saddlebags, for all I care," Lonnie said. "Nothing concerns me right now except freeing this jughead of a mule and seeing how bad he's hurt."

"You can't get him loose too soon to suit me," said Gus, who had been restraining the desperate mule.

"Dallas," said Lonnie, "work that wedge as far into that crevice as it will go and hold it there. We'll never get him loose unless we can widen that crevice."

But it seemed the troublesome mule lacked confidence in their procedure, for he began braying to high heaven.

"Damn it, mule, shut up," Waco said. "Every Paiute within a hundred miles can hear you."

But the mule continued braying, and it seemed he was getting progressively louder. He ceased for a moment as Lonnie began pounding the head of the iron wedge with the sledgehammer. The wedge didn't move, and again the mule began braying his misery.

"Use that hammer on his hard head," said Dallas. "It'll shut him up until we can get him loose."

"Do that," Waco said, as he tried to steady the mule, "and

I'll let you hold the critter up while he's out cold."

"None of that," said Lonnie, as he stopped to catch his breath. "We already have all the trouble we need. Somewhere down deep, this rock may be as big as a house. If it is, we'll need blasting powder to widen that crevice."

"We have two kegs of the stuff," Dallas said.

"And no possible way we can use it without killing the mule in the process," said Gus. "We might as well just shoot the varmint and get him out of his misery."

"He's stubborn, lame, and has a bad case of wanderlust," Lonnie said, "but we need him. I doubt we'll ever widen this crevice with a wedge. I'll try something else."

With all his strength, Lonnie swung the hammer against one side of the crevice. Rock fragments pelted the mule's behind, and he brayed all the louder. It required the combined efforts of Waco, Dallas, and Gus to prevent the mule from further injuring his already swollen and bloody hind leg.

"Steady him," said Lonnie. "A few more blows, and I'll have broken off enough of this rock to widen the crevice."

"Don't be too long," Dallas said. "I reckon that shattered rock digging into his hide feels like buckshot. You want me to take the hammer for a while?"

"I want you to help Gus and Waco hold this damn mule steady," said Lonnie shortly.

"Look," Gus said, pointing toward the sky.

Far above them, four buzzards circled. They awaited death. If not immediately, then for the certainty of its coming.

"Damn," said Lonnie, as he again swung the heavy hammer against the rock. He had struck the rock at such an angle that fragments dug into his face. Blood was running into his eyes.

"Let me have that hammer," Dallas said. "You look like you've been scalped alive. Use your bandanna to stop that blood."

Lonnie needed no urging, for he couldn't see. Dallas swung

the heavy hammer. Again, rock chips pelted the mule, and the animal brayed like he'd been mortally wounded.

"You're some lucky bastard," said Dallas through clenched teeth. "If we didn't need you, I'd favor leaving you here, lettin' the buzzards pick your carcass all the way to your hooves."

The mule brayed all the louder, snaking his head around to eye Dallas. Swinging the hammer, Dallas ignored him. More fragments of rock pelted the mule's hide, and it was all Gus and Waco could do to restrain him. Lonnie was still wiping blood from his eyes.

"One thing for sure," Dallas said, pausing to catch his breath, "if we ever get him out of here, the little varmint's goin' to be hobbled when he ain't hitched to the wagon."

"You'll get no argument from me on that," said Lonnie. "Let me have the hammer."

"No," Waco said. "Let me have a shot at it."

Waco swung the hammer with all his might, splintering more of the rock, but still the mule's hind leg was firmly caught.

"It's goin' to be ticklish from here on," said Lonnie. "We'll have to shatter the rock where it has him trapped. A glancing blow from the hammer could break his leg. Do you want me to take the hammer again?"

"No," Waco said. "I've done some mining in my time, and if it can be done, then I'll do it. I'll swing the hammer true."

Waco again swung the hammer, striking the rock only inches from the mule's trapped leg. The animal broke into a new frenzy of braying.

"It's driving the edge of that stone crevice deeper into his leg," said Dallas.

"It's also chipping away the rock that's got him trapped," Waco said. "Another time or two, and he'll be free."

"Make it quick," said Lonnie, "or he's goin' to break that leg trying to get loose."

Waco swung the hammer again, and there was some movement of the mule's leg.

"Hit it once more in that same place," Lonnie said, "and I believe he'll be free."

Again Waco swung the hammer, chipping away the rock. While Dallas and Gus tried to steady the mule, Lonnie slowly worked the imprisoned hoof out of the rock crevice. The mule immediately showed his gratitude by trying to run away. Dallas locked his arms about the animal's neck, dragging him down. Lonnie seized the lariat from his saddle and, using it for a lead rope, got a loop over the mule's head. The riders started back toward the river, the mule limping along on three legs.

"It'll be a while before he uses that leg," said Waco.

"We'll have a look at it when we reach camp," Lonnie said. "We don't have the time to wait for him to heal. If nothing else, we may have to take another mule from the wagon, replacing them with two horses."*

"There may be some hope for that," said Gus. "Surely among all the horses we took from those *Mejicano* outlaws, there'll be at least two that's pulled a wagon before."

They splashed across the Pecos, the mule limping along behind.

"How badly is he hurt?" Becky asked.

"See for yourself," said Lonnie. "All the way to the bone, likely. Kirby, you and Dirk get a fire started. We'll need some hot water."

"If some of you will hold him, I'll do the doctoring," Becky said. "I don't fancy being kicked in the head. You look like you can use some doctoring yourself," she said, looking at the still-bloody nicks on Lonnie's face.

---

*Because of a difference in stride, a mule wasn't compatible in harness beside a horse.

"I can wait," said Lonnie. "Take care of the mule first. Then we'll cross-hobble him."

"I'll help you doctor him," April said hopefully.

Lonnie was about to refuse when Becky caught his eye. When he said nothing, Becky spoke.

"I'll appreciate your help, April. As soon as that pot of water starts to boil, bring it, and we'll get started."

The mule's leg was cleaned with hot water and then doused with whiskey. When alcohol hit the raw wound, it took six men to throw the mule and keep him from running away. The injured leg was then smeared with sulfur salve, and a bandage was knotted in place. They carefully allowed the mule to get to his feet, and with a length of rope, Dallas quickly cross-hobbled him. With a left front leg hobbled to a right hind leg, he wouldn't be going far. He was then led back to join the other mules and horses.

"Now," said Becky, her critical eyes on Lonnie, "I'll patch you up."

The rest of the outfit moved away, talking to Gus, Waco, and Dallas about what had been done to rescue the unfortunate mule. It afforded Lonnie and Becky some privacy.

"I reckon Kirby and Laura patched things up," said Lonnie.

"They have," Becky said. "All it took was for Kirby to say he was sorry for acting like a sore-tailed grizzly."

Lonnie laughed. "What about Dirk and April? I saw you pass me that 'shut up' look."

"I'm glad you've learned to recognize that," said Becky. "I set Dirk straight, I think, and he convinced April it wasn't her fault the mule wandered away. I thought she would feel better if I allowed her to help doctor the mule."

"You've really got a handle on what other folks are thinking," Lonnie said. "That's just a little scary."

Becky laughed. "Then just be damn careful what thoughts go wandering through your head."

"Oh, I will," said Lonnie. "Round the others up. I'll tell them what we aim to do."

"What *are* we aiming to do?"

"You'll find out when I tell the others," Lonnie said.

The outfit came together, and Lonnie wasted no time in speaking to them.

"That mule likely won't heal for a week or two, and there's no way we can wait until he's able to work again. Today, we're going through all those horses we picked up from those *Mejicano* outlaws. There must be at least two that have pulled a wagon before, and that's the two we're looking for. We'll have to use two horses. Horse beside a horse, and mule beside a mule. We'll tie the other two mules on lead ropes behind the wagon, just so old three-legs don't come down with the wanderlust again."

"He may not be able to walk on that leg as soon as tomorrow," said Becky.

"Then he'll walk on three legs," Lonnie said, "unless you aim to hog-tie him and stuff him in the wagon."

They all laughed except Becky, and finally she joined in. She was changing, and for the better. Lonnie winked at her.

Along the Pecos. July 29, 1853

Having devoted much of the day to finding and freeing the wandering mule, there was little to be gained by continuing the drive before the next morning. Even then, the mule might not be able to stand on the injured leg.

"Justin," said Lonnie, "there's still plenty of daylight left. Take Wovoka with you and scout maybe twenty miles ahead. The rest of us are going to try and find a pair of horses who aren't strangers to a wagon, if we can."

Justin and Wovoka rode out.

"How do you know if a horse can be hitched to a wagon or not?" Becky asked.

"We'll choose some of the calmest ones we can find," said Lonnie, "and they'll have to be geldings. Then we'll hitch them to the wagon and see how they behave."

"They still may raise hell when they find they're hitched up with a team of mules," said Kirby Lowe.

"Maybe not," said Lonnie.

They walked among the grazing horses, ruffling the ears of those coming close enough. One of the blacks particularly impressed Lonnie. He put his arm around the horse's neck, and the animal nickered. Lonnie led him away from the others.

"Here's another," Waco Talley said, leading a second black.

"The rest of you keep looking," said Lonnie. "Waco and me will try these two."

"We goin' to hitch the mules up with them?" Waco asked.

"Not yet," said Lonnie. "If they don't go crazy when we harness and hitch them to the wagon, I think they'll accept the two mules."

"The mules may not accept them," Waco said.

"Then we'll use the pair of mules for the lead team and put blinders on the varmints," said Lonnie. "They won't be able to see the pair of horses behind them."

The horses stood quietly, accepting the harness. Once harnessed, they obligingly back-stepped up to the wagon.

"They're no strangers to a wagon," Waco said.

"We'll go with these two," said Lonnie. "I doubt we could do any better."

Removing the harness from the two blacks, Lonnie and Waco led them back to the rest of the herd.

"We've found a couple more friendly ones," Dallas said.

"Keep them in mind, in case we need them," said Lonnie. "These two blacks have been hitched to a wagon before. We'll go with them."

"Lonnie," Becky said, "before we get into Paiute country, Mindy, April, Laura, and me would like to have a bath in the river."

"I can't help feeling that's a bad idea," said Lonnie. "Some of us would have to go with you and keep watch. That's not . . . quite proper."

"I've been called a gentleman," Kirby said. "I'll go along and stand watch."

"*What* are you going to be watching?" asked Laura suspiciously.

That struck Becky, Mindy, and April as hilariously funny.

"See that bend in the river down yonder?" Lonnie said. "The four of you can go just around that bend, out of sight. Dallas, Dirk, Kirby, and me will be on this side of the bend waiting for you. If you see anything suspicious, get out of there and holler for us."

With blankets for towels, the four women started toward the bend in the river, with Lonnie, Dallas, Dirk, and Kirby following.

"I don't like this," said Dallas. "We're not quite in Paiute country, but we're not out of Comanche country, either. This would be a grand time for Indians to show up."

"Maybe they won't be in the water too long," Lonnie said. "It'll be muddy, with them stomping around."

Lonnie and his companions waited around the bend, near enough to hear the splashing in the water. Muddy as the water was, the women were enjoying its welcome coolness.

"Suppose they're peeking at us through the bushes," Laura said. "Wouldn't that be something?"

"I don't know about Dallas, Dirk, and Kirby," Becky said, "but Lonnie wouldn't stoop that low, and he'd give the others hell if they get any ideas."

"Snake," April screamed, and started for the river's west bank. She slipped, fell, got up, and screamed again.

Becky, Mindy, and Laura stumbled out behind her. But

Lonnie and his companions had heard only the screams.

"Come on," Lonnie shouted. "Something's happened."

The four naked women stood on the opposite bank of the river looking helpless.

"What the hell is it?" Lonnie demanded.

"A snake," said April in a trembling voice. "A big snake."

"You saw it?" Dirk asked.

"I didn't have to see it," said April fearfully. "I stepped on it."

"Where are your clothes and blankets?" Lonnie asked.

"Over there," said Becky, "in the brush behind you."

"Oh, great," Lonnie said. "You'll all have to come back across."

"Not me," said April, shuddering. "I'll stand here naked until . . . until . . ."

"Until everybody's had a chance to see you without your britches," Dirk said.

She had some choice words for Dirk, and the other women, struck by the humor of the situation, laughed.

"Are you crossing this damn river or do I have to come and get you?" Dirk snarled.

"Come and get me," said April defiantly, her hands on her hips.

There was a shallows where the water was only knee-deep. Without a word, stepping into the river, Dirk waded across. Seizing April, he flung her over his shoulder head-down and carried her to the opposite bank.

"Now," Dirk said, standing her on her feet, "get your damn clothes on, and don't be expecting another bath unless it rains."

April's three companions still stood on the opposite bank of the river.

"I reckon Dirk's got the right idea," said Lonnie. "Come on."

He waded across the river, followed by Dallas and Kirby. There was a hint of amusement in the eyes of the three women as they each were shouldered and taken across the river. April appeared to be in no hurry drying herself with a blanket. Dirk stood glaring at her, unsure as to what he should say or do. Wisely, he said nothing. The other three women took their time drying themselves, while Lonnie, Dallas, and Kirby were as silent as Dirk. Finally, when the women were again dressed, they followed Lonnie, Dallas, Kirby, and Dirk back to camp. The four looked grim, and the rest of the outfit decided not to ask any questions as to what might have happened. Lonnie went to the wagon and got two tins of grease. He and his three companions, once their sodden boots had dried, would be forced to grease them. Otherwise, the leather would become as stiff and hard as a shingle from a south Texas barn. Several hours before sundown, Becky, Mindy, April, and Laura began supper. They still had dried apples, and as the fruit boiled, Wovoka and Justin rode in. The Indian eyed the cooking pot in anticipation.

"No Indian sign," said Justin. "Why are you *hombres* wet to the knees?"

"We've been wading in the river," Lonnie said sourly. "By God, don't ask why."

Justin shrugged his shoulders and began unsaddling his horse. Wovoka had unsaddled his mount and sat cross-legged near the cooking fire.

"Look at him," said Becky. "Feed him dried apple pies, and he never speaks an unkind word. I wish all men were like that."

"In snow country, when it's storming, an Indian leaves his squaw outside, bringing his horse into the teepee," Lonnie said. "Maybe the rest of us could learn from him."

"With me," said Becky, "that would happen only once."

The others said nothing, and Lonnie chose not to continue the tirade. Supper was eaten mostly in silence, and when the first watch rode out, April and Laura made no effort to go with it. Dirk McNelly and Kirby Lowe rode together, discussing the afternoon's events.

"Why the hell are they down on us?" Kirby wondered. "It was their idea, taking a dip in the river. We only went down there after April screeched like *el Diablo* himself had hold of her. Was it our fault they was all standin' there jaybird naked?"

"No," said Dirk, "and what burns my tail feathers is why they didn't come out on the riverbank where they'd left their clothes. I ain't makin' any excuses or apologies."

"Tarnation, you're right," Kirby said. "Hell, we don't even know it *was* a snake. Might have been a tree root. We done what we thought was right."

When the second watch rode out, Becky didn't ride with Lonnie, nor did Mindy ride with Dallas. Like Dirk and Kirby had already done, Lonnie and Dallas pondered the unusual circumstances.

"I don't understand why they're put out with us," Dallas complained. "It wasn't like we were spying on them, when April was screeching and howling."

"Sooner or later, we'll have to have it out with them," said Lonnie, "but I'm with you. I don't aim to make any excuses. If she gives me hell, I'll hand it right back. I didn't say anything yet, but I didn't tie the knot with Becky to have here standin' there before other *hombres*, jaybird naked."

"The other *hombres* meanin' Dirk, Kirby, and me," Dallas said.

"Yeah," said Lonnie, "but I don't aim to take it out on any of you. In fact, I reckon I won't say another word about it. Hell, I ain't gonna fight with Becky from here to Utah."

"I reckon you got the right idea," Dallas said. "Let's talk to Dirk and Kirby. Without any of us raising hell about it, we'll see how long these females go on blaming us."

10

Along the Pecos. July 30, 1853.

*A*fter breakfast, Lonnie brought the two horses they had chosen, while Dallas brought a pair of mules. The horses were harnessed to the wagon, while the mules were harnessed ahead of them, as the lead team. Almost immediately, the mules took to peering around to see who—or what—was behind them.

"Dirk," said Lonnie, "get the blinders out of the wagon. We're goin' to need them."

Kirby Lowe brought the remaining two mules on lead ropes. The injured one limped, but no longer walked on three legs.

"Kirby," Lonnie said, "you, Gus, and Waco change that mule's bandage. While you're about it, give him another dose of sulfur salve."

It was Mindy's day on the wagon, and she already sat on the wagon box.

"Mindy," said Lonnie, "we're going to tie these two mules behind the wagon on lead ropes. Don't travel so fast that the one with the injured leg can't keep up."

"How am I supposed to know whether he's keeping up or not?" Mindy asked. "I can't see him behind the wagon."

"Becky, April, or Laura will ride alongside or behind you," said Lonnie, "and they can tell you if you need to slow down."

"Well, do you want one of us, or all three?" Becky asked.

"If it takes all three of you to watch two mules," said Lonnie pleasantly, "then all three of you follow the wagon."

Becky's former cowboys knew something unusual was going on, but they managed to hide their grins.

Gus and Waco tied the two mules behind the wagon on lead ropes.

"The rest of you saddle up and let's ride," said Lonnie, going for his own horse.

When they were ready, Lonnie shouted the command.

"Head 'em up, move 'em out."

Becky, Laura, and April all rode behind the wagon. The mule with the injured leg decided he didn't like his new position, and braying frantically, tried to rear. But he could not, for the rope was taut, and he began kicking and nipping at the other mule beside him. Not to be outdone, the other mule did some kicking and nipping of his own.

"Mindy," Becky shouted, "the mules are fighting."

"Then stop them," Mindy shouted back. "It's all I can do just driving the wagon."

Becky rode her horse between the two mules, and the one with the injured leg sank his big teeth into her right thigh. Becky beat the animal on the head with her fists, and it had absolutely no effect. Meanwhile, the other mules was still kicking and biting, all of which spooked Becky's horse. Nickering, the horse tried to rear. Laura kicked her horse into a gallop, getting ahead of the wagon.

"Stop the wagon, Mindy," Laura shouted. "That mule's about to chew Becky's leg off."

Mindy stopped the wagon. Two of the drag riders—Kirby

Lowe and Waco Talley—had heard the commotion and rode back to see what was wrong. They were dismayed to find Becky and her horse caught between the two mules, one of which still had his teeth in her thigh. The other mule, trying to get to his adversary, was nipping and kicking Becky's horse. The horse tried to back-step, but the mule still had a firm grip on Becky's leg.

"Waco," said Kirby, "untie that varmint from the wagon and get him out of the way."

Waco untied the rope and dragged the ornery mule away, leaving only the one who had a death grip on Becky's thigh. Becky's face was pale, and she was gritting her teeth to avoid crying out. Kirby drew his Colt and slammed it down against the mule's head. When he keeled over, his teeth still sunk in Becky's leg, she was dragged off her horse on top of the troublesome mule. Only then was she able to free her leg.

"Waco," Becky gritted, "let me have your gun. I'm going to kill this son-of-a-bitch, if I never do anything else."

"I don't think so," said Waco. "We already lost a day trying to rescue him, doctoring his leg. Lonnie's the trail boss. Let's wait and see what he has to say."

Furious, Becky bit her tongue. One of the other drag riders had ridden ahead of the herd, informing Lonnie of the problem. He rode back just in time to see the mule, again on his feet, kicking and rearing on the lead rope. Waco held the other mule's lead rope. Becky lay on her back in the grass, her Levi's down around her ankles. Mindy, Laura, and April hovered around, unsure as to what they should do. So fierce had been the mule's grip on Becky's thigh, it oozed blood where the animal's teeth had sunk in. All around the wound, the skin was fast turning a bluish purple.

"Kirby," said Lonnie, "you and Waco get a fire going. Get a pot of water on to boil."

The herd had been headed, and the rest of the riders had ridden back to see what had caused the delay. There was no doubt in anybody's mind what had happened, for the teeth marks on Becky's thigh spoke for themselves. The mule stood there calmly, watching their activities with interest.

"My God," said Dallas, "we should have left the ungrateful little varmint stuck up there in the rocks for the buzzards."

There were murmurs of agreement from the other riders. Becky hadn't spoken a word.

"Well, by God," Lonnie said, "this is my wife, naked from the waist down, and all you *hombres* are gathered around like it's a freak show."

"Sorry," said Waco, "but we knew her before you did, and we were concerned."

"I appreciate that concern," Becky said, speaking for the first time. "All of you remain where you are."

None of the riders moved away, and when Lonnie's eyes met Becky's, they were full of defiance and determination. When the water began boiling, Mindy removed the kettle from the fire and brought it to the wagon. Kirby Lowe had taken the medicine kit from beneath the wagon seat.

"Will you see to her, or do you want me to?" Mindy asked.

"Do what needs doing," said Lonnie. "Just be sure to use plenty of whiskey after you clean the wound."

Lonnie turned away, still unwilling to meet Becky's eyes.

"What do you aim to do with this uncivilized varmint?" Dallas asked, his eyes on the troublesome mule.

"What we should already have done with him," said Lonnie. He drew his Colt and shot the mule through the head.

"No!" April cried.

Mindy and Laura said nothing, their faces pale with shock. Becky's eyes were closed, but tears leaked out under the lids.

"That's two hundred dollars shot to hell," said Dallas.

"I wouldn't care if it was two thousand dollars," Lonnie gritted. "Rope this varmint and drag him away for the buzzards and coyotes."

Dallas roped the dead mule, mounted his horse, and dragged the carcass away.

Mindy had cleaned Becky's wound with hot water, and when she doused it with some of the whiskey, Becky cried out.

"Should I bandage it?" Mindy asked.

"No," said Lonnie, "we can't. It's an animal bite, and it'll have to heal from the inside out. We can't have those Levi's next to the wound, either. Take them off her."

"No," Becky cried, "I can't ride in my shirttail."

"You're going in the wagon with Mindy until that wound heals," said Lonnie. "Mindy, you'll have the wagon for a while."

"I don't mind," Mindy said.

Waco had already tied the surviving mule behind the wagon again. Gus Wilder had unsaddled Becky's horse, finding a place for her saddle in the rear of the wagon.

"I'll turn your horse in with the remuda, Becky," said Gus. "He'll like that better than trailing the wagon beside a mule."

"Part of it was that mule's fault," said Becky. "He was kicking and biting my horse, while the other mule had his teeth sunk in my leg."

"We'll leave the varmint tied to the wagon," Lonnie said. "If he takes to raising too much hell, we'll let the buzzards and coyotes have him, too."

With Dallas helping, Lonnie hoisted Becky up to the wagon seat, careful to keep her weight off the injured leg. Mindy took a blanket from the wagon, covering Becky from the waist down. The riders mounted up, prepared to return to the herd. Lonnie lingered, for in Becky's eyes there was no hostility. Only pain.

"Lonnie," she said, "I'm sorry . . . about the mule."

"Don't be," said Lonnie. "Just make yourself as comfortable as you can. We'll need to make as many miles as we can so there'll be graze for the horses and cattle."

He rode away, again taking his place ahead of the herd. April rode on one side of the wagon, while Laura rode on the other.

"I thought Lonnie was going to raise hell when we took your Levi's down with everybody looking on," said Mindy. "I think he was ashamed of himself when Waco spoke up."

"He's having to learn what Waco and most of the others already know," Becky said. "We're an outfit, and when we reach Utah Territory, we'll be like family, because there won't be anybody else. When Lonnie came along, I was within a few days of losing the old place my Pa homesteaded. Sandy, Benjamin, Elliot, and Justin had already had to go, since I couldn't pay them. Gus and Waco would have been next. Seeing them go hurt me nearly as much as burying what was left of Ma and Pa."

"If that wound's hurting you," said Mindy, "there's laudanum in the medicine kit."

"I can stand it," Becky said. "We may need the laudanum farther on."

Despite the delay, the drive traveled a considerable distance before bedding down the herd for the night. Mindy tried to help Becky off the wagon box, but was unable to do it alone. Kirby Lowe, who had been riding drag, came to help. But as he and Mindy lifted Becky down, a puff of wind caught the blanket, flinging it to the ground.

"I'll get it," said Laura, dismounting.

"When you do," Becky said, "spread it under that pine beside the river. There I can sit with my back to the tree. I'm sorry I'm so useless and can't help with the cooking."

They eased Becky down on the blanket, her back against a pine. When the riders had unsaddled their horses and unhitched the team from the wagon, Lonnie knelt beside Becky.

"I reckon I don't have to ask how you're feeling," he said.

"I feel like I've been bitten by a mule," said Becky, attempting to smile.

"Some of us will be checking on you during the night," Lonnie said. "That wound's bad enough to develop infection. If there's fever, you'll have to take some whiskey."

He got to his feet, preparing to go, when she spoke.

"Lonnie?"

He knelt beside her, taking both her hands in his. Tears crept down her cheeks, and when she spoke, it was no more than a whisper.

"Thank you for caring. It means a lot."

"I care more than you'll ever know," he said. "I reckon it takes something like this to remind me. I swear I'll try to do better."

"You're doing well," said Becky. "I'm sorry we were so . . . cold to you, when you and the others came to rescue us from April's snake. It wasn't the fault of any of you."

"You don't know how glad I am to hear you say that," Lonnie said. "Now I'd like for you to talk to Mindy, Laura, and April. We weren't watching you, and I think Dallas, Dirk, and Kirby felt as foolish as I did, looking at the four of you jaybird naked."

"I'll talk to them," said Becky. "As I've already told Mindy, when we reach Utah, we'll be far away from our families. We'll be more like a family than an outfit, because there'll be nobody else for us to turn to."

Suddenly she laughed.

"What's so funny?" Lonnie asked.

"I'll never forget the expressions on your faces," said Becky, "when you, Dallas, Dirk, and Kirby saw the four of us there on the riverbank without a stitch. It was worth it all, just to see what you *hombres* would do."

"It was an experience," Lonnie admitted. "By the time we reach the Green River range, we won't have any secrets left."

"I know I won't," said Becky. "My God, it's the middle of the summer, and I just can't stand this wool blanket

Mindy's draped over me. Take it away. The one I'm sitting on is itchy enough."

"You need a longer shirttail," Lonnie said, removing the blanket.

"The hell with it," said Becky. "If it gets any hotter, I'll take off the shirt."

Mindy, Laura, and April prepared the supper, and after cleaning up, they took time to see how Becky was feeling.

"You're somewhat indecent," Mindy said. "Where's your other blanket?"

"It was so hot, I couldn't stand it over me another minute," said Becky. "I had Lonnie take it away."

"My God, he's changed," Laura said. "I expected him, Dallas, Kirby, and Dirk to have a mad on from now until we reach Utah."

"He's not the only one that's changed," said Becky. "He's asked me to talk to all of you, to assure you that they weren't watching us in the river. They wouldn't have seen us, if April hadn't screamed about the snake."

"What snake?" April asked innocently.

"The damn snake that caused you to yell your head off, getting the four of them near enough to see us all standing there naked," said Mindy.

"So there wasn't a snake," Becky said.

"Oh, there may be one in there somewhere," said April. "I thought there was."

"So you embarrassed the hell out of all of us for nothing," Mindy said.

"Not for nothing," said April. "I just wanted to see if I could make Dirk jealous, to see if he wouldn't pay more attention to me."

"I wonder what he'd say if he knew that," Becky said. "You don't make a man jealous by bringing him face-to-face with four naked females. It didn't bother you, having him see Mindy, Laura, and me?"

"I . . . I didn't think of it like that," said April. "Ma died when I was young, and Pa went on a permanent drunk. I've had nobody to talk to, nobody to tell me how to be a woman. You won't tell on me, will you?"

"I think I can speak for all of us," Becky said. "We won't tell. I've already told Lonnie it was worth the experience, just seeing the look on their faces when they saw us standing there on the riverbank. All I regret is that you screamed before I had a chance to wash my hair. When this leg heals, before winter comes, I'm going to have a real bath."

"You remember what Lonnie said about that," said Mindy. "You won't get another bath until it rains."

"Oh, I think I can change his mind about that," Becky said. "Next time, we'll take the four of them with us. That snake trick won't work a second time, April."

Despite the delay, the loss of a mule, and Becky's injury, the outfit was encouraged. Lonnie sat down beside Becky and they ate supper together.

"How far do you think we've come?" Becky asked.

"Not nearly far enough," said Lonnie. "From the scale on the map, we're still a good two hundred and fifty miles south of New Mexico Territory. We'll be traveling all the way across New Mexico, and from what I know of it, it's mostly mountainous. There will be times when we'll have to go far out of our way to get the wagon through."

"I'm still glad we brought the wagon," Becky said.

"So am I," said Lonnie. "We can lay over near Santa Fe long enough to replenish the supplies we'll use getting there. I think we'll need some more laudanum and maybe another two gallons of whiskey."

When the riders on the first watch had mounted, they rode by to see how Becky was feeling. Remembering what she had told Lonnie, Becky was especially kind to Kirby Lowe and Dirk McNelly. When the cleaning up was done following supper, Mindy, Laura, and April came to sit with Becky for a while. The strange events of the day had brought them closer together than ever.

"I told Lonnie I didn't need any laudanum," Becky said, "but I've changed my mind. My leg's hurting something terrible."

"I'll get it," said Mindy.

Becky drank some of the laudanum, and her three companions remained with her until she slept. Then they moved quietly away. When it was time for the second watch to begin, Lonnie went to see about Becky. Her face was cool to the touch, and he sighed in relief.

The night passed quietly. At dawn, Lonnie again went to check on Becky, finding her awake.

"You didn't have any fever at midnight," said Lonnie.

"I don't have any now," Becky said. "I changed my mind about the laudanum and Mindy got it for me. We'll surely need to get some more in Santa Fe."

When Mindy, Laura, and April had prepared breakfast and served the outfit, they took Becky's breakfast to her. When the meal was over, they were ready to move out. Lonnie, with Mindy's help, lifted Becky to the wagon seat. Becky groaned.

"That leg's got to be sore," said Mindy.

"Oh, God," Becky said, "I never dreamed I was hurt so bad until you put me in the wagon. This leg's so sore, I'll be lucky if I can walk on it by the time we reach Utah."

Along the Pecos. July 31, 1853

"Head 'em up, move 'em out," Lonnie shouted.

He and Wovoka rode ahead of the herd. Laura and April rode beside the wagon. Mindy did her best to avoid jolting Becky around, but the terrain was such that there was little she could do. Becky gritted her teeth and kept her silence.

"I can tell we're getting closer to the mountains," said Laura. "The air's different."

The herd moved on, the cowboys increasing the gait, and the day's drive was the best they'd had since leaving San Antonio. Again they lifted Becky from the wagon, placing her on a blanket under a tree. As supper was being prepared, there were slivers of golden lightning far to the west.

"We may be in for a storm sometime tonight," said Waco.

"If that's the case," Lonnie said, "we'll all be on watch until the danger of it is past. After the best day we've had so far, I'd hate to see this herd scattered from here to yonder."

"We need to make room in the wagon for Becky before the storm gets here," said Mindy. "She's in no shape to ride watch, and there's no use in her sitting on the ground in a storm. The lightning may be really bad."

"Make a place for her behind the wagon seat," Lonnie said. "Laura, you and April can help. Move things from the front back as far as you can."

Becky said nothing, but she felt like a burden.

The distant storm came closer, until the rumble of thunder could be heard. Lightning galloped across the horizon, and already the longhorns were on their feet, bawling their unease. Picking up on their fear, some of the horses nickered.

"Waco," said Lonnie, "you and Gus get over there among the horses and calm them if you can. The rest of us will do our best to hold the herd."

"We've made room in the wagon for Becky," Mindy said. "If one of you will help me get her in there, April, Laura, and me will help you hold the herd."

"I'll help you with her," said Dallas.

Lonnie said nothing, but he looked upon Mindy with approval. While a stampede could be dangerous and lightning fatal, they needed every rider they could get in the face of the coming storm.

"I feel so damn useless," Becky said as Dallas and Mindy lifted her into the wagon.

"Don't," said Dallas. "We all know you'd be in the saddle if you were able."

The first big drops of rain were pelting the wagon canvas as Mindy saddled her horse. Laura and April were already with the restless herd. Gus and Waco seemed to have calmed the horses, but the longhorns were on their feet, tails to the wind, bawling their unease. All the riders began circling the herd, and some of those who remembered the words were singing some of the old songs. The lightning became almost constant, its golden hues lending a mystical touch to the rugged terrain. Thunder rumbled, each peal colliding with the next, in a virtual drumroll of sound. The earth shook, and as one the herd began to run, heading east. But the riders had been prepared for that, since the storm was coming from the west. Lonnie and Dallas were ahead of the herd, shouting and shooting, but it seemed to have little effect. Mindy, Laura, and April galloped along until they were well ahead of the stampeding cattle. Lonnie and Dallas were still in the path of the stampede. Finally they gave up and rode for their lives. Dallas made it, but fifteen yards behind him, Lonnie's horse stumbled, throwing him. There was no time to help him to safety. Mindy leaped from the saddle, doubling her lariat as she ran. April and Laura, although not quite sure what she was about to do, grabbed their lariats and followed her. When one of the lead steers was close enough. Mindy swung the doubled lariat as hard as she could, belting the animal across its tender muzzle. Laura and April had followed Mindy's lead, and having been stung by the lariats, three of the lead steers reared, bawling. Those behind slammed into the leaders, and the leaders lit out across the thundering front that was the rest of the stampeding herd. Some of the herd followed the frightened lead steers as they turned back the way they had come. The cowboys began to bunch the confused herd. It seemed a virtual miracle that the stampede had turned when it had, for within a few more feet, the thundering herd would have trampled Lonnie Kilgore. The three women sank down on the muddy ground, their lariats still in hand, as the rain poured down on them. Kirby and and Dirk were running, using the frequent flashes of lightning to guide them. They had seen the riderless horses galloping away from the stampede, and they expected the worst. They leaped from their saddles, but Lonnie was there first. He sat in the mud, with his arms around the three women, nobody saying anything. Not until much later would he be able to talk about the stampede that, if not for three valiant women, would have taken his life. But Dallas, out of reach of Lonnie, had seen the daring rescue. When the cattle and horses had been bunched, he wasted no time in telling the rest of the outfit how three women, armed only with doubled lariats, had turned a stampede and saved Lonnie's life. He told Becky first, and she was waiting when Mindy returned to the wagon. There was no need for words. Becky threw her arms around Mindy and wept.

The lightning and thunder ceased, and within an hour, so did the rain.

"We'll go ahead with our watches as usual," said Lonnie. "Those of you on the first watch, keep the herd and the horses bunched. The second watch will relieve you at midnight."

When the second watch took over, Lonnie rode alone. His companions respected his need for silence, allowing him time to sort his thoughts. At the start of the drive, he'd had his doubts about April and Laura, only to see them standing beside Mindy, turning the stampeding herd with doubled lariats. Becky was right, he decided. They were much more than an outfit. They were a family.

Along the Pecos. August 1, 1853.

After the storm of the night before, Becky had remained in the wagon. Mindy had taken her breakfast to her and was on the way to prepare her own meal when Lonnie spoke to her.

"After breakfast, Mindy, we'll harness the teams. There's not much use in doing anything more until we're sure the mud's not enough to bog down the wagon."

Mindy nodded. Having already eaten, Lonnie went on to the wagon. He had no idea Becky had heard of his narrow escape the night before. Becky sat on the wagon seat, eating. She paused when she saw him coming, and before he could speak, she did.

"Dallas told me about last night, Lonnie. I told you we're a family."

"I had all night to think of some of the things you've said," Lonnie replied, "and all I can say is that you're right. When that horse dumped me last night, I landed on my head and shoulders. There was no way I could have escaped that stampede if Mindy, Laura, and April hadn't come between those running steers and me. At one time or another, I've been some put out with all of them. I have some making up to do, and I'm not sure where to begin."

"None of them will expect anything of you," Becky said, "except that you never take them for granted. No more talk about Indians bringing their horses inside while leaving a woman out in the storm."

"After last night," said Lonnie, "I'll never have a hard word to say to any of them. I'd appreciate you talking to them. Nothing I can think of to say seems enough."

"I'll talk to them," Becky said. "They're all like me. We're going to a faraway place, and with no family near, we want to turn to one another, or to any of the rest of you. I don't think I ever thanked you, so I'm thanking you now. You hired Gus, Waco, and the others when I was down and had nowhere to turn. When I was very young, they taught me to ride. They've been family for a long, long time."

"They'd be a credit to any outfit," Lonnie said. "I'm proud to have them with us. Not just because they're excellent hands, but because of their loyalty to you."

The teams had been harnessed to the wagon, and Mindy drove it a hundred yards or so upriver. There was some mud, but not enough to bog down the wagon.

"The wagon can make it," Lonnie shouted. "Let's saddle our horses, bunch the herd, and move 'em out. Justin, I want you and Wovoka to ride twenty miles ahead of us and report back as soon as you can."

Justin and Wovoka already had their horses saddled, and they rode upstream along the Pecos. The rest of the outfit had saddled and mounted their horses. Lonnie shouted out the command for which they waited.

"Head 'em up, move 'em out."

Mindy kept the wagon a little farther behind the drag than usual, and Becky noticed.

"You're getting behind," said Becky.

"Some," Mindy said, "but I'm in a better position to see all the holes and drop-offs. I don't want to bounce you around too much. I know your leg's still sore."

"It's not nearly as sore as it was," said Becky. "Maybe three or four more days, and I can take my turn on the wagon and set my saddle."

The outfit maintained the gait of the day before, and again the herd responded.

"A twenty-mile day," Lonnie said, elated. "If we can just go on like this, we'll be on our Green River range before snow flies."

But trouble awaited them in the mountains of New Mexico, as well as on their Green River range in northeastern Utah. . . .

11

Fort Laramie, Wyoming. August 1, 1853.

*T*wo of the Mormon leaders—Adolph and Bertram—who
had been among the first to help establish the colony near
the Great Salt Lake were taken to Captain Stoddard, the post
commander. Stoddard did not welcome their coming, because
the Mormons had overrun and occupied Jim Bridger's trading
post. Stoddard stood up behind his desk, waiting for one of
them to speak. Bertram did.

"We have been told that much of the range along the Green
River has been sold. Sold to Gentiles. We have come to see
the territorial land map."

It was their right, and Captain Stoddard spread the huge
map out on his desk. Squares had been blocked off along the
Green River, each with a number.

"That's been sold, paid in full with gold," Stoddard said.
"I have the titles in my safe, waiting for the owners to pick
them up."

"You have no right, selling land so near what we have
colonized," said Adolph. "This is our land. We were here
first."

"I know that," Captain Stoddard said patiently, "but it does not allow your taking all of Utah Territory by divine right."

"You are wrong, Captain," said Bertram. "Our God ranks far above you and all of the soldiers of the United States government. In settling here, we have obeyed His command."

"Since you're involving God in this land squabble," Captain Stoddard said, "did he also send you to overrun and capture Jim Bridger's trading post?"

"Bridger's post was abandoned," said Bertram. "We are claiming it."

"Then remove it from that quarter section of land," Captain Stoddard said. "Bridger is the owner of that land, paid for and registered long before you people settled near the Great Salt Lake. I have notified Washington. If you and your people do not voluntarily go, soldiers will evict you."*

Without another word, the Mormons left Captain Stoddard's office. Only when they had mounted their horses and were riding south did Bertram speak.

"We will contest the right of the Gentiles to our land. We will build there and defend our holdings, just as we will defend our possession of Bridger's trading post."

In Captain Stoddard's office, the officer wiped his sweaty face on the sleeve of his blue tunic. By the time he heard from Washington about evicting the Mormons from Bridger's trading post, hell would likely have busted loose along the Green River. He didn't doubt for a minute that the Mormons would try to claim the registered and titled land, but he was equally sure that the Texas cowboys who now officially owned the land would not give up their holdings without a fight. He sighed, knowing they had not had time to return from Texas with a trail drive. The Mormons would have ample time to dig in.

*In 1857, soldiers were sent, driving the Mormons from Bridger's Trading Post.

Along the Pecos. August 1, 1853.

"It's the first day of August," said Dallas, who kept up with such things. "We have just thirty more days of decent weather. Then comes the snow."

"You're a cheerful cuss," Kirby Lowe said. "We might have sun right on through all of September."

"Oh, there'll be sun," said Dallas. "You just won't be able to see it, for snow clouds."

"You *hombres* shut up and eat your breakfast," Lonnie said. "We'll take it a day at a time, worrying about the weather when we have cause. We're going to continue driving the herd at the faster gait, like we've been doing. Instead of ten—maybe fifteen—miles, we're shooting for twenty. We've had delays, barely gaining ten miles. Now we have catching up to do."

Despite her pleas for a horse, Becky still rode in the wagon with Mindy.

"My leg's hardly sore at all," Becky grumbled.

"It's not well, either," said Mindy. "Lonnie's just being sure. You should be flattered."

"I suppose I am flattered some," Becky said, "but I've enjoyed about all I can stand, with only an itchy wool blanket between my bare bottom and this wagon seat. Damn it, I want my Levi's."

"Maybe tomorrow," said Mindy. "We'll see what Lonnie thinks."

"He'd better be thinking of my raw, sore behind," Becky said, "or I'll raise hell."

"Will you?" said Mindy. "You promised there wouldn't be any more cussing and fighting among us. We're a family, remember?"

April and Laura had been riding alongside the wagon, listening to the conversation.

"Mindy's right," Laura said.

"Yes," said April. "We're just going along with what you promised."

"Me and my big mouth," Becky said, trying her best to appear angry.

Justin Irwin and Wovoka continued riding ahead of the drive, watching for Indian sign. They had seen nobody, nor had they seen any Indian sign. They had reined up and were about to ride back to meet the herd when somewhere upriver a horse nickered. Justin's horse answered.

"Damn it," Justin grunted, "now we'll have to face them, whoever they are. Wovoka, we'll talk first. We don't shoot unless they make some wrong moves."

There were four riders, all armed. One of them had his left arm in a sling. They all reined up about a dozen yards away, and the lead rider spoke.

"We wasn't expectin' to see nobody till we got to El Paso. You *hombres* alone?"

"No," Justin said. "We're with a trail drive downriver a ways. We've been lookin' for Indian sign."

One of the men laughed. "You ain't lookin' too close. There's one right next to you."

Justin was watching Wovoka's dark eyes, and he sidestepped his horse until he was between Wovoka and the stranger who had said exactly the wrong thing.

"This is Wovoka, a Shoshone," Justin said. He's part of our outfit, and he don't like being talked down to. I'm Justin Irwin, and I think it's in the best interests of all of you if you ride on."

"Aw," said the man who had laughed, "I didn't mean nothin'. I was just makin' a joke."

"Then don't make any more," Justin said. "The four of

you ride on the way you were headed. Wovoka and me will follow.''

Clearly they didn't wish to do that, but Justin had hooked his thumb in his gunbelt near the butt of his Colt. Wovoka wore a tied-down Colt, and glared at them like he could cheerfully kill them all. Justin and Wovoka sidestepped their horses, allowing the four strangers to get ahead of them. Then they all started downriver. Riding point, Lonnie saw them coming and raised his hat, the signal to halt the drive. He then sat his horse, waiting for the four strangers to reach him. They did, and reined up, Justin and Wovoka behind them.

''They claim to be on their way to El Paso, Lonnie,'' said Justin.

''Do you *hombres* have names?'' Lonnie asked.

''Yeah,'' said one of the bearded men, ''but we don't consider that none of your damn business.''

''In Texas,'' Lonnie said grimly, ''a gent that hides his name is generally a no-account rustler, a bank robber, or a low-down, back-shootin' coyote. Now who the hell are you?''

It was more of an insult than they were willing to take. The man nearest Lonnie went for his gun, only to find himself facing Lonnie's Colt, cocked and ready. The other three hadn't made a move, because Justin and Wovoka were still behind them. The stranger who had his Colt halfway out of the holster let it slide back. Finally he spoke.

''I'm Dobie Aikens. The others is Neal Stubbs, Rye Wimberly, and Fox Presnall. Now are you satisfied?''

''Not quite,'' said Lonnie. ''I'm trail boss for this drive, and I don't like the looks of any of you. Circle wide of the herd and go on your way.''

''You might at least have given us an invite to supper,'' growled the man with his left arm in a sling. ''You're one unsociable son-of-a-bitch.''

''I'll go considerably beyond that,'' said Lonnie, ''if you

don't move on. You've just seen the good side of me. Now ride.''

The four of them rode on, circling wide around the herd. Not until they had passed the drag riders did they notice the women. Becky and Mindy were on the wagon seat, while April and Laura rode alongside the wagon.

"Thunderation," said Dobie Aikens. "Females."

He reined up his horse, but only for a moment. Waco and Gus had left the herd and had started toward the four strangers. Aikens trotted his horse, catching up to his three companions.

"Aikens, you're a damn fool," Neal Stubbs said. "This is a salty Texas outfit, and that trail boss could of filled your gut with lead before you got your pistol out. Forget them females and let's ride on while we can."

"A trail boss will bleed just like anybody else," said Aikens, "and the bastard's got to sleep sometime. So have them females."

"Well, if you got any thoughts of ridin' back," Rye Wimberly said, "you're damn well goin' to divide the gold we took in that robbery in Santa Fe."

"Yeah," said Fox Presnall, his slitted eyes on Aikens. "I was the only one that was shot, and if you even look like you aim to weasel me out of my share, I'll kill you. Just remember, this ain't my gun arm in the sling."

Aikens said nothing, and the four rode on.

Justin joined the drag riders, while Wovoka rode to the point position with Lonnie. Gus and Waco trotted their horses along, Justin between them.

"Who was that sorry-lookin' bunch?" Waco asked.

"I don't know," said Justin. "My horse nickered, and there was no way Wovoka and me could avoid them. The best we could do was force them to ride on ahead of us. When Lonnie insisted on knowing who they were, one of them tried to draw on him. I've never seen a man pull iron as quick as Lonnie. He buffaloed the four of them without firing a shot.''

"I saw them slow down when they saw the wagon and the women," said Gus. "I think we'll have to be careful while we're on watch tonight. None of our guns will save us if we're bushwhacked from behind in the dark."

April and Laura left the wagon and joined the drag riders, seeking to learn who the four strangers had been.

"Wovoka and me ran into them upriver," said Justin. "The best we could do was force them to ride on ahead of us. After one of them went for his gun and Lonnie outdrew him, they gave us some names that may or may not be their real ones."

"If looks mean anything," April said, "I'd hate to be left alone with any one of them."

Having learned all they could, April and Laura dropped back to ride beside the wagon. Becky and Mindy were anxiously awaiting some explanation regarding the strange riders.

"I saw them looking at us before they rode on," said Mindy. "I hope they'll keep going wherever they're headed."

"I think Lonnie will have something to say to us after we bed down the herd for the night," Becky said.

The herd traveled on another ten miles before Lonnie judged it was time to call it a day. After his usual signal, they bedded down the longhorns beside the river, and their horse remuda just a few yards farther upriver. Lonnie rode over to the wagon where Gus and Waco were unhitching the teams.

"Mindy," said Lonnie, "do you think Becky's leg has healed enough for her to get back into her Levi's without tearing off the scab?"

"Maybe," Mindy said. "We can try, if Becky's willing."

"I feel like my bare behind's grown to this wagon seat," said Becky. "I'll endure anything I have to just to get back on my horse."

"I reckon you'll be on the wagon seat a few more days," Lonnie said. "Mindy's had the wagon all the time you've been laid up."

"Oh, God," said Becky with a groan, "I owe you a week."

"At least you won't be sittin' here in your shirttail," Mindy said. "That is, if we can get your Levi's on over that sore leg."

"They'll go on," said Becky. "Get them now. I want to help with supper."

"Becky," Lonnie said, "don't rush it."

"Get me my damn britches," Becky said, "or I'll go looking for them myself."

"They're in the back of the wagon," said Mindy.

"Get them," Lonnie said. "We might as well find out if she's in as good a condition as she thinks."

Working together, Lonnie and Mindy managed to ease the Levi's on, being careful not to hurt the scabbed-over wound. Triumphantly, Becky buttoned the Levi's and stood up. She would have fallen if Lonnie hadn't caught her.

"You've been sitting so long, you'll have to practice walking again," said Lonnie. "I'll help you down and you can hang on to me."

"And I think you'd better let April, Laura, and me get supper," Mindy said.

"I think so, too," said Lonnie, "and you may not be ready to take over the wagon just yet. We'll see how you're feeling in the morning."

They left Becky lying on a blanket beside the river, and she had to content herself with the return of her Levi's. Supper was ready well before dark, and when they all had eaten, Lonnie called them all together.

"All of you saw the four *hombres* that rode by here today," Lonnie said. "Maybe they rode on, but we can't gamble on that. They could return sometime in the night."

"Since Becky's leg's well enough," said Mindy, "I think all of us should sleep as near one another as we can. We can keep our guns handy."

"I'll go along with that," Lonnie said. "Gus, I want you and Wovoka among the horses, and except for Wovoka, the rest of us will circle the herd. Wovoka, I want you circling the camp afoot all night. *Comprende?*"

"*Sí,*" said Wovoka, drawing his Bowie from beneath his waistband.

A dozen miles south along the Pecos, the four riders had dismounted and unsaddled their horses. It was still light when they built a fire and prepared their meager supper. It was Neal Stubbs who said what was on all their minds.

"We're far enough from Santa Fe. I want my share of the gold right now."

All eyes turned to Dobie Aikens, for they expected him to disagree. His manner, when he spoke, was surprisingly mild.

"We'll divvy up after we eat. I ain't goin' on to El Paso. I once had some trouble with the Rangers, and I ain't about to let the Texas law get its hands on me. I aim to ride west to Arizona Territory."

"Damned considerate of you to tell us," said Rye Wimberly. "The Rangers might string up the rest of us just on general principles, if they caught us ridin' with you."

"Don't you go bad-mouthin' me," Aikins growled. "You're a damn thief just like me."

"True enough," said Wimberly, "but I ain't a killer, hidin' out so the law can't find me and stretch my neck."

Besides Rye Wimberly, Neal Stubbs and Fox Presnall were looking unfavorably toward Aikens. The bearded outlaw laughed, and it was an unpleasant sound. Then he spoke.

"So none of you don't like old Dobie. You was quick enough to throw in with me back in Denver when I had plans for takin' that bank in Santa Fe."

"That was one thing, but likin' you is something else," Rye Wimberly said. "I decided I didn't like you after you slit that saloon girl's throat in Denver. Now that we got that Santa Fe bank job behind us, if you don't split with us and go your way, then I aim to go on alone. It's one thing to be facin' a robbery charge, an' another to be dodgin' a noose because you killed for no reason.''

''Then lay down a blanket and we'll split the gold right now,'' Aikins said. ''I've had all I can stand of you gutless *hombres*.''

The gold coins were emptied from all their saddlebags, and they all sat cross-legged in a circle around the blanket. Aikins began separating the coins in four separate piles, one before each of them.

''Now,'' said Fox Presnall when the dividing was done, ''let's count it.''

''No need for that,'' Aikins said. ''You all saw me divide it equal.''

''Then you count yours and I'll count mine,'' said Rye Wimberly. ''Then we'll compare.''

Neal Stubbs and Fox Presnall were looking at Dobie Aikins in a way that suggested if he refused to count his share, he had somehow managed to cheat the rest of them.

''All right, damn it,'' Aikins said, ''but I'm only doin' it once. Keep your eyes open and your mouths shut.''

Aikins began stacking the double eagles, ten of them to a stack.

''Five thousand and forty dollars,'' Fox Presnall said when Aikins had finished.

''Now I reckon I'll saddle up and ride,'' said Aikins.

''I reckon you won't,'' Rye Wimberly said. ''Not until I count mine.''

To the disgust of Aikins, his three companions counted their shares. Satisfied the split had been equal, the three men returned the gold to their saddlebags. Aikins was the last to gather up his. He then saddled his horse, took the saddlebags, and rode downriver.

''That ain't the way to Arizona Territory,'' said Neal Stubbs.

"Hell, let him ride on to El Paso where the Rangers can get him," Fox Presnall said.

The three outlaws doused their fire before dark and lay down, their heads on their saddles. It was nearly midnight when a shadowy figure on foot approached the sleeping men. Pale starlight glinted off the Bowie knife in Dobie Akins's upraised hand. He visited each of the sleeping men, slashing their throats. He then drove the Bowie into the ground, cleaning the blade. He took the saddlebags with all the gold that had belonged to the three dead men, and secured all the saddlebags to the saddle on one of the horses. He then mounted his own horse, and with the packhorse on a lead rope, started north along the Pecos.

The night had been quiet. Some people in the camp dozed while others circled the drowsing herd. Kicking off her blanket, Mindy sat up.

"What are you doing?" Becky asked.

"I have to go to the bushes," said Mindy.

"You know what Lonnie said about that," Becky said. "Squat where you are."

"Oh, for heaven's sake," said Mindy, "we have to sleep here the rest of the night and cook breakfast here in the morning. I'm only going over there in that bit of brush."

Mindy was barely out of sight when all hell broke loose among the horse remuda. The animals nickered in terror as Gus and Waco fought to hold them. Some riders galloped to the rescue, while others mounted their horses on the run. But all the turmoil ended as quickly as it had begun. There was only silence.

"All of you gather at the wagon," Lonnie said quietly.

Quickly they gathered around in the darkness, and it was Waco who spoke.

"We don't know the reason for it," Waco said, "but me

and Gus found the cause. This headless six-foot rattler was flung in among the horses.''

"You didn't see anybody, then," said Lonnie.

"No," said Gus. "We was fightin' like hell just to hold the horse remuda. They might have run even then if Wovoka hadn't been close enough to jump in and help us."

"I hate to suggest it," Lonnie said, "but this has all the earmarks of an Indian trick, although they generally run a horse through camp with a fresh cougar hide roped to it."

"Mindy's gone!" said Becky.

"Gone?" Lonnie said. "How? Where?"

"She went to the bushes just a little before the commotion began among the horses," said Becky. "We forgot about her when the horses started nickering."

"Damn it," said Lonnie, "that explains the diversion."

"Becky," Dallas said softly, "show me which way Mindy went."

Becky led him to the place where they had last seen Mindy. Kirby Lowe had gone to the wagon for the lantern, which he lighted.

"All of you stand back," said Dallas. "Lonnie and me will look for tracks."

Among the old dead leaves there was little hope of finding any tracks, but Lonnie and Dallas refused to give up the search. Finally, on a short stretch of bare ground, there was a single boot print.

"It's not Mindy's," Dallas said.

They went on, occasionally finding some small sign. Finally they found where at least two horses had been tied. The horse tracks led south along the river.

"Them bastards that was through here today," said Dallas. "I'm goin' after them."

"You're not going alone," Lonnie said. "There's four of them. Anyway, we won't find them in the middle of the night."

"First light may be too late for Mindy," said Dallas bitterly. "They'll have had time to use her, kill her, and move on. I'm going after them as soon as I can saddle my horse."

"I understand," Lonnie said, "and I don't blame you. I'll ride with you, and we'll take Wovoka with us."

Dallas said nothing, allowing Lonnie to speak to the rest of the outfit. They were quiet as Lonnie, Dallas, and Wovoka mounted their horses.

"Hold the herd and the horses here until we return," said Lonnie.

"Oh, God," Laura said, "I wish we had done something to keep Mindy in our sight. I feel like it's our fault."

"Well, I don't," said Becky. "Lonnie told us to get in one place and stay there. Mindy heard him, just like the rest of us."

"Let's don't argue among ourselves about who was wrong," April said. "Let's all stay awake and pray that Lonnie, Dallas, and Wovoka can find them while there's still time for Mindy."

The camp was wide awake, but there was little talk. Each of them had their guns handy, but there was a sobering realization among them that their precautions were in vain, that nothing they could do would save Mindy.

Downriver, Wovoka rode ahead, Lonnie and Dallas following. They had gone almost a dozen miles when a horse nickered. Wovoka reined up, raising his hand in the starlight. The three of them dismounted. Wovoka pointed downriver, then to himself. He would go and investigate. Lonnie and Dallas had to satisfy themselves with that, because not only might their presence endanger Mindy, a dangerous ambush was a possibility.

Wovoka moved like a shadow, his Bowie gripped in his right hand. Ahead, there was a nicker, and a horse stomped its hooves. Wovoka paused and then went on. The moon had just risen, and eventually Wovoka could see the shadowy forms of two horses. His eyes roamed the small clearing between him and the horses, and that's when he saw the three bodies. There was no movement, and quickly Wovoka returned to his waiting companions.

"Dead *hombres*," said Wovoka, holding up three fingers.

"Maybe three of the four," Dallas said. "Let's see who they are, and then we'll know which of the bastards we're looking for."

Leading their horses, the three riders reached the grisly scene of death. The moonlight was such that they could see each dead face.

"The missing one is the varmint calling himself Dobie Aikens," said Lonnie. "I don't see how he managed to slit the throats of all these men, even if they were sleeping."

"God only knows how many others he's killed," Dallas said, his voice trembling, "and he has poor Mindy."

"We have one thing in our favor, and so does Mindy," said Lonnie. "He's likely to ride all night, expecting us to follow. We'll catch the varmint before he's had time to have his way with Mindy."

"Horse," Wovoka said, pointing to the two animals in the shadows.

"Horse be damned," said Dallas. "That murdering bastard has Mindy. Come on."

"You can take the horses on the way back, Wovoka," Lonnie said. "We must first find this killer and take Mindy from him."

"*Sí,*" said Wovoka. He mounted his horse and rode out, Lonnie and Dallas following.

The three riders stopped only to rest their horses. Nothing was said, because none of them were certain that Mindy's abductor had continued downriver. It was frustrating, because waiting until first light, when they might see tracks, would put them farther and farther behind, perhaps costing Mindy her life.

A few miles downriver, Dobie Aikins rode ahead, the other horse following on a lead rope. On the second horse, he had tied the saddlebags containing the gold behind the saddle. Across the saddle, belly-down, he had tied Mindy. Her wrists were bound to her ankles under the horse's belly.

"You dirty bastard," Mindy shouted, "my outfit will be coming for me."

Akins laughed. "You won't be alive to see it, girlie. Come first light, we're goin' to find us a good hidin' place, and you're goin' to entertain me for a while. I'll be across the border before your bunch can catch up."

It was a disturbing thought, and Mindy's heart was frozen with fear. She became silent, so her captor wouldn't realize just how afraid she was.

Not far behind, Wovoka, Lonnie, and Dallas rode on. The eastern sky had begun to gray. Within minutes, they would know if they were actually following a trail. When they came to some bare ground, Wovoka reined up and dismounted. Lonnie and Dallas waited while the Indian studied the ground. When he faced them, he held up two fingers, pointing south.

"The varmint's headed for El Paso or the border," said Dallas, "but it's not likely he'll be taking Mindy with him. We have to catch them while she's still alive."

Wovoka took the lead, kicking his horse into a gallop. Lonnie and Dallas followed. At regular intervals, Wovoka dismounted, studying the ground. Finally, getting to his feet, he pointed west across the Pecos. Quickly he mounted his horse. Lonnie and Dallas followed him across the river, and in the first bare ground they came to, they could easily see the tracks of two horses. Wovoka slowed his horse to a walk, holding up his hand.

We're getting close," said Lonnie. "He's looking for a place to hole up for a while."

Dallas said nothing, his haggard face grim. Slowly the trio rode on until Wovoka again held up his hand.

"Stay with horse," Wovoka said. "I find."

Wovoka was gone only a few minutes. He beckoned to Lonnie and Dallas, and quietly the three of them advanced on foot. Ahead there was a small canyon with a blind end. As they approached, there was a terrified scream, and Lonnie had to seize Dallas.

"Go," said Wovoka softly, pointing toward the mouth of the canyon. In his hand he held his Bowie knife. He said no more, working his way silently along the canyon's rim until he reached the blind end.

"Come on," Lonnie said quietly. "Wovoka has a plan. There's nothing we can do without the risk of him killing Mindy."

Lonnie and Dallas made their way to the mouth of the small canyon, only to find the outlaw had heard them coming. His arm was around a naked Mindy, a Colt in his hand.

"Come any closer," said Aikins, "and the little lady gets her head blown off."

12

*Y*ou murdering son-of-a-bitch," Dallas shouted, "that's my wife."

Aikens laughed. "She might of been, bucko, but she ain't no more. Now you *hombres* turn around and go back the way you come, and just maybe I'll leave her alive when I'm done with her."

A dozen feet above Aikens, on the rim of the blind canyon, stood Wovoka, Bowie in his left hand. When he leaped to the canyon floor, it was almost on silent feet, for his moccasins made little sound. Aikens turned his head enough to see Wovoka, but the Indian was too quick for him. Wovoka seized Aikens's right arm, drawing the outlaw's Colt away from Mindy's head. The weapon roared, blasting lead into the canyon wall. The Indian twisted Aikens's right arm until the outlaw cried out in pain. He dropped the Colt and in an instant, Mindy broke loose and ran to Dallas.

"So it's knives you want, you bastard," growled Aikens. With his free hand he drew his own Bowie from beneath his belt.

He drove his blade at Wovoka, but the Indian wasn't there. They circled one another, each seeking an opening.

"I'll kill the bastard," Dallas said, reaching for his Colt.

"No," said Lonnie. "This is Wovoka's show. We don't buy in unless Aikens overcomes Wovoka. This varmint kills with a knife, and it's only fitting that he taste the blade himself."

The struggle went on, each man grasping a knife in one hand and fending off his opponent with his free hand. Suddenly, instead of pushing the outlaw away, Wovoka used his grip on Aikens's arm to draw his adversary toward him. Wovoka's iron grasp still kept Aikens from getting to the Indian with the knife. Wovoka drove his knee into the outlaw's groin, and Aikens grunted, dropping his Bowie. Once, twice, three times Wovoka drove his Bowie into Aikens's belly. After the third thrust, the outlaw fell and didn't move again. Wovoka drove the blade of his Bowie into the ground, cleaning it. He then thrust it under his waistband.

"Mindy," said Dallas, "I'm sorry you had to see this."

"I'm not," Mindy said. "I think that's what he had planned for me, after he . . . finished with me."

"Where are your clothes?" Lonnie asked.

"I don't know," said Mindy. "While I was tied across a saddle, he cut them off me."

"This would be a good time for me to take a switch to you," Dallas said. "Damn it, all of you were told not to wander around camp in the dark."

"I know," said Mindy meekly, "and I've learned my lesson."

"Lonnie," Dallas said, "do you think I ought to switch her behind?"

"No," said Lonnie, "she's been through enough. Experience is the best teacher. Get her a saddle blanket to wear back to camp."

"Not until I thank Wovoka," Mindy said.

The Indian had said nothing, listening to the three of them argue. He was startled as Mindy walked toward him. She

threw her arms around him, kissing him full on the mouth.
Wovoka was embarrassed beyond words. He stood there, his
eyes on the ground, and he said nothing until Mindy backed
away and spoke.

"Thank you, Wovoka."

"Ugh," said Wovoka. "Find horse."

While Dallas found a blanket for Mindy, Wovoka led Aikens's horse and the packhorse into the clearing.

"I have an idea those saddlebags are going to tell us something," Lonnie said. "Maybe we'd better wait until we reach
the herd before getting into them. Wovoka, I'll lead these two
horses. You can lead the other two that belonged to these dead
coyotes. Now let's ride. I doubt anybody's been in the mood
for breakfast, and that will delay us a while."

The four of them reached the Pecos, following it upstream
along the east bank. When they reached the place where the
three dead outlaws lay, Lonnie and Dallas spared Mindy the
sight by riding wide of it. Wovoka soon caught up to them,
the remaining two horses on lead ropes.

"Having started off with not even half enough horses, we
ain't done bad," said Dallas. "Besides what we had, we now
have thirty-one horses that didn't cost us a thing. We'll have
the makings of one hell of a herd by the time we reach the
Green River range."

"Unless the Rangers or a U.S. marshal catch up with us
before we're out of Texas," Lonnie said. "We can't prove we
didn't take every one of those horses from their original owners. I don't much like the penalty for horse stealing."

"Well, I ain't for turning any of 'em loose," said Dallas.
We *know* we took them from outlaws that wanted us dead.
They just all got a dose of their own medicine."

"*Sí,*" Wovoka said. "Keep horse."

"We aim to, Wovoka," said Lonnie. "We have enough
stolen stock already to get all of us hanged ten times over.
What's four more?"

When Lonnie judged they had ridden half the distance back to camp, they reined up to rest the horses.

"Mindy," Dallas said, "do you want to get down and stretch your legs?"

"No," said Mindy, "as much as I'd like to. I'm sitting on the edges of this blanket, and I don't think I'd ever get it back into place."

The four of them rode on, and well before they reached the wagon, the outfit heard them coming.

"Who are you?" shouted Waco Talley.

"Lonnie, Dallas, Mindy, and Wovoka," Lonnie replied.

Becky, April, and Laura were there to help Mindy off the horse, disregarding the fact that she was only modestly covered by a horse blanket.

"Will one of you please get me a new pair of Levi's and a shirt from the wagon?" Mindy begged.

Becky began rummaging around in the wagon, seeking Mindy's clothing. Lonnie, Dallas, and Wovoka unsaddled their own horses and then unsaddled the four horses that had once belonged to Aikens and his companions. Lonnie spread out the horse blanket that Mindy had been wearing, and removed one of the heavy saddlebags from Aikens's packhorse. He up-ended the saddlebag, and double eagles tumbled into a pile on one corner of the blanket. The procedure was repeated with each of the saddlebags, resulting in four piles of gold coins.

"Thunderation," Justin Irwin said, "that's a fortune."

"It is," said Lonnie, "and it's unlikely these varmints got it without stealing it. Worse, they may have killed for it."

"They seem to have divided it equally," Dallas said. "We can count one pile and have some idea how much is there."

"Justin," said Lonnie, "you, Elliot, Dirk, and Kirby each count a pile. I think this is the reason Aikens slipped back in the dark and murdered the other three outlaws."

"Mindy," Becky said, "come over here and talk to Laura,

April, and me while we get the breakfast ready. We want to know all about what happened.''

"What's the verdict?" Lonnie asked when the cowboys had counted the double eagles.

"Five thousand and forty dollars," said Elliot Graves.

"The same here," Justin said.

"Same thing here," said Dirk.

"That's what I got, too," Kirby said.

"So for some reason, they split up," said Lonnie. "Likely Aikens slipped back during the night and murdered the others for their shares."

"Now," Dallas said, "what are we going to do with it? If we get caught with this and it's identified, we could get life in Yuma."

"That's the trouble," Lonnie said. "There's nothing we can tie this back to. Generally, a bunch of varmints with this much coin got it by sticking up a bank. But we don't know where it came from. We'll take it with us, and maybe there'll be a sheriff in Santa Fe who can shed some light on it."

"Maybe there won't be," said Kirby. "That's enough to buy the rest of the Green River range, or a hell of a lot more cows and horses."

"I reckon," Lonnie said, "but nobody ever came to a good end by using what he took, stealing from somebody else. Unless there's no proof of ownership, we're returning every dollar to the gents it was stolen from. I reckon it'll depend on the sheriff."

April, Laura, and Becky soon had breakfast ready. Mindy wore her new Levi's and a new shirt, and seemed no worse for her recent experience. When Wovoka came through the breakfast line, they filled his tin plate to overflowing, and then filled a second plate for him.

"I don't know about other Indians," Mindy said, "but Wovoka's a man from the soles of his feet to the top of his head."

After breakfast, Lonnie rolled the mass of gold coins into

a blanket, making a place for it in the back of the wagon. Becky was already on the wagon box, her first time to handle the teams after being attacked by the mule. April, Laura, and Mindy already had saddled their horses. The outfit was ready when Lonnie shouted the command.

"Head 'em up, move 'em out."

Wovoka rode beside Lonnie, while on his other side Justin Irwin rode.

"Justin," said Lonnie, "you and Wovoka cover at least twenty miles. More, if you find any reason to be suspicious."

Justin and Wovoka rode on ahead and soon were out of sight. Lonnie had given the order to increase the gait, and the herd had responded. The number of their horses had increased to the extent that the horse remuda had been bunched up at drag directly behind the cattle. It allowed the drag riders more control and with the horses directly behind the herd, it discouraged the longhorns who might otherwise have bolted down the back trail. The weather continued hot and the sky cloudless. As the day wore on, it became obvious that the drive was going to cover more than the usual twelve to fifteen miles. April, Laura and Mindy rode beside the wagon.

"You're awful close to the horse remuda," said April. "If something scared the horses and they decided to run, you couldn't possibly get out of their way."

"I know," Mindy said, "but this is the way Lonnie wants it. He thinks, with the horse remuda in between the tag end of the herd and the wagon, there'll be less chance of the cattle stampeding."

Justin and Wovoka rode what they believed was twenty miles, without finding anything but four sets of tracks—of shod horses—heading south.

"This has to be the tracks of the four coyotes that showed up at our camp yesterday," said Justin.

Wovoka nodded his agreement, and they rode on a little farther before turning around and riding back to meet the herd.

Justin and Wovoka rode alongside Lonnie long enough to tell him of the tracks heading south.

"Since they're following the river," Lonnie said, "it looks more and more like they were headed for El Paso or the border. It also looks like the robbery might have taken place in Santa Fe, since they were traveling almost due south from there."

Justin rode on back to join the drag riders, leaving Wovoka with Lonnie.

"I was kind of hoping that gold hadn't been stolen in Santa Fe," said Dirk McNelly. "It might be ours."

"Lonnie's almost sure it was taken in Santa Fe," Justin said, "and unless something changes his mind, he aims to find out who it was stolen from."

With the herd bedded down for the night and supper being prepared, Lonnie spread out the big government map they had been using. There were few landmarks, except the rivers.

"I figure we're just about here," said Lonnie, pointing to a position along the Pecos.

"Another week as good as today," Dallas said, "and we'll be close to Santa Fe. I'd say we're maybe a hundred and fifty miles south."

"In a way, I hate to get there," said Becky. "It's been nice, following the Pecos and always having plenty of water."

"According to the map," Lonnie said, "we'll do well not to follow the Pecos all the way to Santa Fe. A few miles from there, we can turn to the northwest, reaching the Rio Grande. We can then follow it on into southern Colorado Territory."

"There's a string of mountains just after we enter southern Colorado," said Dirk, "but they don't seem to have a name."

"That should be the Continental Divide," Lonnie said. "If we're due to have trouble with the wagon, I expect it to come while we're crossing these mountains."

"Just south of Santa Fe," said Justin, pointing to the map,

"there's a thin line leading west. That must be the cutoff to the Rio Grande."

"You and Wovoka will be taking some long rides, Justin," Lonnie said. "Once we leave the Pecos, we need to know how far it is to the next sure water. We can't be sure the Rio Grande is close enough for us to reach it with a day's drive."

"Once we're near Santa Fe," Becky asked, "who's going in to the store?"

"I reckon we all can, as long as we don't go at the same time," said Lonnie. "I think we'll take the wagon in first, replenishing supplies which are low or have been used up entirely. I don't know what can go wrong, but if something does, I'd prefer not to have the wagon in town any longer than necessary."

"I think we'll surprise a lot of folks," Waco said. "I'll bet this is the first trail drive that's ever come up the Pecos bound for Utah Territory."

"I just hope we don't find another bunch of rustlers there, wantin' to take over our herd and the horses," said Elliot Graves.

"If we do," Lonnie said, "we'll treat them just like we treated the others."

Along the Pecos. August 6, 1853.

As had become their custom, Justin and Wovoka continued riding at least twenty miles ahead every day. This day, they were about to return to the herd when Wovoka pointed ahead. He trotted his horse to investigate, Justin following. The ground was bare, but the tracks of the four riders who had been riding south along the Pecos were no longer there.

"Let's backtrack until we learn where they turned off," said Justin.

Finally, some fifty yards to the south, where the ground

was covered with fallen leaves, they found all the evidence they needed. The four riders had come in from the west, then following the Pecos south.

"Since they were outlaws," Justin said, "I'm guessing they followed the Rio Grande for a ways and then cut across to the Pecos, maybe to confuse a posse. I think we'd better go on until we reach the Rio Grande, to see if there's water and graze between here and there."

Reaching the Rio Grande—a distance that Justin estimated at twenty-five miles—they rode upstream a ways. As Justin had expected, the four sets of tracks they had seen leading south along the Pecos had turned west, leaving the Rio Grande.

"That's what they done," said Justin. "They lit out along the Rio Grande, and then—maybe after dark—they cut across to the Pecos. It's time we was gettin' back."

Wovoka nodded. They turned their horses and rode back toward the Pecos. There they took notice of landmarks, so that the herd could take the short route to the Rio Grande.

"I think you're right, Justin," Lonnie said, when Justin had explained what he believed the outlaws had done. "Tomorrow night should be our last night on the Pecos. Once we've left it, we'll have to keep the herd and the horses moving so we can reach water before dark. I was hoping it wouldn't be that far from the Pecos to the Rio Grande."

"Well, it is," said Justin, "and we didn't cross any streams between the Pecos and the Rio Grande."

After the herd had been bedded down and supper was being prepared, Lonnie told the outfit what Justin and Wovoka had learned.

"Twenty-five miles in one day?" Kirby Lowe said. "We'll have to run the legs off the cattle and the horses, and then might not make it."

"It's that or a dry camp," said Lonnie, "and if you've

never experienced one, I can assure you that you won't like it.''

''We'll have to get an early start and push like hell,'' Dallas said. ''Once we reach the Rio Grande, how far will we be from Santa Fe?''

''The Rio Grande, flowing in from the north, bypasses Santa Fe,'' said Lonnie, ''and I'm hoping it'll be far enough from town so that our herd and horse remuda won't draw any unwanted attention. We should be near enough to wind up all our business in Santa Fe in one day. Not more than two.''

The next day, Wovoka rode with Lonnie ahead of the herd. It was late afternoon when Wovoka held up his hand. They had reached the place where the four outlaws had ridden in from the Rio Grande. Lonnie raised his hat, signaling the flank, swing, and drag riders to head the herd and bunch them for the night.

''This will be our last night on the Pecos,'' Lonnie said, as the outfit gathered while supper was being prepared. ''Tomorrow, it's west to the Rio Grande, and as some of you know, Justin figures it's a good twenty-five miles. Staying on the Rio Grande, we should pass almost within sight of Santa Fe. If we make the long drive tomorrow, we should be close enough for us to ride in the day after tomorrow.''

To the Rio Grande. August 8, 1853.

The sky was still gray in the east when the outfit bunched the cattle and the horses.

''Head 'em up, move 'em out,'' Lonnie shouted.

The drag riders were on the very heels of the horse remuda, keeping the remuda tight, so that, looking back, the longhorns could see only an advancing wall of horses. Several of the drag steers, seeking to quit the herd, found themselves being nipped on the flank when they tried to slow down, their behinds colliding with a horse's muzzle.

It was Mindy's day with the wagon, and she had her hands full trying to keep the wagon up with the horse remuda. Not liking the increased gait, one of the remuda horses reared. His hooves came down hard on the rear of the horse ahead of him, who retaliated by snaking his head around and snapping at the offender. Cows bawled and horses nickered, but the cowboys kept them moving. Despite their haste, it was dark when they headed the horses and longhorns, bedding them down along the river. After supper, Lonnie sought out Justin Irwin.

"Tomorrow," said Lonnie, "I want you and Wovoka to choose us a campsite along the river to the north of Santa Fe."

There was considerable excitement among the riders, as they looked forward to a visit to town. It might be months—or years—before they had another such opportunity.

Along the Rio Grande. August 9, 1853.

The following day, Justin and Wovoka rode out, seeking a place along the Rio Grande that was near town, where they could bed down the herd and their horse remuda. The pair soon returned.

"It's maybe twelve miles," said Justin, "and the graze looks better than any we've had so far. It's close in, but not within sight of the town."

"*Bueno,*" Lonnie said. "I think we'll stay there a couple of days so our herd and our horses can take advantage of the good graze."

After supper, there was a lively discussion about who would be first to visit the town.

"I don't want to sound selfish," said Benjamin Raines, "but I'm out of plug, and I'm near dead for a chew."

"Why don't we let Gus, Waco, Sandy, Benjamin, Elliot, and Justin go in first?" Dallas said. "The rest of us can take the wagon the next day, and maybe before the town finds out we're here we can be gone. It'll still be early. They could ride in after supper."

"That might be a good idea," said Lonnie. "Then tomorrow, the rest of us will go in, taking the wagon."

But after supper, when she and Lonnie were alone, Becky had a chance to talk to him.

"Why are you letting the riders go into town ahead of us? Do you know something about this town that the rest of us don't?"

"No," said Lonnie, "I've never been to Santa Fe, and I don't know a thing about it. I'd say we can let our six riders go in first without anyone being aware that they're part of a trail drive. If the rest of us went in first, with women and a wagon, it would be a dead giveaway. Stocking up with provisions at the store would be enough to convince certain people that we have money, that we're worth robbing."

"They'll all see the rest of us and the wagon the next day," Becky pointed out.

"True," said Lonnie, "but by then we'll be past with the town. We'll keep a close watch on the herd and the horses at night, and we should be able to get away from here without any trouble."

Santa Fe. August 10, 1853.

The outfit maintained the faster gait, and the drive reached the graze that Justin and Wovoka had selected well before sundown.

"We won't take the wagon in for supplies until tomorrow," said Lonnie. "Gus, Waco, Sandy, Benjamin, Elliot, and

Justin are welcome to ride in right now, unless you want to wait for supper."

"I'm needin' some plug a lot more than I'm needin' supper," Benjamin Raines said. "I'll ride in and get enough to last me a while."

"I don't think it's a good idea for one man to ride into a strange town alone," said Waco. "I think the rest of us should go with you."

The others quickly agreed. The six riders saddled fresh horses and headed for town.

"I know they're good men, and that there are six of them," Mindy said, "but I can't rid myself of the idea there may be trouble. Most of our horse remuda's stolen, and more than twenty thousand dollars in gold is in the wagon."

"I reckon it's a chance we'll have to take," said Lonnie. "I've warned them about the saloons, and if they're thirsty for a drink, to satisfy it with a beer or two."

Having been founded by the Spanish, Santa Fe was an old town. Streets were narrow, with every place of business shoulder-to-shoulder with others on either side. First, the six cowboys found a mercantile, where they filled their saddlebags with tobacco, shells for their weapons, and clean socks. They then went in search of a cafe. They found one—the Henhouse—that looked interesting.

"Let's try this one," Waco suggested. "With such a name as that, they just might have fried chicken. It's been months since I've tasted that."

"Let's find out," said Justin. "If they don't have it, we can always leave."

But they found fried chicken was the house speciality, and the six of them took the largest table in the place.

"Bring us two platters of fried chicken, with the fixings that go with it," Waco said when the waiter arrived.

"Yeah," said Gus, "and get some more to cooking. This may not be enough."

First the waiter brought coffee cups and a large blue-granite coffeepot. Cups filled, the cowboys settled down to enjoy the coffee while waiting for their food. After devouring three platters of fried chicken, they decided they'd had enough. They left the cafe.

"Well, we've had ourselves a mess of fried chicken, and we've been to the store," Gus said. "Where do we go from here?"

"Let's check out the saloons," said Sandy Orr.

"You heard what Lonnie said about the saloons," Justin said.

"I heard," said Sandy, "and I ain't goin' there to drink. It's been years since I had a few dollars to set in on a poker game. I won't risk more than twenty. When I lose that, we'll go."

"You don't seem very confident," Benjamin Raines said.

"I got no reason to," said Sandy. "I've always loved the game, but I never seem to draw a good hand."

"You ought to be more careful who you set in with," Waco said. "Somebody may have been slick dealing you."

"If we can find a saloon with a game goin' on," said Sandy, "why don't the rest of you have a beer and watch? Maybe you can give me some advice."

"I'll do better than that," Waco said. "If we're limiting it to twenty dollars, I'll sit in with you. I'm no expert, but I win more than I lose."

The Pecos appeared to be the largest saloon in town, as well as the most affluent. It was still early, but already the place was doing a thriving business. The mahogany bar was a good fifty feet in length, and men were backed up three-deep waiting to be served. Two poker games were in progress. A young man stood up at one of the tables and shouted at one of the bartenders.

"More whiskey over here, and make it quick."

One of the sweating bartenders hurried to the table with a

full quart bottle. The kid with the big mouth said something, and his companions laughed. It was at this table that two men folded, withdrawing from the game.

"We'll set in for a few hands, gents," said Waco, as he and Sandy took chairs across the table from the noisy kid.

"Set in as long as you like," the kid said. "Just so you don't mind me takin' all your money."

"Take it if you can," Waco said, without a smile.

"That's Billy, the son of Sheriff Al Singleton," one of the others whispered to Waco.

That explained the huge pile of chips Singleton had before him, and likely his arrogant shouting at the bartenders. Nobody wished to bring down on himself the wrath of the sheriff by putting the man's loudmouth son in his place. The cards were dealt around the table, Billy Singleton dealing. To Waco's surprise, he had three aces.

"Damn," Sandy whispered, "it's time to raise."

"I'm standing pat," Waco said.

Billy Singleton won the pot with four kings. He also had the fourth ace, making his hand virtually unbeatable.

Waco and Sandy lost five straight pots, while Singleton won four of them.

"Barkeep," Waco shouted, "a new deck."

"What the hell's wrong with this deck?" snarled Singleton.

"I didn't say anything was wrong with it," Waco said mildly. "I just asked for a new deck. Does it bother you?"

Some of the onlookers laughed, and it didn't help Singleton's disposition. The seal was broken on the new deck, and Sandy Orr won the first pot. Waco took the second and the third, and a pair of townsmen the fourth and fifth. As the game continued, Singleton's stack of chips diminished. When he finally won a pot after losing ten, he got to his feet and glared across the table at Waco.

"You been cheatin', you bastard, and I'm calling you."

13

Except for Sandy Orr and Waco, the men at the table turned over their chairs getting out of the way.

"Nobody's been cheating since we opened a new deck," Waco said. "Gus, get that last deck from the bartender."

"Leave that damn deck out of it," shouted Singleton. "This is the deck we're usin' now."

But the barkeep surrendered the old deck, and Gus brought it to the table. With considerable skill, he fanned the cards out, flowing from one hand to the other. Then, knowing where every jack, queen, king, and ace was, he placed them on the table.

"If anybody cares to look at those cards," Gus said, "you'll find the edges have been shaved. Any cheating was done with this deck, not the new one."

Billy Singleton's face went red and he leaped to his feet. Waco waited until he had his Colt halfway out of the holster. Waco then drew his own Colt and shoved it under Singleton's nose.

"Everybody stand back," Gus ordered, his Colt in his hand. Nobody at the bar moved.

"Now," said Waco, "I'm willing to forget you tried to

draw on me, if you'll turn and walk out of here.''

"I'm goin', damn you," Singleton said, "but you ain't seen the end of this."

As Waco kicked back his chair to get up, his companions were watching Singleton as he started for the door. Suddenly Singleton turned, dropping to one knee, a Colt in his hand.

"Waco," Gus shouted.

Waco seemed to fall sideways, drawing his Colt as he went. Singleton fired twice, his lead splintering two of the slats in the ladder-back chair where Waco had been sitting. But Waco fired only once. The force of the slug flung Singleton backward, his head striking one of the saloon's batwing doors.

"My God," said one of the onlookers, "now you've done it."

"I defended myself," Waco replied. "I have plenty of witnesses. Somebody go after the sheriff and let's settle this."

When Sheriff Al Singleton entered the saloon, he paused for a long moment, looking into the dead face of his son. Billy Singleton still clutched the Colt in his hand.

"Billy started it, Sheriff," said one of the bartenders. "He shot twice before the other gent pulled a gun."

"Shut up, Rufe," Singleton snapped. "I want anything from you, I'll ask for it."

Waco had reloaded his Colt and had returned it to its holster. He stood with his foot on the rung of the chair whose back had taken the force of Billy Singleton's slugs. He was calm, and his eyes met those of Sheriff Singleton.

"I reckon you done the murdering," said Singleton.

"Wrong," Waco said. "I killed a man who was trying to kill me. He fired first. See the back of this chair?"

"So you provoked him," said Singleton.

"I did not," Waco said. "I called for a new deck of cards, and he took it personal."

"That's the same as calling a man a cheat," said Singleton.

"He was a cheat," Gus said. "Aces, kings, queens, and jacks in the old deck had shaved edges."

"Just who the hell are you?" the sheriff demanded.

"Gus Wilder. Waco here's a lifelong pard of mine."

"Then I'll lock the both of you in the same cell," Singleton snarled.

"I don't think so," said Gus. "There's five of us with Waco, and we saw it all. So did the rest of these *hombres*. It was self-defense. That young coyote was called a cheat only because he was. Now stand aside. We've had enough of your town."

"You ain't goin' nowhere," Singleton said. "There'll be an inquest in the morning. Then we'll find out just what these witnesses have to say. You and your gunslinging friend are going to spend the night in jail. Unbuckle your gunbelts and drop them on the floor."

Sandy Orr, Benjamin Raines, Elliot Graves, and Justin Irwin had their hands near the butts of their Colts. But when they caught Waco's eye, he shook his head. They would have to do as Sheriff Singleton demanded.

"Sheriff," Elliot Graves asked, "what time's the inquest?"

"Nine o'clock," said the lawman shortly.

"Waco," Justin said, "we'll see you and Gus in the morning."

Waco and Gus were marched out of the saloon ahead of Sheriff Singleton. Justin Irwin turned to the men who had witnessed the shooting.

"You gents saw what happened," said Justin. "Will you testify in court tomorrow?"

There was an uncomfortable silence as men looked away. Several began inching toward the door.

"You, barkeep," Justin said. "You told the sheriff that Singleton drew first. Will you testify to that in court?"

The barkeep opened his mouth to speak, but no words came out. In his eyes was the look of a trapped animal. Without responding, he sank down on a stool behind the bar. Without another word, Sandy, Benjamin, Elliot, and Justin left the saloon. There was but one thing they could do, and they did it. They rode back to the herd and told the rest of the outfit of the injustice done Gus and Waco.

"We'll be there in the morning, and free them," Becky shouted angrily.

"I wish the whole damn bunch of you had stayed out of the saloons," said Lonnie. "It's always a risk, gambling with strangers. I'm afraid this is a situation where the sheriff's son has been getting by with cheating because the town's been buffaloed by his pa. It's a bitter pill for a man to swallow, having his son branded a cheat, and then gunned down after shooting first, trying to shoot his opponent in the back."

"I think we're in big trouble," Justin Irwin said. "None of the bunch that was there in the saloon offered to tell the court what really happened."

"I think you're right," said Lonnie. "The town's been enduring the cheating of Billy Singleton because he's the son of the sheriff. Now, for the same reason, we may not be able to get an honest testimony."

"This ain't a trial," Dallas said. "This is to prove or disprove the need for one. I believe I could drag the truth out of one of those *hombres* that saw the shooting."

"Maybe we should have a lawyer," said Becky.

"Why bother?" Lonnie said. "In a town intimidated by a sheriff, how many lawyers are going to defeat him in court?"

"Such a strong sheriff might also buffalo the judge," said Justin.

"I don't want to get on the bad side of the law," Lonnie said, "but Gus and Waco are not going to be victims of a prejudiced court. Tomorrow we'll leave Wovoka, Becky, Mindy, April, and Laura with the herd. The rest of us are going to be at that inquest in town. Waco and Gus will be riding back with us, if we have to shoot our way out."

There were shouts of approval from the rest of the outfit. When the watches changed at midnight, Becky still hadn't slept. She and Mindy saddled their horses, prepared to ride with the second watch. Becky trotted her horse alongside Lonnie's. Finally she spoke.

"If you have to shoot your way out, you'll be outlawed, won't you."

It was more a statement of fact than a question, and Lonnie didn't seek to avoid it.

"Many a man has been outlawed when confronted by unjust lawmen. There has to be a way out of this, if only we can find it. I think it's all going to depend on the judge."

In the Santa Fe jail, Gus and Waco stood looking out the small barred window.

"I reckon Lonnie's cussing us up one side and down the other," said Gus.

"It's likely he may be put out some, us gettin' into this mess, but I'm looking for him and all the others at that inquest in the morning," Waco said. "We're a Texas outfit, and right or wrong, none of us will ever stand alone."

Santa Fe. August 11, 1853.

Gus and Waco were brought their breakfast at half-past seven. Despite the forthcoming inquest, they were hungry. A waiter from a nearby cafe had brought their breakfast, and he returned for the empty dishes.

"Pardner," said Waco, "where's the courthouse? Can we see it from here?"

"Yeah," the waiter said. "It's half a block down, on the far side of the street."

Somewhere in town, a tower clock struck eight times. At

eight-thirty, when it struck the half hour, eight horsemen rode up before the courthouse.

"I told you," Waco shouted. "They're here."

At the courthouse, Lonnie and his companions dismounted, looping the reins of their horses about the hitch rail. Then they all sat down on the courthouse steps. Gus and Waco, hearing the door to the cell block open, turned to face their barred door.

"Time to go," said Sheriff Singleton. Reaching through the bars, he handcuffed Waco's wrists. He then secured Gus's wrists in the same manner. He unlocked the cell door and, standing back, allowed the two prisoners to emerge. In his hand was a cocked Colt.

"Here they come," Dallas said, getting to his feet.

The rest of the outfit stood up, facing the approaching lawman and his captives. Lonnie stepped out, confronting the sheriff.

"Sheriff," Lonnie said, "I'm Lonnie Kilgore, trail boss, and these men are part of my outfit. I hope you have no objection to us attending this inquest."

"None," said Singleton, "as long as there is no disturbance. Disrupt the proceedings, and the judge will clear the courtroom."

Sheriff Singleton marched Waco and Gus in ahead of him. Lonnie and his companions followed. There weren't more than a dozen people in the courtroom, and the judge had not yet taken the bench.

Sheriff Singleton led Waco and Gus directly to a narrow table facing the bench. Lonnie, Dallas, Dirk, Kirby, Sandy, Benjamin, Elliot, and Justin took the row of chairs directly behind them. Waco and Gus looked around the room. Leaning back as far as he could, Waco whispered to Lonnie.

"That gent in the derby hat was the house dealer last night, and beside him is Rufe, one of the barkeeps."

"No talking," said Singleton. "All stand."

Judge Elias Guerdon entered the courtroom and took his seat. He immediately spoke.

"This is an inquest, not a trial. Whether or not there is a trial will depend on how the defense pleads and on the evidence presented. What are the charges?"

"Gus Wilder and Waco Talley provoked my son during a poker game. Talley shot and killed my son, Billy."

"Ah," said Judge Guerdon, "and how does the defense plead?"

"Not guilty, sir," Waco said, getting to his feet. "I fired only in self-defense after the Singleton gent had shot at me twice."

"I suppose you have witnesses," said Judge Guerdon.

"I do," Waco replied. "The four friends who were with me and Gus."

"I object to that," shouted Sheriff Singleton. "They are prejudiced. They'll each repeat what the prior witness said."

"Overruled," Judge Guerdon said. "None shall hear the testimony of the others. Those four men the defense calls as witnesses, please stand."

Sandy Orr, Benjamin Raines, Elliot Graves, and Justin Irwin all stood.

"You will testify first," said Judge Guerdon, pointing to Sandy Orr. "The other three of you will wait in the corridor, each of you testifying in turn. Bailiff, remove those three men. "You," he said, pointing to Sandy, "mount the box and take the oath."

Sandy stated his name, took the oath, and repeated the incident of the night before, as it had happened. Sandy was dismissed, and one by one, Benjamin, Justin, and Elliot took the stand and repeated the same story. The judge wiped his brow. It was highly unlikely—perhaps even impossible—that four men could relate the same story, with none of them having heard the testimony of the others. Judge Guerdon took the only possible door that was open to him.

"I understand that this whole thing happened after one Waco Talley asked for a new deck of cards?"

"That's what it amounts to," Waco said. "Gus got the old deck, and after he had taken out the jacks, kings, queens, and aces, we could see those cards had been shaved. Billy Singleton drew on me then, but I was ahead of him. I offered to forget the whole thing if he would leave peaceful. Before he reached the door, he turned and fired twice. I was saved only because one of my pards yelled at me."

"So you shot him," said Judge Guerdon.

"I did," Waco said. "It was my life or his. I didn't do a thing any other man wouldn't have done."

"I see," said Judge Guerdon. "Does the defense have other witnesses?"

"Judge," Gus said, "I see last night's house dealer and one of the bartenders are here. "I'd like for you to hear what they have to say. Rufe is the bartender, but I don't know the dealer's name."

"Rufe Elkins and Ernie Gordon," Sheriff Singleton said, "but I object to their being called. Rufe was a considerable distance away. When I arrived, Ernie Gordon's spectacles were lying on the table, and he can't see without them."

"Overruled," Judge Guerdon said. "The court wishes to hear the testimony of these unprejudiced witnesses. Mr. Gordon, will you take the stand?"

Gordon did so, looking into the stormy eyes of Sheriff Al Singleton.

"Now," Judge Guerdon said, after the house dealer had been sworn in, "suppose you tell the court what you saw last night."

"I saw a man who had been branded a cheat try to shoot his accuser in the back," said the house dealer. "I can't add anything to what those who have testified have already said."

"You lying son-of-a-bitch," Sheriff Singleton roared, "you'll never work in this town again."

"Nor will you, Sheriff Singleton," said Judge Guerdon coldly. "It's becoming more and more evident that Billy Singleton—your son—was shot and killed while trying to do some killing on his own, and you're attempting to cover up his wrongdoing. Mr. Gordon," he said to the house dealer, "do you have that doctored deck of cards?"

"I do," Gordon said, placing them on the podium before the judge.

Every eye was on Judge Guerdon as he fanned out the cards, separating jacks, queens, kings, and aces. His cold eyes on Sheriff Singleton, the judge spoke.

"These cards speak for themselves, Sheriff. Would you care to look at them?"

"No," said Singleton in a choked voice.

"Are there more witnesses for the defense?" Judge Guerden asked.

"Elkins, the barkeep," said Waco.

"Rufe Elkins, take the stand," Judge Guerdon said.

Nervously, his eyes on Sheriff Singleton, Elkins made his way to the stand and quickly was sworn in. He spoke reluctantly, stumbling along, but he told the same story the judge had already heard repeatedly.

"Does the prosecution want to question this witness or any of the others?" the judge asked. "If not, the witness may step down."

His relief obvious, Elkins left the stand.

"I have reached a verdict," Judge Guerdon said. "All stand, and the two accused will approach the bench."

Gus and Waco stood up and approached the bench.

"Based on what I have heard," said Judge Guerdon, "and the fundamental right every man has to defend his own life, I am declaring this a case of self-defense. Sheriff, you will remove the cuffs from these men. After that, we stand adjourned, and Sheriff, I want to see you in my quarters immediately."

Sheriff Singleton's eyes were stormy as he removed the

irons from the wrists of Waco and Gus. The lawman then did a strange thing. Ripping the star from his vest, he dropped it before the judge. When he spoke, his voice was bitter.

"You want my badge, damn you, here it is."

With that, he walked out of the courtroom. Gus and Waco were congratulated by their comrades, and they hurried to catch up to the house dealer and the barkeep who had testified on their behalf.

"You gents have done this town a favor," said Ernie Gordon, the house dealer. "I am ashamed of myself for having kept silent for all these years about Billy Singleton's cheating with marked cards. We put up with him because we were afraid his daddy would come down on us. The sheriff can drum up enough reasons to close a saloon, if he's a mind to."

"The question is," Rufe Elkins said, "what's he goin' to do now that he's given up his star? He's liable to sneak around and shoot Gordon and me."

"If he goes after anybody," said Gus, "I expect him to come gunning for Waco and me."

"One problem there," Waco said. "Tomorrow we'll be on our way to Utah. I reckon we messed things up for you, Lonnie. It might not be safe bringing the wagon into town for supplies."

"I think it'll be safe enough," said Lonnie. "As soon as we return to the herd, we can harness the teams, load up the ladies, and come back to the mercantile. Tomorrow we'll be on the Green River Trail again."

They returned to the herd and a joyous welcome. Even Wovoka shook their hands, although he wasn't quite sure what the occasion was.

"Now," Lonnie said, "the rest of us are going into town to load the wagon with some of the supplies we're out of, or nearly out of. I want the six of you to remain here with the herd and horse remuda. Wovoka, scalp anybody that tries to leave."

The Indian grinned, a rare thing for him. It was the kind of joke he understood.

"Stay out of the saloons," Justin shouted as the wagon rolled away.

Becky drove the wagon, while Lonnie, Dallas, Dirk, Kirby, and the other three women rode alongside. They reached town without difficulty, with only a few citizens pausing to watch them. Reaching the mercantile, Becky expertly backed the wagon up to the store's loading dock.

"Who's goin' in?" Dallas asked.

"We all are," said Lonnie. "We're an outfit, and we're not broke. Just keep in mind we have only so much space in the wagon, and we need to devote most of it to grub to see us through the coming winter."

Becky stopped to admire a long dress that had numerous petticoats beneath it, and beneath them, ankle-length pantaloons.

"What would you do if you saw me in that?" Becky said.

"Likely not what you'd expect," said Lonnie. "If I had to fight my way through all of that, I'd probably just forget it."

Mindy was nearby, had heard the exchange, and was laughing. Despite their fleeting interest in women's finery, it was the women who chose the supplies to restock their wagon. They bought all the dried apples the store had in stock, added a barrel of flour, a barrel of meal, five cured hams, and half a dozen sides of bacon.

"I got fresh eggs," said the storekeeper.

"How many?" Becky asked.

"Seven dozen," said the merchant.

"We'll take them all," Becky said. "How about coffee beans?"

"They're in ten-pound bags," said the storekeeper, "and I got twenty bags. That's two hundred pounds."

"We'll take a hundred pounds," Lonnie said. "We may not have room for all that."

"I ain't settin' through a High Plains winter without hot coffee," said Kirby Lowe. "Not even if each of us has to thong a bag of it behind his saddle."

"That's kind of how I feel," Dallas said, "and I reckon the *hombres* with the herd will agree. Some things a man just can't do without."

"I hate to say this, as opposed as I am to whiskey," said Becky, "but we ought to buy another two gallons for snake-bite."

"Don't forget the laudanum," Mindy said. "We only brought one bottle, and you've had most of that after the mule bit you."

"Damn it," Becky hissed, "don't be talking in public about that blasted mule biting me. Having the rest of the outfit know is embarrassing enough."

"Good thing you was in the saddle," said Dallas. "If the critter had chomped down on your behind, you'd have been sleeping standing up."

Lonnie, Dallas, and Mindy were laughing. Becky blushed furiously and walked away. It took them more than two hours in the store to replenish their supplies in the wagon. Their departure from town seemed as unnoticed as their arrival.

The herd of longhorns and the horses were grazing peacefully, and the riders were taking advantage of the occasion. They were relaxed, drinking coffee. Wovoka went to the fire and filled his cup, draining the pot.

"The *hombre* that drains the pot has to make the next pot of coffee," Sandy Orr said.

"Ugh," said Wovoka, shaking his head. "Squaw work."

"The squaws ain't likely to be back for a while," Waco said. "I'll swallow my pride for as long as it takes to boil some more coffee."

Waco emptied the grounds out of the two-gallon granite pot and started for the nearby Rio Grande. Suddenly there was a shot, and Waco stiffened, stumbled backward, and fell on the grassy riverbank. By the time his companions reached him, blood had begun soaking the left side of his shirt just above his gunbelt. His eyes were closed, his breathing shallow.

"I'll get some mud," Gus shouted. "We have to stop the bleeding."

Sandy Orr, Benjamin Raines, and Elliot Graves quickly removed the bloody shirt, and they looked at one another with tragic eyes. The wound was low down. Suddenly there was the patter of hooves as Wovoka rode east toward the Pecos.

"Wovoka's goin' after the dry-gulching bastard," said Justin Irwin. "Waco's hit hard enough to need a doctor, and I'm riding to Santa Fe to find one. I'll likely see Lonnie and the others there, or meet them on their way back. I'll tell them what happened. Those of you that ain't scared to talk to the Almighty, say some words that old Waco will be alive when the doc gets here."

Justin kicked his horse into a fast gallop, and by the time he was halfway to town, he could see the approaching wagon, with his comrades riding beside it. Becky reined up, for she had recognized Justin.

"Dear God," said Laura, "something's happened at camp."

"Waco's been bushwhacked," Justin yelled, reining up in a cloud of dust.

"How bad?" Lonnie asked.

"Plenty bad," said Justin. "Low down, and bleedin' something awful. Gus and the rest are trying to stop the bleeding with mud. Wovoka's gone after the yellow coyote that shot him."

"What direction?" Lonnie asked.

"East, toward the Pecos," said Justin.

"Dallas," Lonnie said, "I want you to ride back to Santa Fe with Justin, in case there's some trouble getting a doc to Waco. Hog-tie him, if you have to. Kirby, I want you and

Dirk to accompany the wagon the rest of the way to camp. I'll be there as soon as I can. I aim to take whatever trail Wovoka's following. I think I know who we're looking for, and I can promise you it'll be his last trail.''

"*Vaya con Dios,*" Becky shouted as Lonnie galloped his horse eastward, while Justin and Dallas rode toward Santa Fe. Kirby, Dirk, Mindy, Laura, and April rode close to the wagon, while Becky urged the teams to a faster gait.

"Here comes the wagon!" Gus shouted, as he saw the vehicle and its outriders coming at a gallop.

"I don't see Lonnie or Dallas," said Sandy Orr.

Becky reined up the teams and all but fell off the wagon box. The rest of the riders were out of their saddles in an instant, hurrying to the blanket-covered Waco. It was Becky who raised the blanket, revealing Waco's terrible wound. She caught her breath and expelled it with a sob. The wound had begun bleeding again.

"Mindy," said Becky desperately, "get me the medicine chest from the wagon. Some of you bring more mud—plenty of mud—from the river."

Becky covered the bleeding wound with a slab of mud three inches thick. Over that, to hold it in place, she wrapped a bandage all the way around Waco's middle.

"Where's Lonnie and Dallas?" Benjamin Raines asked.

"Lonnie sent Dallas back to Santa Fe with Justin," Dirk McNelly said. "Lonnie's riding east, hoping to pick up Wovoka's trail. They're going to ride down the bushwhacker."

"I reckon some of us should have gone after him," said Elliot Graves, "but Wovoka had already lit out, and it looked like Waco needed all the help he could get."

"You did the right thing," Becky assured him. "Whoever did this won't get away."

Lonnie pushed his horse as hard as he dared, stopping to rest the animal when he had to. Eventually he came upon the wagon tracks that led from the Pecos to the Rio Grande. There were two new sets of horse tracks, one virtually on top of the other, heading east toward the Pecos.

A few miles ahead, Wovoka rested his horse and rode on. He had his Bowie slipped under his waistband and his fully loaded Colt in his left hand. These whites had treated him as an equal, and now one of them lay dead—or nearly dead—as the result of a cowardly gunman shooting from cover. Ahead, he saw a small cloud of dust, and he urged his tired horse on. The rider ahead of him twisted around in the saddle and fired three times with his six-gun. But the range was too great, and the two horses galloped on. Slowly but surely Wovoka's horse gained on the weary horse ahead.

Two or three miles behind, Lonnie heard the three pistol shots and urged his horse to an even faster gait. Finally there was a fourth shot, and all was silence.

"Damn it," Lonnie groaned. "Damn it."

His own mount was staggering and he dismounted, sparing the animal. Whatever was going to happen already had. Finally, far ahead, there came a horse. Lonnie recognized the horse and Wovoka. As the Indian drew nearer, Lonnie could see that he had a horse on a lead rope. Wovoka reined up and Lonnie went to the led horse. A man lay belly-down over the saddle. Taking him by the hair, Lonnie raised his head and found himself looking into the dead face of former Santa Fe Sheriff Al Singleton.

"*Bueno*, Wovoka," said Lonnie. "You're one *hombre* to ride the river with."

"Waco my *amigo*," Wovoka said. "Kill this *cobarde*."*

*Coward.

14

Lonnie and Wovoka rode into camp, Wovoka leading the horse with Singleton's body.

"Is that who we think it is?" Kirby Lowe asked.

"Former Sheriff Al Singleton," said Lonnie. "Wovoka got to him before I did. How is Waco?"

"I managed to get the bleeding stopped," Becky said, "but he's still in a bad way. He was hit in the side, and the lead's still in there."

"There's nothing we can do except wait for the doctor," said Lonnie.

"It's a pretty good ride," Benjamin said. "I just hope he'll come."

"He will," said Lonnie. "Dallas and Justin will see to that."

"We got to do somethin' with this dead coyote," Dirk McNelly said. "You aim to take him back to town?"

"No," said Lonnie. "He's no longer a lawman. We'll bury him here beside the river so the coyotes and buzzards can't get at him. That's more than he deserves."

"Elliot," Gus said, "let's get the shovels from the wagon and start digging the grave."

The outfit waited impatiently for almost an hour before a distant cloud of dust rose, marking the return of Dallas, Justin, and a man in a buckboard with a black bag beside him on the seat. Reining up his team, he stepped down from the buckboard. Lonnie was the first to reach him, and the doctor had some hard words to say.

"I'm tired of being fetched out of town to patch up some bullet-riddled outlaw. I want all of you to know that I'm here under protest."

"Sorry to inconvenience you," said Lonnie, "but we're not outlaws. We're Texans, with a herd of Texas cattle on our way to Utah. A bushwhacker shot one of our riders, and it seems he's in a bad way. I'm Lonnie Kilgore, trail boss."

"I am Dr. Bennigan," the medic said. "Show me to the wounded man."

Lonnie led him to the pile of blankets under which Waco rested. The doctor drew back the blankets and removed the huge slab of mud from Waco's side. The wound immediately began to bleed again.

"Hot water, and plenty of it," Dr. Bennigan said. "That lead has to come out."

"We got whiskey, Doc, if you need it," said Dallas.

Dr. Bennigan said nothing, waiting for the hot water. Laura and April brought two big pots of boiling water.

"You stay here and assist me," Bennigan said, pointing to April. "The rest of you stay back out of the way."

Timidly, April moved in beside the doctor, while the rest of the outfit gathered a few yards away. Elliot and Gus returned with their shovels, having buried Al Singleton. Almost an hour passed before Dr. Bennigan got to his feet, and when he spoke, there was an urgency in his voice.

"I got the lead out, but I can't promise you he'll make it. He's lost a lot of blood. I have a small hospital, and it may help his chances if we take him there. At least I can see that he's free of infection and that the bleeding doesn't start again.''

''Take him there, Doctor,'' Lonnie said, ''and don't spare any expense. We can pay.''

''Leave him on those blankets and cover him as best you can,'' said Dr. Bennigan. ''If you like, some of you can sit with him until he improves or . . .''

''He left the sentence unfinished, but they all knew what he meant.

''We've been pards a long time,'' Gus said. ''I'll ride in and stay with him tonight.''

''I'll be there to take over in the morning,'' said Justin.

''You can count on all of us, Doctor,'' Lonnie said. ''On behalf of us all, I want to say thanks for coming.''

Lonnie extended his hand, and instead of shaking Dr. Bennigan's hand, he placed five double eagles in the surprised medical man's palm.

''That's far too much, and not necessary at this time,'' said Dr. Bennigan.

''Doc,'' Lonnie said, ''if Waco pulls through, that's not even half enough.''

Gus, Dallas, Justin, and Kirby had lifted the blanket-wrapped Waco as gently as they could. It was Gus who spoke to the doctor.

''Doc, the four of us will ride in with you and help get him into the house.''

The doctor nodded, mounting to the seat of his buckboard. Lonnie said nothing, knowing that only Gus would remain with the wounded Waco. The buckboard whirled away in a cloud of dust, two of the four men riding on either side of it.

''He has to live,'' said April with a sob. ''The Green River range won't be the same unless we are all there.''

''We'll all be there,'' Lonnie said, with a confidence he didn't feel.

Dallas, Justin, and Kirby soon returned from town.

"We got Waco there and into the doc's house," said Waco. "He said if Waco makes it through tonight, he'll likely recover. If there's any change for the worse, he'll send Gus to let us know."

"God, I hope we don't see Gus tonight," Justin Irwin said.

The others remained silent, for Justin had spoken for them all. Afternoon slowly faded to night as a chill wind swept in from the north. Supper was mostly a silent affair. Lonnie and Becky took the first watch, filling in for Gus and Waco. Becky rode beside Lonnie, and despite his reluctance, he was forced to talk to her.

"Even if Waco lives," said Becky, "it'll be a week or two before he can ride. That may hurt our chances of reaching the Green River range ahead of the winter snows. What can we do?"

"We'll wait and take our chances with the snow," Lonnie said irritably. "Don't you think Waco's worth it?"

"You know I do," said Becky. "I'd spend the winter here and go on in the spring, if it took that long for Waco to heal."

"I expect we'll know something when Gus returns in the morning," Lonnie said.

Sante Fe. August 12, 1853.

Justin Irwin rode out at dawn, prepared to sit with the wounded Waco during the day. Other riders had already volunteered for the next two days and nights, if needed. Reaching town, Justin knocked on the door and was admitted by Dr. Bennigan. The doctor's eyes were red, as though he'd had little or no sleep. He led Justin into the sickroom, and Gus looked as weary as the doctor.

"He's had a bad night," Dr. Bennigan said. "We've given him everything, including whiskey, and he's had a raging fever. It's dropped in the last hour, and that could be a good sign.''

"I'll watch him today, Doc," said Justin, "and Dallas Weaver will be here tonight. You need some sleep. Lie down somewhere, and I'll holler if there's trouble.''

"Within the next hour," Dr. Bennigan said, "if he still has any temperature at all, get some more of that whiskey down him.''

Gus rode back to camp, and all of the outfit gathered around, looking for some sign that their comrade had survived. Quickly, Gus told them the little that he knew.

"We couldn't break his fever," said Gus, "and we tried everything, including a quart of whiskey. It came down a little this morning before daylight, but the doc said it wasn't near enough. He aims to see that Waco gets more whiskey every hour until his fever breaks.''

Gus unsaddled his horse and then sank down on his saddle, burying his face in his hands. It seemed so long ago and so far away that he and Waco—neither quite twelve—had wrestled maverick cows out of the Brazos River brakes in south Texas. Silently he did something he had done only once or twice in his life. He prayed.

"Gus," said Becky softly, "we saved you some breakfast.''

"Thanks," Gus said, "but I don't feel like eating.''

"Perhaps some coffee, then," Becky persisted.

"Coffee, then," said Gus.

Becky brought the tin cup and set it down beside him, but with his head resting on his knees, Gus was asleep.

"I reckon it's good news," Dallas said when noon came and went without Justin riding in. "I'm bettin' that by tonight Waco will whip that fever.''

An hour before sundown, Justin still hadn't returned, and Dallas saddled his horse and headed for town. When he knocked on Dr. Bennigan's door, it was opened by Justin.

"His fever broke just a little while after Gus rode back to camp," said Justin. "The doc is gettin' a few winks. He's been up for two nights straight."

"Ride on back to camp and take them the news," Dallas said. "Now that his fever has broken, we might not have to sit with him all the time. But if I'm not back by suppertime, have one of the others ride in to replace me."

"I will," said Justin, "but the doc's official word is that if Waco gets plenty of rest and good food, he'll recover."

Breakfast was in progress as Justin rode into camp, but all activity ceased as the outfit all gathered around.

"Waco's fever broke this morning," Justin said, "and the doc believes that with plenty of rest and good food, Waco will be all right."

That brought some glad shouts from the outfit. There was even a look of relief on the haggard face of Wovoka. They all resumed eating with renewed appetites.

"Waco's goin' to hate it, us losing this much time on the drive," said Sandy Orr.

"I hate it, too," Lonnie said, "but it's not Waco's fault. We'll wait for him as long as we have to."

It was still early afternoon when Dallas rode in from town. His horse trotting, there was no evidence of urgency. Dallas dismounted and, before unsaddling his horse, spoke to the gathered outfit.

"Waco talked to me a while ago and said the hangover from all that whiskey is worse than the gunshot wound. The doc's wife fed him two bowls of soup. We can visit him a few of us at a time, but we don't have to set with him."

"Did you tell him we got the bastard that shot him?" Lonnie asked.

"I told him Wovoka ran down the bushwhacker," said Dallas. "Waco said he'd marry that Indian, if he wasn't so damn ugly."

The outfit shouted with laughter, Wovoka joining in. After

supper, Lonnie brought up something had been bothering him.

"Tomorrow we're going to be forced to move upriver. The graze here is gone, and in another day or two, the cows and horses will be racks of bones."

"That won't be a problem," Dallas said. "We can just move a couple of miles each day until Waco's on his feet."

"It may be more of a problem than you think," said Gus. "Doc Bennigan told me that to the north of here—the way we're headed—there's some almighty big herds of sheep depenin' on that graze."

"Then when we reach the sheep range," Lonnie said, "we'll just have to drive beyond it. We're just passing through, and I can't see involving ourselves in a range war."

The following day, they moved their camp two miles north along the Rio Grande. The graze would be adequate for maybe two days. The outfit took turns riding in to visit the fast-healing Waco. When Lonnie rode in, it was Waco who spoke of the many sheep in the area and of a possible shortage of graze for their cattle and horses.

"I got to get out of here," said Waco, "and we got to get far enough north that these damn woolies ain't a problem. Find Doc and ask him when I'll be able to get up and out of here."

"Two more days," Dr. Bennigan said, "and even then, no exerting yourself. Break that wound open and start it bleeding, and you'll have to endure this whole thing all over again, including the whiskey."

"I reckon I can't ride, then," said Waco.

"Not on a horse," Dr. Bennigan said, "but you have a wagon, don't you?"

"Yeah," said Waco without enthusiasm, "but it'll never replace a horse and saddle."

"You can always remain here another week until you're fully healed," Dr. Bennigan said slyly.

"Thinkin' about it," said Waco, "maybe that wagon seat wouldn't be so bad, me settin' there with Becky one day and

Mindy the next. Two pretty girls can make a man swallow his pride and like it.''

On the day the wagon passed the closest to Santa Fe, Becky was at the reins. Gus and Justin accompanied the wagon, and Becky drove into town. Waco was anxiously awaiting them, looking thin and hungry. Becky stepped down from the wagon, while Gus and Justin gave Waco a hand getting aboard.

''Dr. Bennigan,'' Becky said, ''Lonnie wants you to have this.''

She dropped five more double eagles in the surprised doctor's hand.

''That's entirely too much,'' said Dr. Bennigan.

''Take it, and remember us,'' Becky said. ''We're Texans, and we look out for people who have proven themselves. You have, and we're obliged.''

Mounting the wagon box, she drove away, Gus and Justin trotting their horses alongside the wagon. They soon caught up to the slow-moving herd, and the wagon fell in behind the horse remuda. The outfit waved their hats at Waco, and he waved back. Instead of riding beside Lonnie, Wovoka turned his horse and rode back to the wagon. Dropping back, Gus allowed the Indian to get close to Waco.

''*Amigo,*'' said Wovoka. ''*Bueno hombre.*''

The Indian extended his right hand, and Waco took it. Wordlessly, Wovoka kicked his horse into a lope, rejoining Lonnie at the head of the herd.

Come sundown, the drive was twelve miles north of Santa Fe along the Rio Grande.

''After supper,'' Lonnie said, ''we'll have to study that map some. As I recall, we'll be leaving the Rio Grande tomorrow and following the Rio Chama for a ways.''

''What are we going to do about that gold we took from them owlhoots that stole it in Santa Fe?'' Kirby asked.

''I haven't forgotten it,'' said Lonnie. ''The town will have to appoint another sheriff to serve until next election day. There's no sign of any storm on the way, and the drive has settled down. In the morning, I'll choose one of you to ride with me. We'll load all the gold on a horse and return it to town. If no new sheriff's been appointed, then maybe we can talk to Judge Guerdon.''

But before dark, a horseman rode in from the south. On the left pocket of his flannel shirt was a lawman's star. Reining up, he spoke.

''I'm Elkin Potts, the new sheriff.''

''I'm Lonnie Kilgore, trail boss,'' said Lonnie. ''Step down and I'll introduce you to the rest of the outfit.''

''That won't be necessary,'' Potts said stiffly. ''I came here for some information. Al Singleton and me growed up together, and he was my *amigo*. I ain't sayin' what he done was right, but I want to know what you done with him. I know he rode after you.''

''He did,'' said Lonnie, ''and he bushwhacked one of my riders. You'll find him maybe a dozen miles south on the west bank of the Rio Grande. We buried him.''

''I'm obliged for that,'' Potts said, reining his horse around to depart.

''One other thing,'' said Lonnie. ''Before we left the Pecos, we met four *hombres* heading south. They looked like a bad lot. We figured you'd like to know, in case they'd been up to something here in town.''

It was an opportune time for Potts to tell them of the stolen gold, if in fact it had been stolen in Santa Fe, but Potts did not. When he spoke, his voice was hard and cold.

''If there'd been any law work that needed doin', Al Singleton would of done it. He was a good sheriff, and I reckon he wouldn't want a bunch of strangers buttin' into the town's business. Neither do I, so don't do us no favors. Just go on the way you're headed, and don't none of you come back. You ain't welcome.''

He wheeled his horse and rode back the way he had come.

"Well," said Dallas, "are you still ridin' back to Santa Fe in the morning?"

"I reckon not," Lonnie said. "I've just been told I'm not welcome."

"But what about the gold?" Becky asked.

"It goes with us," said Lonnie. "If they refuse to claim it, then they don't get it. Once we're settled on the Green River range, I'm thinking we can use that money to bring us a herd of those blooded Spanish horses from California. It could become the grandest horse ranch in the West, and it would be jointly owned by us all. Anybody object to that?"

"Lord, no," Gus Wilder said, "if you're sayin' what I *think* you're saying. You would take in Waco, Sandy, Benjamin, Elliot, Justin, and me as pardners?"

"That's exactly what I'm saying," said Lonnie, "and I think we'll have to make plans to include Wovoka. He won't fool with cows, but I don't think he'll feel like horse ranching is for squaws."

"Horse *bueno*," Wovoka said.

"Nobody objects, then," said Lonnie.

"You could have lived a lifetime and never come up with something as grand as that," Dallas said. "What about it, everybody?"

There was hand-clapping and shouts of approval. The six cowboys who had hired on for wages shouted the loudest, for they had before them a future that might have been forever denied them in Texas.

"Now," said Lonnie, "all of you on the first watch saddle up, and let's get this night behind us. I want us to move on tomorrow. I can't believe this acting sheriff would go so far as to try and take revenge, but the sooner we can remove the temptation, the better."

After Waco's replacement on first watch had ridden out, Lonnie brought the big map near the fire. Dallas, Benjamin,

Elliot, and Justin gathered around as Lonnie studied the map.

"My hunkers ain't back to normal," said Waco. "I'll go along with what the rest of you decide needs doing."

"I'm beginning to think that following the Rio Grande is more trouble than it's worth. Tomorrow," Lonnie said, "we'll leave the Rio Grande and follow the Chama River for maybe thirty miles. It looks like maybe twenty-five miles after we leave the Chama to the next stretch of water, which is unnamed on this map."*

"There," said Dallas, "we follow the Animas River maybe seventy miles to the north, where it passes Durango, and from there, it looks like maybe seventy-five miles until we reach the confluence of the Animas and the Gunnison. There we should be able to follow the Gunnison all the way to the Colorado. We'll follow it maybe twenty-five miles and then cross it into eastern Utah. From there we won't be more than thirty miles south of Willow Creek, which is a runoff from the Green. When we reach Willow Creek, we're maybe forty miles from home."

"You reckon he's right about them distances, Lonnie?" Dirk McNelly asked.

"Close, I reckon," said Lonnie. "We don't know how accurate this map is, or whether or not we can depend on the scale being right."

"Why don't we add up the total miles, anyway?" Mindy suggested. "I'd like to have an idea as to how far we still have to go."

"I've been adding," said Waco, scratching on the ground with a stick. "Looks like we are maybe 220 miles miles out of Durango. From there, it's 325 miles to our Green River range. From here, we're still maybe 545 miles away."

"My God," Becky cried, "we'll never make it ahead of the snow."

*Present-day name of this is Cañon Largo, a tributary of the San Juan.

"We'll keep to the fast gait," said Lonnie. "It's all we can do."

The Chama River. August 18, 1853.

The day dawned clear and hot. By the time the sun was two hours high, horses, cows, and humans were dripping sweat. According to their calculations, they would follow the Chama for thirty miles. Waco was well enough to ride, and took pleasure in being back in the saddle. It was near sundown when Lonnie judged the river deep enough and the graze good enough for their camp.

"Some of this water across western New Mexico and southwestern Colorado might not be as plentiful as we think," said Justin Irwin. "From what I've heard, water to the High Plains comes mostly from melting snow."

"If the map shows a river or creek," said Lonnie, "I feel sure there'll be some water."

"I don't feel that sure," Dallas said, "but I'm hoping. Except for us ridin' back to Texas from California, we don't know this territory."

"No," said Lonnie, "we don't. We're far enough from Santa Fe for the Paiutes to take notice of us. I'll have Wovoka ride twenty miles or so each day, looking for any Indian sign."

The first watch mounted and rode out. Laura and April rode with Kirby and Dirk. All seemed serene, and the wind from the northwest had a chill bite to it. The rest of the outfit had rolled in their blankets to get what sleep they could before the start of the second watch. When midnight came, the second watch saddled up. Becky joined Lonnie, and Mindy rode with Dallas. So much had happened, there had been little time for conversation. The women had not ridden watch while Becky and Waco had been injured. Now they felt a need to talk.

"We still have more than five hundred miles ahead of us,"

Becky said, "and I'm afraid of what might happen. Either before we reach the Green River range or after we get there."

"I think we're doing right well, taking care of anything that happens along the way," said Lonnie. "The most troublesome unknown factor is how those Mormons are likely goin' to object to us movin' in."

"Then whatever happens between here and there, we'll still have a fight on our hands when we arrive," Becky said.

"I expect so," said Lonnie, "but we're not ridin' in with our defenses down. Before we reach our range, I aim for Wovoka and me to have a look around, so we'll know what we are up against before we ride into the midst of it."

"I understand the need for that," Becky said, "but if they know we're claiming a large part of the Green River range, how did they find out? Maybe we can move in and settle down before they know we're coming."

"I wish I could believe they don't know," said Lonnie, "but there's a big land map of Utah Territory at Fort Laramie. Every claim that's been filed for has been marked off. The Mormons may not know who's coming, but they'll know somebody is. I wish I could talk to Jim Bridger. He'd have some idea as to what might be about to happen."

Mindy was having an equally disturbing conversation with Dallas.

"I suppose I'm expecting too much of the government and its soldiers, where Indians are concerned," said Mindy. "There must be thousands and thousands of them. But surely there's not so many Mormons that they can just take over a territory."

"If Bridger was right and they did overrun his trading post," Dallas said, "I expect the first thing the government will do is force them to give up Bridger's place. Maybe then the army will help us, but we can't wait. Someday the frontier will become civilized and the law will say what's right and what's wrong. But I doubt any of us will live to see that day.

We'll have to go on stomping our own snakes."

Dallas was more right than he knew, for at that moment, Wovoka dismounted near the river. He had heard something. Listening, he heard it again. There was some slight movement within the water that was almost totally drowned out by the gurgle of the river. The moon had set, and there was only starlight. Wovoka drew his Bowie and flattened himself on the ground. Slowly, a man's head rose above the riverbank. There was little or no disturbance of the water as he climbed out of the river. The stranger wore only a loincloth, and Wovoka grinned in savage glee. It was one of the hated Paiutes! Wovoka drew his Bowie and lunged, but his adversary was quick and sidestepped Wovoka's thrust. The Paiute countered with a thrust of his own, but Wovoka was just out of reach. Like the head of a darting rattler, his blade flashed in the pale starlight, but the Paiute seized his arm, while attempting to thrust his own Bowie into Wovoka's belly. But Wovoka used his right knee to good advantage. He slammed it into the Paiute's groin, and with a groan of anguish, he released Wovoka's arm. Three times Wovoka drove the Bowie into the Paiute's belly, and he collapsed to move no more.

"Haaiii," Wovoka grunted.

Lonnie and the rest of the outfit had heard the brief scuffle on the riverbank and had witnessed Wovoka's victory.

"*Bueno*, Wovoka," said Lonnie. "The Paiutes know we're here, and this one was sent to take our measure."

"*Sí,*" Wovoka said, pleased. "Kill Paiute."

"I doubt they'll try anything else tonight," said Lonnie, "but we'll strictly have to keep our eyes open until we're out of their territory. If it hadn't been for Wovoka's keen ears, this gent might have stampeded the cows as well as the horse remuda. Wovoka, I'll want you to ride quite a ways ahead in the morning. The rest of this *hombre*'s tribe may be closer than we think."

"*Sí,*" Wovoka said, pleased.

The second watch mounted their horses and again began circling the cattle and horses.

"That's the first time I've ever seen a man die by the knife," said Becky in a slightly trembling voice.

"I'm sorry you had to witness it," Lonnie said, "but Wovoka did what he had to."

"You could have shot the Paiute, helping Wovoka out of a dangerous situation," said Becky. "Why didn't you?"

Lonnie laughed. "Wovoka would have hated my guts. He did battle with an enemy and won, knife against knife. It would have shamed him to have had one of us shoot and kill his opponent. Besides that, there's the chance a gunshot might have stampeded the herd."

The rest of the night was peaceful, and the outfit was ready for breakfast when the first gray light of dawn shone in the east. Wovoka had gone to find the dead Paiute's horse.

"Gus," said Lonnie, "I want you and Justin to get some shovels from the wagon and bury that Paiute. Try to cover the grave with leaves as best you can. Once they learn their scout is dead, they'll be hell-bent on revenge."

"They'll know he's dead when he don't come back," Kirby Lowe said. "By tonight, I'd say we'd all better be on watch."

"You're right about that," said Elliot Graves.

"We'll take care of tonight when it gets here," Lonnie said. "Wovoka will ride along the Chama for at least twenty miles, looking for sign."

"If they're smart, they won't leave any sign along the river," said Sandy Orr. "They'll ride far enough from the river to avoid us finding their sign."

"That won't stop Wovoka," Lonnie said. "Once he's ridden the twenty miles, if he's found no Indian sign, he'll ride half a dozen miles parallel to each bank of the river. The Paiutes are going to learn a hard lesson, I think, because it's Indian against Indian.''

"*Sí,*" said Wovoka. "Kill Paiute."

15

On the Chama River. August 19, 1853.

*W*ovoka returned in time for breakfast, leading the horse that had belonged to last night's dead Paiute. He loosed the animal with their own remuda. Breakfast over, Lonnie spent a few minutes with Wovoka. The Shoshone had learned enough English until it had become much easier to communicate with him. He mounted his horse and rode out, following the Chama. Within minutes, the outfit had the herd moving, with the horse remuda at their heels. Becky was on the wagon box, while Mindy, April, and Laura rode close to the wagon.

"Dallas said we're supposed to watch the back trail," Mindy said. "With all our horses back here behind the herd, the Indians might hit the drive from behind. I think all of us ought to arm ourselves with some of the Colts taken from that bunch of outlaws who tried to bushwhack us."

"Good idea," said Becky. "Here."

From beneath the wagon seat, she passed Mindy one of the gunbelts with a loaded Colt in the holster. Laura and April made similar requests, and were each handed one of the gun rigs with its Colt.

"This belt's too big," April complained. "It'll slide down around my feet the minute I dismount."

"Loop it around your saddle horn," said Laura. "That's what I'm doing with mine."

Dallas, Gus, Sandy, Benjamin, Elliot, and Justin rode drag, bunching the horses close on the heels of the herd of longhorns. Long without rain, the ground was dry, and in the air, clouds of dust hung stationary, as though they might remain there indefinitely. The herd, the horses, and the riders were sweat-soaked. Becky wiped her sweating face on the sleeve of her shirt and made an unladylike comment her three companions thought uproariously funny.

"I need to go to the bushes for a minute or two," Mindy said, "but I'm afraid to go by myself after having that outlaw carry me away."

"I don't see how you could have any moisture left in you, the way we're sweating," said Laura. "Dallas is riding drag. You can get him to stop with you."

"Damn it," Mindy said, "I don't want the whole outfit knowing."

"Then why go anywhere?" said Becky. "Nobody's going to know it's not sweat."

April laughed. "I'll spread the word that you sweated more than any of us."

"You do," Mindy said ominously, "and I'll tell Dirk some of the things you've told me about him."

"Do that," said April, "and I won't wait for an Indian attack to use this pistol."

Almost a dozen miles ahead of the drive, Wovoka reined up, listening. Hearing nothing to arouse his suspicion, he was about to ride on. Then, several hundred yards upstream, he saw a covey of birds dip down toward a thicket, only to rise again and fly away. There was trouble ahead, and Wovoka suspected it was more than he could handle alone. It was his duty to return to the trail drive and warn them in time to prepare for attack. Quickly he wheeled his horse, kicking the animal into a fast gallop.

"Aaaaiyeee," came a shout from behind him.

Looking over his shoulder, Wovoka could see a dozen mounted Indians pursuing him at a fast gallop. Some carried lances in their hands. Wovoka's horse was already running at a gait that would soon exhaust the animal, allowing his pursuers to ride him down. While he was tempted to turn and fire, he knew that accuracy with a gun from the back of a galloping horse was difficult. He would save his ammunition. He had learned from the cowboys that three quickly fired shots was a call for help, but he felt he was still too far ahead of the drive for the shots to be heard. On he galloped, aware that his weary horse had begun to heave. He would soon be forced to take a stand, and he began looking for some cover. But time had run out, and fate took a hand. The left front hoof of his horse plunged into an invisible stump hole full of dead leaves. Wovoka was thrown over the animal's head, and behind him he could hear the victorious whoops of his pursuers. Wovoka had but one chance and he took it. The riverbank was high enough that water had eaten into the bank, leaving a two-or three-foot overhang. A shelf. Wovoka rolled off the bank into the water, and as far under the overhang as he could get. While his enemies couldn't get at him from his side of the river, he would be in plain sight from the opposite bank. He drew his Colt, prepared to sell his life as dearly as possible. Upstream, he could hear splashing as the riders plunged their horses into the river. Wovoka fingered the deerskin bag on a leather thong around his neck. In it were enough paraffin-coated loads to fill the loading gate of his Colt five more times.* But he was at a disadvantage. The opposite bank of the river had a dense thicket that would provide cover for the attackers, and they

---

*Prior to metal cartridges, loads were prepared and paraffin-dipped for waterproofing.

wasted no time taking advantage of it. An arrow thunked into the muddy riverbank, quickly followed by two others, all narrowly missing Wovoka. He fired three times into the thicket and there was a cry of pain. But the arrows kept coming, one of them slashing through the buckskin legging into Wovoka's left thigh. But the wind was out of the west, and the three shots had been heard.

"Head 'em," Lonnie shouted, waving his hat.

Some of the others had heard the distant shots, and the nearest riders—Dirk, Kirby, Gus, and Waco—galloped their horses to where Lonnie waited. Dallas was the first of the drag riders to arrive.

"Wovoka's in trouble," said Lonnie. "Dallas, you're in charge. Dirk, Kirby, Gus, Waco, and me will get to him, if we can."

Dallas nodded as his five companions galloped along the river. Eventually they heard two more shots, closer this time.

"He's got just one more shot," Waco shouted. "Then the varmints will be rushing him before he can reload."

When Wovoka fired his sixth round, his companions were close enough to see the puff of smoke rise above the riverbank.

"Fill that thicket with lead," Lonnie shouted.

The five of them each fired five times, saving one shot. There was no response from the thicket and none from beneath the riverbank's overhang, where Wovoka had taken refuge. The silence dragged on, evidence that the attackers had obviously retreated. Then Wovoka cautiously raised his head above the riverbank.

"*Bueno amigos,*" said the Indian. "Follow. Kill."

"Not this time," Lonnie said. "You have an arrow in your leg. Mount up behind me and we'll get you back to the wagon."

But Wovoka seemed not to have heard. He had thumbed open the loading gate of his Colt and was reloading the weapon. Finished, he thrust it under his waistband and set off across the river.

"That don't strike me as bein' a smart thing to do," said Kirby.

"They're gone," Lonnie said, "and he knows it. He wants to know if we hit any of the varmints."

Wovoka disappeared into the thicket and almost immediately reappeared, leading a dead Paiute's horse. He held up just one finger.

"One lucky shot," said Gus. "Wonder how many there were?"

"Not many," Lonnie said, "or they wouldn't have run."

Wovoka had splashed back across the river. Climbing out, he held up both hands, all fingers extended. He then raised two more fingers.

"Twelve of them, minus one dead," Waco said. "I'd bet my boots and saddle they're part of a larger party. They just took advantage of Wovoka because he was alone."

"I'm afraid you're right," said Lonnie. "We'll catch hell farther on."

Wovoka mounted the dead Indian's horse and they started back to meet the herd. Just a mile distant, they found Wovoka's horse limping along, grazing as he went. Waco caught the animal, using his lariat for a lead rope.

"He's just lamed," Lonnie said, "and he'll be all right after a rest."

But the worst was yet to come. Dallas, Justin, Sandy, Benjamin, and Elliot rode a slow circle around the bunched horses and longhorns. Mindy, Laura, and April had remained with Becky and the wagon. It was April who made a startling discovery.

"Indians behind us!" she shouted.

On they came, more than two dozen of them. The lead rider shouted at the others and they kicked their horses into a fast gallop, spreading out. Becky was the first to recover from the shock. Leaping down from the wagon box, she cut loose with her Colt. While the Paiutes were still out of gun range, the shots alerted the riders circling the herd.

"Come on," Dallas shouted. "We can't let them get close enough to stampede the herd and the horses."

Several miles away, Lonnie and his companions heard the shots.

"Let's ride," Lonnie shouted. "The varmints are attacking the rest of the outfit. They just created a diversion to draw some of us away."

The shooting continued as Lonnie and the rest of the outfit galloped to the rescue. The Paiutes were close enough that their arrows were ripping into the wagon canvas. But to the evident surprise of the attackers, the four women beside the wagon were demonstrating a remarkable accuracy. By the time Dallas and his riders joined the fray, four of the Paiutes were down. The others seemed to pause, undecided, allowing Dallas and his companions to gallop within range. With the increased fire, four more Indians went down. That seemed to make up the minds of the others, and they galloped their horses back the way they had come. By the time Lonnie and the rest of the outfit arrived, it was all over.

"Anybody hurt?" Lonnie shouted, leaping down from his saddle.

"Nobody," said Dallas, "and we owe this one to the ladies. They cut loose before the rest of us was in range, pickin' off four of the varmints. That confused them long enough for the rest of us to get four more of them."

"I think we just turned their hole card upside down," Lonnie said. "They reckoned we'd ride to help Wovoka, and figured to attack the herd while only a few were here to defend it. Great shooting, all of you. Before we move on, Wovoka has an arrow wound that needs tending."

"I'll tend to it," said Becky, taking a blanket from the

wagon seat. "Peel off those buckskins, Wovoka, and stretch yourself out on this blanket."

Clearly embarrassed, Wovoka shook his head.

"Mindy, you, April, and Laura vamoose," Becky said. "He doesn't want all of you seeing him without his britches."

Again Wovoka shook his head, pointing to Becky.

Mindy laughed. "He doesn't want any of us seeing him without his britches."

"The four of you make yourselves scarce for a little while," said Lonnie. "One of us will see to the wound."

"I'll start a fire and put some water on to boil," Becky said. "That is, if Wovoka has no objection."

None of them had ever heard Wovoka laugh before, and it came as a surprise when he did. It was a strange guttural sound.

"I swear that Indian understands everything we say," said Becky, after hanging the pot of water over the fire.

"He has more manners than any man in the outfit," Mindy said. "After the mule bit you and you were sitting around in your shirttails, he hardly looked at you at all."

"I don't know if I should feel grateful or insulted," said Becky.

"Maybe he's not old enough to be interested in females," Mindy said. "I think he likes horses best."

The object of their conversation sat quietly while Lonnie and Waco tended the wound. It wasn't serious, and the shaft didn't have to be driven through the flesh. With a bandage on his leg, Wovoka pulled on his buckskin leggings. He stood up, walking without a limp.

"I reckon we can move on," said Lonnie. "We still have half a day of daylight."

"We still have more of those Paiutes somewhere ahead of us," Waco said, "and I don't doubt the rest of this bunch that attacked from the back trail have joined forces with them by now. That's enough to lay a pretty solid ambush."

"I think they misjudged us and our firepower considerably," said Lonnie. "Altogether, they lost nine men, while we lost none. I'd be more concerned if they were armed with guns. Their daytime attacks having failed, I expect them to try something else, like maybe stampeding the herd and the horses during the night."

"Kill Paiute," Wovoka said. "I go, I find."

"Not this time, Wovoka," said Lonnie. "They'll have it in for you, after losing one of their warriors and having you escape. You'll ride with me, and if we see any evidence of an ambush, we'll all ride in shooting. A man alone is too much temptation for them, and I don't want you shot full of arrows."

"They'd dearly love to separate us and pick us off one at a time," Gus said. "That's the way the Comanches in Texas operate, and all the more reason why we'd better all stand watch at night until we're out of Paiute country. They know if they scatter the herd and the horses from here to yonder, we'll have to split up for the gather."

"I'd say you're right," said Dallas.

"That means no sleep for God knows how long," Dirk said.

"Better without sleep than without hair," said Kirby.

"Once we're out of New Mexico and into southern Colorado, we should be pretty much clear of Paiute country," Lonnie said. "We should leave the Chama tomorrow, and if we're figuring right, we shouldn't be far from the Animas River."

In the twilight, Lonnie had the entire outfit—including the women—in the saddle and circling the herd and the horse remuda. Midnight came and went without any disturbance, and quietly Lonnie called all the riders together.

"This is gettin' on my nerves," said Lonnie. "We all know damn well they're out there somewhere, but we don't know if there's fifty or five hundred. Wovoka, I want you to go with me and find their camp if we can. At least we'll know how many we're up against. The rest of you keep watch just as you've been doing.''

''No moon,'' Waco said. ''They'll be hard to find, if they've put out their fire.''

''They can't see us any better than we can see them,'' said Lonnie, ''and we're downwind. We can hear a horse stomp its foot half a mile away.''

Nobody else said anything. Seeking out the Paiute camp could be extremely dangerous, but the uncertainty, the not knowing, was taking its toll on them all. Lonnie and Wovoka rode away in the darkness.

''He's right,'' Gus said. ''The varmints might wait two or three days, knowing we're on watch all night. Then they'd hit us at dawn, when we was all hungover from no sleep.''

''I just hope Lonnie's impatience won't prod him into taking any unnecessary chances,'' said Becky.

''Don't let that bother you,'' Waco said. ''He's got Wovoka with him, and he's a damn savvy Indian.''

''We owe Jim Bridger for insisting we bring Wovoka with us,'' said Dallas. ''I believe when him and Lonnie return, they'll know where the Paiute camp is and how many of them we're up against.''

Lonnie and Wovoka kept their horses to a walk, lest the sound of their coming alert the Paiute camp. The wind—from the northwest—had increased, and brought with it the distinctive smell of rain from somewhere beyond the distant mountains. By the stars, they had been riding for close to two hours, and as though by mutual agreement, Lonnie and Wovoka reined up, listening. They heard nothing, but just as they were about to ride on, Lonnie felt Wovoka's strong hand on his arm. Wovoka dismounted, Lonnie following. For just a moment, the night wind brought the faint odor of wood smoke. Just as abruptly as it had come, it was gone. They waited, but the smell of smoke didn't come again, and there was only the sigh of the wind in the trees.

"Leave horse," Wovoka said quietly, looping his reins around a convenient limb.

Lonnie tied his horse beside Wovoka's and, allowing Wovoka to lead out, followed. It seemed to Lonnie the Paiute camp would be near the river, but that didn't appear to be the case. In the meager starlight, Wovoka found a shallows in the river, and there they waded across. They were part way through the river when Wovoka paused, Lonnie right behind him. Somewhere ahead, a horse snorted.

"You stay," said Wovoka softly.

It was a touchy situation, and Lonnie remained where he was. Wovoka quickly vanished in the murky shadows beneath the trees. He crept down a slope to the south of the river, pausing often to listen. Finally, in a puff of wind, a spark rose. It was from a near-dead fire and lasted only seconds, but it was enough to tell Wovoka where the Paiute camp was. He circled around the sleeping camp to the south, and there—alongside a small tributary to the river—horses grazed. Quietly Wovoka made his way to the nearest horse. Getting his arm around the animal's neck, he calmed it. Keeping his head down, he gently led the horse among its grazing companions. The horse appeared to be moving naturally, and since it did not spook the rest of the horses, it allowed Wovoka to remain no more than a shadow as he tallied the number of grazing horses. He held his Bowie in his right hand, expecting to find some of the Paiutes on watch, but to his surprise, there were none. Quietly, he led his captive horse far enough from the others so that he could avoid spooking them. Then he swiftly made his way back to where Lonnie waited. He touched Lonnie's arm, and in the starlight Lonnie watched him raise both hands with spread fingers five times.

"Damn," Lonnie grunted. "Fifty of them."

"Ugh," said Wovoka. "Horse run, Paiute walk."

"Good thinking," Lonnie said. "If we can stampede their

horses, it might gain us time enough to get out of Paiute country. But we'll need more riders.''

''Horse run now,'' said Wovoka.

''I see what you mean,'' Lonnie said, his eyes on the starry heavens. ''We don't have much time. It'll be first light in about two hours.''

''Ugh,'' said Wovoka. ''We go now.''

Taking the reins of their horses, they started, Wovoka in the lead. Lonnie wondered if there had been sentries, but knew better than to ask. If there had been Paiutes on watch, they now lay dead. His and Wovoka's was a dangerous task. They were far enough from their outfit that if they failed to stampede all the Indian horses, the Paiutes might ride them down, even in the dark. But it was a move just daring enough that the Paiutes might be taken by surprise, for even after their losses, their numbers were far superior to those of the men with many horses and a herd of *feo* brutes with long horns. Wovoka led the way to the south of the camp. There he paused, taking Lonnie's arm.

''Leave horse,'' Wovoka said.

Lonnie left his horse beside Wovoka's, hoping neither animal would sense the presence of the Indian horses and nicker a greeting. But it was a risk they had to take, for if they were to successfully stampede the horses of the Paiutes, they needed their own mounts. It was a mystery to Lonnie what Wovoka intended to do, but he followed the Indian's lead. Wovoka eased in among the grazing horses, going to those nearest the Paiute camp. With calming whispers, he got his left arm around the neck of one of the horses. The animal did not cause any disturbance, and Wovoka repeated the procedure with his right arm around another horse. Slowly he led the two horses several hundred yards south of the Paiute camp. Wovoka's ability with horses was uncanny, and gritting his teeth, Lonnie set out to follow the Indian's example, if he could. The stomping of a hoof, a nervous nicker—anything—might alert the sleeping Paiutes, pitting himself and Wovoka against fifty hell-raising Indians. Should even one of the horses sound an alarm, it would be all but impossible for Lonnie and Wovoka to reach their mounts and escape. The first horse Lonnie approached raised its head and seemed about to nicker in alarm when Lonnie caught its muzzle. He stroked the animal's neck until it resumed grazing. Getting his other arm around a second horse wasn't quite so difficult, and the pair allowed him to lead them slowly southward, until he could see those Wovoka had taken ahead of him. Lonnie fully understood Wovoka's intentions. Leading the horses as far away as possible would lessen the chance that any of the sleeping Paiutes could capture a horse before all had been stampeded beyond their reach. Such a distance would pretty well assure the inaccuracy of Indian arrows in the dark. Again Lonnie looked at the stars, and it seemed less than an hour to first light. But Wovoka didn't hurry, and neither did Lonnie. He breathed a long sigh of relief when they finally led away the last of the Paiute horses. But the worst of it wasn't over. Had there been more riders, stampeding the horses would have been a cinch, but there was only Lonnie and Wovoka. Returning to their own horses, no talk was necessary. Mounting, they circled wide of the Paiute camp, coming in well between it and the grazing horses. Seeking to minimize the noise at the start of the stampede, they doubled their lariats and rode in among the herd, slapping the flanks of the first few horses. Nickering, the animals broke into a gallop, and the stampede was on. Lonnie and Wovoka drew their Colts and began firing over the heads of the running horses. Behind them, they could hear the growing angry clamor among the Paiutes. Since it was all but impossible to reload their Colts in the dark on galloping horses, Lonnie and Wovoka used their doubled lariats as whips, shouting and screeching like demented souls straight from hell. The herd of galloping horses responded accordingly. To Lonnie's immense relief, they hadn't scattered, but were galloping on as a herd. It would prevent the Paiutes from catching a few and using them to gather the others. Lonnie and Wovoka spared their horses, slowing them to a slow gallop. Their shouting was enough to keep the stampede going.

"Dear God," Becky cried, as the night wind brought the sound of distant shots, "the Paiutes are after them."

"Maybe not," said Dallas. "I counted a dozen shots. They're not going to empty their Colts in a single volley when they'd have to reload in the dark."

"I suppose that makes sense," Becky said, "but I'm still afraid for them. Can't some of us ride and join them?"

"Lonnie told us all to stay with the herd," said Mindy.

"You *would* say that," Becky snarled. "It's not your man out there with a damn bunch of bloodthirsty Indians shooting him full of arrows."

"I didn't mean it that way," said Mindy.

"Maybe not," Becky said angrily, "but that's how it looks to me."

"Shut up, Becky," said Waco, "or I'll turn you over my knee like I used to when you were a snot-nosed kid."

"If you don't, I will," Gus said. "Us yelling at one another won't change a thing. If we went gallopin' off in the dark without knowing what's goin' on, we might find ourselves in more trouble than Lonnie and Wovoka."

"I'm sorry, Becky," said Mindy. "I have all the faith in the world in Lonnie, and just as much in Wovoka. I don't think either of them will get themselves into anything they're not able to get out of."

"All right," Becky said shortly, "all of you have made your point. I was wrong."

"There's nothing wrong with being scared when there's cause," said Dallas, "but we're all a long way from home. We can't afford the luxury of fighting among ourselves when it gains us nothing. Let's keep our faith in Lonnie and Wovoka strong. We're not that far from first light. If we don't have

some word by then, we'll decide what to do. For now, I think
we should obey Lonnie's orders and begin circling the herd
again.''

Even Becky was silent as they mounted their horses and
followed Dallas.

Far to the south, as first light brightened the eastern horizon,
Wovoka reined up his weary horse. Lonnie reined up beside
him.

"Them Paiutes have a long walk ahead of them," Lonnie
said. "You think it's enough?"

"*Sí,*" said Wovoka. "Two, maybe three suns."

"Then let's get back to the herd," Lonnie said. "The others
may have heard the shooting, and they won't know if we're
alive or dead."

"*Sí,*" said Wovoka. "Much hungry."

"You're not by yourself," Lonnie said. "I think we've
earned the right to set down to a good breakfast, even if it
costs us a couple of hours."

Wovoka pointed to the west, beyond distant mountains,
where dirty gray clouds had lifted their heads above the horizon.

"Tarnation," said Lonnie, "that's just what we need. Rain
to create enough mud so we can't move the damn wagon before those Paiutes gather their horses. Come on."

While they rode back to camp, preparations for breakfast
were under way. Nobody had anything to say, for dawn had
arrived, and all Becky's fears seemed justified. Mindy's sad
eyes were on Becky, but she seemed not to notice. The rest
of the outfit looked grim. Not one of them wanted to think of
life on the Green River range without Lonnie and Wovoka.
The August sun already had them sweating when they saw the
two horsemen coming. Lonnie and Wovoka trotted their
horses along the river. Reining up, they dismounted, and for
a moment, nobody spoke. Becky broke the silence, running to

Lonnie, tears streaking the dirt on her face. Ignoring it all, Wovoka headed for the wagon, where breakfast had been prepared on the wagon's tailgate.

"Eat," said Wovoka.

"Like hell," Kirby Lowe said. "Not until we find out where you *hombres* have been all night and what you've been up to."

"Let him eat," said Lonnie. "He's earned it. I'll tell you what a fool thing the both of us did."

Quickly he told them of Wovoka's idea of stampeding the Paiute horses, and how just the two of them had accomplished it.

"So if they attack us," Waco said, "they'll be afoot. I don't expect that, us armed with guns and them with bows and arrows."

"Neither do I," said Lonnie, "but from the looks of those clouds over yonder, we may be in for enough rain to muddy the ground so's we can't move the wagon. That could hold us up long enough for the Paiutes to round up their horses."

"I reckon it's safe to say they'll be mad as hell," Gus said.

"There's only a few things in life that are dead certain," said Lonnie, "and that's one of them. Let's eat and cover as many miles as we can today. Tomorrow, the wagon may be stuck in the mud, and we may all be on the watch for killing-mad Paiutes."

16

With no immediate Indian threat, the outfit enjoyed a good breakfast. It was Mindy's day on the wagon, and Gus and Waco harnessed the teams. Wovoka had gone to see about his horse that had been lamed the day before, and when he led the animal from the herd, it still limped.

"Tie him behind the wagon," Lonnie said. "It won't help him heal if one of the others should kick that sore leg."

Wovoka nodded, and the rest of the riders looked upon him with approval. Concern for a horse wasn't characteristic of all Indians. Some simply rode an animal to death, and when it dropped, got another.

"Head 'em up, move 'em out," Lonnie shouted.

The drag riders bunched the horse remuda close behind the herd, and Mindy followed with the wagon. Gus and Waco were among the drag riders, and when the drive was well under way, the two cowboys rode side by side.

"That was some hell of a thing Lonnie and Wovoka pulled off last night," said Gus. "I didn't want to bother everybody with what's bothering me."

"But you don't mind bothering me with it," Waco said. "I'm obliged."

"Oh, hell," said Gus, "don't lay that 'hurt feelings' act on me. We been together just too long."

"Then tell me what kind of burr you got under your tail," Waco said. "It might be the same thing that's botherin' me some."

"So far," said Gus, "we've had a clash with maybe sixty Paiutes. I've never been in any situation involvin' hostiles when there was so few of them. Where do you reckon the rest of the tribe is?"

"Since we ain't run into 'em," Waco said, "I reckon they're somewhere ahead of us. I'd say something to Lonnie, but it might prove embarrassing. I just don't believe him or any of the others is green enough to believe we're done with the Paiutes."

"We'd better wait until tonight," said Gus. "Lonnie believes there may be Paiute trouble until we're out of New Mexico, and that's another four days at least, even if we ain't slowed up by rain and mud."

Wovoka rode ahead of the herd with Lonnie, and there was no sign of Indians. After bunching the herd for the night, while they waited for supper, Lonnie spoke to them.

"I reckon we'd be foolin' ourselves thinking we're rid of the Paiutes. We'll have to be constantly watching, because we don't know how many of them are in the territory. They may be behind us, or somewhere ahead of us. Don't expect to get much sleep for the next four nights. We'll all be in the saddle."

They ate a silent supper, for clouding the minds of each of them was the grim possibility that they might yet face even greater numbers of Paiutes. Jagged shards of golden lightning romped grandly across the western horizon, while a cooling west wind brought with it the pungent smell of rain. After supper, although it wasn't quite dark, the riders began saddling their horses. The lightning was visible more often now, and thunder rumbled away into silence, only to rise to greater heights. Already the longhorns had begun to mill uneasily, and some of the horses had begun nickering. It was Wovoka who rode among the horses, ruffling their manes, speaking to them in some strange tongue only they seemed to understand. Slowly they settled down, but not the herd of longhorns. One bawled as though setting the tone, and others joined in, creating a grim, melancholy chorus.

"Sing to the varmints!" Lonnie shouted.

Kirby and Dirk began their off-key version of a bawdy song unfit for female ears, but such was their predicament that nobody seemed to notice or care. Lonnie, Dallas, Gus, and Waco had worked their way beyond the horse herd, for if there was a stampede, it surely would be away from the storm, along the back trail. It was the most dangerous position, for if a rider's horse fell or threw him, he might be trampled to death. The possibilities of such a tragedy were not lost on the rest of the outfit. The other riders—including Becky, Mindy, Laura, and April—were riding in the direction they expected the herd to run.

"No," Lonnie shouted, waving his hat. But the rising wind whipped his voice away.

Thunder rumbled closer, and gray sheets of rain rode in on the wind. The horses, as well as the longhorns, had their backs to the storm, wanting to drift with it. Wovoka did his best, but the horses were becoming more and more difficult to control because of the pushing and shoving of the uneasy longhorns. Suddenly thunder shook the earth, and some of the horses broke away to the southeast. The direction was totally unexpected, and none of the riders were able to head the leaders. There was an explosion and a flash of light as lightning struck a huge boulder almost directly ahead of the stampeding horses. Shards of rock—like shrapnel—struck the lead horses, sending them rearing and screaming. Horseshoe fashion, they turned, galloping back the way they had come, into the face of the wind and rain. The frightened longhorns followed. With

Wovoka in the lead, the riders began to head the lead horses, and soon the entire mass of horses and longhorns milled about, confused. The thunder receded and the lightning died away to an occasional flicker, the worst of the storm having passed. It took some doing, in darkness and pouring rain, but slowly the riders were able to separate the horses and longhorns. Finally all the animals settled down. Riders slid out of their saddles, leaning against their horses, exhausted.

"This would be a damn good time for the Paiutes to attack," said Dirk wearily.

"How'd you like to have your throat cut with a dull knife?" Kirby snarled.

The rain soon ceased, but the wind remained brisk, and with their wet clothing, every rider's teeth chattered with cold.

"Somebody get some wood from the wagon's possum belly," said Lonnie, "and let's get some coffee started."

"What about the Paiutes?" Mindy asked.

"Damn the Paiutes," said Dallas. "We'll fight the bastards when they show up. Get that coffee brewing."

"Horse hurt," Wovoka said, when he led one of the horses near the fire.

There was blood on the animal's chest and legs, obviously from the particles of rock flung by the lightning.

"Check the others out, Wovoka," said Lonnie, "and lead them near the fire, one at a time. Becky, bring me a tin of sulfur salve from the medicine chest."

"They'll heal," Dallas said. "Blowflies shouldn't be a problem at this altitude."

"We'll doctor them anyway," said Lonnie. "It'll be a miracle if some of them aren't blinded."

Lonnie smeared sulfur salve on the wounds as Wovoka led the horses near the fire. Of the five horses, none was seriously injured. Once the riders had finished off two pots of hot coffee, they saddled up and again began circling the herd. The wind had died, and its absence took the chill out of the night. As their clothing began to dry, the spirits of the outfit rose considerably. An unexpected quirk of fate had spared them a stampede, with the dreaded lightning heading and confusing the herd. The sky had cleared, and the expanse of purple glittered with millions of distant stars.

"Two o'clock," Lonnie said. "Where's Wovoka?"

"I got no idea," said Dallas. "Last time I saw him was when he led those horses in for doctoring."

Lonnie spoke to all the riders, and none of them knew what had become of Wovoka.

"He's likely out scouting," Waco said. "I reckon he heard us wondering if there was more of them Paiutes that might come looking for us."

"Maybe you're right," said Lonnie. "He moves in the dark like a shadow."

But Lonnie grew increasingly anxious, for it was almost two hours before Wovoka returned. Like a phantom, he stepped out of the shadows, silencing Lonnie with the touch of his hand. Wovoka spoke softly.

"Many Paiute come."

"How many?" Lonnie asked anxiously, "and where are they?"

Wovoka said nothing, raising his right hand over his head and moving it in a circle. It was a single answer to both Lonnie's questions. There were enough Paiutes to surround them. Dallas and Waco stood behind Lonnie and, having heard his questions, fully understood Wovoka's answer. Dallas whistled long and low.

"We're in for it," said Waco. "I reckon the number ain't important, if there's enough of them to surround us."

"We have maybe an hour until first light, to convince them our medicine's stronger than theirs," Lonnie said. "Wovoka, watch them as close as you can without them knowing. Dallas, you and Waco get back to the herd, and I'll join you in a few minutes. There may be a chance for us. Tell Becky, Mindy,

April, and Laura I want to see them at the wagon, pronto."

Wovoka had already vanished in the darkness, and without question, Dallas and Waco returned to the herd. Dallas told Mindy only that Lonnie wanted the four women to come to the wagon. It would be up to Lonnie to tell them of the growing danger and to set them to whatever task he had in mind. The four of them picketed their horses, and when they approached the wagon on foot, Lonnie spoke quietly, repeating what Wovoka had told him.

"Oh, Lord," said Becky, "what do you want us to do?"

"We dare not light a fire or a lantern," Lonnie said, "so you'll have to work as best you can in the dark. One of you get that bolt of muslin cloth from the wagon, along with a blanket to spread on the ground."

"Why?" Becky asked.

"No time for questions, damn it," said Lonnie. "Get it. Then I'll tell you."

Becky scrambled to the wagon seat, tossing down a blanket, which Mindy spread on the ground beside the wagon. Finally she handed down the bolt of muslin. Lonnie dropped it on the blanket, and when Becky climbed down from the wagon, he spoke.

"Here, take my knife. I want you to cut off ten pieces of that muslin. It's a yard wide, and I want each of these ten pieces cut at three-foot intervals. Get started on that while I get one of those kegs of black powder."

None of them said anything, knowing there was more he had yet to tell them. The kegs of black powder had been loaded so they wouldn't shift, and it took Lonnie a while to move all the goods securing them. Finally, the forty-pound keg under his arm, he climbed down from the wagon.

"Hand me the knife," he said, placing the keg of powder on the blanket. The lid had been screwed down and was difficult to remove in the dark. Finally it came loose.

"The muslin's been cut and is ready," said Becky.

"Take one piece at a time, spreading it out on the blanket so it lies flat," Lonnie said. "Then take a double handful of the black powder and put it exactly in the center of the muslin square. Then pull all four corners together until you have a kind of sack. See that the black powder is bunched in the bottom. Then, with a strip of muslin, tie it around the neck of the sack, holding the powder tightly in the bottom."

"Are we allowed to know what you're going to do with it?" Mindy asked.

"Eventually," said Lonnie. "For now, you only need to know that we have to convince those Paiutes our medicine is stronger than theirs. When you're done with this, keep your Colts handy and stay here beside the wagon. Don't be moving about. Wovoka's out there somewhere. When it's first light—as soon as you can see—I want you to build a roaring fire behind the wagon, just as though we intend to have breakfast."

Then he was gone, and Becky swore under her breath.

"Whatever he has in his mind, he's not telling us the worst of it," said Mindy. "That tells me it's dangerous enough to get somebody killed."

"Yes," Becky said, "and that's why he's told us to stay beside the wagon. We're being kept out of it."

"Well," said Laura, "should we feel flattered that he thinks that much of us, or should we be insulted because he doesn't think we can live up to whatever he has in mind?"

"I suppose I'm a coward," April said, "but I'm not sure I could do what he's thinking of doing. This stuff's explosive, and somebody's got to get awful close for it to do any good."

"My God," said Mindy, "that's why he had us cut these large muslin squares, and his reason for a big fire. They're going to set fire to those lengths of muslin and ride to meet the Paiutes."

"That sounds exactly like something Lonnie would do," Becky said, "and if the Paiutes have us surrounded, they won't just stand there. They'll shoot so many arrows, they won't all miss."

"What are we going to do?" cried April.

"Oh, hell," said Becky wearily, "I don't know what's going to become of us."

Suddenly Mindy began heaving and gagging. Rolling away from the blanket, she turned over on her belly, throwing up in painful spasms. Spent, she lay there breathing hard.

"Lord," Becky said, "did what I say cause that?"

"No," said Mindy's muffled voice. "I've been feeling sick for two or three days now. My belly hurts, and I just feel like hell."

"Not *that*," Becky said. "Not now."

"What are you talking about?" Mindy demanded.

"You're in the family way," said Becky. "That's the first sign."

"No," Mindy said. "When Dallas and me sleep together, all we take off is our hats."

"You're forgetting something," said Becky. "While we were at the Kilgore Ranch, we didn't sleep on the ground. We had beds. Did you only take your hat off *then*?"

"I . . . I guess I took it all off," Mindy said.

April and Laura laughed.

"You picked the wrong day of the month," said April.

"Shut up, both of you," Becky said. "Any one of the three of us may be next. We had as much opportunity as Becky did."

"Oh, God," cried Mindy, "by the time we reach Green River, I'll be as big as any cow in the outfit. Dallas will have a fit."

"No, he won't," Becky said. "He was there when it happened."

"He'll make a fuss over me on the wagon, helping with the cooking and everything," said Mindy. "He'll fidget around me like an old hen."

"You'd better hope he does," April said. "My pa was off on a drunk when I was born, and he didn't know I existed for two weeks. Then he didn't give a damn."

"Whatever else happens," said Mindy, "don't breathe a word of this to Dallas. I'll tell him at . . . some . . . better time."

"When you're big as a cow," April suggested.

"April," said Becky, "please shut up. We have enough problems. Don't worry, Mindy, we'll keep your secret as long as we can."

"Until I'm big as a cow and can't hide it any longer," Mindy said unhappily.

As first light neared, all the riders came together. It was time for Lonnie to tell them what he had planned to do, what he hoped might save them from an overwhelming force of Paiutes. At that precise moment, Wovoka arrived, and he didn't bring good news.

"Paiutes come," Wovoka said.

"Wovoka," said Lonnie, "I'd like for you to remain near the wagon. Under the seat you'll find some of those Colts we took from the outlaws. The women will be with the wagon, and the Paiutes may try to rush them. The rest of us are going to try and convince them our medicine is better than theirs. All of you come on, and bring your horses."

"What about the herd?" Dallas asked.

"If we don't rid ourselves of these Paiutes," said Lonnie, "the herd won't matter."

Becky and Laura had the fire going behind the wagon. Lonnie knelt beside the wagon, reaching into the possum belly. He brought out a handful of resin-rich pine splinters a foot long. He lighted the end of one, waiting until it was burning strong. Then he took one of the muslin bags loaded with black powder and mounted his horse. Only then did he speak.

"There's nine more bags of black powder there. As these

Paiutes move closer, I aim to use this one to give them a good dose of it.''

"Lonnie," said Becky, "no—"

But several dozen of the Paiutes had ridden closer, almost within arrow range. Lonnie kicked his horse into a run, heading straight at the startled Indians. He touched the blazing torch to the loose neck of the muslin sack. The cloth flared up, and Lonnie held it until the last possible second. Then he threw it. The powder exploded before it hit the ground, and horses reared, screaming. Dazed Paiutes were thrown to the ground, while their horses galloped wildly away. As some of the Indians staggered to their feet, Lonnie cut loose with his Colt. Seeing three of their comrades fall, the other Paiutes broke and ran.

"It's working," Dallas shouted. Quickly he lighted one of the resinous splinters, took one of the bags of muslin-wrapped powder, and leaped to the saddle. A group of Paiutes approaching from another direction stood undecided as a result of the first explosion. It was this group that Dallas went after, galloping his horse recklessly close. As Lonnie had done, Dallas lighted the muslin, throwing it at the last moment. With a burst of fire and smoke, it exploded over the heads of the Paiutes, and the results were even more dramatic. Horses galloped away riderless, and many of the fallen Paiutes didn't move. Those who did found themselves within range, as Dallas cut loose with his Colt. When he rode back to the wagon, the remainder of the mounted Paiutes had turned their horses and were well out of gun range.

"Damn," said Waco, "I didn't get a chance at 'em."

"Neither did any of the rest of us," Kirby complained. "Lonnie, why didn't you tell us, instead of just galloping off on your own?"

"Because I wasn't sure it would work," said Lonnie. "If they'd got me, I wanted the rest of you to have a chance. I had the ladies make plenty of those, in case we needed them."

Wovoka appeared delighted when the Paiutes had been frightened away, and at the same time, he was irked because he hadn't been involved.

"The question is," Gus said, "have they given up on us for good, or just until they get up the nerve to try again?"

"We'll have to wait and see," said Lonnie, "but I managed to gun down three of them, and Dallas got two more. There's quite a few others that haven't moved. They're dead, or they've had their senses knocked out. We'll move on and allow them to gather their dead. We'll put the rest of those black-powder bombs in the wagon for later use, if we happen to need them. Now let's get ready to move out."

The rest of the outfit seemed amazed at what Lonnie had accomplished, while several of them eyed Dallas with envy, for he had been quick to take part. Wovoka said nothing. He mounted his horse and, when the herd was moving, took his place at the head of it next to Lonnie. Dirk and Kirby were the swing riders, while Dallas and Justin rode flank. The others rode drag, while Mindy followed with the wagon.

"We been just too lucky, too often," said Waco, riding beside Gus. "That lightning bolt struck just at the right time, saving us from a stampede, and we've stood up to every one of the Paiute attacks. Even with the rain we had, the ground wasn't too muddied for us to move the wagon. That kind of good fortune can't go on. Just when you start believing in Lady Luck, she turns out to be a cantankerous old heifer who'll kick the props from under you and then, when you're belly-down, stomp you."

"I wish I could disagree with you," Gus said, "but I'm afraid you're right. I've kept my trap shut because all I know is what I've heard, but that Colorado River is said to be hell to cross because it runs mostly through deep gorges. I once talked to a puncher who rode with a herd from Santa Fe to California along the Old Spanish Trail."*

*THE OLD SPANISH TRAIL. Trail Drive #11.

"But they crossed the herd, didn't they?"

"Yeah," said Gus, "but only after finding the lowest banks, and then diggin' the steepest parts away with picks and shovels."

"I reckon that might work," Waco said, "but did they have a wagon?"

"I don't know, and didn't think to ask," said Gus. "It'd take us until spring to dig far enough into those banks to cross a wagon. I reckon there'll be time enough to think about that when we get there. When we finally get there, we won't be more than a hundred miles from the Green River range, if Lonnie's map is right."

"Yeah," Waco said. "Once we're that close, we'll find a way to cross."

Becky, Laura, and April rode beside the wagon. After Lonnie's unexpected and dangerous ride against the Paiutes, Becky had said little.

"Becky," said Laura, "you should be proud of Lonnie. That was a brave, daring thing he did. Not many men would have taken that chance."

"Most men would have had better sense," Becky said shortly.

"Well, I'm proud of Dallas," said Mindy, who had heard the conversation.

"You might not be so proud, if he'd been shot full of Paiute arrows, leaving you in the family way," Becky said grimly.

"Like Lonnie, he did what had to be done," said Mindy. "He's my man, and I'm proud of him."

Becky said nothing, and from the way Laura and April looked at her, it was clear that they agreed with Mindy. With the herd moving at a faster-than-usual gait, they made good time, for they had left the Chama River, and according to the map, the next nearest water was Cañon Largo, more than twenty miles distant. The sun was noon-high when the right rear wheel of the wagon slid off a rock shelf, splintering the wheel. April kicked her horse into a run, catching up to the drag riders.

"Broken wagon wheel," April shouted.

"I'll ride ahead and stop the drive," said Waco.

"The wagon's down," Waco shouted, when he was close enough for Lonnie to hear.

Slowly the drive ground to a halt, and the riders began bunching the herd.

"Gus and me can replace the busted wheel," said Waco.

"Not until you find the spare wheel and the wagon jack," Lonnie said, "and God knows how much of the load we'll have to move. I'll go along and help. Wovoka, you stay here and keep watch."

"I'm sorry," Mindy said, when Lonnie and Waco reached the wagon. "I saw that rock shelf and missed it with the front wheel."

"Not your fault," said Lonnie. "After you guided the front wheel away from it, could be that the team veered back a little. We'll get the spare wheel on there, pronto."

But it was easier said than done. Much of the wagon's load had to be shifted before they found the spare wheel and the wagon jack.

"If I had it to do over," Lonnie said, "I'd bolt this damn spare wheel to the outside of the wagon box and rope the jack to its rim."

Waco laughed. "Men are stubborn varmints. They do things cockeyed and left-handed half their lives, until they finally figure out the best way."

Nobody laughed, for suddenly they had nothing to laugh about. A band of screeching Indians came galloping at them from the south, while a similar horde galloped in from the north.

"The black-powder bombs are in the wagon," Mindy cried.

"No time," Lonnie shouted. "They're going to rush us. Everybody pull your guns."

Dirk, Kirby, Justin, Dallas, and Wovoka were at the far side of the herd, too far away to be of any immediate assistance. They came galloping to the rescue when they saw and heard the attacking Indians, but the first charge was over by the time they arrived. Mindy lay on the ground, a Colt in her hand and an arrow in her left side. Lonnie, who had cut down three of the attackers, lay belly-down, an arrow in his back. Waco had a wound in his left arm, and blood dripped off the tips of his fingers. Seven of the attackers lay dead, while those who had ridden away had reined up well out of gun range. In an instant, Dallas was off his horse beside Mindy. Becky stood over Lonnie as though frozen in shock, with huge tears rolling down her cheeks.

"Kill," Wovoka shouted. Leaping off his horse, he seized three of the Colts from under the wagon seat, shoving them under his waistband.

"Wovoka, no," Dallas yelled. "There's too many of them."

But Wovoka might not have heard. Mounting his horse, he galloped toward the distant band of Paiutes.

"Come on," said Gus. "They'll kill him."

In an instant, Sandy Orr, Benjamin Raines, Elliot Graves, Justin Irwin, Dirk McNelly, and Kirby Lowe were galloping to catch up to Gus. His hand dripping blood, Waco had his foot in the stirrup when Laura caught his good arm.

"Don't go," Laura said. "You're losing blood."

"I'm needed, woman," replied Waco as he yanked his arm free from her grasp.

Although the several dozen Paiutes were obviously surprised by the hard-riding cowboys, they stood their ground, nocking arrows to their bowstrings. Leading the attack, Wovoka cut down two of the Paiutes before the others began loosing their arrows. But all the attackers had their heads down against the necks of their horses, and their combined fury was evident in their grim faces and deadly aim. Suddenly Gus was galloping his horse next to Wovoka, and their combined efforts produced a formidable fire. Emptying one of the Colts, Wovoka seized another. When an arrow grazed his horse, Gus was thrown, and belly-down, he continued firing until he had emptied his Colt. The attack, though vastly outnumbered, fought like devils, forcing the Paiutes to run for their lives. Amazingly, no less than seventeen Paiutes had been killed in the furious attack, while none of the attacking force had been hit. There was a gash from an arrow along the flank of the horse Gus had been riding, and Kirby Lowe caught the animal.

"My God," said Waco, as the attackers returned to the wagon, "I never saw the like. How many of 'em did you get?"

"Seventeen," Benjamin Raines said, "but how bad have they hurt us?"

"I got a bad arm wound out of it," said Waco, "but Lonnie and Mindy may be really in a bad way."

Dallas had removed Mindy's shirt and was trying to stop the bleeding. Becky, Laura, and April knelt around Lonnie. His shirt had been cut away, and blood still oozed out of the wound around the shaft of the arrow.

"We're still miles away from the next water," said Gus, "and we still have to replace that wagon wheel. I reckon you're next in command, Dallas. What are we going to do?"

"There's enough water in the barrel on the side of the wagon for a while," Dallas said. "Lonnie and Mindy must be cared for right now. Some of you get a fire going. Becky, get the medicine chest from the wagon. Justin, you and Elliot jack up the wagon. Kirby, help them replace that wheel. It's been bad, but the worst may be ahead of us."

17

Justin, Elliot, and Kirby jacked up the wagon and soon had the wheel replaced. Once a fire had been lighted and water was boiling, it was time to remove the cruel arrows from Lonnie and Mindy. With Lonnie badly wounded, the outfit looked to Dallas.

"Dallas," said Gus, "I'll tend to Waco's wound. Lonnie and Mindy are hurt one as bad as the other. If you'll care for Mindy, Justin can take that arrow out of Lonnie, I reckon. He's had experience with Comanche arrows."

"I'd be obliged," Dallas said. "Will you, Justin?"

"I'll do it," said Justin. "Becky, fetch me a pot of that boiling water."

There was only one way to remove a barbed arrow, and that was to drive the shaft on through the flesh. Dallas began working over Mindy. Breaking off the feathered end of the shaft, he unloaded his Colt and began using the butt of it to drive the shaft on through. Even though unconscious, Mindy cried out in pain. From a distance, Laura and April were watching fearfully. As Justin began the same tedious procedure on Lonnie, Becky hovered near, wringing her hands.

"Becky," Justin said patiently, "go over yonder and wait with April and Laura."

Becky seemed not to have heard.

"Damn it, Becky," Justin shouted, "this is hard enough. Get away from here."

Laura took Becky's arm, leading her away. Justin and Dallas continued their gruesome task, their shirts wringing wet with sweat. They wiped their sweaty faces on their already sodden shirtsleeves. Dallas finished first, dousing Mindy's wound with disinfectant. Then he turned to the three frightened women.

"I need one of you to bandage her wound while I support her."

Without a word, Becky went to help him. Justin still labored over Lonnie, fearful that the arrow might puncture a lung. If it did, Lonnie Kilgore was a dead man. Gus already had bound Waco's wound when Justin finally drove the shaft of the arrow through.

"Gus," said Justin, "I'll need some help. We'll have to pack this wound tight, front and back, to stop the bleeding."

With Gus holding the thick cloth pad in place on Lonnie's back, Justin turned him over and applied a similar cloth pad to the exit wound. Lonnie's face was pale, his eyes squinted in pain, but there was no bloody froth on his lips.

"Thank God," Justin said. "The arrow missed his lung."

"It's going to hurt," said Gus, "but we got to raise him up, pour disinfectant into the pads, and bind them in place."

Justin nodded, readying the bottle of disinfectant. Elliot came forward to hold the pad over the wound in Lonnie's back, when Gus raised him up. Quickly, Justin soaked both the pads with disinfectant and then bound them tightly in place with muslin wrapped around Lonnie's torso. Dallas had covered Mindy with a blanket, and brought another, with which he covered Lonnie. Justin was still on his knees, too weak to rise. He felt a hand on his shoulder.

"Thank you," said Becky in a small voice.

It was a trying time, with two of their comrades so seriously wounded, but someone had to make the decision to go on, and Dallas did.

"We'll have to make room for Lonnie and Mindy in the wagon. Dirk, Kirby, Benjamin, and Sandy, get started clearing space. When you're tired, some of the rest of us will take your place."

The four men labored for nearly an hour before climbing wearily down.

"There's just too damn much stuff in the wagon," said Sandy Orr.

"Then we'll just have to remove some of it," Dallas said. "We still have those canvas squares and plenty of rope. We'll make packs of some of the things that can go on a packhorse. Wovoka, choose four or five of the gentlest horses that will carry packs."

Wovoka nodded and went for the horses. Dallas climbed into the wagon, handing down anything that might safely travel on a packhorse. The cowboys were more asccustomed to packhorses and pack mules than wagons, and they quickly assembled five packs for those horses Wovoka believed would safely carry them. When the packs were loaded on the five horses, blankets were spread on the portion of the floor that had been cleared in the rear of the wagon. Lonnie and Mindy were carefully placed upon the blankets.

"We'll need you on the wagon, Becky," Dallas said. "Are you up to it?"

"Yes," said Becky. "I'm sorry I haven't been much help."

"Nothing to be sorry about," Dallas said. "I know how you feel. Mindy's in there, too."

But before they could move out, there was a cry of pain from the wagon. Mindy was conscious.

"Becky," said Dallas, "give her a big dose of laudanum. Give Lonnie some, too. Maybe they can sleep through the next few hours."

He didn't have to remind them they were still many miles

from the next water, and that there was little or no graze for the herd and the horses. Dallas and Wovoka rode to the point position.

"Head 'em up and move 'em out," Dallas shouted, waving his hat.

There was no supper, for their one water barrel was dry by suppertime. The horse remuda became unruly and the longhorns cantankerous as the sun slid below the western horizon. It was the day's end, a time to graze, a time to rest. But the weary riders pushed on, keeping the horses and longhorns bunched, until they became so exhausted they no longer attempted to quit the herd. Three hours after dark, there came a light breeze out of the west, bringing with it the smell of water. The longhorns forgot their exhaustion, and in a horn-clacking, bawling frenzy, stampeded west. There was no stopping them, and all the horses—even the five packhorses—followed at a fast gallop. The riders could only get out of the way.

"Damn," said Justin Irwin, "I don't believe a lightning bolt could have stopped them this time."

"We'll have a gather on our hands," Dallas said, "but there's water, and if there's any graze, they won't scatter to hell and gone."

"Yeah," said Benjamin Raines, "and while we're there, it'll allow Lonnie and Mindy a rest from jolting around in the wagon."

Almost two hours later, they reached Cañon Largo, a tributary to the San Juan. There was plenty of water, and more graze than they had expected. In the starlight, the riders could see the dark shapes of grazing horses and cattle.

"What next?" Kirby Lowe asked.

"We're going to have our fill of hot coffee and grub," said Dallas. "Then we'll divide what's left of the night into two watches. Tomorrow, we'll start our gather."

"Lonnie and Mindy's still sleeping," Becky said.

"We'll let them sleep until they have fever," said Dallas. "Then we'll have to pour some whiskey down them."

Cañon Largo. August 22, 1853.

Each of the riders managed to get a little sleep during the night. Near dawn, Lonnie and Mindy were feverish and had to be dosed with whiskey. Immediately after breakfast, Wovoka mounted his horse and rode out.

"Where's he going?" Elliot Graves wondered.

"I haven't sent him anywhere," said Dallas, "but I reckon he's looking for Indian sign."

"He's as natural a scout as I've ever seen," Justin said. "He knows what needs doing, and he's three jumps ahead, doing it. On the frontier, an outfit can't have a better edge than that."

When the outfit began their gather, it was much as Dallas had predicted. The hungry, thirsty herd was pretty well bunched, since there was water and graze. Wovoka was gone most of the day. When he returned, his explanation was simple.

"Paiute no follow," he said, pointing to the back trail.

"Sign?" Dallas asked, pointing toward the northwest.

Wovoka shook his head.

"Thank God," said Becky.

By suppertime, their fever diminished, Lonnie and Mindy were awake. Dallas was leaning over the wagon's tailgate, grinning at them.

"Where are we?" Lonnie asked.

"Cañon Largo," said Dallas. "The herd smelled the water last night and stampeded, but they didn't scatter. We gathered the whole bunch—horses included—today. Becky, April, and Laura will have supper ready pretty soon. Is anybody hungry?"

"No," said Lonnie, "but if I don't eat, this hangover's likely to kill me."

"That's about the way I feel," Mindy said.

"What happened to all those Paiutes?" Lonnie asked. "I reckon they didn't just get so tired they left?"

"After you and Mindy were hit and the rest of the outfit left the herd, you wouldn't believe what happened," said Dallas. "Wovoka grabbed three Colts from the wagon and lit out after about two dozen Paiutes. Gus and most of the others followed, and after they shot down seventeen, the others just seemed to lose interest."

Dallas stepped aside when Becky and Laura showed up with tin plates of food for Mindy and Lonnie.

"Why is there so much room in the wagon?" Mindy asked. "You didn't leave anything behind, did you?"

"No," said Becky. "Dallas had Wovoka choose five horses to carry packs. That's where the rest of it is. Dallas did everything that needed doing. I'm afraid I wasn't much help."

The Animas River. August 28, 1853.

The outfit rested six days, allowing the herd ample opportunity to graze and water. The drive then headed north, toward southern Colorado Territory. Dallas kept the herd and the horse remuda at a steady gait, and Becky followed with the wagon. While the outfit waited for supper, Dallas took out the big map they had been following, and some of the riders gathered around.

"We'll follow the Animas a hundred and forty miles, until we reach the Gunnison," said Dallas. "From there, it looks like we can follow the Gunnison west, all the way to the Utah Territory line. Then we'll have to cross the Rio Colorado, and I reckon that's goin' to be a hell of a job, from what I've heard. Thank God Lonnie will be healed enough to take over as trail boss by then."

Becky laughed. "He says you've done so well, he's going to let you trail-boss the outfit the rest of the way to the Green River range."

"Like hell," said Dallas. "I'm going to get him out of that wagon and in his saddle."

"With that much river ahead of us," Waco said, "we ought to average a good twenty miles a day. Maybe more."

The leaves were turning red and gold, and there was a chill in the air at night, but the sun rose hot in the morning sky. The weather remained favorable, and the average Waco had predicted was not only met, but improved upon. On the first day of September, they were seventy miles along the Animas River and well into southern Colorado Territory.

It was a celebrated occasion in more than one respect, for Lonnie and Mindy were able to gather around the supper fire. Tomorrow, Mindy would again take over the wagon, and Lonnie would return to the head of the drive. The cattle had actually begun to gain some weight, for graze in the high county—especially along the river—was good. Wovoka had been scouting ahead daily, but found nothing to alarm him.

"After supper," Dallas said, "we can unload the packhorses and put all those goods in the wagon again. We owe your Pa, Lonnie, for suggesting we bring a wagon instead of a bunch of pack mules, which we didn't have anyhow."

"It would have been hard on Lonnie and me, wounded, to ride draped over a couple of pack mules," said Mindy. "The rest of you would have had to go on without us, or wait a week for us to heal."

"That would have been something for both of you to tell your grandchildren," Dallas said. "How you traveled to Utah Territory, shot through with Paiute arrows, drunk and belly-down over a mule."

Utah Territory. September 2, 1853.

Eight Mormon leaders had gathered to discuss the eight sections of land that had been sold and titled along the Green River. The senior member of the group—Adolph—spoke.

"We have begun our empire with occupation of land in this territory, and we must not allow the Gentiles to gain a foothold. Therefore, we must occupy these sections of land by building on them. Bertram, Cyrus, Eli, and myself will each occupy one of the four grants along the eastern bank of the Green River. Gabriel, Zachary, Joab, and Ichabod, each of you will occupy one of the four sections along the west bank. Each of you are to employ as many members of our colony as may be necessary to construct a dwelling, well before a party of Gentiles arrive."

"It has been almost three months since they have filed," said Ichabod. "Perhaps they do not intend to settle here after all."

"Do not question my authority," Adolph said. "They will be coming. I command each of you to construct a log dwelling before the first snow."

The seven men left Adolph's cabin, and with mixed emotions set about recruiting the friends and family members needed for the construction. They had their doubts about the legality of what Adolph had proposed, for their occupation of Jim Bridger's trading post had accomplished nothing except to arouse the ire of government officials in Washington.

The Gunnison River. September 8, 1853.

"We can't be more than fifty miles from the Rio Colorado," Lonnie said, "and then we should be within maybe thirty miles of Utah Territory."

"If this good weather will just stay with us two more weeks," said Dallas, "we'll make it. That is, if we can get the wagon and the herd across the Colorado."

"If, hell," Lonnie said. "The Colorado's been crossed before."

"Maybe not with a wagon," said Becky.

"Well, it's going to be crossed by one this time," Lonnie said, "if we have to build a damn bridge from one bank to the other. We didn't come this far to let that stop us."

"You've purely got to admire his determination," said Gus.

"He generally don't want word of it gettin' out," Dallas said, "but his great-great-great-granddaddy on his pa's side was a Missouri mule. Lonnie gets his stubborn naturally."

"All right, damn it," said Lonnie, "but if we have to build that bridge, I know at least two *hombres* that'll be cuttin' logs for it."

There had been no further Indian sign, but Wovoka continued to scout ahead each day. Their second day on the Gunnison, the setting sun flamed crimson behind gray clouds that stretched from one horizon to the other.

"Like it or not, we're about to get some rain," Benjamin said.

"That's all right," said Lonnie, "as long as there's no thunder or lightning, and not too much mud for the wagon."

Justin laughed. "You're a mite old to still believe in Santa Claus."

They all laughed, but there was nothing humorous about the night that followed. There was no thunder or lightning, but having grown up in perpetually dry south Texas, there was rainfall such as the cowboys had never seen. Three hours into the first watch, heavy gray clouds swept in, almost touching the treetops. The rain, when it began, was so heavy the riders couldn't see one another just a few feet away. There was no thunder and no lightning, but just enough wind to give the longhorns and horses a sense of direction. It was their nature to want to drift with the storm, and turning their backs on it, they did their best. The riders got ahead of the horse remuda, attempting to head the animals, but behind the horses, pushing and shoving with their deadly horns, came the cattle.

"Separate the horses," Lonnie shouted.

He didn't know if anyone heard him or not, but Wovoka seemed to know what needed doing. The Indian was seeking to drive the horses far enough ahead of the herd for the riders to get in between, where they might head the longhorns. The rain slacked a little, and the other riders joined Lonnie and Wovoka. Slowly but surely, the horses were driven away from the longhorns. With Wovoka and several riders seeking to control the horses, the others turned on the longhorns, swatting them with doubled lariats. While the brutes didn't want to face the driving rain, neither did they like being struck on tender muzzles with whiplike lariats. To everybody's dismay, the rain didn't let up, but continued for the rest of the night. Everybody—including the women—was in the saddle. The horses were not so difficult to control, for there weren't so many of them, but the longhorns seemed determined to turn their backs on the slashing rain and drift back along the Gunnison. The dawn broke gray and dreary, with no letup in sight. There was no breakfast, just as there had been no sleep, and with little prospect of either. The mud was unbelievable. When his horse slipped, Kirby was thrown face-down. When he got to his feet cursing, he was just unrecognizable. He managed to catch his horse and mount, but in his muddy clothes, he slid out again. An old steer charged Becky's horse, and she was thrown into the mud. On hands and knees, she was saying some very unladylike things to the steer, who just stood there looking at her. Lonnie leaned over, seized her by the waistband of her Levi's, and carried her from the path of the herd. There he dropped her back into the mud and rode back to try and head the troublesome longhorns. Mercifully, the rain ceased. Finally the longhorns allowed themselves to be herded together and bunched. Wovoka had the horse remuda under control. The Gunnison River had overflowed its banks, and there was run-off everywhere. Every rider—even those not thrown into the mud—had been virtually covered with mud slung by the hooves of the horses and longhorns. Wovoka slid off his horse and simply lay down in one of the fast-flowing runoffs from the river. It seemed like the logical thing to do, and removing gunbelts, boots, and hats, the rest of the outfit followed his example. With the passing of the rain, the sky cleared rapidly, and the sun began to steam the sodden earth.

"Tarnation," said Lonnie, sitting on a rock trying to pull on his sodden boots, "I don't know what I need most—a little sleep or a lot of grub."

"Eat," Wovoka said.

"I'm with him," said Waco. "If I lay down, I'm so weak I might not be able to get up again."

"Somebody see if there's any wood left in the possum belly," Becky said, wringing the water out of her hair.

Gus and Sandy went to the wagon and began rummaging through the possum belly beneath it. They dragged out what kindling and wood was left.

"That's all of it," said Gus. "There won't be any for supper tonight, or breakfast in the morning."

"We haven't eaten since breakfast yesterday morning," Lonnie said. "Get a fire going and let's eat."

Wearily, Becky, Mindy, April, and Laura began preparing the meal. When the coffee was ready, everybody took time for a cup of the steaming brew. The sun had begun to dry their clothing, and their situation didn't look quite so hopeless. The food did wonders, and when they had eaten, Lonnie spoke.

"That wagon won't be going anywhere until the sun dries up some of the mud. I'd say we'll be here at least through tomorrow night. For now, we'll take turns sleeping two or three hours.''

"In all this mud?" Becky asked.

"Only if you prefer it," said Lonnie shortly. "Otherwise, you can take some of those lengths of spare canvas from the wagon and spread them on the grass. I'm going to take an axe and try to cut some dry wood from the downside of a fallen tree.''

"I'll take the other axe and go with you," Gus said.

"I'll keep watch," said Dallas, "if a couple more of you will join me. The rest of you can get some sleep.''

"I watch," Wovoka said.

"So will I," said Elliot Graves.

Taking the axes from the wagon, Lonnie and Gus set off upriver, looking for fallen trees that might yield some dry wood.

"I reckon we won't have to worry much about dry weather in this part of the world," Gus said.

"I reckon not," said Lonnie, "if the last few hours were a sample of it.''

Several wind-blown trees didn't rest entirely on the ground, and the branches cut from their undersides yielded dry wood. With little else to do, Lonnie and Gus cut enough of a proper length to replenish the wagon's possum belly. By suppertime, the entire outfit had been able to get enough sleep to keep them going. Now with an ample supply of dry wood, they had supper and the first watch mounted their horses. With a starry, cloudless sky above them, the night was peaceful, and they all greeted the dawn in a better frame of mind. But the ground was still too muddy to move the wagon, and they all spent a long, restless day. The graze had begun to play out, and they had no choice except to move the herd and the horse remuda farther upriver.

"I know there's been no Indian sign," said Dallas, "but I don't like the idea of this.''

"Neither do I," Lonnie said, "but the herd and the horses need graze. With any luck, the ground should be dry enough by tomorrow for the wagon."

Southwestern Colorado Territory. September 11, 1853.

There was more than the usual chill in the air as the outfit greeted the dawn. Along the Gunnison River, where the recent rain had overflowed the banks, the ground was still muddy.

"We should be able to make it," Lonnie said, "if we keep the wagon far enough from the river. As chill as the nights are becoming, I think we'd better try."

"I'll do my best," said Becky, whose turn it was with the wagon.

The sun no longer seemed as hot, and the unseen fingers of the wind plucked dead and dying leaves from the trees. Within them all was the uneasy feeling that time was running out, that one day soon, the big gray clouds from the west would not bring rain, but snow.

"Head 'em up, move 'em out," Lonnie shouted.

With Lonnie and Wovoka riding ahead, the outfit moved out. Becky pulled the wagon in behind the horse remuda, careful not to get near the still-muddy riverbank. It seemed, after the endless hours of rain and a veritable sea of mud, that their good fortune had returned, for Lonnie estimated the drive had covered at least thirty miles. Another day of similar good fortune would take them to within thirty miles of the Utah territorial line, where they would then have thirty miles in which to find a suitable crossing of the dreaded Rio Colorado.*

"The wind's colder than it was yesterday," Dallas observed, as they sat down to supper at the end of the day.

---

*They reach the Rio Colorado near the present-day town of Grand Junction, Colorado.

"We've been lucky," said Justin Irwin. "Last time I was in this high country near this time of year, that wind was blowin' snow ahead of it."

"Suppose we do reach Green River ahead of the snow," said Laura. "We'll still have all the winter ahead of us, with no shelter."

"I've been thinking of that since we left Texas," Lonnie said, "and I don't really know how we'll weather this first winter. I think we'll be forced to build a single log shelter for us all on one of the claims, and another for the horses. I've been hoping we still might get there in time to accomplish that ahead of the first snow. Now I'm not so sure."

"I wish we had followed the Green south when we left Fort Laramie on our return from California," said Kirby Lowe. "All we know is, we've got eight sections, four on each side of the river. There might be a cave, high riverbanks, or maybe a canyon."

"Cañon," Wovoka said. "Wovoka know."

"There is a stretch of the Green that flows through a canyon?" Lonnie asked excitedly.

"Sí," said Wovoka. "Rim. Much grass."

"That could be the saving of us all," Becky said, "but suppose it isn't on our land?"

"I don't care a damn *whose* land it's on," said Lonnie. "If there's a long enough stretch of the river flowing through a deep canyon, those canyon rims can protect us, the horses, and the herd from the snow until spring."

"I'm more excited than when we started the drive," Mindy cried.

"We find soon," said Wovoka, pleased that he had contributed to the excitement of his companions.

"I want to keep moving until we reach the Colorado," said Lonnie. According to the map, we can follow it maybe thirty miles into Utah Territory before we have to cross it. Once we reach the Colorado, we shouldn't be more than a hundred miles from Green River.''

The outfit kept the herd bunched, moving them at as fast a gait as they could. Before the sun sank below the western horizon, they left the Gunnison and found themselves on the high banks of the formidable Rio Colorado.

"Well, we made it," Dallas said. "Now the question is, how far along it do we have to go before we find the banks low enough to get the herd to water?"

"Maybe too far, before dark," said Lonnie. "We're going to backtrack to where we left the Gunnison, so there'll be water for the herd tonight. Tomorrow, I want you riding point. Wovoka and me are going to ride the Colorado until we find a place we can cross the herd and the wagon."

"Suppose there isn't such a place?" Becky asked.

"Then we'll look for banks low enough to get the herd and the horses to water, and on across to the other side. Then, if there's no other way, we'll find a narrow enough place and build a log bridge for the wagon."

"You're serious about that, I reckon," Dirk McNelly said.

"I am," said Lonnie, "unless you can think of a better way."

"Well, I hope we ain't still cuttin' logs for that bridge when the snow comes," Kirby Lowe said.

"If we are," said Lonnie grimly, "you'll just have to work harder. It'll help to keep you warm. Now let's turn this herd around and move it back to the Gunnison for the night."

"Why didn't he think of this before we left the Gunnison?" April whispered to Becky.

Becky laughed. "Two reasons. He's a hardheaded Texan, and he's Lonnie Kilgore. He was hell-bent on reaching the Rio Colorado today, and he did."

"A stubborn man," said April.

"Stubborn, hell," Becky said. "He's beyond that. He's been known to take his britches off over his boots."

18

The Rio Colorado. September 12, 1853.

*D*allas," said Lonnie as he and Wovoka prepared to ride out, "keep the drive moving at as rapid a gait as you can. Somewhere within the next twenty-five or thirty miles, we must at least find a place where the Colorado's bank is low enough for us to water the herd and the horses, and we don't know how far along the Colorado that will be."

"Yeah," Dallas said. "I reckon I'd better not ask what we're goin' to do if you ride a thirty-mile stretch without finding a low enough bank for us to reach the water."

"I reckon you'd better not," said Lonnie. "This is a high-stakes game we can't afford to lose. Just don't let any grass grow under your feet."

"Head 'em up, move 'em out," Dallas shouted as Lonnie and Wovoka rode away.

Dirk and Kirby were the swing riders, Gus and Waco the flankers. Sandy, Benjamin, Elliot, and Justin rode drag. Mindy kept the wagon right on the heels of the drag, while Becky, Laura, and April rode beside the wagon.

"Lord," said April, "those riverbanks are awful steep. I

hope they're not like that for the next hundred miles.''

"No matter," Becky replied. "You heard what Lonnie said."

"I heard him," said Laura, "and I suppose we can build a bridge for the wagon. But he can't take the cows and horses across a bridge unless he leads them one at a time."

"That's not very amusing," Becky said. "He might do exactly that, if there's no other way."

"But we'll need water for the cows and horses tonight," said April.

April's companions looked at her without responding. It was the gospel truth, and none of them dared consider what might be the result if, at day's end, the only water was at the foot of the Colorado's steep banks.

Lonnie and Wovoka had paused to rest their horses. The animals had been kept at a walk, and Lonnie estimated they had ridden five miles. The Colorado's banks seemed about as steep as ever. Lonnie was tempted to ask Wovoka what he thought of the situation, but a look at the Indian's impassive face told him Wovoka likely had no ideas at the moment. They rode on, Lonnie becoming more uneasy all the time. As they progressed, the river's banks became more rocky, with an occasional ledge reaching out from their bank toward the opposite one. It was just such a ledge—or the collapse of it—that brought Lonnie a ray of hope. The rock ledge had slid into the river, taking with it other stones and quite a portion of the riverbank. Lonnie reined up, Wovoka beside him.

"I know we can't take the wagon down that bank," Lonnie said, "but the cows and the horses could get down."

Wordlessly, Wovoka pointed toward the opposite rocky bank, which looked every bit as formidable as ever. It was a valid observation, but Lonnie was looking at the results of the landslide from their own bank. Rocks and dirt had created a barrier, raising the water level of the river considerably.

"If we could bring that other bank down," said Lonnie,

"we could cross the herd and the horses here."

"No wagon," Wovoka said.

"Not without some work," said Lonnie, "but we'll have the beginning of a bridge. This is likely the best we're going to find. Let's ride back and meet the drive. I want that bolt of muslin, a keg of black powder, and a shovel."

Wovoka said nothing. He had been profoundly impressed when Lonnie had used the black powder to intimidate the hostile Paiutes. It was with considerable anticipation that he followed Lonnie back the way they had come. He wanted to see the white man's magic take down the far bank of the mighty Colorado to the equal of that which had been leveled by a landslide.

"Keep the drive moving, Dallas," Lonnie said, when they met the herd. "The bank on our side of the river's been cut down by a landslide. We're going after some black powder, hoping we can equalize the situation."

"*Bueno,*" said Dallas. "Can we cross the wagon there?"

"Not without considerable work," Lonnie said, "but if we can bring down that opposite bank, we can water the stock and drive them across."

Lonnie and Wovoka rode around the herd, waiting until the wagon reached them.

"Mindy," said Lonnie, "stop just long enough for me to get a keg of black powder, a shovel, and some muslin. The drive's going on, and you can catch up."

"What are you going to do?" Becky asked.

Quickly, Lonnie explained, while Mindy went into the wagon after the items Lonnie had requested. She found the powder first, and Wovoka took it. Then she handed down the muslin, followed by the shovel. With his knife, Lonnie estimated and cut half a dozen three-foot lengths of muslin, each a yard wide. The rest of the bolt he returned to Mindy.

"Now catch up to the herd," said Lonnie. "Maybe we'll

have a place to cross the herd and the horses by the time you get there.''

The wagon soon caught up to the drag. Becky, April, and Laura rode along with the drag riders long enough to tell them what Lonnie hoped to accomplish.

"I've never seen as hell-bent an *hombre* as Lonnie Kilgore," Justin said admiringly. "If he decided to tackle hell with a bucket of water, I reckon I'd grab a bucket and follow."

"He does have a way about him," said Sandy Orr, "and I think he's the kind it'll take to settle this frontier. I'm looking forward to this Green River ranch."

Lonnie and Wovoka reached the place where a landslide had caved in the riverbank. They dismounted, and using his knife blade, Lonnie removed the screws from the wooden lid of the keg. The ground being dry and grassy, he spread out one of the muslin squares. Upon it, he poured a large amount of black powder. Pulling the muslin's four corners together, he knotted them into a sack. Wovoka had spread out the other muslin squares, and Lonnie quickly made three more bags of the explosives.

"We'll hold off on the other two," Lonnie said. "We may not need them."

He then studied the farthest bank of the river. Among the many stones, there was an upright one—like a huge finger— that stood almost as tall as a man. Taking his lariat from his saddle, Lonnie built a loop. After several failed casts, he got the loop around the tall stone. The lariat had barely been long enough.

"Wovoka," said Lonnie, "after I've climbed up onto that other bank, I want you to tie these bags of black powder to the rope so I can pull them up. Then send me the shovel."

"*Sí*," Wovoka said.

Lonnie checked his shirt pocket, finding his oilskin-wrapped matches there. He then tied a loop in the lariat, passing it over his head and under his arms. Even after the landslide, the water was above his waist. Removing his gun-belt, he hung it around his neck. Taking a firm grip on the rope, hand over hand, he raised himself to the edge of the farthest riverbank. Scrambling up to firm ground, he removed his gunbelt and buckled it around his waist. He then loosed the lariat, and with one end still looped over the vertical stone, dropped the free end of it to Wovoka. He caught it, and securely tied it to the neck of one of the bags of black powder. Quickly, Lonnie drew that one up, and Wovoka sent up the others in similar fashion. Last came the shovel.

"Now," Lonnie said, "go back to the other bank and lead the horses back far enough so you're out of reach of any flying rock."

Lonnie began studying the ground, seeking a place where the first blast might prove the most effective. A dozen feet back from the edge of the river's bank was a fissure that ran parallel to the river for a few yards. It was narrow, requiring some hard work with the shovel to make room for a bag of the black powder. On second thought, Lonnie dug a second powder placement near the other end of the fissure. There was a huge mass to be moved, and even two charges might not be enough. Lonnie paused. There was one element he hadn't considered. He must light both muslin bags and still reach a safe distance before the explosions.

There was a light wind from the west, sufficient to extinguish a match. He removed two matches from his oilskin pouch, just in case. Kneeling with his back to the wind, shielding the match with his hat, he popped it alight with his thumbnail. Even with protection, the flame flickered as he touched it to the mouth of one muslin bag. The flame caught quickly with the wind fanning it, and Lonnie ran to the next charge. As he had half-expected, his movement sucked out the flame of the match. Not knowing how much time he had, he knelt by the second charge. Again shielding the match with his hat, he lit it and touched it to the muslin.

Then, hat in hand, he ran for all he was worth. Even then, he was barely in time. The first explosion shook the earth, and like an echo, the second one followed. The concussion threw Lonnie to the ground, and he was showered with dirt and hunks of rock. He sat up, unable to hear, and only half-conscious. A stone the size of his fist had struck him in the head. He could feel blood running down to mix with the dirt on his face. Unsteadily he got to his feet, wiping his eyes on the sleeve of his shirt. On the other bank, he could see Wovoka. He had left the horses, approached the river, and regarded the devastating result of the explosions with awe. Lonnie examined his handiwork with considerable surprise. Apparently the fissure had run much deeper than he had thought, for the river's bank had been collapsed to the level of the opposite one. The new debris had combined with that of the landslide to create a hump a dozen feet wide across the river. While it still wasn't level enough for the wagon, there was more than a foundation for a bridge. Quickly the river's water had backed up, and was already flowing across the added obstruction. Lonnie was able to walk across to the other bank, and the water wasn't over the tops of his boots.

"*Grande,*" said Wovoka.

"It was a mite impressive," Lonnie said. "Let's empty the rest of this black powder back into the keg. Then we'll ride back to meet the herd."

Within five miles, they met the oncoming herd.

"How much of that powder did you use?" Dallas asked. "It sounded like the world was coming down on our heads."

"Maybe too much," said Lonnie, "but two charges of it got the job done. Without any work, the herd and the horses can drink, as well as cross to the other side. We'll have to level it some more for the wagon, though."

"You and Wovoka can take over the point," Dallas said, "and I'll return the shovel, and that keg of powder to the wagon."

"*Bueno,*" said Lonnie, "and on your way, you might as well tell the others that likely the hardest part of our problem is solved."

When the herd reached the newly created crossing, Lonnie waved his hat. After the herd and the horses had been headed, the rest of the outfit approached the blast area.

"Just a little more," Waco said, "and it would have been leveled enough to cross the wagon."

"I don't think so," said Lonnie. "With the river flowing across the newly blasted dirt, the wagon would mire up hub-deep. As difficult as it may be, we're goin' to have to cut some logs, snake them in, and lay a ribbed bridge across the part where the water flows."*

"I reckon we'll take the herd and the horses across first," Justin said.

"Yes," said Lonnie. "The wagon can stay on this side for as long as it takes us to cut the logs and build the bridge. There's a considerable amount of rock in what's slid into the riverbed, and with the herd and the horses crossing first, they'll pack down that dirt and rock some. Then maybe the logs we'll put there won't sink into the mud. Even if they do, we'll only have to cross the wagon once."

"We'll have to take the herd and the horses across before sundown, then," Dallas said. "They'll need water, and with so narrow a crossing, there's no way they can all water at the same time."

"We'll take the horse remuda across first, watering them as they go," Lonnie said, "and then we'll take the herd across a few at a time, watering them as they cross. Waco, you and Gus help Wovoka take the horses across first. Then we'll split up into five teams of two, each taking maybe fifty head of cows across at a time. Once they've watered, don't let any of

---

*In modern-day terminology, a "corduroy" bridge, with logs placed side by side.

them wander up- or downstream. Swat them on their behinds and take them on across, making way for the next bunch.''

The horses were watered and crossed without difficulty, but the longhorns proved far more difficult. Cowlike, they wanted to linger, watering when the notion struck them. One unruly bull leaped off the newly created crossing into water up to his eyes. Up on the far bank of the river, it took three mounted riders with lariats to drag the stubborn animal out of the river.

''Dallas,'' said Lonnie, ''I'm going to mount my horse and get into the water on the upstream side of this crossing. I want you to mount up, get in the water, and cover the downstream side. Double your lariat, and any varmint lookin' like it wants to take a dive into deeper water, just swat the hell out of it.''

That helped, but when the last of the herd had crossed, the gray of twilight was upon them, and first stars twinkled far away. Supper had long since been ready, but the riders had to finish crossing the herd.

''Those of you on the first watch, go ahead and eat,'' Lonnie said. ''The rest of us will watch the herd and the horse remuda.''

Dirk, Kirby, Gus, Waco, and Sandy went to supper. Lonnie and the rest of the outfit began riding around the bunched herd and the horse remuda.

''I reckon we'd better keep a close watch on them all night,'' said Dallas. ''Somebody might get thirsty and head for the river.''

''Tarnation,'' Justin said, ''we don't want that. It's enough that we got to water them all again in the morning before we move out.''

''I don't know if we should do that or not,'' said Lonnie. ''Do it again, and we won't be taking them across to the other bank. We'll be driving them back to this one, and it just might take us most of the day.''

''They've been watered tonight,'' Dallas said. ''I say we head them out at a trot just as early in the morning as we can get the wagon across. When they get thirsty, a little wind from the west will get them the rest of the way to the Green, even if it's fifty miles.''

"That's the truth, if I ever heard it," said Justin.

"For whatever it's worth," Benjamin Raines said, "I think we'd better get this drive to Green River just as quick as we can and find or build some shelter. Notice how cold that wind is already?"

"Yeah," said Elliot Graves. "The next bunch of clouds blowin' in, I'd say they won't be bringin' rain."

"Besides shelter," Justin said, "we're gonna be needin' firewood, and plenty of it."

"I'm inclined to agree with all of you," said Lonnie, "but it's going to take some time to get the wagon across the river. I'm figurin' half a day. How many of you still think we can reach Green River tomorrow?"

"Maybe late tomorrow night," said Dallas. "The only other choice might be for five of you to take the herd and move on, with all the women riding drag. The rest of us could work like hell, maybe get the wagon across, and catch up."

"No," Lonnie said, "we're not going to split up the outfit. If the Mormons are hostile enough to take over Bridger's trading post, we may yet have a fight on our hands, and we won't be in any position for that, with half the outfit back here trying to get the wagon across the Colorado. We'll all remain here until we get the wagon across, and then we'll all move on together. Even if it takes us all night to reach the Green, keeping the herd moving won't be any more difficult that holding them in a dry camp."

"I reckon I'll have to agree with you on that," said Dallas. "If there's any wind, they'll smell the water and stampede hell-bent-for-election anyhow."

"That's how the stick floats, then," Lonnie said. "No matter how long it takes us to get the wagon across, we're going on to Green River, be it thirty miles or fifty."

When the riders on the first watch returned, Lonnie and his companions rode across the river to the wagon.

"We kept the supper as warm as we could," said Becky.

"It won't matter," Lonnie said. "It'll taste damn good, compared to tomorrow night, when there won't be any."

"Why?" April asked.

"I'm glad you asked that," said Lonnie. "Now all of you gather around and listen. I'm in no mood to go through this more than once."

Quickly, he told them of his decision to get the wagon across the river, and then to take the drive on to Green River, regardless of how long it might take.

"I think it's what we must do," Mindy said, "however troublesome it may be. I have a feeling if we delay much longer, the snow will come before we get there."

"I have that same feeling," said Becky. "But what about watering the herd and horses in the morning?"

"No time," Lonnie said. "They'll have to make it on to Green River."

Eastern Utah Territory, September 13, 1853

"Wovoka," said Lonnie, "I want you to stay over yonder with the horses and see that none of them wander back toward the river. Becky, I want you, Mindy, April, and Laura circling the herd until we're able to get the wagon across the river. That will leave ten of us to cut trees, lay that bridge, and bring the wagon across. We should be ready to move out before the herd becomes too restless."

There were four axes in the wagon. Lonnie, Dallas, Benjamin Raines, and Elliot Graves each took one of the axes. They chose trees about four inches in diameter so the men could work swiftly. After the trees were cut and trimmed, the rest of the riders snaked them to the river crossing and put them in place. Two hours before noon, Lonnie judged the makeshift ribbed bridge would hold up for a single crossing of the wagon. To the relief of them all, the wagon crossed safely.

"Head 'em up, move 'em out," Lonnie shouted.

The herd again took the trail, the wagon directly behind the horse remuda. Too soon, it seemed, the sun slid below the western horizon. The longhorns became troublesome, but the riders kept them bunched and moving at a fast gait. The west wind blew cold, numbing ears and fingers. But the wind also brought the smell of distant water, and as the herd became weary and thirsty, they began bawling their frustration.

"The varmints are gonna run," Dallas shouted, as the drag steers lunged left and right.

There was nothing the riders could do except ride for their lives. The bawling, horned avalanche was unstoppable. They ran, the horse remuda on their heels. Lonnie and Wovoka waited until the rest of the riders and the wagon caught up.

"One thing for damn sure," said Waco. "They'll reach Green River tonight."

"So will we," Lonnie said.

They moved on, until under glittering stars and in the pale moonlight, they began to see grazing longhorns and horses. When at last they could see the river, they reined up. It was their promised land, and nobody spoke. There was no sound, except the weeping of one of the women.

Green River, Utah Territory. September 14, 1853

"Wovoka," said Lonnie after breakfast, "I want you to take me north to the canyon you spoke of."

"*Sí,*" Wovoka said.

"After we've had a look at that canyon," said Lonnie, "we'll gather the herd and horses and take them there."

"How are we going to know where our holdings begin and end?" Becky asked.

"I may have to ride to Fort Laramie for our deeds and such," said Lonnie. "It won't be a problem, if we can winter in this canyon. We can begin our building in the spring."

Lonnie and Wovoka rode almost twenty miles, and the canyon, when they reached it, was even more than Lonnie had expected. It was wide, with high rims. The Green flowed through it, and protected as it was, there was lush grass along both banks of the river as far as the eye could see.

The sudden roar of a rifle seemed twice as loud in the silence. The lead struck the ground a dozen feet ahead of Lonnie and Wovoka, and in an instant they were bellied down in the grass. Then came a shout from the canyon's west rim.

"Turn back. You're not welcome here. This is homesteaded Mormon land from here to the north, along both riverbanks."

"We're not turning back," Lonnie shouted. "We've bought and paid for land you claim, and we have deeds and title. If you want a fight, then you'll get one."

There was only silence. Lonnie and Wovoka mounted their horses and rode back to the outfit. Lonnie's report was grim news.

"Damn," said Dallas, "there may be hundreds of them. How in tarnation are we goin' to hold so much land when there's so few of us?"

"Find Bridger," Wovoka said. "Bring Shoshone."

"Bridger and the Shoshone are in Wyoming," said Lonnie. "This is our fight."

"Bridger and the Shoshone are *compañeros*," Wovoka said. "I go, they come."

"Would you do that for us, Wovoka?" Becky asked.

"*Sí,*" said Wovoka. "Maybe ten suns."

"I'm beginning to understand why Jim Bridger wanted Wovoka to come with us," said Kirby Lowe. "If Wovoka thinks Bridger and a band of the Shoshones will ride to join us, what do we have to lose for the asking?''

"Ten days," Lonnie said. "We may be neck-deep in snow by then."

"Not if we move the horses and the herd into that canyon," said Dallas. "Tonight we can ride those canyon rims and be sure none of that bunch is holed up there. Sounds like our land—and what they're claiming—is north of the canyon anyhow."

"It does," Lonnie said. "Wovoka, we can use the help of Bridger and as many of your Shoshone *amigos* as are willing to join us. We have plenty of beef, so they can winter here without going hungry."

"Sí," said Wovoka. "I go now."

"Not without grub," Lonnie said, "and you can take an extra horse. Becky, fix Wovoka enough grub for ten days."

Becky hurried to the wagon, Mindy, April, and Laura going with her. Within an hour, Wovoka rode north, leading an extra horse, a pack of food lashed to its back.

"Dear God," said Laura as they watched Wovoka ride away, "our very lives may be depending on an Indian."

"I never met a white man I trusted more," Becky said. *"Vaya con Dios,* Wovoka."

After supper, when darkness had fallen, Lonnie gathered the outfit around the wagon.

"Dallas," said Lonnie, "I want you to take Dirk, Kirby, Gus, and Waco, and ride that canyon's west rim until the canyon plays out. Sandy, Benjamin, Elliot, and Justin will ride with me along the east rim. No shooting unless you're fired upon. I don't think they'll try to do more than keep us off our own land, but we can't be sure. Tomorrow, I want to get the herd and the horses into that canyon. Becky, Mindy, April, and Laura, I want all of you to remain here with the wagon, keeping your Colts handy. We'll return as quickly as we can."

There was nothing more to be said, and the ten men rode

north. It was still early and the moon had not risen. Lonnie and his four companions rode along the canyon's east rim, seeing nobody. There was no disturbance from the west rim, a fair indication that Dallas and his men had encountered no difficulty. The canyon rim began to level down.

"Far enough," Lonnie said. "Let's turn back."

They did so, returning to the wagon just minutes ahead of Dallas and his companions.

"Nobody on the west rim," said Dallas. "How long do you reckon that canyon is?"

"Near ten miles," Lonnie said, "and from what I saw of it in daylight, there's plenty of good grass. Tomorrow, we move the herd and the horses into the canyon and establish our camp there against the west rim. It slants inward enough until snow can't touch us. A bushwhacker on the opposite rim would have a long shot, and in plain view."

Green River, Utah Territory. September 14, 1853.

The drive upriver into the canyon went smoothly.

"We'll take turns, half of us dragging in dead trees for firewood, leaving the rest in camp with the herd," Lonnie said.

The wind had become increasingly colder, and the necessity of having an adequate pile of firewood was all the more evident. Day after day, they continued, with those remaining in camp chopping the dragged-in dead trees into convenient lengths. Lonnie finally decided they had enough.

"Damn good thing," Dallas declared. "We've dragged in every dead tree within a good five miles."

The first and second watch continued as usual, and still nobody disturbed them. There was little to be said, and while nobody said anything, their eyes were constantly turned to the north, for from that direction might come their friends or their enemies. Not until the fifteenth day following Wovoka's departure was there any change in their circumstances. At sundown, as they were eating supper, Becky cried out, pointing north. The Indians rode four abreast, military style. Leading the columns was Wovoka and Jim Bridger. Lonnie ran to meet them, taking Bridger's hand before the bearded mountain man could dismount. As Wovoka dismounted, Becky threw her arms around him, an act his Shoshone companions found highly amusing.

"Wovoka said you needed some help, and I expected that," Bridger said, "so I brought some Shoshone friends to winter with us."

"Bless you," said Lonnie.

"There's a hundred or so," Bridger said. "They volunteered, because they don't like this bunch that took over my trading post, and now seem determined to claim all of Utah, as well as parts of Wyoming. We shot a couple of deer to help out with the grub."

"We're by no means broke," said Lonnie. "If we can make it ahead of the snow, we can take the wagon to Fort Laramie for another load of grub."

"Not a bad idea," Bridger said. "While you're there, you can get your papers on your claims from Captain Stoddard. You might also tell him these Mormons have log buildings on every section of land you own. We saw them on the way downriver."

The night became an event none of them would ever forget. On October 1, 1853, Lonnie, Dallas, Wovoka, and five Shoshones started for Fort Laramie, taking the wagon. Their future seemed as bright as the sun in the blue of the Utah sky, at the end of the Green River Trail.